GW01548398

ASIN: B01MG5TVZ1

Table of Contents

"Now, my own suspicion is that the universe is not only queerer than we suppose, but queerer than we <u>can</u> suppose."

J.B.S. Haldane 1927

Chapter 1

Royal Observatory, Blackford Hill
Edinburgh, Scotland
Sunday, 7 May 2017 16:03

It came down to twelve neatly stacked pages, the only order in a room scattered with books, journals, and overflowing waste baskets. Professor Simon Millar slowed his breathing as he looked on the product of an insane period of work. They were nothing to look at, just one pile of papers among so many others, but they represented the scientific immortality he had craved his entire life. He had no way of knowing they would lead to his death that very night.

Millar looked away from the papers and cradled his head. The background noise was becoming intrusive; he pulled out his computer's power cord, and welcomed the silence that followed an abrupt mechanical whine.

Only three hours remained until his guests arrived and he would broadcast his work through a hastily arranged web conference to colleagues at CERN, the European Organisation for Nuclear Research based in Switzerland, and the Perimeter Institute of Theoretical Physics in Ontario, Canada.

Scientific breakthroughs were rarely announced on Sunday evenings, but his reputation had lecture halls waiting expectantly at both institutions. Many prominent scientists were making time in their weekends to discover whether they had been invited to share in some outstanding new work, or to satisfy the vanity of a man known to hold himself in high regard.

Whatever their concerns, Millar knew his discovery would catch the global imagination and guarantee his place among the scientific elite. Like Newton, Bohr and Einstein, his name would live on until man was no more.

As is so often the case with scientific enquiry, the breakthrough was entirely accidental, not that it mattered as he was in good company. Becquerel inadvertently discovered radioactivity and shared a Nobel Prize for his efforts, and even Nobel himself discovered gelignite by chance.

The Large Hadron Collider at CERN promised to transform man's understanding of the physical world, but no-one could have guessed such a stunning discovery would come so soon from the most complex machine ever created.

Images flooded Millar's mind, as he visualised the huge twenty-seven-kilometre circumference of the main tunnel buried one hundred metres beneath Switzerland and France. The collider's sole purpose to accelerate beams of particles in opposing directions, increasing the velocity to near-light speed, before bringing them together in head-to-head, high-energy collisions. Data analysis of the resulting debris, the shattered particle fragments, held the key to a new understanding of the universe.

He felt an overwhelming wonder for the world, from the simple warmth of the sun on a summer's day, to the mathematical elegance embedded in the physical world.

Millar shook his head; he would rise above the fatigue and complete one last review of the data. The conclusions were sound, but as he reached the summit of his profession, a simple oversight could so easily turn triumph into ridicule.

There was the issue of the test message. He should never have allowed such a reckless act, but his mind would soon be at ease over its content as the decryption engine was working to reveal the full transmission.

He crossed the hallway to the main computer lab and signed into the UNIX grid system. The decryption engine was still decoding the message, the on-screen timer tracking a relentless brute force attack that would eventually break the code.

Millar would have to be patient; the program would report when it had found the elusive key that unlocked the plain text. In the meantime, he needed to prepare for his guests. There had been little time for friends in recent years, and he hoped this discovery would bring the sense of achievement he needed to take time for a life outside his work.

The computer emitted a ping and Millar could see the decryption engine reporting the high probability of a message recovery. It scored the result of each decryption attempt, all but one produced garbage, random streams of jumbled characters, but the alert on a high score meant the decryption engine had broken the cipher once more. Millar selected the option to translate, print, and then collected the copy from a row of printers.

His legs gave way as he read, he slumped down beside a stack of printer paper where his mind cleared and came to a complete focus. He'd heard the radio news earlier that day, only the headlines, just for the time it had taken to buy the carton of milk that had been his breakfast. He made his way back to a desk, logged in, and loaded the BBC News website. He stared at the main headline then back to those twelve pages: and knew he was so terribly wrong.

Chapter 2

Edinburgh, Scotland
Sunday, 7 May 2017 19:10

The taxi passed the King's Buildings campus of Edinburgh University before turning into a side road leading up to the Royal Observatory's home on Blackford Hill. The driver continued a one-sided conversation about football, receiving an occasional nod from a passenger whose thoughts were on a brother he hadn't seen in over two years.

The outline of the observatory buildings came into view as tarmac roads and streetlights were exchanged for a gravel track and the deepening darkness of the hillside. The driver switched on the headlights, adjusted the speed for the loose surface, and followed the road as it wound upwards. The track ended at a car park, where the observatory's high stone walls were lit up by the blue lights of police cars parked up in a hurry outside the compound's main entrance.

Ben Millar paid the driver, and stepped out into a public car park popular with dog walkers and those wanting a view over the city from the south. Lighting up a cigarette, he spotted the black 1967 Rover P5B Coupe, a car Simon had owned since his undergraduate days. Ben had never understood the attraction, it was a big, boxy saloon most famously used by government ministers and members of the Royal family. In fact, the car was plain ugly, but Simon loved his 3.5 litre Rover and while girlfriends and a wife had come and gone, the staid old car remained.

A small crowd surrounded a cop controlling access at the observatory's main gate. Ben walked on to a low iron fence where he could see small groups had come together as though waiting for the end of a fire drill. They were mostly students, the campus busy with end of year exams.

The observatory resembled a small fortress, with high walls and low iron fencing ringing an open courtyard. The Victorian section was impressive, the red sandstone building laid out in a T-shape, with towers at each end and a library extending out from the centre. Both towers were unusually shaped as cylindrical drums rather than the standard domed hemispheres commonly found on observatories around the world. They were topped with weathered copper and ornately decorated with stone carvings and numerous inscriptions. The staff and students were lucky to work in such a place, even those, like his brother, situated in the awkward, stone-clad annexe tacked onto the west side.

Ben decided to head for the annexe, where there was a number of police standing outside. He vaulted the fence, and continued past an ambulance directly outside the east tower's visitor's centre. He glanced through the open doors to find a young woman, dressed in black, sitting by a medic. He couldn't help but stare, and turned away when she caught his eye. She looked totally lost, the streaked mascara, and short black hair highlighted the paleness of her complexion, the distinctive silver stud on her left lower lip making her look even more vulnerable. He kept on walking, wondering what she'd been through. There was no obvious sign of injury, but he feared the worse as there was little security in or around the campus buildings. Her presence explained the police, and his initial concern that Simon was somehow involved started to pass, but he'd been called here for a reason, and he needed to find out why?

Ben made his way to the Institute of Astronomy building, and the waiting cops. As he approached, an officer stepped forward, his hand barring the way.

"Can I help you, sir?"

"I'm looking for my brother, he works here," Ben said.

He felt the cop look him over; the waxed-cotton Barbour jacket looked smart enough with jeans, t-shirt, and a blue v-neck jumper. The downside was the bruising to his face, still visible through a deep tan, and a missing tooth on his upper left jaw.

The cop took out a notebook, "Did you just get out of a taxi?"

Ben nodded.

"Did you speak to the officer at the gate?"

"No, he was busy."

"This is a crime scene, no-one should have got past the gate," he said shaking his head, he looked at Ben closely "You're not a reporter, are you?"

"I received a call from the university an hour ago saying my brother, Professor Simon Millar, had some kind of breakdown. They had my number as an emergency contact, and I'm here to find out what's going on."

The cop paused, "Wait here a moment," he said before walking a few paces away to speak into his radio.

After a short conversation he turned back to Ben. "Can I see some ID?"

"No problem," Ben replied reaching for his wallet.

Ben waited as a stretcher was wheeled out of the building, a police sergeant leading the way. The trolley was empty, and the sergeant shook his head to another cop at the door.

"What's happening?" Ben asked.

"You'll have to speak to one of detectives," the cop replied not looking up from Ben's driving licence.

"It's obvious my brother's involved. You got on the radio the moment you heard my name."

The cop compared Ben to his licence photo, "There's been an incident, your brother is involved, he's with paramedics-"

"How bad?" Ben interrupted.

"I can't tell you anything else, but someone will be coming out to talk to you."

That reply told Ben the cop knew more than he was saying, and the rest wasn't good. He stubbed the cigarette out on a bin, and nodded towards the ambulance, "I'll wait for the detective over there."

The cop nodded, "I'll ask him to be as quick as he can."

Ben sat on stone steps outside the library. He remembered seeing Simon's face on TV and reading an article which mentioned him as leading one of the experiments at the new particle accelerator in Switzerland. He'd been proud to hear it, and wished their parents had been alive to witness another success. The ten-year age difference had left a gap neither brother had tried to bridge; they had little in common, and were more like distant cousins who collided at the occasional family event. He couldn't remember the last time they'd spoken.

Two uniformed cops stood on the other side of the ambulance and Ben heard Simon's name. He shook his head, and tried to listen in, but the conversation had moved on. Three men in suits passed by, the last one having a close look over at him.

"Look out, Special Branch's arrived," One of the cops said.

"That was quick," the other replied.

Ben shuffled along to hear them clearly.

"What'd you expect? That professor called 999 to claim responsibility for the dirty bomb attack in Germany."

Ben could hardly breathe, the Ohrdruf attack was all over the news.

"I'd heard a rumour, who told you?"

"The sergeant. There was a queue of people wanting a chat with the professor about that."

"Who'd have guessed?"

"Too right, he cut his own wrists... lost a lot of blood. They're all too late, he won't be talking to anyone again."

Ben sat on the cold, lifeless stone, and took in what he'd just seen and heard. An empty ambulance stretcher pushed casually out of the building, no emergency, no-one in a hurry, the overheard words - Simon was dead.

He closed his eyes, he'd learned to accept death, his past was littered with it, his mother gone while he was still a kid, close friends lost in training accidents or enemy contacts, but however remote their relationship had been, Simon was the only family he had left.

Ben wasn't sure how he felt, but realised the overwhelming emotion was confusion. He knew Simon hadn't cut his wrists, that was simply impossible. Simon was a man of few doubts, a man whose life meant something. Thoughts of suicide would never occur to him, and then there was the terror claim, had he heard that right? Nothing added up, he needed to talk to the girl, she was part of this, and she must know something.

The radio on one of the cop's shoulders crackled into life. Ben glanced around; something familiar had cut through the noise above the chatter. He scanned the immediate area, then it struck him - it was a distinctive sound from an engine designed over fifty years earlier, it was the sound of Simon's car.

Ben skirted around the police, following the east tower wall to where he'd last seen the old Rover parked up. Exhaust fumes billowed out from the cold engine of the vintage car.

It jerkily reversed a few feet, then stopped suddenly. Ben checked to see if the cops had noticed, but there was no reaction, so he made directly for the car. Simon was dead and someone was taking his car.

Ben ran flat out towards the gates, a solitary student watched as he changed direction, angling his approach to make it difficult for the driver to see him.

The car swung out from its parking space in a violent motion, the driver making sure there was no second stall. Ben slowed to a walk as the car turned to face him, he was unable to see behind the glare of its headlights. As it passed, he reached for the passenger door, but missed, recovering to pull on the rear door handle, open it, and throw himself onto the back seat. The car accelerated hard, then braked heavily, plummeting Ben into the rear foot well before accelerating once more. He twisted immediately to pull himself upright.

A female voice screamed, "Get out! Oh no, oh please no!"

He got onto his knees to see the cop on the gate jump for his life. Ben held on as they skidded sideways and skipped across the car park and onto the dirt track leading back down to the city.

Ben reached for the handbrake, if that didn't stop them, he'd go for the driver.

"Get out of my car!" she shouted as her left elbow snapped back. He tried to slip the impact but caught a glancing blow under his left eye. He instinctively reached for her hair, but stopped short of closing his fist. His anger gave way to fear - they were heading for a stone wall.

"Watch out!" Ben shouted, pulling at the wheel and bracing as they just made the corner and accelerated towards the next.

"This isn't your car," Ben shouted. "Pull it over... now!"

To his surprise, the car screeched to a halt, and he was thrown back into the worn, brown leather he'd first sat on as a teenager. He didn't know what to expect next, but his eyes widened when she turned to face him. He was seeing her face for the second time that evening - the pale white skin was exaggerated by the jet black hair. The remains of the dark mascara that still ringed her eyes from having found Simon dead or dying.

"You were in the ambulance!"

"Who are you?" she shouted. "Tell me quickly, the police are coming..."

Ben looked through the rear window and saw that cops were sprinting towards the stationary car.

"My brother owns this car, so I think you'd better stop this right now."

He leaned forward, pulled the handbrake on, and held it.

"Simon's brother, the soldier?"

"Not any more."

She considered him for a moment, "We have to go, I'm doing this for Simon."

"Doing what?"

The cops were barely twenty metres from the car.

"Simon was attacked, I'll tell you everything, but we have to go now."

He released the handbrake and sat back, she blinked, then turned as the car jerked forward, accelerating away.

Ben watched as the cops pulled up, their hands going for their radios.

Chapter 3

Major Peter Kessler read the message summoning him to a meeting with the newly promoted commander-in-chief of German naval forces, Admiral Donitz. Kessler checked his watch and then his uniform. The former told him it had been close to twenty hours since he'd slept, while the latter was torn, blood-stained and beyond repair.

He nodded to the waiting sergeant who pulled the Frenchman's head from the iron table where the pliers had torn out his teeth. The boy had nothing more to give. A recent recruit to the resistance aged barely nineteen, he knew nothing of value - nothing they hadn't already obtained from his comrade whose naked, flayed body hung from a hook in the centre of the cell. That sight had caused the boy to piss himself, and he'd begged to talk before a blow was struck.

The young man had been blessed with a strong, athletic frame, but his shattered leg twitched uncontrollably as though unable to comprehend any impulses other than pain. There was no reason for pity, good men died the previous day, and Kessler had nearly been one of them.

He motioned to end the interrogation and walked out as the sergeant aimed a final punch that swept the boy to the floor. He'd be left to lie in his filth until dragged to the gallows later that afternoon.

Kessler made his way to his quarters where he dressed and shaved. He checked his reflection in the full-length mirror; he'd hardly gained any weight since his competitive boxing days, the result of hard, regular training.

Donitz's visit to the U-boat base was no real surprise. As a submarine captain in the last war, his affection for U-boats was known well enough. While a man of that rank was free to go where he pleased. Kessler, as the officer responsible for security in the Lorient sector, should have been informed of his imminent arrival. Who else knew he was here? And more importantly, could he have been the real target of last night's attack?

Kessler met his adjutant, Captain Karl Muller, ten minutes before the appointment. They walked together down the stone steps, out onto the courtyard and a waiting car.

"Good morning, sir, did you get anything out of the partisans?" Muller asked.

"Nothing of importance, did you have better luck?"

"I caught up with the girl on the edge of the town," Muller replied, "There was a capsule hidden in her mouth. She actually smiled as she bit down."

"Damn, she was the one, the British bitch behind all this," Kessler said. "We needed her alive."

Muller shrugged, "They all told the same story - the target was any German in uniform. The operation was days in the planning, and they knew nothing about a visiting admiral. An attack twenty minutes earlier might have gotten them one."

Kessler shook his head, "I lost three good men. Round up twenty locals, they can hang alongside their countrymen and the English girl. Take another twenty as hostages. Let's remind them resistance has a price."

Muller acknowledged the order, "And now the admiral has called. Any idea what he wants, sir?"

"I hoped you would tell me. For once, we are both in the dark. Come, my friend, we will find out together."

The SS men's car approached the waterside Chateau that had been Admiral Donitz's headquarters before the previous year's disastrous British commando raid on the port of St Nazaire. That attack gave Kessler responsibility for the security of the largest U-boat base in France, with the Fuhrer's authority to execute the survivors from any future commando missions. The British would know from his treatment of the local resistance that anyone captured faced immediate execution.

It was British desperation to counter the U-boat threat that led to the suicidal raid on St Nazaire. So many Englishmen died destroying the port's dry dock, but they would consider the raid a success, and so a similar attack was a possibility. Kessler had turned Lorient into a fortress, but it was still deemed prudent to move the U-boat command, and the admiral, to Paris.

During the Napoleonic wars, the French had used this port to defend their shores against an enduring British foe. It was being used against the British again, this time to cut their lifeline to the United States. The naval blockade they had planned to defeat the Fatherland had been shattered by the U-boat wolfpacks housed in their pens across the waters to the north.

Their car passed through wrought iron gates into the Chateau grounds. Sentries stood smartly to attention, as despite the poor light, they instantly recognised the tall, slim major. One of Donitz's aides, a young naval lieutenant, waited as they approached. They were led inside where Kessler handed the lieutenant his leather coat. He studied the sailor's immaculate uniform, contrasting it with the generally unkempt appearance of bearded U-boat officers and men. The junior staff officer had a good chance of seeing the end of the war, but Kessler would have preferred the chance of an Iron Cross on a U-boat command.

"Sir, the admiral wishes to see you right away," the young officer said in a clear controlled voice. Kessler could feel his discomfort.

"Then, you had better take us to him."

The SS officers followed the lieutenant up a staircase to the first floor where they were shown into a large drawing room. Admiral Donitz stood around a desk with two of his senior men studying a map. He briefly raised his head as the door closed behind Kessler. He waved them to come forward before going back to whatever they had interrupted.

Kessler walked to the centre of the room, he knew Donitz reasonably well, but their relationship was cool. Kessler was left with the impression the man didn't care for his methods. Whatever the admiral's view, it was easy to kill through a periscope or the sights of a rifle. It was very different close up with a knife. He considered the admiral a hypocrite; his U-boats killed men, women and children in the thousands. He just didn't have to look at the faces, or hear the screams when his orders set the seas alight.

The SS men waited in silence for a full minute before Donitz looked up. He seemed to have reached a decision and issued a series of commands before dismissing his men.

Donitz picked up a single sheet of paper from the desk, and glanced at Kessler before reading the contents. Only then did he stroll over to the stone fireplace, and finally address the new arrivals.

"I hear you survived an attack, Major," Donitz stated. "I take it you are well?"

"Very well, thank you," Kessler replied, fully aware that the man had little interest in his wellbeing. "I was concerned you might have been the target, but no-one knew of your visit – even I was not informed."

The admiral's face was taut, there was anger, and Kessler held his gaze waiting to find out why.

"Major, I would like to know what you can tell me about this?" Donitz said, as he walked back and placed the sheet of paper on his desk. Kessler moved forward and read a message received hours earlier. The main section was still encrypted. He removed his right glove and pushed the message towards Muller.

"Sir, this is news to me. What does the remainder say?" It would be so much easier if he wasn't forced to play these games.

"What about this?" The admiral handed Kessler another sheet of paper; it contained a technical description, and looked like an excerpt from some scientific manual.

"I have no idea," Kessler replied hardly looking at it, "can we speak plainly?"

"Very well, Major, the first message was received a few hours ago. It is an unauthorised message transmitted on the naval Enigma and addressed to you. How did the sender know the current naval Enigma codes? I would very much like you to enlighten me, Major? This is a serious breach of the very security that you are responsible for maintaining."

Kessler expected signals sent to him to use the army Enigma, Donitz was paranoid about communications security, so much so, his variant of the Enigma machine had an extra rotor to increase the complexity of the encryption. The extra rotor had not been taken up by the other services as the standard machine was considered completely secure.

"I know nothing of the message. Please have the full message decrypted and sent to my office. I will start an investigation immediately."

"The rest of the message is irrelevant. All I require from you is an explanation of who sent that message, and how they knew the codes?" Donitz replied.

"Sir, as I have already stated, I had no knowledge of this message before this meeting, or who could have sent it. I have no access to naval codes and neither do any of my men. I will start an investigation, but you must understand - I need the clear text of the full message to continue," Kessler repeated.

"Thank you, Kessler, I have started my own enquiry, so your help is not required-"

"But sir-"

"Do think me a fool? I will not allow your henchmen to use systems vital to the Reich. My investigation will discover those responsible, and they will pay a heavy price. Now, if we have no other business, please resume your duties."

The admiral turned his back in a sudden dismissal.

Kessler eyes widened at the rebuke, but that was the only outward sign of a quick temper.

"Sir, the message is addressed to me, and says the source has important information. Regardless of any other investigation, I request the full text of the message once more. There is a possibility the contents have some value."

The admiral turned to Kessler, a derisive expression on his face, Kessler stared him down, forcing himself to remain calm.

"Major, communications security is paramount, and I will not allow another, unreliable investigation. Has it not dawned on you that our enemies could be reading our signals? I would ensure that your house is in order with regards to this message. We have been forced to change our Enigma codes across the entire fleet, and I intend on making an example of the cause - whoever that may be. You asked for plain speaking - I have decided the contents of the message will be destroyed, as will anyone I find connected to it. Good day, Major!"

The admiral turned away once more, and was already looking out the next matter in need of his attention. Kessler didn't reply as he caught Muller's eye and motioned towards the door. They walked in silence to the top of the staircase at which point Kessler stopped: "I want to know all about that message. Someone sent it to me for a reason. Get a copy and find the naval codes we need to decrypt it, and Muller, I don't care how you do it."

Chapter 4

Edinburgh, Scotland
Sunday, 7 May 2017 19:41

Ben felt for a seatbelt as they gained speed, but the car was in original condition and they'd never been fitted. Whatever the ambulance girl hoped to achieve, they couldn't get far. The heavy car with its big 3.5 litre engine would be easily outperformed by anything remotely modern. The performance, and the fact it was so distinctive, made it a terrible getaway car.

"Slow down, you're going to crash," Ben shouted.

"I know how to drive, and we're not going far."

"I hope you know what you're doing," Ben replied, bracing as the car swerved to narrowly avoid a stationary van.

She studied him through the rear mirror, "You look nothing like Simon."

"That suits me, but he's my brother all the same."

"What are you doing here?" she asked.

"I got a call about some problem with Simon," Ben checked his watch, "I arrived about seven minutes ago, and was waiting to talk to the cops when I overheard some stuff I didn't understand, and then this car's engine starting up. The cops think he cut his own wrists-"

"That's bullshit," she snapped.

"We agree on that, but I need to know why my brother is dead."

As the car rolled back onto tarmac, their eyes met through the mirror once more, and Ben could see tears running down her face.

"The way things are, the cops aren't going to let us get far, they'll want to know why you've taken his car, and I need to know too?"

"OK, I understand."

"Then who are you?" Ben asked, as the car shifted under braking.

"Lily Taylor, I worked with Simon."

Ben studied her, who was this girl? The all-black uniform of skin-tight army trousers, converse baseball boots, and faded shirt. She was tall, close to his height. She was athletic rather than thin, with an interesting, pretty face framed by a layered bob with a strong, angular fringe. A tattoo showed below the shirt sleeve at her right wrist, and she had several prominent piercings.

"OK, we're introduced," Ben said. "What makes it a good idea to run from the cops?"

"I know what I'm doing!" She replied. "I'll explain, but we need to get away from here now."

Ben knew the area around the observatory; narrow streets with cars jammed into every available parking space. It would take less than a minute to join a major road.

The car accelerated, and although they were only doing forty miles per hour, the speed was dangerous for the road, and Ben lent forward, tempted to hold the wheel straight and go for the handbrake before someone got hurt.

As he got closer, he heard her voice, it was quiet, barely a whisper, "I don't want any of this." The car jerked forward as her foot pressed further to the floor. As he was about to speak, she glared at him, then braked hard without warning, as though getting herself and the car back under control.

Ben held on tight, "How far?"

"Close..."

Ben sat back, the car was still travelling too fast. Sirens were coming from all around them, and they'd be stopped soon enough. He wanted time to talk to her before the police caught up with them. They just made a green light and joined a main road, bottoming out the suspension, as the car snaked and skidded towards the affluent residential areas of Morningside and the Grange.

They headed up a slight incline before turning left, Ben knew this road, it led to Morningside with high walls stretching the length of the street on either side. The well-spaced electric gates and entry intercoms were the only giveaway that some expensive homes lay behind the otherwise anonymous stone walls. They had barely turned in before the old Rover shuddered to a halt.

"Damn, wrong way!" Lily said as she clunked the gearbox into reverse and spun the car around. They moved off, and to Ben's relief, stopped briefly at a junction before crossing to a street where the large, elegant houses faced out proudly for all to see. The police sirens were closer now, and the wrong turn could only hasten their capture.

Lily suddenly dropped their speed and drove slowly. She pulled the car into a driveway and continued around to the rear of a large detached house before coming to a stop.

Security lights illuminated a generous, landscaped garden which bordered the paved parking area. They were hidden from the road.

"You live here?" Ben asked.

"Yeah, right. Like I could afford a house in the Grange on an academic salary. I can hardly afford anything in this city, that's if I could get a mortgage after the economic meltdown, and the fuck up that is Brexit."

"Well, whose is it then?"

"No idea, but I pass here daily, it's been up for sale for months. It's my dream home, but at offers over £1,200,000 - I'll have to pass. I guessed it'd be empty, so it was worth the risk to come here."

Ben looked at his watch; it was only a few minutes since they'd left the top of a hill barely a mile away. A police siren wailed close by, Ben waited for a patrol car to pull in behind them. A moment later the siren faded, leaving them in the clear for now.

He turned back to find Lily's eyes closed, while she repeatedly clasped her hands together.

"Are you OK?"

"Do I look OK?" she snapped, "I don't think I'll ever be OK after this."

"Can you tell me what happened?" He asked.

"I don't like thinking about it... He was covered in so much blood."

She stopped, realising she was talking to someone close to Simon.

"I'm sorry, I wasn't thinking, this must be hard for you."

"Go on, and don't spare any details."

"I didn't know how to help him. I don't think he was in pain, he was hardly moving - like he was trying to conserve his energy... trying to hold on for help."

"Did he say anything? I told you the police think it's suicide..."

"He was murdered, there's no way he would take his own life."

He nodded his agreement, "Did he say anything at all?"

"I couldn't make it out, I don't think he knew I was there."

"I was hoping for more than that."

"You think I didn't want more?" She replied. "I was in his office to get answers."

"To what questions?"

"He phoned me earlier - what he said didn't make a lot of sense."

Ben frowned, "Did he say anything about Ohrdruf?"

"The place in the news?"

"Yes, and that's the part I don't understand, when I heard two cops talking, they said he made a phone call claiming responsibility for yesterday's terrorist attack at Ohrdruf in Germany."

She leant back against the car, shaking her head as he offered a cigarette.

"What attack?" she asked. "What are you talking about?"

"It's been on the news all day, a dirty bomb attack outside Berlin."

"He claimed responsibility? But that's impossible..."

"Not according to the police, Special Branch had arrived to question him."

"I don't understand..."

"What did he say when he phoned you?" Ben asked.

"He was going to make a big announcement, but there might be a problem. He wouldn't explain, but if anything happened to him, I would find an envelope in his car and I was to take it to James Munro, that's the head of his department."

"Have you got the envelope?"

"I haven't had time to look," she said pulling the glove compartment open.

Ben flicked his cigarette into the garden, and looked at her impassively as a powerful car entered the driveway.

Chapter 5

Andrew Shaw did not need the training of a Secret Intelligence Service officer to conclude the Detective Chief Inspector Ian Whyte was not best pleased. The stream of orders, punctuated by curses and threats, made that clear to all who found themselves in the dead man's office.

The professor's body lay behind the desk, eyes open, looking blindly at investigators charged with making sense of a life that had drained away through crude wounds to the lower arms and wrists.

A Special Branch liaison officer called him over to the ill-tempered DCI, and he wondered what he'd done to deserve chasing some ridiculous confession on the fringe of the Ohrdruf investigation.

He carefully passed the forensics team who continued to work despite the surrounding drama. Shaw stared into the dead eyes trying to understand why on earth a man like this would contact the police and claim responsibility for a terror attack.

"I was told you were coming," DCI Whyte said without welcome, "What's MI6's involvement? The phone call made by our friend here?"

Shaw nodded, "I won't take up much of your time, Chief Inspector. That call is the only reason I'm here. I travelled a long way to interview him."

"You're a little late," Whyte said looking to the body.

"What can you tell me about his death?" Shaw asked.

"Let's make sure we understand each other first - I'm running this investigation, so any information you turn up relevant to this inquiry is disclosed immediately - is that understood?"

"I'm hoping to wrap this up by the end of the day. It doesn't seem likely he's involved in Ohrdruf. I'll be on my way when I have something to rule him out."

The DCI turned to examine the body, "Professor Millar isn't known to us, not even a speeding ticket. What have you got?"

Shaw had read the professor's file on the way over, and took up the invitation to share.

"As a prominent scientist, he's on record," Shaw said, "but there's little of interest: he's well regarded in his field, nothing to suggest he's a security risk, his finances are in order, he's never been politically active, and the medical history's clear. That's the extent of his file, apart from this phone call, there's nothing to put him on our radar."

The DCI grunted seemingly satisfied.

"Well, what I have so far is right in front of you: alcohol, slashed wrists and a crazy phone call."

"Self-inflicted?" Shaw asked as he noted the empty bottle of Jack Daniels lying on the floor.

"I like simple explanations."

"Anything to back that up?"

"Apparently Millar's been acting out of character, working crazy hours, and pushing himself hard. Who knows what was going on in his head when he made that phone call? Suicide's a definite possibility, but I'll know more when the pathologist makes her report."

"Is anything missing?" Shaw asked, looking around the office.

"There's no sign of a robbery-" Whyte replied, before being distracted by a uniformed sergeant who was making directly for them.

"Sir, the girl that found the body has just driven off in the victim's car!"

"Tell me this is your idea of a joke."

He shook his head, "Sorry sir, and they nearly ran over some uniforms as they left."

"They?" Shaw asked.

The sergeant glanced at Shaw, Whyte nodded for him to continue, "She took off with the victim's brother, Ben Millar."

He's going to explode, Shaw thought as the DCI's colour brightened.

"Ben Millar?" Shaw asked.

"The victim's brother, he was supposed to be waiting for me outside," Whyte replied, "I take it, we're chasing them down?"

"Yes, sir."

"Get them into custody. I do not want to have to explain how a witness managed to drive off in the victim's car, I will look like a fucking idiot, so find them and do it fast."

The sergeant hurried away.

"Bad luck," Shaw said.

Whyte forced a smile, "As I was saying, Millar still had his wallet, and the piles of papers and books everywhere are apparently normal. So for what it's worth, I doubt he's linked to your terrorist event. It's more likely he lost his way and topped himself."

"So suicide is your main line of inquiry?"

"All lines of enquiry are open, Shaw, so if you'll excuse me."

"Just one last question, you don't seem too concerned about the missing witness?"

Whyte stopped for a moment, the colour rising again.

"The girl's in shock after finding this mess. One thing I do know, they'll be found soon enough."

Shaw watched as the DCI left the soiled office then followed him out. His mind churned over the possibility of a suicide and it fitted what he'd heard so far. When incidents such as Ohrdruf hit the media the crank calls rose in proportion to the news exposure, and the professor's call came after hours of blanket TV and radio coverage. Shaw would have to wait until morning to get a flight back to Berlin, but he'd need the story on the brother and missing witness before returning to the real investigation leaving him behind on the continent.

Chapter 6

Edinburgh, Scotland
Sunday, 7 May 2017 19:59

A large, silver-grey Mercedes estate stopped behind the Rover. Lily stepped forward, waving to the driver, as Professor James Munro stepped out of the car and greeted them with a tight smile. He was a tall, thin man with piercing blue eyes and immaculate hair that colour-matched his car. The formal, tailored jacket worn with jeans and a fashionable, expensive shirt were more media executive than academic. Munro certainly gave the impression of being extremely certain of himself, something Ben welcomed as they needed someone who could handle people fleeing a murder scene.

"Lily, I can't believe any of this, it's a terrible, terrible shock, and you having found him - it's too dreadful for words," Munro said taking both her hands.

Lily acknowledged Munro with a hesitant smile before introducing Ben.

"James, this is Ben Millar, he's Simon's brother," she said, her voice quiet.

"I'm so sorry about Simon, I can't quite believe it," Munro said putting his hand on Ben's shoulder. "I worked with Simon for a long time, he mentioned you now and then. He told me you'd been injured while serving abroad, he was so worried about you."

Ben nodded, but Simon only knew he'd been injured after the recovery, and they'd never talked about his service life.

"You look well enough now, it was the Royal Marines, wasn't it? Did you return to active duty?" Munro asked.

"It was, but I've been out two years," Ben replied.

"What are you doing now?"

"Diver, working in oil and gas."

Munro smiled, "Well, you must be fit enough now, I'm glad to hear it."

They were interrupted by the sound of ripping paper.

"Simon left this for me," she said as they both looked over.

She was holding an opened envelope, a wad of bank notes, and a thin sheaf of stapled A4 paper. She looked curiously at the cash, placing it on the bonnet of the Mercedes.

"That must be over a grand," Ben said.

"More, there are fifty pound notes too," Lily replied as she scanned the accompanying papers.

"What's going on?" Munro asked.

"I had to call you," Lily replied holding out the sheets. "Simon wanted me to give you these papers, I think they're related to his murder - they have to be."

"Murder?" Munro said, "The police think it's suicide."

"You know him better than that," Lily said handing him the papers.

Munro patted his jacket pockets, "Oh dear, we'll need to go back to my house, I've left my reading glasses in the hurry to get here."

"We can read them to you," Ben suggested.

"That won't work at all," Munro replied looking around them, "and I assume we're trespassing?"

"Did you see any police on your way over?" Ben asked.

"There were a few cars-"

"They're looking for us," Ben said. "We left the observatory in a hurry."

"The choice of meeting place made it obvious that things weren't exactly above board," Munro said.

"But I owe it to Simon to help out if I can, but I'm not prepared to do anything illegal and I won't lie to the authorities, I hope that's acceptable?"

"I'm going to publish Simon's paper, and we have nothing to hide," Lily replied.

The two men exchanged glances as she flipped back and forward through the pages, totally focused, immersing herself in Simon's work. Her eyes widened, and Ben stepped forward waiting for anything that might explain why they were here, but she simply continued, ignoring them both.

"What?" Munro asked impatiently.

Her eyes never left the page as she replied.

"He says he's found something... something the government won't want disclosed. Anyone who has worked on the project won't be safe until his work is in the public domain... he asked me to enlist your support to publish the papers... I've to use the money to go away for a few days. I'll be able to come back once Simon has worked things out."

Ben leaned against the car, "Whatever he was involved in, he didn't expect it to kill him."

A siren sounded in the distance, it was only a matter of time before the police realised they must have stopped and a systematic search was carried out.

"What's in those papers?" Munro asked Lily.

She held up a dozen printed pages.

"It's a research paper entitled 'Closed Timelike Curves and Causality'."

"Do you understand it?" Ben asked.

"Some of it," She replied giving him a sharp glance, "I'm a software engineer in the astronomy department."

"She also has a degree in electronic engineering, and a masters in mathematics," Munro said.

"Yeah, but my main thing is software," Lily added.

"What happened tonight?" Ben asked.

She gave a long sigh, "Simon called me today and asked if I could run some files through the decryption engine. I was surprised as he'd never asked before."

"The decryption engine?" Ben asked.

"Simon lined up some work for me through a friend, and the project developed software called the decryption engine. I usually work on open source code, but this was good gig, good enough to pay off my credit cards. The software ran on the physics department's grid system."

"Really? That system is exclusively used for our own projects." Munro said.

"You didn't know about it?" Lily asked.

"First I've heard of it," Munro replied. "It took us years to secure the funding. Neither Simon or myself would have allowed it."

"Well, Simon did," Lily replied.

"OK, what happened next?" Ben asked moving them on.

"Simon said he'd allowed something pretty stupid to happen... that he'd have to straighten things out, it was all in the package he'd left for me."

"And..." Ben said.

"He wouldn't go into it, and as I've told you already, he made me promise that if anything happened, I was to look in his car for a package and get it to James."

"What the hell did you say to that?" Munro asked.

"What could I say? He wouldn't talk over the phone, so I came to see him in person, and found him barely conscious."

They looked at each other through a brief, uncomfortable silence.

"What does the decryption engine do, on this grid?" Ben eventually asked.

"It's designed to decipher documents, to break codes," Lily replied, "Simon let it run on the grid, which is just a network of machines used to collaboratively model complex systems".

"Its power would be perfect for code breaking," Munro said, "What was being decrypted?"

"There was a vast amount of archive data from lots of sources. Some of it became available after the fall of the Iron Curtain. The system decrypted the messages into their native languages - it's pretty smart."

"And, it was only used for older messages, nothing current?" Ben asked.

"I don't think so. I was told the material was all pre-1960s, and the cipher strength is low by today's standards. Those documents can be broken by trying out every possible key combination in a brute force attack. The decryption engine uses artificial intelligence techniques to inspect each of the millions of decryption attempts and score them on whether a result looks like a recognised language. If the score is high enough it informs the user of success, the idea is to reduce the search space, speeding up the decryption process. It'll be pretty basic by GCHQ and NSA standards, but it does the job. It's mainly used on Russian archives containing radio signals captured over a number of decades, the Russians were only able to decode a small fraction at the time, but kept all intercepts on file."

"So, what was your part in this?" Ben asked.

"They wanted to speed up the computer code, and I've done that sort of work before. Most programmers don't have the necessary background to fully optimise or develop algorithms."

"Why decode those archives? Who wanted it done?"

"I don't know why, but the who is a historian called Charles Rae. He acquired the archive data and bankrolled the project. I'm not sure what he gets from it."

"I've met Charles Rae," Munro said, "but I had no idea he was using our systems."

"My worry is the decryption engine found something it shouldn't have, and that's why Simon was killed. I was worried enough to warn Charles just before I arranged to meet James here."

"You think it's possible Simon was murdered because of some old messages?" Ben asked.

"It's one possibility," Lily replied.

"Why take the car and run?" Ben asked.

"Someone killed Simon - I wanted to get away, and I thought I could do so without being noticed, but I didn't count on you."

"You can hardly blame me."

"I don't," she replied.

"Right," Munro said, "things are way out of hand, and we're going to have to let the police deal with this. The way you left in the car... it looks bad, they could think you're involved in Simon's death. The truth is, running away will make things more difficult for everyone."

Lily's face coloured, but she answered quietly.

"What if the police seize all of this as evidence?" She asked, holding out Simon's envelope. "Don't you want to read this before making a decision?"

"Of course I do, but it might have been better if he had trusted the authorities," Munro reasoned. "Lily, this couldn't be more serious. We have to go to the police eventually."

"The decryption engine deals with government signals-"

"Are you really suggesting the government had him killed," Munro interrupted.

"I don't know," she snapped back. "I don't trust any government? They routinely spy on our emails, the sites we visit, our interactions on social networks, and they monitor our texts and voice calls. Why should I trust them? You both know Simon, he wasn't weak or prone to panic. He was worried enough about me to have provided all this," she said lifting up a handful of bank notes. "You know him - that must mean something?"

"I know him well enough," Munro replied, "he could come across as selfish and arrogant, but he was no-one's fool."

"Then you'll understand why I'm doing this," Lily said, "Wait, this looks like a message from the archives, the one he asked me to process earlier today." She held out a single page.

"It doesn't look like modern cipher text, these characters are alphabetic in groups of five," she continued, "the industry standard algorithms such as 3DES and AES produce a jumble of characters outside the ASCII range."

"I'll have to take your word for it," Ben said.

"There are standard encryption libraries, and you don't have to understand them to use them. The world is full of script kiddies who testify to that. Modern encryption algorithms are almost impossible to break, but these repeating groups of five characters are most likely to be a World War Two German Enigma message," she said pointing to the text, "and that's a different story altogether."

"Are you sure, this looks Russian?" Ben asked, pointing to a date.

04.фев.1943

"That's just a header with the date the message was intercepted, and it's the same date as the one I decoded for Simon earlier. It was intercepted by the Soviets in February 1943, and will definitely be Enigma," she replied.

She took another page from the pile, "There's another one," she said. "Same date... but there was only one this morning?"

"Did you see the decrypted version?" Ben asked.

"No, I just set it running and told Simon where to find it after it had been cracked."

"OK, what's the plan now?" Ben asked.

"James' house, we need his glasses?" Lily asked.

"Well, let's go then," Munro replied. "We can plan our next move once we know what we have," he started walking to his car. "We'll pass the observatory, hopefully the police are looking for you everywhere, but there."

Munro reversed carefully back onto the road, Ben had a last look at Simon's old Rover, then scanned both ways to find the road was clear.

"It's a short journey," Munro said speaking to Lily as he shifted the automatic gearbox into drive. "I have to ask - did you hear about the Ohrdruf incident?"

"We know Simon made a call to the police," Ben replied. "He appears to have claimed responsibility."

"That's what the police told me, they wanted my opinion on Simon's mental state-"

"And what did you say?" Lily asked.

"I said he'd been driving himself hard lately, but I didn't think for one moment he could have lost his senses. That didn't sound such a convincing argument after they told me about that phone call. I hope you don't mind me asking," Munro said, "but could the wounds have been self-inflicted?"

From the rear seat, Ben could see Lily's face harden, she took a deep breath before replying.

"Simon would never do that, and you should know better than to ask."

"I had to ask... claiming responsibility for a dirty bomb attack thousands of miles away, does raise questions," Munro replied.

"Which we're hoping you can help answer," Lily said.

"I'll try, but we need to keep open minds."

"Not on that, we don't," Lily said turning away to look out of the car.

Munro focused on his driving while Ben shared a silence that left him with a feeling of growing unease. There were so many questions: why had Simon claimed responsibility for a terror attack, why had he been so distrustful of the authorities, who was Charles Rae, and what had the decryption engine really found?

The Mercedes drove on past affluent houses where their car was yet another luxury vehicle. They skirted around Blackford Hill and were slowing for traffic lights when their headlights caught the extensive reflective markings of a stationary traffic car. It was parked up on the pavement with a clear view of all approaches to the junction. Munro didn't react, and they were still rolling when the lights changed in their favour. As Munro coolly accelerated away, Ben could feel the cops scanning the passing car, but he'd already looked away in the same way quite innocent people tried to fade into the background when passing through customs.

He waited for the squeal of tyres, or a blaring siren to stop them dead, but they continued on until the car turned into a quiet street.

"I've never been stopped by the police in my life," Munro commented. "I look far too respectable for any of that."

Chapter 7

Lorient, France
Thursday, 11 February 1943 12:15

It took less than five minutes by car from the Kerovan submarine pens to the restaurants on Lorient's Rue du Port. Karl Muller was unsurprised to find the major sitting at the same table they'd survived a deadly attack barely twenty-four hours earlier.

It was the care Kessler took when visiting the town that saved them. His bodyguards prevailed against a fierce assault, but not without taking losses.

It was pure luck the resistance missed killing the architect of the Atlantic war; Donitz had left the cafe a few minutes earlier and may well have been the real target of the attack. Was the admiral a large enough prize to risk the carnage that would follow? They must have realised hostages would be taken, and a number executed in retaliation. The captured Frenchmen certainly knew nothing of the admiral's presence, believing they were part of a random action, but their ignorance didn't necessarily extend to the mission planners?

The major was letting the locals know he would go where he pleased, and visiting the day after the attack was simply another reminder of who controlled their town.

The car pulled up and Muller watched the proprietor buzzing around Kessler's table playing the genial host. He played the part well, his practised warmth may have fooled the idiots and drunks, but Muller knew the man hated every German uniform, and feared them more. The major had insisted the cafe open as normal, but as expected, there were no other patrons this lunchtime. It would take a strong stomach to eat across from the broken bodies that hung on a makeshift frame directly across the street. There was no attempt to hide the violence of their deaths, and the torture was obvious on the semi-naked bodies of the young men. Only the English spy was fully clothed and unmarked. She hung like an obscene doll, her alabaster skin drained of blood, soon to discolour and decay. Muller paid her no more attention, another corpse among the countless he had witnessed these past years.

Major Kessler understood the proprietor's position, and said he was a brave man in his own way, continuing with family life as best he could, while the new order formed around them. Muller caught the major's eye and was invited to take a seat. The major poured Muller a glass of red wine while staring openly at their host's daughter, she was as aware of this as her father, and was anything but afraid. That would change when she was dragged from her bed that night and questioned. Guilty or innocent, her family's fate was already sealed, and the coming days would see many more would pay for the failed attack.

"Muller, you have the message?" Kessler asked.

"Yes sir, I had one of our men approach a radioman and ask for a copy. He explained it was a delicate situation, and our radioman was able to help," Muller replied.

"This must not come to the attention of the admiral."

"An informant told us of liaisons between a local man and the radioman, both were due to be arrested, and so he had no choice but to cooperate, and do so quietly."

"Make sure of that - have him disappear. You have seen the message contents?"

"Yes sir, they look sensational, but admiral is apparently unimpressed."

"Don't make me wait any longer, man - the message?" Kessler held out his hand for the typed page.

IMPORTANT, THIS MESSAGE IS FOR THE ATTENTION OF MAJOR PETER KESSLER. DO

NOT DECODE THE FOLLOWING SECTION WITHOUT AUTHORISATION.
   ***

I MAKE THE FOLLOWING OFFER WHICH IS NON-NEGOTIABLE. I HAVE ACCESS TO TOP-LEVEL INFORMATION REGARDING THE DEVELOPMENT OF AN ALLIED SUPER WEAPON - AN ATOMIC BOMB.

I AM AWARE GERMAN SCIENTISTS REJECTED THE FEASIBILITY OF DEVELOPING SUCH A DEVICE FOR USE IN THE CURRENT CONFLICT, BUT THE ALLIES ARE A MATTER OF MONTHS FROM ENRICHING THE FISSILE MATERIAL REQUIRED FOR SUCH A WEAPON, AND TESTS ON A DELIVERY MECHANISM ARE AT AN ADVANCED STAGE.

I CAN SUPPLY INFORMATION TO ALLOW YOUR SCIENTISTS TO COMPETE DIRECTLY WITH THIS EFFORT. I CAN PROVIDE THE LATEST THEORETICAL PAPERS AND PRACTICAL RESULTS FROM THE TOP SECRET MANHATTAN PROJECT WHICH COMMENCED IN 1941.

IN RETURN, I WILL TAKE POSSESSION OF A CERTAIN ARTEFACT WHICH IS CURRENTLY IN THE CARE OF THE GERMAN REICH. MY MOTIVES ARE PURELY PERSONAL; I HAVE NO INTEREST IN THE OUTCOME OF THE WAR - MY ONLY INTEREST IS THE COLLECTION OF FINE ART.

MY PRICE FOR THIS VITAL INFORMATION IS CATHERINE THE GREAT'S AMBER ROOM. IT WAS REMOVED FROM THE WINTER PALACE IN ST PETERSBURG IN 1941.

PROVIDING MY TERMS ARE MET, A FULL DOSSIER ON ALLIED NUCLEAR TECHNOLOGY WILL BE SENT IN AN ENIGMA SIGNAL THIRTY DAYS FROM NOW.

THE LAWYERS LISTED BELOW ARE ACTING AS INTERMEDIARIES. THEY HAVE NO KNOWLEDGE OF MY IDENTITY. ANY ATTEMPT TO INTERFERE WITH THEM WILL RESULT IN THE DESTRUCTION OF THE DOSSIER WITHOUT TRANSMISSION.

AN EARLY THEORETICAL PAPER FOLLOWS THIS TEXT TO PROVIDE THE NECESSARY PROOF OF THE QUALITY OF THE INFORMATION. THERE WILL BE NO FURTHER CONTACT. YOU HAVE THIRTY DAYS TO TRANSFER THE AMBER ROOM.

The major sipped his wine as he leafed through the remaining pages.

"You are right, Karl, this cannot be ignored. Any possibility of an enemy super weapon must be investigated. Have you any evidence the admiral has passed this to Berlin?"

"No, I am told he believes the message is worthless, sir?"

"I will not rely on his beliefs, the authenticity of these documents must be verified one way or the other. Now, is there anything else?" Kessler asked.

"Yes sir, the lawyers are based in Zurich, I assume whoever sent this message has taken care in his dealings with them."

"No doubt, but you never know. Have them checked, nothing obvious. Let it be known we are travelling to Berlin for a few days, the admiral will think we are going to complain about being excluded from the investigation."

"Where are we going, sir?"

"To find our country's nuclear scientists. If they consider this document is genuine, then we will follow on to Berlin and make our case against the admiral's negligence complete. So find where nuclear research is carried out and arrange transport, make it later this evening as we have to round up a few more of these partisans."

"Yes sir," Muller replied standing up and quickly draining the wine.

Kessler topped up his own glass and absentmindedly re-read the main message. He called after Muller.

"One last thing, reserve a place on the next train east for the radioman's friend... no, wait, hang him with the others for the murder of a German radio operator, and add his family to those taken hostage."

Chapter 8

Edinburgh, Scotland
Sunday, 7 May 2017 20:06

Andrew Shaw left the dead professor's office to get some air. Why had his section chief, David Sykes, ordered him here? Surely a police report would have been enough to rule Simon Millar out of the Ohrdruf investigation? Sykes caused more problems than he solved, and this would be some arse-covering exercise so he could tell the chief that every avenue was being pursued. That would be fine if Shaw wasn't the one wasting his time.

Sykes would want an in-depth report that would end up filed unread, as it would soon be obvious that Millar was as responsible for Ohrdruf, as he was for the terror attack on 9/11. Shaw sighed, Sykes had to be retiring soon, the service had evolved over the past two decades, and the old boy's club was now a modern, professional organisation. Well most of it had, relics like Sykes held onto their networks, resisting any attempts for more accountability, and despite whatever good work he'd put in over the years, the service would be in a better place without him.

Shaw pulled out his phone and called the imposing MI6 headquarters at Vauxhall Cross on the south bank of the Thames. He selected Sylvia Bartlett's, number and pressed to connect.

"Hi, can I help you?" replied a male voice.

"Alan, it's Andrew Shaw. Is Sylvia about?"

"Nope, in a meeting, anything I can do?"

I'm on an investigation in Edinburgh, I need some information on the brother of a dead professor, the brother's name is Ben Millar. Also, anything you've got on a Lily Taylor who works for Edinburgh University. I'll email their details now."

"I'm working on some stuff for Sykes that can't wait. I'll leave Sylvia a message to see what she can find for you, but I'll send the basics to get you started."

Ben thanked the analyst and ended the call.

He turned to go back into the building when DCI Whyte burst out of the door, with the Special Branch man tagging along behind him.

"Shaw, I need a word," Whyte bellowed, "What do you know about Ben Millar?"

Shaw checked his phone, "Nothing yet, what's happened?"

"I've asked around, only a couple of Simon Millar's colleagues knew he had a brother, and none had met him."

"So?"

"He's worked here for close on twenty years, does that sound reasonable to you?"

"It doesn't sound unreasonable?"

Is he one of yours?"

"What?"

"I said, is he one of yours?"

"I have no idea what you're talking about."

Whyte moved closer.

"I asked you if you were holding out on me, is it really a coincidence you arrive around the same time as a man claiming to be Millar's brother, and he disappears with a witness?"

"I've got nothing to do with it. Ben Millar is supposed to be the victim's brother, I just asked for a background check, so let's just hold on until we know the facts."

Whyte snorted, "If I find out you've lied, I'll arrest you for attempting to pervert the course of justice, and don't think I won't - you got that, Shaw?"

"You've made it perfectly clear," Shaw replied.

DCI Whyte's phone rang, and he stood back to answer it. The Special Branch officer mouthed a sorry to Shaw who shrugged, and checked his own phone. There was an email waiting. He entered his passwords and read the text. Whyte had finished his call and was storming off.

Shaw's phone vibrated.

"Whyte," Shaw called after him. The DCI stopped and turned around.

"This is what I've got. Ben Millar, 29 years old, ex-royal marine... served seven years... this is interesting, four of them were in special forces, in the SBS."

Whyte through his hands up, "Are you kidding me? A member of the Special Boat Service, and he's not one of yours. I'm supposed to believe that?"

Shaw angled his phone to allow the DCI to read the screen.

"We have ex-SBS in the service, but he's definitely not one of ours. Look, he's been working as a saturation diver since he got out, and was recently deported from Zambia for police assault.

As for Lily Taylor, 26 years old, masters degree from Edinburgh in mathematics, with a first class degree in engineering from Cambridge. She works here as a research assistant. However, she's affiliated with a number of left-wing groups, and is an activist concerned with Internet privacy. She's contributed to free software to hide people's online activity... GCHQ have an interest in her. That's it for now, more should follow."

Whyte considered Shaw for a moment, "OK, Shaw, but just remember what I said. I've been fucked about by your lot before, I don't intend on letting it happen again."

Chapter 9

The Mercedes estate turned off Grange Loan into a street where the houses were grander and set further back from the road. James Munro pulled into a semi-circular driveway, and parked in front of a detached double-garage decorated with a battered basketball hoop. Lily and Ben followed him through a heavy, dark-red door that led into the kitchen of his large house.

"First things first," Munro said as he placed a large iron kettle on top of a gleaming Aga range - the smell of hot metal pervaded the room. They were surrounded by books, most neatly stacked, but many lying out, dog-eared and well-used. The walls were haphazardly covered in photos, many stuck up without frames, the majority featuring the smiling faces of children. It was a visual history of happy times and holidays. A few photographs were important enough to sit framed on a side table, they spanned the years starting with two grinning infants and finishing with two graduations.

Munro invited them to sit around a sturdy kitchen table, where he quickly set out a teapot and some mugs.

"I suspect we could all do with something stronger, but there's work to do. Help yourself to the fridge if you're hungry."

Lily remained seated, but Ben helped himself to a banana from a bowl on top of the fridge. Lily's brow furrowed, she seemed to be questioning how he could eat at a time like this. Ben shrugged, marine training had taught him to eat and sleep when he could, compromising your ability to function made no sense, and it made no difference to how he felt about Simon's death.

They waited for Munro to read the papers, Ben sensed the professor wouldn't take kindly to being rushed, and Lily looked prepared to wait, so he decided to push some of his own questions.

"You said your department's grid system shouldn't have been used for anything other than physics research?"

"It's exclusively used for our own projects," Munro replied firmly as he placed a tray with milk, sugar and a plate of biscuits on the table.

"None of this makes sense," Munro continued, "Simon was always so focused on his own area of study, when it came to say, art and history - I'm sorry to say, he was quite ignorant."

Munro moved a couple of books to clear a space for the papers.

"I don't think he was closely involved," Lily replied. "He provided the introductions for Charles Rae, it was only when I heard it would run on the grid that I asked about it again. He simply said there was spare capacity, and it might as well be used."

"But that definitely wasn't the case?" Ben asked Munro.

"It's fully booked - has been since it came online," Munro replied, shaking his head as if trying to find an acceptable explanation.

"Let's consider what we know about today," Munro said, "we know Simon made an inexplicable phone call, and that he called a meeting for tonight, and that you had the terrible ordeal of finding him in his office... but what else?"

"He called me earlier today," Lily replied. "He was asking about the decryption engine, he'd killed a software process running on the grid by mistake, and stopped a document being decoded. He'd been unable to contact Charles Rae, so asked me to restart the system and place the document at the top of the queue. I still had access, and could do that. I also showed him how to check if the file had been processed, but I didn't wait for the decoded version. There are two messages in the envelope Simon left for me alongside the paper, I think one is the message he interrupted, and we need to know why they are here."

"Can you decode the messages?" Munro asked.

"Yes," Lily replied, "I intended to do just that after I'd heard your view of the paper, but I'll have to go to my office, you need a password for the decryption engine, and mine is on a post-it note back there."

"Which makes this a good time for me to read these documents," Munro said holding them up, "I'll start right now."

Lily moved to sit across from Munro as he slowly read through the pages. Ben saw her properly for the first time under the bright kitchen lighting. Was she normally conscious of her looks? She hadn't taken the time to straighten her hair, and she'd only quickly wiped away what little mascara had been left after her tears. Finding the body must have been a terrible shock, but given similar circumstances, he knew his last girlfriend, Eva, would have found a bathroom by now, even if her mother had died she'd have found a bathroom by now. He couldn't help comparing Eva with Lily. Eva was stunning, and he was still a little surprised she'd fallen for him. Lily was beautiful, not in a conventional Eva sense, but on her own terms. Her intelligence made her all the more attractive. Her hand shook slightly as she took a sip from her cup. Ben held out his own hand which was steady. He raised his head and found her watching him.

"I'm sorry," he said dropping the hand. "I was checking my nerves."

"I suppose the adrenaline must be wearing off," Lily replied. "I nearly ran over a cop."

"Yeah," Ben smiled. "You did."

Munro pushed the papers away and peered at them over his glasses.

"I'm sorry to say this, but I'm not sure there's much of a connection between this paper and Simon's death, it appears totally irrelevant."

"But he says it must be published," Lily replied, "There must be something?"

"There certainly is something, but it's incomplete. There's a reference to some test message without further elaboration, and what remains seems to suggest Simon has experimental evidence on the existence of closed timelike curves... I'm afraid this is worse than I feared, he may have had some sort of breakdown."

Ben expected Lily to react, but she just sat staring at the pages across the table.

"A closed timelike curve?" Ben repeated. "What does that mean?"

Munro explained, "Well, they're nothing new; Gödel, and more recently, Gott, have shown how these curves can, in theory, exist under general relativity. I have to say, I doubt they exist anywhere other than in the minds of theoreticians-"

"But what if they did exist?" Lily cut in, she'd rolled up the sleeves of her shirt exposing an intricate Japanese black and grey tattoo.

"Well, they would open up the possibility of a physical route back to an earlier point in spacetime, but that has nothing to do with your decryption engine, old government signals, or whatever else we have."

"I don't get it?" Ben said, "Why leave a theoretical paper?"

Munro pushed the papers over to Lily who turned them towards her and started reading again.

"I can't answer that, but the existence of closed timelike curves would throw up so many complications: for example, the principle of causality expects that an event is preceded by its cause. If these curves did exist, causality cannot be taken for granted - an event could happen in the same instant as the cause, or an event could even trigger itself, the cause and the event would be a single entity."

Ben shook his head, "So, there would be a breakdown in cause and effect?"

"Exactly," Munro replied, "time can loop back on itself, an event can occur before its cause, and the hand of time is able to revisit a point already passed, it's sensational stuff, and the most sensational way to describe it is time travel."

Ben's eyes widened at those words, Munro quickly raised his hand and laughed softly.

"Please don't get excited by any of this, this is theoretical and no-one will ever travel back in time. There's no argument about that, and Simon isn't proposing anything as preposterous as that. I can give you a basic explanation why-"

Ben held up his hand, "I'm way over my head already. A more relevant question is: what does this have to do with Simon's death?"

"One would have to say nothing at all," Munro replied.

"Could he have put the wrong paper in the envelope?" Ben asked, "What else was he working on?"

"The CERN experiments, and there was some work with our American colleagues on pulsars..."

Ben knew the name but must have looked puzzled as Munro started to explain, "Pulsars are another name for neutron stars - they spin rapidly while emitting radiation, and if the path of radiation tracks towards the earth, we can see the light pulsing on and off, hence the name. It's a bit like watching the rotating beam of a lighthouse."

Ben thought Munro's tone was probably reserved for the department head's more disappointing students.

Lily pushed one of the printed sheets back to Professor Munro. "James, what's this?" She said pointing to a section, "He's talking about Centauro effects?"

Munro paused and re-read the passage.

"If I remember correctly, Centauro effects were first detected in the upper atmosphere, high above South America. The detected signature is bottom heavy - it looks a bit like a centaur from Greek mythology, hence the name. No-one really knows what causes the effect; some say they are the product of high energy cosmic rays colliding with other particles while others suggest they are tiny black holes which explode showering particles after a brief, unstable life."

"Sounds like we're back in the world of science fiction," Ben added.

"Believe me, that is no fiction," Munro replied. "CERN's Large Hadron Collider is able to produce collisions with enough energy to create these particles, so we'll know much more about their properties shortly," Munro paused momentarily, "The energy levels reached by Simon's experiments were high enough to create them, but they weren't the focus of his research."

"Is he suggesting they can generate closed timelike curves?" Lily asked, taking Munro back to the paper.

"Yes, he's proposing they're a possible conduit, but that makes no sense, they are rather small at around 20 micrograms, very unstable and so only exist for milliseconds, apart from that we know very little about them."

"Twenty micrograms?" Ben repeated.

"Yes, that's twenty one millionths of a gram, in layman's terms, that's about a tenth of the weight of a human hair," Munro replied.

"James, Simon has been running experiments in the LHC for nearly a year now, he could have found out more about them?" Lily said.

"That's possible, but please don't get excited by all this. Even if Centauro effects could facilitate a closed timelike loop, then as I explained, they would be so unstable that nothing could pass through them. The same problem applies on a larger scale. If we were ever able to engineer some sort of wormhole to try to visit our great grandparents for tea - and that really is a fantasy - it would simply collapse as soon as anything tried to enter it. Time travel is impossible and certainly not through the tiniest of black holes - even if that's what they actually are."

"You know Simon - he's not prone to exaggeration - he valued his reputation far too highly for that, there has to be more to this," Lily replied.

"There's nothing new in this paper and you know full well that academic staff publish work regularly to boost departmental ratings and attract funding. Twenty-years ago, a single complete paper on a topic would be published, now you may get ten or more with none really significant on their own. That's how things are done today, and while there may be more to Simon's work, it's not here."

"How can you be so sure?" Lily asked.

Munro cleared his throat and looked up, "I'm sorry, we can't publish this-"

"But we must-" Lily said.

"Now hold on, Lily, hear me out," Munro replied, "This work isn't finished, these are notes on an interesting topic, but there's no evidence of any kind. There are some references to an experiment, but I can find no detail. The pages aren't numbered, so some of it may be missing, but publishing something like this after his death serves no purpose. It might even damage his reputation, and possibly mine, if I was involved-"

"OK, so there's disagreement on the paper," Ben interrupted, "but it tells us nothing about his death."

"We can't say that either." Lily replied, "From my reading, Simon is suggesting minuscule black holes created and destroyed during the Centauro effect are able to transport electromagnetic waves to another part of spacetime, a destination that could be earlier in the timeline than the source of the transmission. Is that right so far?" She asked Munro.

"Yes, that's the example given, but it's some claim without proof."

"He's talking about a Kerr singularity," Lily said.

"Did Simon discuss this with you?" Munro asked.

"No, but Kerr was a mathematician, not a physicist, and I understand the concept from a mathematical point of view," Lily said.

"Is this really important?" Ben asked.

"Yes, it is important. The original black hole model was static, and the singularity was a point that marked the end of time as we know it. The Kerr variety has the singularity as a spinning ring. This ring marks the end of space, but not time, and if you enter the ring at a certain angle you could travel through it to another part of the universe or to whatever lies inside it, of course no-one knows what that is, including physicists," Lily explained looking to Munro.

"We certainly do not!" Munro replied. "Simon was full of admiration for you, and I'm beginning to see why."

"And why is this important right now?" Ben asked.

"If a Kerr singularity exists it could pass messages through time," Lily replied holding up the Enigma signals.

Ben blinked hard.

"Oh Lily, you can't be serious? You're saying a Kerr black hole - which exists for a time period so small it can hardly be measured - is connecting us to a point in the past?" Munro asked, "Come on, those are stunning claims, and you need hard evidence to make them."

"You just said that general relativity allows for the existence of timelike curves. We know astronauts on missions experience time at a slower rate than people on the Earth's surface because of the high speeds they travel. We can prove that. But there's so much we don't know yet. There is no unified theory of physics, and if one is ever proposed, who knows what we'll be asked to believe? Would you find what Simon is saying so hard to accept if you had the proof? Is it so bizarre? The Large Hadron Collider has been described as a black hole factory - you must have been waiting for something like this to happen? Surely you expect something extraordinary in return for the billions of dollars it has cost to build?"

Munro stood and slowly removed his glasses and placed them on the table.

"You need more than this," Munro replied. "This paper would be seen as nothing more than pure speculation... and possibly junk science. No respected journal would publish this as it is. We need proof, without evidence, all we could do is post it on the Internet, and I can't see what that would achieve."

"Maybe we have the proof already," Lily replied. "He put the Enigma messages in the envelope for a reason, and they would have been transmitted as electromagnetic radio waves, Simon was too good a scientist for us to dismiss them, they must be decoded."

Munro shook his head.

"If you can find proof, it would win him his Nobel Prize, but there's not enough here. If this is more than theory, and he's seen this effect, then this would be the biggest discovery in a century. If coherent information could be passed between time periods, it would simply be stunning, but I couldn't agree with Simon's assertion that the messages are already part of our present, and can have no further effect. My guess would be our time line could become fragile, and there would be a tipping point where interference in the past would cause a seismic shift – we may well be standing on extremely dangerous ground," Munro replied. "But consider this, Simon deserves to be remembered as the brilliant man he was, so be careful about the claims you make in his name."

Chapter 10

Airfield, North of Lorient, France
Friday, 12 February 1943 01:20

A tanker heavy with fuel drove slowly past the triple-engine Junkers transport aircraft. The strong smell of high-octane gasoline wafted across the runway, blown by the propellers of a Messerschmitt 109 fighter readying for a night patrol.

Kessler pulled up his collar against rain falling in sheets as he continually scanned the runway for the party of army officers whose flight would take them to Frankfurt.

Kessler had briefly considered ordering his own flight, but while Frankfurt left them a long drive, it also covered their tracks nicely. If Admiral Donitz knew they were going to the nuclear research facility at Ohrdruf, then he would also know they had read that morning's contentious Enigma message. It was better accept an extra journey, especially when the admiral discovered the radioman's death.

Kessler checked his watch once more; the army officers were attending a banquet for one of their generals, and were obviously in no hurry, as the flight should have left five minutes ago bound for Berlin with the stop at Frankfurt. The pilot shrugged and said he would have to sit on the tarmac until they arrived. Kessler would give them another ten minutes before requisitioning the plane. If he was right about the message, there would be no need to worry about upsetting some Wehrmacht officers. Everything depended on the validity of the sample supplied with the message. If those documents were genuine, the Fatherland was in danger, and the admiral had made an unforgivable mistake.

The drive from Frankfurt would extend north to Gottingen, and an audience with the physicists of its famed university. He would seek to verify the documents before going on to the concentration camp at Ohrdruf where Muller had discovered the Reich's nuclear programme was based. If strong enough support could be gathered from either location, he would travel to Berlin to report the atomic threat and the admiral's incompetence.

Kessler checked his watch one more time, just as the air raid sirens produced an ear-splitting wail. Searchlight beams immediately sent columns of light to probe the blanket of clouds above.

Anti-aircraft guns spun on their platforms searching for targets, before suddenly releasing volley after volley of high explosive shells. The sound of high-altitude bombers droned between the bursts of fire. Apparently engine noise alone was enough for the crews to determine friend from foe. Kessler hoped the Junkers' engine had a distinctive voice, and he didn't want to think about the utter futility of death at the hands of men trying to differentiate between aircraft engines in dark skies over the thunderous roar of 37mm cannon.

Kessler could wait no longer, and signalled to Muller who approached.

"Tell the pilot we're leaving now."

Muller rolled his eyes, "Sir, is it wise to risk angering the army and the navy on the same day?"

Kessler laughed, "We can worry about the admirals and generals when we find this is all a hoax, but until then, we go where this message takes us."

The change in air pressure woke Kessler during the descent, he checked his watch, despite the noise, he'd been sleeping for close on four hours. Muller was still awake, he was one of the bravest men Kessler had known, but his fear of flying meant he would only sleep on the longest of flights through sheer exhaustion.

Kessler understood those fears when they were in range of enemy fighters, but this was Frankfurt, deep inside the Reich, and the airport they approached was a heavily-defended Luftwaffe base.

They disembarked, thanking the young pilot who had reluctantly accepted Kessler's written orders to requisition the flight.

There was enough light to see the outline of a small guard house with a ubiquitous Volkswagen Kubelwagen parked up outside. The small open-topped vehicle was similar to the Jeeps sent to England by the Americans, and to the bottom of the North Atlantic by U-boat torpedoes.

The SS men threw their luggage onto the back seat. Muller's torch found no key in the central ignition switch, so Kessler lent on the horn until he heard some activity inside the building. The door rattled on its hinges as a large sergeant filled its frame ready to roast whoever had the nerve to summon him in such a way. He peered at the uniforms in the poor light before snapping to a salute.

"Sergeant, I've had to divert here on important business," Kessler said slowly pointing his torch at the man's face. "Get this car fuelled and ready to go."

"I must clear it with my captain, sir," the sergeant replied.

"I don't have time to wait, you can make your report later," Kessler said as he started to erect the canvas roof and fix it in place.

The sergeant looked closely at their uniforms once more, and the glint of Kessler's Iron Cross 1st Class caught his eye. Kessler could see the decision was made.

Minutes later they drove out of the airport's main entrance, Kessler checked the map and found the road to Gottingen. Dawn wouldn't break until after 0700 so they would see little of their journey other than a few metres of road through blinkered headlights.

Kessler ordered Muller to get some sleep, the drive was over two hundred kilometres, and they would arrive in time for breakfast. The rest of their morning would be spent finding one of the university's many Nobel Prize winning scientists and discover whether it was wise to risk all on a message the admiral had dismissed without a second thought.

Chapter 11

James Munro and Lily continued to argue over the significance of Simon's papers, but Ben was preoccupied with the coded messages, why had Simon wanted them decrypted, and why were they here now?

Finding those answers would explain his brother's death.

"Sorry to interrupt," Ben said, "Lily, do we need to go to your office to decrypt the messages? Won't Charles Rae already have them?"

"I'll call him," Lily replied, "I promised to call him anyway."

Ben watched as she walked through to a large room with two sets of full height windows looking out to the garden. The light outside was failing, but the garden was partially illuminated by street lighting from beyond the far wall. Lily pressed the mobile phone to her ear, Ben frowned, how long would it take the police to intercept and track its position? He took his out and turned it off, he'd tell her to do the same as soon as she'd finished her call. They needed to stay out of police hands until they could read the messages.

With Lily out of the way, Ben turned to Munro who sat with Simon's work symbolically at arm's length across the kitchen table.

"I don't believe he'd hurt himself, and I know he's not responsible for a terror attack," Ben said quietly, "But I haven't seen him in a while, so what's your real opinion?"

"We can't know what other people are thinking," Munro replied, "but I'm inclined to agree with you on both counts. The only problem is the phone call, that's harder to explain."

Ben sat back, "I don't understand the call either."

"I'm sorry you've lost him," Munro said shifting in his seat, "he was a good man."

They sat quietly for a moment, and Lily's voice drifted in from the other room.

"I didn't really know him," Ben said eventually, "he'd left for university when I was seven, and I joined up when I was seventeen. We rarely got in touch."

"If you don't mind me saying, you seem very like him, detached, quite cool..."

"Lily mentioned we don't look alike, I suppose we had to have something in common."

Lily interrupted as she came back into the room.

"I talked to Charles, he's going to send someone for us, and we can use his office to decrypt the messages."

"Did he say how long?" Ben asked.

"Within the hour," she replied. "Can we put the TV on? Charles says there's lots of news coverage."

"There's one through there, help yourself," Munro replied, pointing back into the room where Lily made her call.

Ben walked through the wide doorway to the adjacent room, looked out the windows and immediately noticed the garden was lit up by harsh halogen light.

"Your security lights are on; are you expecting someone?" Ben asked, stepping back.

"No," Munro replied, "unless your Mr Rae has arrived earlier than expected?"

"Too soon," Lily replied. "It could be the cops. We should go, you may be in trouble if we're found here."

"Don't worry about me," Munro replied, "but you should talk to the police, they're trying to find out what happened too."

"No!" Lily replied. "If we stay here we'll be arrested, and the messages will never be decoded."

"OK, where are we going?" Ben asked.

"My office, where else?"

A doorbell rang from the other end of the house, Munro waved at them to be quiet, "Follow me, my study is through here. There's a french window out to the garden, the key is in the lock. Follow the high hedge that runs down to the bottom of the garden, if you get behind it, you can't be seen from the house. You'll reach a wall, the road on the other side leads down towards the Meadows. Call me later, and good luck."

The Meadows was a large public park, close to the city centre and bordered with old hospital and university buildings. Ben knew they could disappear amongst the students, locals and tourists who passed through the tree-lined paths and open fields.

Lily leant forward and kissed Munro on the cheek, he patted her shoulder, looking like a father not quite ready to let his little girl go.

The doorbell rang once more.

Munro urged them on and Ben led the way. He turned the key in the door, opened it a fraction then held Lily back. A man was standing back from the house, illuminated by security lights.

There was no way he'd be able to see into the darkness behind the halogen beam, but Ben didn't want to move as while they couldn't be seen, they could definitely be heard.

Lily made to pass him, but he raised his arm forcing her to stop. The man remained in place. He was powerfully built, about the same height as Ben's 6' 1", but much heavier. Ben still ran three times a week and knew he could outpace the larger man over a distance, and possibly over a sprint, but with Lily, they would be run down.

The man's physical size didn't worry Ben, it was the way he slowly scanned the area, it was if he knew they were there and was waiting for them to run. The head turned and stopped, he was looking straight at Ben who held his breath. Suddenly, they heard Rae's voice, and the man moved towards it and out of view. Ben took Lily's hand and pulled her out into the garden, gently closing the door behind them. She moved ahead, and he followed her into the shadow of the laurel hedging Munro had described.

Ben took the lead and had almost reached the boundary wall, when he instinctively knew something was wrong. He turned to catch a glimpse of Lily as she disappeared behind the evergreen foliage on her way back towards the house.

Ben ran to the edge of cover just as she emerged from the french window once more and made her way to him.

"What was that all about?" Ben hissed.

"I left the Enigma messages and Simon's paper on the kitchen table," she replied. "I had to get them."

"Did you see Munro?"

"No, he must be in one of the front rooms."

Ben shook his head and retraced his steps away from the house, Lily grabbed his hand.

"You OK?" she whispered.

"Yeah, but you shouldn't have run off like that."

"There wasn't time for a debate."

"Fine," Ben snapped. "I just hope Munro doesn't take too much flak. He said he wouldn't lie to the cops, so he'll be telling them everything about us."

"James didn't mean that. He's really quite sweet, but we'd better get away from here, whatever happens, he'll give us enough time to get clear."

They reached a wall about six feet high, so Ben knelt to give Lily a leg up. She leaned over the wall, looked both ways then dropped from sight. Ben followed her on to an empty street where the only sign of life was a few lights from terraced houses on the opposite side of the road. The rattle of a diesel engine approached, and Lily stepped out, hand raised to stop the oncoming taxi.

"Edinburgh University, King's Buildings please," Lily said.

Ben looked back and thought he saw a face look up from behind the wall, but when he looked again, it had gone.

Chapter 12

Gottingen, Germany
Friday, 12 February 1943 08:34

Night gave way to morning, and the dawn revealed a hard frost covering the rolling hills and fields approaching Gottingen. Kessler had cautiously adapted to the slippery road surface and the little Kubel made good progress with the majority of traffic, mostly military, heading in the opposite direction back towards Frankfurt.

An old man on a bicycle nodded as they passed, his breath rising like steam from a train. Kessler stopped and called out for the distance to the town centre. The man pointed to a railway bridge, once they'd passed under it, there was only a few kilometres left to go.

Passing inside the old city wall, they drove onto the grey cobbles of the market square which were laid out in a checked pattern with perpendicular courses of darker stone. The statue of the 'Little Goose Girl' sat at the centre, having recently found a new role accepting the kisses of students on their graduation.

The town hall ran the length of the square, and was bordered at each end by white, half-timbered buildings with red-tiled roofs. A few well-wrapped traders were routinely setting out stalls while pigeons wandered around in search of breakfast. There was no sign of the war here. There were no bombed buildings or sullen-faced refugees. Kessler remembered that among the many Latin inscriptions on the town's buildings, one translated as 'No life outside Gottingen', it was a vain statement, but there was an element of truth. Their country was waging war on two fronts, but there was little sign of it here.

Kessler pulled up at the town hall, he slammed the door shut bringing Muller's sleep to an abrupt end. He left his colleague to waken as he took in the surroundings. Moments later Muller shuffled to his side.

"Enjoy the journey, Karl?"

"Yes sir, the best kind, I slept through it all."

"Good, we will breakfast first," he looked around, "that cafe over there."

They headed off towards a small cafe. A young waitress could be seen through the thick glass of the mullioned windows absentmindedly arranging the tables and chairs. She turned as though feeling their eyes upon her, and hurried, shooting glances in their direction as they stepped inside.

The wonderful aroma of fresh bread combined with a tangy onion soup welcomed them, and once seated, they ordered bread with eggs, cheese and coffee. Muller lit a cigarette, Kessler found the habit disagreeable, especially at the start of the day. He shook his head at Muller's coughing, and the gratitude to the cigarette which was obviously the cause of his discomfort. Officially SS men were prohibited from smoking on duty, but Karl had earned the right to enjoy his addiction.

The girl reappeared from the kitchen with rough bread and thinly-sliced cheese, promising to return shortly with the rest of their meal. The owner came out and bid them good morning, and Kessler motioned for the man to stay.

"Can you direct us to the university's science faculty?"

"I'm unsure, but my wife's friend works in the main building, the Auditorium Maximum. It is a short walk from the far end of Weender Strasse," he said nodding towards the square's north-east corner.

"She passes each morning, and she would know."

"What time?" Muller asked.

"A quarter to nine, Herr Captain, and you can set your watch by her."

"Thank you, when she passes, please ask her to join us," Kessler replied, "and one more question: is there a police station nearby?"

"Yes, Major, just behind the town hall. Can I help with anything else?"

Kessler waved the man away, sitting back as he looked out on the market square. He would wait until the day was fully underway before trying to track down his man, for now, he would enjoy a simple meal in his homeland.

The town was coming to life as more people went about their business. A prim, petite woman, who dressed dowdily and looked older than her years, crossed the square. Kessler checked his wristwatch, it was 0843, and slow if the woman's punctuality was to be believed. He caught the owner's eye and the man motioned to her as she approached the cafe. Kessler drained his coffee as the woman was directed to their table.

"May I present, Frau Schiller, she is an administrator at the university."

"Please be seated," Kessler said.

"How... how may I help you?" she replied almost tripping as she took the nearest chair.

"I'm looking for directions to the science faculty, more precisely, the department of physics?"

Frau Schiller looked unsure.

"Is something troubling you?" Kessler asked.

"I'm sorry, but the last time soldiers were here... I gave a list of all the Jews, there is no-one left, I did not miss anyone out, I am sure..."

"Madam, I am here for information, not Jews," Kessler explained.

"I'm sorry, I just assumed...," the women said becoming flustered, "it was an unsettling time... but I fully understand it was necessary-" she quickly added.

"Let us have no more talk of politics," Kessler interrupted, he had no wish to hear of her devotion to National Socialism. "Where can I find your physics department? I need their help and nothing more."

"I know everyone who works there, who do you want to see, what speciality?"

"There is a physics research facility at Ohrdruf, the man I'm looking for would have worked there, possibly led the research team?"

"Professor Lenz, he keeps his own hours, but I can send a porter to fetch him?"

"Please, as quickly as possible," Kessler replied.

"I will send him here."

Kessler smiled graciously, he had been ready to enlist the help of the police to find the man, but this woman seemed anxious to help, possibly to make amends for the clumsy behaviour of moments earlier, but whatever the reason, it was probably the quickest way to find the scientist.

"Thank you, Madam, we will await his arrival."

Kessler watched as Frau Schiller walked away as fast as she could manage. How many of the expelled Jewish scientists had fled to America? How many had contributed to the papers he carried, and how many were working, at that very moment, on the super bomb to destroy his country?

Kessler patted his SS dagger, these were dangerous men, and he wouldn't have allowed a single one to leave Germany alive.

As Kessler finished the excellent breakfast, a figure appeared, hurriedly running then walking across the square. The university porter arrived, and spoke quickly between pauses to catch his breath. The man was delighted to help them, and told how he had stood shoulder-to-shoulder with the students who demanded the removal of Jewish scientists from the university staff. He was a typical veteran of the Great War, who having spent years feeling betrayed, now had his pride restored by a country that had risen once more.

The porter was confident they would find the professor in his office - he generally worked from there on a Thursday, and so they marched to an imposing building a few minutes walk from the cafe.

They were led into a large hall, and the porter fussed before eventually finding chairs for them to sit by a dusty table, while he went off to search the building. Kessler took out the message and removed the first page leaving the technical data for the scientist to examine. He sat back to wait. Perversely, it suited his interests for the message to be genuine, but that meant the enemy were building a super weapon to destroy the Reich, he decided it would be better if the admiral was right after all.

Kessler thoughts were interrupted as the porter reappeared followed by a tall, immaculately dressed man in his forties with short greying hair. The SS men stood as the professor strode forward to shake their hands. The porter bowed and made to leave, Kessler thanked him knowing the man would appreciate that small courtesy.

"Welcome to the university, Major, my name is Helmut Lenz, we haven't met. I have an excellent memory for faces, terrible for names, but faces I remember well. What can I do for the SS this morning?"

"My name is Kessler, you have worked on the nuclear research at Ohrdruf?"

"You have the right man, Major"

"I need your help on a technical matter," Kessler said.

"Of course, I am at your service."

"I need you to explain the significance of a scientific document, you can read English?"

"Yes, of course, you have the document here?" The professor replied extending a hand expectantly.

Kessler passed him three folded sheets.

He read them one after the other at a slow pace. Kessler wondered if he was having difficulty understanding the science, or just found it difficult to read in English. The officers exchanged glances.

"This is very interesting, Major," The professor said finally. He dropped the papers and slowly raised his head, "Where did you get these?"

Kessler paused before answering; the professor's involvement in top secret research would come with a high security clearance, but he had no reason to know any more than the paper's content.

"What you are holding is a sample. A source has offered us more. I want to know if these papers are genuine?" Kessler replied. "Can you explain their contents?"

"As well as anyone in Germany, you have heard of a fission chain reaction?"

"Only what I've read in the press," Kessler replied, remembering some vague headlines.

"Well, this paper is the summary of a conference held in September. Nuclear fission was first shown experimentally in 1939, by Hahn and Strassmann in Berlin. Einstein's work on the conversion of matter to energy set the theoretical background, there is some disagreement on the validity of the work, but that is unimportant."

Kessler took a deep breath, the memories of the staff clearance may well have been fresh in the professor's mind.

"I am aware of the question of Jewish physics, it has always struck me that truth knows no race or religion. Please speak freely as I am here for your help, not to examine your loyalties."

"I agree, Major, some of my colleagues used the new race laws as a way to attack work they did not understand, it was politics not science."

"Good, let us concentrate on the science, please continue," Kessler said.

"Well, the relationship between energy and mass means that a relatively small mass of a fissionable material - one that can support a chain reaction - has the potential to release a massive amount of energy. Each reaction must invoke a greater number of subsequent reactions until the increase is exponential. This effect forms the chain reaction. With enough material, an uncontrolled reaction will lead to a huge release of energy, and a massive explosion can be the only outcome."

"If you know this already, what do the papers add?"

"Most of this is completely new, Major, fission has only been a research topic for the last decade at most, the very idea of a critical mass was proposed fairly recently. This critical mass is the minimum amount of material required to produce an explosive energy release. This document states that America is producing fissionable material in amounts that make a super bomb feasible in the short term. They are manufacturing atomic weapons for use in this war."

Kessler had guessed the paper was important from the start, but the professor's words stunned him.

"Could it be misinformation, counter-intelligence?" Muller asked, failing to contain his excitement. It struck Kessler he was really asking whether this was too good to be true.

"You have more than just conference notes. Your paper states a controlled chain reaction was achieved in Chicago last December . The paper was co-authored by Oppenheimer, a Jew who obtained his doctorate at this very university twenty years ago. No, gentlemen, everything about what you have brought me this cold February morning is very, very real."

"What would be the effect of such a weapon?"

"Total devastation. One bomb could consume a small town, and if used on larger cities, it would cause huge initial casualties with many more dying from radiation poisoning and the breakdown of civil order left in the aftermath."

"Why do you so easily accept this as factual?" Kessler asked. "Can they really be close to obtaining this weapon?"

"I helped evaluate the possibility of building an atomic weapon for the Reich. We faced many difficulties that led us to believe it was impossible to produce a weapon in the next ten years. That conclusion led to resources being switched to other areas of research and production, however, I always believed it was possible to build a weapon."

Had Admiral Donitz known of the nuclear research decision? Was that the reason he dismissed the message so causally? If so, he had seriously underestimated the allies.

"Why then do the Americans think it can be done?" Kessler asked.

"One of the first problems in producing a bomb is procuring the fissionable material. You must either separate uranium-235 from the relatively abundant uranium-238, or produce plutonium-239 from processing the uranium-238. One of the biggest problems faced by researchers, in both cases, is the yields have been tiny, only a few flakes at most. These papers have an abstract that outlines their production methods and has an extract from a discussion on two designs for the actual detonation. This alone gives us enough information to make progress immediately."

"Could you produce a weapon in acceptable timescales?" Kessler asked.

"That would be my hope, these papers are remarkable, but we must get any others as soon as possible. We must try to develop a weapon, and this information is enough to restart our efforts."

"I will take this to Berlin," Kessler said quickly. "You really have no doubts whatsoever? I mean there are only a few pages of text, is there really enough here?"

"Major, many of the great discoveries of science can be explained by schoolboys. For example, prior to Newton it was thought that a prism did something to white light that produced a spectrum of colours. Newton put another prism behind the first and the spectrum combined to, once again, produce white light, it showed for the first time that white light was a combination of the other colours, no-one had thought to do that before, and it changed our understanding of light-"

"That's very interesting, Professor, but I fail to see the connection?" Kessler said

"The point I'm trying to make is, Newton's experiment was simple and can be explained in a few words. This paper summarises two years of American effort, we can follow that work without having to duplicate their mistakes. I neglected to tell you, but it seems appropriate now. The reason I know controlled fission is possible is that we have already achieved it at Ohrdruf. The Americans will tell us how to continue. We must produce the material needed for the critical mass, and with that material, we would be months away from a usable weapon. We have some advantages over the enemy; we already possess advanced delivery systems in the V1 and V2 rockets, and although conventional bombers can also be used to deliver an atomic blow, unmanned rockets travel at very high speeds and are very difficult to stop, as London knows all too well."

"But how long will it take to get that material?"

"Within twelve months - that would be my goal."

"And you can do this at Ohrdruf?" Kessler asked.

"Yes, it is still a research facility, there is a labour camp close by. When I first saw you, I thought you must be on the staff there. I would suggest you enlist the help of the commanding officer, Major Bohm, he will realise we would have no defence against this weapon and we must produce our own. The only problem is, he left two days ago for Berlin, and I do not know when he returns."

"Does he have a deputy?"

"I hope you do not mind me saying that his deputy is better suited to maintaining order in a work camp than concerning himself with tasks such as this, No, I would not trust something of this importance with him."

"What do you suggest?"

"You send a message to Bohm in Berlin, I will write a letter, and we press him to take action."

There was the possibility other top-level figures in Berlin would form the same conclusion as the admiral and reject the whole subject out of hand. Kessler had to talk to them directly, make them see that whoever produces this weapon first will win this war. He would deliver Lenz's letter in person.

Chapter 13

Edinburgh, Scotland
Sunday, 7 May 2017 20:45

The taxi gained speed as Ben moved forward from the rear bench to a fold-down seat allowing him a view of the road behind. The streets were quiet, and he wished they could be caught up in traffic, another black cab among the hundreds on Edinburgh's streets.

He turned momentarily as the taxi driver slid the partition open.

"You heard the news about the observatory then?" the driver asked.

"No, what's happened?" Lily replied glancing at Ben who didn't respond. He hoped this wasn't another cabbie who did as much talking as driving.

"At first the radio said there'd been an attack," the driver continued, "then the police released a statement saying there'd been a death, but there's been nothing since. You've never seen so many police. The TV cameras are turning up too. Makes you wonder what's going on, it looks like half the bloody force is up there."

Ben kept watch on the road as he listened, the first 'official' announcement of his brother's death. At least their own names and descriptions hadn't been broadcast to the world just yet.

"That's horrible," Lily replied nudging Ben's knee, he nodded his agreement.

"Listen, I hope you don't mind but it'll be quicker if we go past Cameron Toll then loop back," the driver said, "the roads are blocked around the observatory all the way down that side of the King's Buildings. It's pretty quiet tonight, but no point going that way unless you want to?"

"We'll go your way," Ben spoke up, "we're already running late."

The taxi entered Edinburgh University's King's Buildings by the commercial science park. The King's Buildings were a mixture of the Victorian, such as the school of zoology, and the modern office blocks of the science park. Flashing blue lights could still be seen from the top of Blackford hill.

Lily gave the driver instructions to follow the road around to her office. Ben paid, as the driver was eyeing up Lily, her face and piercings would make them a memorable fare for the rest of the evening.

They made their way into the wide hall of a contemporary office building. A key card was required to access the shared areas and a traditional lock and key for Lily's office door. There was no-one to be seen on the short walk up a flight of stairs and along a single corridor. The whole building was in semi-darkness and Ben hoped any extra police patrols would focus on the open, unsecured areas of the university rather than staff buildings such as this.

As they entered the office, Lily made straight for a desk on the right, Ben pulled up a chair as she turned on the large LCD screen which clicked out of sleep mode and prompted for a UNIX system login. Unlike personal computers, which most home users turned on and off like televisions, these machines hosted sessions 24/7 for users on the university network, and the academic world beyond.

Lily typed away, and a banner appeared across the screen for a remote login to the powerful physics grid system.

"We're in," she said smiling.

"What now?" Ben asked.

"We have to get the messages into the decryption engine," she handed him the pages, "take them and put them on that scanner, it'll read and load them into the system."

"How long will it take once they're scanned?"

"It queues the documents, but we can jump to the front. We have the intercept date, so the system will try any Enigma settings it has on record for that time period. If that doesn't work, it will try and crack them, and that can easily take two hours..."

"So we wait?" Ben asked.

"You got a better plan?" Lily shrugged. "Ben, could you do me a favour, there's a small kitchen down the hall on the right, could you get me a glass of water?"

"Sure," Ben said, getting up.

The kitchen turned out to be a small cupboard with a sink and microwave cooker off the main walkway. He squinted as he looked for a glass. The corridor was dark, but the permanent lighting from the nearest stairwell was enough to see what he was doing.

He found a cup and rinsed it before refilling with water. As he walked back, he switched on his phone to find no missed calls, he switched it back off, unsurprised as few people had his number.

He placed the cup in front of Lily who looked away from the computer for the first time since they'd arrived, she pointed at the screen.

"What is it?" He asked, leaning towards her.

"Look at our messages," she replied angling the monitor towards him, "they've already been processed."

Ben could see two highlighted messages in a list that filled the screen.

"So soon, are you sure they're ours?"

"When a document is scanned, it's contents are hashed to give it a unique identifier. The hash becomes the document's signature or fingerprint. Every time you try and decode a new document, its signature is calculated and checked against those in the system to make sure it hasn't already been cracked, and guess what?"

"The messages have already been decoded?"

"Exactly, but although the system processed them earlier, the original cipher text and the decoded plain text files have been deleted."

"How do you know that?"

"Each document has a history: when work began on it, how long it took to decode, and in this case, when it was deleted."

"And when was that?"

"Today at 16:13. It was deleted by Simon."

Ben ran both hands through his hair and glanced out of the high windows onto a drab concrete wall.

"Are you sure it was him?"

"It shows against his login ID, it was him or someone who knew his password."

"Can we decrypt them again?"

"Whoever deleted them couldn't have known the system tracked documents by their signatures, and deleting the messages wouldn't delete the Enigma key that was found by decoding them. The key is added to the system's store and reused on other messages intercepted around the same date range."

"Can you get the messages back quickly?" Ben asked.

"In a few clicks."

"What are you waiting for?"

"Give me a minute," Lily replied. "I'm doing it."

Suddenly Lily turned towards the door. Ben sat up and mouthed "What?"

"I heard footsteps," she whispered. "There's someone outside?"

"Well, you'd better hurry up then," Ben replied, he stood behind the door and listened. He couldn't hear a thing so shrugged, and Lily turned back to the screen.

"Look," she said quietly. "We've got the first one. The description says it was decrypted using an existing Enigma setting from February 1943; it's a German wartime naval signal. I'll load up the plain text."

"You read German?" Ben asked.

"I don't need to, the program translates it."

Ben watched as Lily sent commands to initiate the translation process, an instant later, the text was redrawn.

"That's it. OK, it's a signal from a wartime German major. These are orders to ready a consignment for collection. The consignment contains something called the Amber Room," she looked at Ben who shook his head. "It was to be picked up on 16th February 1943," Lily said.

"What's the Amber Room?" Ben asked.

"No idea, I'll Google it..."

Lily opened a web browser and loaded the search site. She set the search to look for the exact phrase and hit enter.

"Over 200,000 hits," she said, "and I was worried we wouldn't find anything."

She followed the first link and started to summarise the page out loud: "It's an ornate room... a gift to the Russian royal family to Peter the Great... it was originally situated in the Winter Palace in St. Petersburg. It was moved outside the city by Catherine the Great... walled with Amber and other precious stones. It was looted by the Germans when they overrun the city during the Second World War and is still missing, presumed destroyed. It's reckoned it would be worth $150 million today."

"$150 million would be a hell of a motive," Ben said.

"A motive to kill Simon? Do you think the decryption engine has found it?"

"In many parts of the world, a few bucks would be enough to have you killed. $150 million is enough anywhere."

"We'll have to contact, Charles Rae, he must know something," Lily said.

"We should call Munro too, but what about the other message?" Ben said, "We've only got half the picture."

Ben watched over her shoulder as she issued commands to retrieve the next message. German text appeared on-screen momentarily before being overlaid with the translation. They both scanned the screen, Lily spoke first, "Well, we now know why this major wanted the Amber Room," she said. "According to this, it was to be exchanged for nuclear weapons technology."

"Is this real?" Ben replied,

"I think so," Lily said, "it's an offer to trade 1940s nuclear secrets for the Amber Room. I've never heard about that before, have you?"

"No, that's what I mean," Ben replied, "I'd have remembered it."

"Yeah, that's weird, I'd have remembered it too," Lily said.

"Every government controls information. Documents can be sealed for 100 years in this country, and some are never released," Ben replied. "The question is: why would something from seventy years ago matter now?"

Ben knew of traitors like Burgess, MacLean, Philby, and there were post-war scientists with Soviet sympathies who passed the nuclear secrets that gave Stalin the atomic bomb, but if someone had tried to do the same thing for the Nazis, it would have to be well-known, it would have been reported many times.

"Could you give James Munro a call, tell him what we've found?" She asked.

"Sure, and we can find out what the police had to say," Ben replied.

He pulled out his phone, "You got the number?"

Lily flipped through a desktop diary and rattled off a local number.

Ben keyed it in. He let the call ring out before leaving a message. As he pocketed the phone, Lily tugged his arm. He took a moment to react, so she pulled much harder before pushing him towards the window. He took a step back and peered down to the ground floor. A figure stood in the shadows across from the key card entrance.

"Time to go," Ben whispered.

Lily was right behind him as he opened the door.

Ben pitched back at the shock of the beaming face in the doorway; his eyes were drawn to the gleam of gold in the smile. He raised his hands, ready to fight, just as the taser gun electrodes pierced his chest. Intense pain ripped through his body dropping him to the ground, a few, agonising seconds later it stopped abruptly, just before a boot struck his head. Ben heard screaming as he tried to get up, but with darkness closing in, there was nothing he could do.

Chapter 14

Admiral Donitz paced back and forward in front of the large stone fireplace. If any of his aides felt sorry for Kessler's slightly shaken, recently departed young lieutenant, none were prepared to say so. The admiral stopped suddenly and walked to his desk.

"Kessler, has gone too far this time," he snapped. "Make out a warrant for his arrest. I want him back here to account for the radio operator."

"Sir, what proof do we have?" ventured his chief of staff.

"I will tell you what proof we have! Kessler receives a message using my encryption codes, the following day, one of my radiomen is found murdered, and Kessler is off on some trip to Berlin... and you ask me for proof."

"Sir, forgive me, but this is inconclusive, and he is not directly accountable to the navy, if he was a naval officer-"

"I do not care about the SS. Where do you think Kessler is now? I will tell you - he is in Berlin - reporting a message he considers of some importance. He thinks he will discredit me. If Kessler has that message I have all the proof I need, and I will have his head."

The chief made another attempt to intervene but was stopped before he could say a word.

"No more discussions. Have you found out how he travelled?"

The chief knew the admiral's mind was set, and there could be no further argument.

"He commandeered a plane which took him to Frankfurt. They took a car from the airbase, and we discovered his adjutant was seeking information on transport to Gottingen, so that's a likely destination, sir."

"Gottingen, of course - he will want a scientific opinion on the document. He is wasting his time - our scientists have already decided it is not possible to produce a weapon within ten years. Kessler obviously knows better. Send a message to Gottingen ordering his arrest and return to this base, and do it right now."

"Yes, sir."

There was a knock at the door, and a junior staff officer entered the room snapping to attention.

"What is it?" asked the admiral.

"Sir, you wanted to know the whereabouts of French male arrested in connection with the murder of the radioman."

"Yes?"

The officer continued reading from a note.

"He was originally to be transported to a work camp in Poland, but was then held on suspicion of the murder. Major Kessler ordered an example to be made, and he was publicly hanged in Lorient last night."

Donitz snorted and waved the man away.

"And another loose end has been conveniently tidied up. When Kessler is arrested, make sure he is searched and all papers in his possession are taken, that applies to anyone with him. He is to be held until he is brought before me. Tell his lieutenant I want a full report about the Frenchman, he can present it in person at 1100. That is all, Gentlemen."

Chapter 15

Central Scotland
Sunday, 7 May 2017 21:14

Ben's eyes opened to see a battered plywood floor. It was as if he'd surfaced from a deep dive, slowly realising his mouth was gagged, and his hands bound behind his back.

The events before he lost consciousness returned in a rush, he looked for Lily who lay beside him also bound with cable ties and crudely applied duct tape spun around her mouth and head. Ben turned on his side, the damaged, splintered surface of the flooring smelt strongly of solvent. Had something been accidentally spilt, or had it been used to clean up something far worse?

There was a stab of pain as he traced his tongue inside his mouth - the kick had left him cut and swollen. There'd been no time to defend himself against what had been a professional attack. He ignored the strong chemical smell and the sense of being smothered, he overcome those sort of fears long ago, and was more worried how Lily would handle the claustrophobia.

Lily turned towards him and although similarly trussed up, didn't look to have suffered any harm.

Towards the front of the van, they could see the driver's head through a small window. Lily inched over to him, flipping over until his face rested against her hip as she twisted against him. She moved down and he felt her fingers tugging at the tape on the back of his head. He turned back towards her, stretching his neck until her hands were at the corner of his mouth. Each time she buried her fingers to get a better grip brought more pain, but he held the position, making it as easy for her as possible. Finally the tape gave way and his mouth was free. He whispered, with one eye on the window, "OK, your turn."

They arranged themselves as best they could, Ben found her face and started to peel the tape back, he felt her stiffen and realised her hair was caught up too. He kept at it with small movements until he heard her voice.

He turned until they faced each other, the only light came from the window up ahead. The steady stream of oncoming traffic illuminated their compartment with an irregular rhythm. He looked into her eyes momentarily as the headlights of an oncoming car lit them up as it passed. She was terrified.

He whispered gently, "We'll get through this."

"I'm sorry... sorry I got you into this," she said.

"He was my brother, you didn't get me in anything," he replied quietly. "Take it easy, we'll find a way out of this."

The removal of the tape moved the main discomfort from his face to his hands. The thick, white plastic ties were pulled tight, locking the wrists together.

"Lily, your hands or feet, can you get them apart at all?"

"No, my hands are numb, thanks for reminding me," she replied with the trace of a smile.

"Was I out for long?"

"Not really, I didn't know what had happened, you just collapsed shaking, then I saw the wires and he kicked your head. You groaned when they lifted you, but they moved us out of there fast."

"How many are there, did they say anything?" Ben asked.

"There were three at the office. After you went down another man came in, and he picked you up and carried you out. The guy that tasered you grabbed my throat to stop me screaming. I don't like him, the look on his face, I was nothing to him - I think he killed, Simon."

"We'll get out of this, if they wanted us dead, we'd be dead already."

Ben had never felt so helpless. His mind flashed back to a time when he was around twelve years old.

Older boys tried to rob him on one of the first times he'd travelled into town without his parents. They tried to pull him down a side street, away from his friends, and he called out for his mother. That got people's attention, so they let him go, laughing and calling after him. He'd felt ashamed and surprised at calling for his mum that day. He never called on her again, choosing to face his fear and take a few beatings as a result. He was angry they'd caught him out, he'd been ready to fight, but it was better to be hit by electrodes than bullets.

He lay quietly for a moment with his thoughts and the engine noise.

"Are you OK?" Lily whispered.

He nodded, "I'm fine, I wouldn't recommend being tasered though."

"It was so scary when they took us. They never spoke a word to each other."

Ben didn't reply, the flashes of light from outside were becoming less frequent, it was either the hour of the night or they were travelling out of town - probably both. He felt tired, figured it was a reaction to however many thousand volts had pulsed through his system. He wanted the journey to be over - whatever it brought them – he'd never liked waiting, the wait was usually worse than what was coming.

They were increasingly thrown across the floor as the road became a series of tight turns, forcing the driver to go up and down the gears to maintain speed. They hadn't passed an oncoming vehicle for a while now, they were being taken somewhere remote, and there was no point speculating why.

Eventually the van slowed to a crawl and turned sharply, before suddenly coming to a halt. The engine cut out, and Ben realised how loud it had been - this was a commercial vehicle, not a Mercedes saloon. The driver got out slamming the door shut.

They waited for the back doors to open. They waited, but nothing happened. Ben strained his ears, listening for any movement. The dull knocks of the cooling engine block and Lily's rapid, shallow breathing pounded in his ears.

A flash of light momentarily filled the compartment followed by the sound of tyres crunching on gravel.

"Do what they say, try and remain calm, and remember we're going to get out of this," Ben said as he moved between Lily and the door, whatever was coming, he would face it first.

Chapter 16

Vending machine coffee was never good, and Andrew Shaw grimaced as he took a sip before pushing the cup to one side.

He sat back, and watched as the police took statements in the observatory's cafeteria from a procession of staff and students.

DCI Whyte had allowed him to sit in on the interviews, and it hadn't taken long for a consistent story to emerge. Professor Millar had been acting out of character, he'd appeared dishevelled at times, and his intensity and obsession with his work had become a matter of concern among his more vocal colleagues.

The suicide theory was sounding more and more plausible, and a rubber stamp from the pathologist would signal an end to Shaw's interest in the police investigation. He pulled out his phone to check for return flights when a plain-clothes detective entered the room and shouted for all officers to gather around him. There was obvious surprise on their faces as a message was passed around. Shaw joined the group.

"What's going on?" he demanded.

"Sorry sir, I can't discuss this outside the investigation team."

"I'm already cleared by DCI Whyte," Shaw argued.

"Then, I suggest you take it up with him," the detective replied, "and you'd better hurry as he just called for a car."

Shaw rushed down the single flight of stairs and made for the door leading out to the courtyard. DCI Whyte was getting into an unmarked car lit up like a Christmas tree by LED lights hidden behind the front grille.

Shaw pushed forward and called out. Whyte frowned momentarily then motioned to the opposite side of the car. They pulled away as soon as both men were seated.

"I take it this trip is related to the jaws dropping in the cafe?" Shaw asked.

The briefest of smiles crossed the DCI's face.

"We're going to the home of Professor James Munro, another scientist who worked at the observatory."

"He's involved how?" Shaw asked.

"He's dead, and he was Millar's boss."

Shaw glanced at Whyte who was looking out a cigarette.

"What do you know so far?"

"Nothing much, other than this death is no suicide. If you know any more about this business than you've already told me, I need it now," Whyte said lighting up and blowing smoke out of a tiny gap in his window - his only concession to the no smoking sign on the car's dashboard.

"Is that why you've brought me along?" Shaw asked. "You think I'm holding out on you?"

"You'll have your own agenda. You people always have."

"What about the absent witnesses," Shaw asked softly blowing the cigarette smoke back towards Whyte. "Any chance they're involved?"

"It crossed my mind," Whyte replied. "Let's see what we've got when we get there."

The car came to a halt, and the middle-aged detective was out the door the second the wheels stopped turning.

Shaw ran to catch up, and then fell in a couple of paces behind, happy to keep a distance and the man's co-operation. They entered the impressive old house. It was beautifully preserved, tastefully decorated and so obviously a family home. All the happy memories the Munro family had of this place would be destroyed by one dreadful night.

The body lay uncovered on the kitchen floor. A photographer was taking shots while Whyte talked on the phone, his mind elsewhere as he looked through those around him.

Shaw glanced at the body laid out on the dark stone tiles, the head was almost severed, an island centred in reflective pools of blood. The stench was overpowering. Two deaths in as many hours would have Edinburgh's duty pathologist earning his or her pay tonight.

Someone called out for DCI Whyte above the background chatter, and the detective pocketed his phone.

"Sir, you'd better hear this," a young officer said pointing to an answer phone sitting on an elegant Edwardian table.

"Everyone, quieten down," Whyte barked as he quickly crossed the room, indicating for the messages to be played.

A male voice spoke, "James, it's Ben Millar, can you pick up..."

They continued to listen as Millar paused, waiting for a reply. After a few seconds of static, a female voice could be heard just as the message ended.

"Sergeant, find out where that call came from," Whyte ordered. "Everyone, listen up. That's the people we're looking for - Ben Millar, the victim's brother, and Lily Taylor - and we need to bring them in right now. We are looking at two murders tonight."

"You've given up on suicide then?" Shaw asked.

"You heard what I said," Whyte replied, "and I hadn't settled on any theory."

"Yeah, but two murders... Millar and Taylor don't fit the profile?"

"Munro was Simon Millar's boss, and he was visited tonight by his brother and Lily Taylor. I don't know why they were here, but they were both seen leaving this house over a garden wall before jumping in a taxi. A neighbour called it in, and the uniforms who attended found a lot more than a suspected burglary... and now we have the phone call..."

"You think he called knowing he couldn't answer?" Shaw asked.

"Millar must have known he'd been seen leaving, so the call is his idea of cover."

Shaw didn't reply. Something was going on here. He'd have to stay and find out if it was relevant to Ohrdruf.

Whyte headed out of the house with a cigarette packet in hand, he turned back to the MI6 man.

"Shaw, since Millar turned up, the two men he's been in contact with are dead - whatever you know about this, or whatever your fancy training has you thinking - Ben Millar is up to his neck in it, and that's one thing I do know for sure."

Chapter 17

Scottish Highlands
Sunday, 7 May 2017 22:45

A car pulled up close behind the white Renault van. Two men took their time getting of the car before signalling to the van driver who was looking out across the loch to the lights of a small town. The man extinguished his cigarette and opened the van's rear doors. At the flick of a switch, the car's headlights flooded the van's interior, and Ben squinted at the three shadowed figures standing over them. Ben had been through interrogation training, and knew it was best to comply and wait for a chance to escape. He didn't resist when dragged forward by the largest man and pulled to sit up on the tailgate. Lily was moved in a similar manner until they were side-by-side.

For the first time there was a clear view of their captors, the two that held them looked unremarkable, one was older, possibly late-thirties with bad skin, the other maybe ten years younger. They both wore close-cropped hair, casual clothes and heavy boots - they were ex-soldiers, working together, each man covering the other's every move.

The third man's appearance couldn't have been more different, he swept shoulder length hair from his face and smiled at them, a number of gold teeth glinted on the lower, right side of his mouth. Ben blinked, this was the man who'd tasered him in Lily's office.

He was dressed in an expensive suit, and was certainly handsome, but with piercing, cold eyes. Lily was right to be afraid of him. This man was obviously in charge and the others waited on his command. He didn't leave it long as he spat out an order in Russian.

Ben saw the six-inch blade after it had cut the cord at his ankles, a similar motion freed Lily. They were put on their feet, and the man with gold teeth switched to English.

"Follow me, please." He spoke softly as though they had a choice.

"You followed us to James Munro's house in Edinburgh," Ben stated. "Where is James now?"

"Who are you?" Lily added.

The man paused for a second before replying.

"You can call me, Vadim," he replied, "and you will understand very soon."

As they turned away from the van, they were led along an overgrown path, past an assortment of rusty, broken-down vehicles and semi-derelict greenhouses.

Lily suddenly stopped, and Ben turned to her. She nodded back towards the van.

"That's Simon's car," she said, "they've come in Simon's car?"

Ben looked back, he hadn't been able to make it out while standing in its headlights, but he could see it was Simon's Rover, the car they'd left behind hours earlier.

"Let me go!" Lily demanded as she struggled with her guard.

Another command and Ben was firmly held while Lily was pinned down and her mouth bound tight with thick black tape once more. Ben shouted for her to be released before Vadim stood patiently before him, an index finger on his lips.

"You are a trained man, but no match for my friend," Vadim said. "No match at all..., so you walk... now."

Ben stumbled, but his captor used one hand to push his arm up his back then reached around with the other to grip Ben's face, pulling his head back and forcing him to take backwards steps as he was led away.

After a few steps, Ben was allowed to walk properly again, he had stumbled to test their response, and he had been expertly restrained. He'd expected that, what he hadn't expected was their knowledge of who he was, what had been meant by 'trained man', did they know the full extent of his military background?

They passed through a wooden door into a well-maintained, walled garden. The box hedges were laid out in perfect squares, the lawn recently cut, and borders were filled with spring flowers in bloom.

The far end of the garden bordered the wide turret of a small castle. Vadim lead them past the huge, crumbling coat of arms which adorned the turret wall. The castle had been extended with a later section, presumably in more stable times as the large windows would have offered no protection from raiders. Distant mountains could be seen through tall fir and larch trees on the skyline. Ben tried and failed to recognise the mountain tops, the only thing he knew for sure was they were in the Scottish Highlands.

As they approached the castle, a heavy wooden door swung open. Lily fought against her ties at the appearance of the man in the doorway. Ben didn't recognise him, but her reaction made it plain she had. Whoever he was, he certainly looked the part, wearing a sandy-coloured tweed suit, with yellow waistcoat and polished brown brogue shoes. The man looked to be in his fifties with a ruddy face that spoke of a love of the outdoors, but carrying the weight of someone who also enjoyed his food and drink. Ben looked back to Lily confused by the strength of her reaction while her guard shrugged, easily holding her in place.

Their host stepped out to meet them, "Lily, so nice to see you again," he turned to Ben, "and Ben Millar, it's good of you to join us. My name is Charles Rae, do come in."

Chapter 18

Laing Castle, Scotland
Sunday, 7 May 2017 22:51

The castle entrance opened out to a large reception hall complete with a huge stone staircase that branched left and right to the upper floor.

Ben memorised every detail: the suits of armour, the paintings, the flags and pennants, and any potential weapons. He took it all in as they were led to a grand public room. Charles Rae stood beside a carved stone fireplace. A coal fire burned at the base, the walls were a deep red, and the style of the furniture was in keeping with the period of the building. The whole room must have been recently restored and was finished to an exceptionally high standard, the quality usually found in a top-end hotel.

The fireplace sported a smaller version of the turret's weather-beaten coat-of-arms on a prominent centre plaque. Ben added the extra clarity of the design to his memory, a shield with a diagonal banner containing three stars, a knight's helmet above, and scrolls framing the shield to either side. There was no attempt to hide any of their captor's faces or where they had been taken. Ben took a deep breath and let his eyes fall on Charles Rae.

"Remove the cords and tape," Rae ordered as Lily and Ben were pushed back onto a large settee.

"We are going to remove your gag, Lily," Rae said, "I advise you to be civil as there's no possibility of being heard outside this room. We sit in a private estate, one hundred and twenty-five acres of it to be precise, and the external walls are several feet thick renovated with triple-glazed windows. So no-one can hear you and I have no time for hysterics."

"Lily will be fine," Ben said slowly. Rae had offered yet more information about their current location; he didn't care what they knew about this place.

"Why are we here?" Ben asked.

"Ah Ben, I hope you behaved for Vadim and his men," Rae replied pouring himself a glass of sparkling water. "I apologise for the taser gun, but we wanted to get you here unharmed."

"They were no trouble," Vadim said as he pushed his hair from his eyes and held up the Enigma message printouts.

"We found these at the woman's office. They have been searched, we found some money. We have their phones. There is nothing in the car."

Vadim crossed the room and handed the messages to Rae before leaning against a wall, there were a series of soft clicks as the Russian inspected Lily's smart phone.

Ben peeled the remaining tape from his mouth and face. Lily's gag had also been removed, and Ben was glad she was holding her temper.

"What do you want from us?" Ben asked steadily, controlling his anger at Lily's treatment and the knowledge these men were responsible for Simon's murder.

Rae started to reply, "I brought you here to answer my questions-"

"Did you kill Simon?" Lily interrupted.

Rae looked thoughtfully at her.

"I can understand you have questions of your own. You've had quite a night."

"Did you kill him?" she asked again, "And what about James Munro, where is he?"

"I'm afraid we stumbled onto something that is bigger than anyone could have imagined."

"Charles, you killed him," Lily said tears running down her face, "I phoned to warn you, and it was you all along. That's how these bastards knew to come to James' home, and how they knew I'd be in my office."

Rae gave a small shrug, "Simon left me little choice. Munro became a problem when I found out you were talking to him. He was too much of a risk to leave unchecked. He was a dead man the moment you made contact."

"Dead?" Lily gasped.

Ben's let his head drop, he'd known they were in danger, but any denial of their position vanished with Rae's casual admission of murder. There was no emotion in the man's voice; there was no attempt to shock or threaten - he was simply stating a fact. Ben turned to Lily whose face was wet with tears.

Without warning, Lily sprang up at Rae. The guard was waiting for such a move and pulled her back by the wrist.

"You're fucking insane," she screamed. "You've murdered two innocent people! The police will find you, and you'll rot in jail for the rest of your fucking life!"

Rae nodded to Ben's guard whose cupped hands slapped Ben's ears causing him to fall to the floor. Lily stopped struggling as she watched Ben roughly thrown back on the sofa, his eyes streaming and his hand clamped to the side of his head.

Once Ben was seated, she turned and stared defiantly at Rae.

"Now I have your attention," Rae said. "Please just answer my questions or things will get much more unpleasant for Ben. Do you understand me?"

Lily nodded, Rae had reminded her who was in control and Ben could see her fight replaced by a fear of what was to come.

"The police do not concern me, they will find what I want them to find," Rae continued.

"And what does that mean?" Lily asked her voice quieter now.

"Let's move on to the reason you've been brought here," Rae replied as he held the Enigma messages up. "You've accessed these messages through the decryption engine. What did you make of them? Who else has seen them?"

Lily cleared her throat nervously glancing at Ben.

"All we know is that the messages are from the 1940s, and a German major tried to locate an item called the Amber Room to exchange for nuclear secrets..."

"Does anyone else know about them?" Rae asked.

"No-one," Lily snapped, "no-one knows any of this, we found out just before these men arrived at my office. Who are they?" she asked, her eyes on Vadim.

"My associates, they assist me in the search and recovery of lost artefacts, you might consider us to be modern-day treasure hunters."

"Is that the decryption engine's purpose," Ben asked, "to find treasure?"

"I was able to procure a vast store of Soviet government archives. The records spanned a period from 1930 to well into the 1960s. While they have a genuine historical interest, I was convinced they would be helpful in the search for future acquisitions. Have you any idea of how much of Europe's art and wealth is still unaccounted for seventy years after the end of the Second World War?"

"No, I don't," Ben replied. "How did you involve Simon?"

Rae took another sip of water, "Have some patience. Let me put things in context; a significant portion of my Russian consignment contained encrypted German military signals from the Second World War. The Soviets had been unable to decode them, but they still stockpiled them month-after-month, year–after-year.

Once decoded, many of those signals accurately recorded the movements of goods. The German stereotype for bureaucracy and order is well deserved, and so I believed some of the signals must have covered items of value. To the victor goes the spoils, and the Nazis systematically looted every museum, palace and art gallery in occupied Europe. So I put my efforts into having them deciphered."

Ben could feel Vadim watching them. He tried to ignore the barely contained smile on the man's face as

Rae continued his lecture.

"The decryption engine was developed by some talented academics, the kind of people who spend literally all of their time in front of computers. They were delighted to find someone willing to pay well for work they found so fascinating."

"But why the killings, what did the decryption engine uncover?" Ben asked.

Rae pondered a moment at the question, when he looked up he seemed to come to a decision.

"It's obvious we intercepted you in time as you seem to know very little," Rae said flatly.

"We can tell the police you're a murderer," Lily spat out.

Charles Rae nodded to his men, suddenly Lily and Ben were held fast, and cable ties slipped over their wrists and ankles again.

"I needed to know if anyone else was involved, but I'm convinced you've acted alone, and so you can now play the part I'd originally planned for Simon. It will lead the police to what will be a satisfying conclusion for them."

"It can't hurt to tell us - why Simon?" Ben shouted as he was held for Vadim to bind him.

"Simon had to die because he wanted to expose who had sent the Amber Room messages to the Nazis," Rae replied.

"But why would that matter after so long?" Ben asked, his head was jerked back and tape wound around his mouth.

"Careful with Millar," Rae barked at the guard, "Tape up the girl first, leave their mouths."

Ben was totally bewildered by the order and just stared at Lily helplessly as the tape was removed from his face and applied to Lily.

Rae waited until the guards finished.

"Ben, most people are happy to live pathetic lives; consumed with their next conquest, their office jobs with pension and health care, and the illusion of a meaningful life. They drink themselves senseless at weekends, copulate like animals and live through reality television.

That could never be enough for me. I'm an excellent historian, but I want the good things in life, it's not enough to be barely comfortable in a tenured university position like your brother or James Munro. I choose to follow history in a way that both excites and allows me to prosper..."

Rae took a sip of water, as Ben watched Lily who had slumped onto the floor.

"If you really want to know how your brother was involved, you'll look at me," Rae demanded.

Lily sat up purposely controlling her breathing, and after a moment, she nodded to Ben who slowly turned back towards Rae.

"You ask why Simon was involved, I was lucky it was someone with such ambition and self-importance. He insisted on total secrecy as he wanted to be the man who discovered where the past and present met - I couldn't believe my good fortune."

"Are you talking about the paper he wrote?" Ben asked, "It was just an academic paper, he was just postulating. Munro said-"

Rae shook his head, "Just as I expected James Munro would, but he would have accepted the truth eventually and so he had to be dealt with."

"What truth? Are you doing this because you think you can find the Amber Room through some time loop? Do you know how stupid that sounds?" Ben snapped.

Rae didn't reply immediately, his small, dark eyes stared at Ben as though daring him to speak again.

"No more insults, Ben, let's continue our discussion without any more outbursts. Now, will you agree that scientists are trained to make observations and provide explanations within an accepted framework or theory?"

"Yes," Ben replied.

"Well, I gave Simon something I thought he might have a bit of difficulty explaining."

"I don't understand?" Ben said.

"That's the point, no-one does. I showed Simon messages from my Russian archive, they all occurred repeatedly in batches between 1941 and 1943. The thing was all the messages were the same, they all said: 'ASTRAEUS-PYTHIA-8 error, aborting run'."

"Why show them to Simon?"

"ASTRAEUS-PYTHIA-8 is a unique phrase if you search for it on the Internet, you find those words come together in an experiment run at CERN on the new Large Hadron Collider. Simon told me that Astraeus is the name of his experiment, and pythia is some computer language they use. That message is broadcast when an error occurs."

"And you're saying there's some kind of link between them?" Ben asked slowly trying to work out where this was heading as Rae stepped closer to them.

"No, I'm saying there's more than a link. I'm saying they are the same messages, I'm saying that error messages originating no more than one month ago from CERN were intercepted in the early 1940s."

Chapter 19

Gottingen, Germany
Friday, 12 February 1943 1052

Passengers on the opposite platform stood as a steam train approached the station. The heavy locomotive pulled up in a shroud of heat and smoke. Kessler could feel the weight of the engine as it shuddered to a halt. The smell of engine oil and hot metal cut through the cold, crisp air.

Checking his watch, he realised that for all its Swiss quality it still needed to be wound, he smiled, it was something he rarely forgot, but his mind was on other things today.

Muller appeared from the station office and walked slowly towards him, there was no urgency as he marked time with the other travellers waiting on their connections. A single glance was enough to know something was wrong. A young soldier strolled onto the platform and looked around casually, but the tight grip on his rifle and the way he avoided looking at the SS men betrayed the feigned indifference.

"Do we have a problem?" Kessler asked as Muller sat down.

"I passed the time of day with the station master. He was nervous and kept looking behind me, next thing the boy arrives, and I can only assume others are on the way."

"He looks like he's shitting himself," Kessler observed.

Muller lit a cigarette as he faced Kessler and glanced back towards the town.

"Unfortunately, our time is running out, a military police truck has just pulled up."

Kessler glanced over his shoulder, the crescent-shaped breast plates of the Feldgendarmerie flashed in the sunlight as the military police started to dismount from the truck and form up.

"Follow on after I've dealt with him," Kessler said as he set off towards the lone guard who continued to avoid eye contact with the approaching SS major. Although the soldier's eyes only left Kessler for a moment, it was enough time for him to draw his dagger and hold it against his forearm. The guard positioned himself badly with his back to an open door leading to the ticket office and rest rooms. Kessler walked behind him, and unaware help was so close - the young soldier maintained the pretence he was on a routine patrol and let Kessler pass.

Muller watched the guard closely, their eyes finally met just as his neck snapped back, and the dagger was held against his throat.

Muller moved quickly, acutely aware the police unit would be on the platform in seconds. Kessler had dragged the boy through a side door into a stairwell. Muller joined them, looking for something to bar the door.

"Your orders, now!" Kessler hissed the soldier's ear.

"Major, you are to be detained on sight. That is all I know."

"Who called the chain dogs?" Muller asked, using the Feldgendarmerie's nickname.

"Sent for by the station master, he pressed me to watch you until they arrived. I was simply passing."

"If you want to live, be silent," Kessler said pushing him back to sit on a step.

They listened, an NCO barked orders, but was drowned out as another train arrived on the platform blocking out the light from the ceiling-high wall of thick and dirty, opaque glass.

Kessler turned to the soldier.

"Is there an exit on the other side of these stairs?"

The boy nodded rapidly before Kessler flicked a strong jab at his chin leaving him a crumpled heap at their feet. "Come on, we have our chance," Kessler called out.

As they made to climb the narrow stairway, heavy boots kicked the door off its hinges, leaving it at an angle blocking the passageway.

Kessler bounded upwards ignoring the shouts from below and threw himself into the upper corridor where he sprawled across a worn, varnished floor. He lay there for a moment before the realisation hit him that he was alone.

Angry shouting came up from the stairwell, but there was no sound of an advance. Kessler drew his pistol and poked his head out to take in the situation. Muller must have lost his footing and was face down, a handful of stairs from the top.

Rifles were trained on his adjutant who had no chance of escape. Kessler shouted down, ordering them to lower their weapons, he looked out once more and caught Muller's eye, he knew that look, and watched in disbelief as his comrade tried to dash up towards him. Gunshots echoed in the confined space as Muller was shot down before he took a step. Further shots were directed towards Kessler which he returned instantly before pulling back from the splintered door frame. He smashed the butt of the pistol into the wall, and called out curses to the men below, it was unbelievable they would open fire on their own countrymen. His anger was also with Muller for trying an escape with no possibility of success.

"Cease fire, I am a SS major, and I demand you to cease fire now!"

The shooting stopped.

"I know who you are and we have orders for your arrest, Major Kessler," a voice replied. "Throw down your weapon and surrender or we will be forced to storm your position and more men could die."

Heavy footsteps at the far end of the corridor told him that exit was now covered. The only escape would be to shoot out the filthy glass panels and try to reach the platform.

The shouts came from below once more, "Your captain is alive, but needs medical attention. We cannot help him until you put down your weapon and surrender. This is your last chance, Major!"

Kessler's risked another look. He was sure Muller was dead. His friend's body lay motionless, but if there was a chance he could be saved, he would take it.

Kessler stepped out into full view and slowly placed the pistol on the floor before raising his hands to the side of his head.

Chapter 20

Laing Castle, Scotland
Sunday, 7 May 2017 23:04

"The error message was intercepted in the 1940s..." Ben repeated, staring at Charles Rae, his mind trying to make sense of what he'd just heard. Lily was no longer struggling, but was open-mouthed, staring at Rae.

"You're saying modern day error messages from CERN have turned up in signals from the 1940s? Simon wouldn't have believed that, it has to be a mistake?" she said.

"He didn't believe it at first," Rae replied, "but the evidence was there, so what could he do? The first problem was the number of messages and their temporal spread. There had only been three occurrences of that error broadcast at CERN, but there were hundreds of identical intercepts from the forties. That concerned Simon, but he was soon able to explain it by some harmonic effect. I wasn't interested in the details, only with the practical uses of this discovery. I could see beyond the science as I didn't have his preconceptions, and so the truth was obvious to me - messages had been passed between periods in time - I didn't care how, but Simon assumed the conduit was these microscopic black holes, these Centauro effects."

Ben saw his shock at Rae's explanation mirrored in Lily's eyes.

Rae continued, "Can you imagine the surprise when the DNA helix was discovered, or the atom split? We believe these fantastic things because we're told they are true. Only a tiny fraction of the world's population take the time to fully understand man's greatest achievements, take the time to satisfy themselves they are correct. The human race has just built the world's most powerful particle accelerator - the most complex machine ever constructed. For me, it's simply another tool that strips nature bare. However, with new discoveries comes scepticism and scientists are trained to be cautious. Simon initially chose to ignore the obvious... well, until tonight that is."

"What happened tonight?" Ben asked.

"He realised the truth. I had convinced him to send another message, one he would compose. The experiment that caused the original error message was repeated, and when the warning was triggered, this time we would transmit a signal of our choosing. I convinced him it would have to be encoded, or it might be discovered by one of his rivals at CERN. So he gave me his message which I threw away, and replaced with my own."

Lily slumped forward, "I think you may have gotten it, my dear."

Rae laughed, "Simon was going to expose me as the man who tried to sell the Nazis nuclear secrets seventy years ago. Can you imagine how he felt? He was ready to announce his discovery to the world, but any triumph would mean nothing after his complicity in sending that message was known. His ambition fed that message into the decryption engine, and it guaranteed he'd keep his mouth shut until he had irrefutable proof the effect existed."

"I can't believe he'd do that," Lily said.

"Of course you do," Rae replied. "You know science is as competitive as any sport and how scientists will hide their work until it's ready to publish. Science is carried out in secret for fear someone will get there first, or for fear of the humiliation on one of your peers finding an unnoticed error. Simon was worried the time loop was a hoax, and he would be remembered as a fool. That was what made him so easy to manipulate. We talked about the unforgiving nature of the scientific community and the ridicule that surrounded the cold fusion debacle. That fear drove him to decrypt my message as he could leave nothing to chance on the approach to his crowning achievement. He finally became suspicious, and I was forced to act."

Lily tried to stand up, her guard moved to pull her back. Rae regarded her for moment, he flicked his finger towards her, "If she makes a scene, tape her mouth and eyes."

Ben looked at her, the tape had left blotchy red marks on her pale face. Vadim caught Ben's reaction and the grin grew a little wider. Rae turned to her, "You have something more to say?"

"I can't believe any of this - how can you send a message back through time and be able to target a specific date or person, it's impossible."

"I have no idea how this works," Rae replied. "I have no idea how a computer works either, just that it does. Simon devised the means of targeting a time period. Government interception of signals traffic started in the early 1900s and has grown exponentially over time, the Americans, with GCHQ's help, seem to have expanded that to all messages, so people like me are particularly careful. Simon explained a transmission could only be detectable if it fell within certain periods. So, if we sent a message back to the Jurassic era, it would be a wasted effort. So for the purpose of the test, we needed a period when signals intelligence was actively collected. The fact that the initial signal was found in 1940s Europe gave us a perfect target. Reports from the period showed many ghost signals were retransmitted repeatedly for weeks on end. Simon thought they could well be the result of the Centauro black holes and the harmonic effect I mentioned. The difficult thing was to target a particular day, month or year to find our test message once it had gone. Simon realised possessing valid German Enigma settings for a particular day meant it didn't matter if a message was received over and over again, as long as it was received during the time period the Enigma code was valid. If so, the message could be understood in that time slot..., if not, it wouldn't decode with the current key and be discarded as junk."

Lily shook her head, "But what if sending something to the past affects the present? I can't believe Simon would agree to send a test message... it's insane."

"You mean the Grandfather Paradox? If someone goes back in time and stops his grandfather meeting his grandmother, that person would no longer exist. It is considered by many to indicate the impossibility of time travel. Simon's understanding was that these messages had already had an effect, they were already woven into our timeline-"

Lily tried to stand again but was restrained once more.

"Sending any message, even a test message from CERN is bad enough," she shouted, "but sending atomic secrets back in time... that's unforgivable."

"Following Simon's reasoning, and don't forget he is one of the world's pre-eminent physicists, it makes no difference what is sent as it's already part of our past. I sent the biggest bait possible to get the Amber Room. The war was turning against the Nazis in 1943 and what could be a bigger prize than the atomic bomb. The first message offered it to them, the next, which will be sent from CERN tomorrow, will deliver all the blueprints from the Manhattan project. The Amber Room has been an interest of mine for decades, and it makes a much grander experiment than what Simon eventually agreed to try."

Lily mouthed a reply. She looked dumbfounded.

"You don't know anything about it," she said coldly, "other physicists believe that quantum effects could, in theory, allow time travel, and if messages got to the 1940s through tiny black holes, then no-one know what that means. Don't you understand? You can't say it won't affect us because you can't know! I can't believe Simon would have done this. How can you believe you'll find the Amber Room? It's utter madness."

A smile played across Rae's thin lips as he refilled his glass with more water.

"I don't think Simon ever believed it would really work," he said. "He thought the messages that got through were total flukes. He thought it would be difficult to repeat, but if we were going to attempt it, then I decided it was going to be something worth sending. The Amber Room disappeared sometime before the end of the war, and if I'm correct, it was placed in the vault of a certain Swiss bank on my instructions. I just have to find the reply to my message with details on how to access it. But think of what this technology means: how can you trust what happened yesterday wasn't decided tomorrow? But that's my problem... yours is more immediate."

The guard's grip tightened on Ben.

"You can't get away with this," Ben said. "It's too big - you can't hide something like this – you must realise that?"

Lily cut in, "Simon says he's responsible for Ohrdruf. Your message caused the nuclear contamination – you must have seen the news, your messages are changing the present, you can't send any more."

Rae turned back to them, "I don't think so. Simon made it clear that couldn't occur."

"Well, if you hadn't killed him, you might find he changed his fucking mind," Lily shouted.

Rae looked them over, "As I said, you will both be playing a part I originally devised for Simon. However, when we examined his history, we found you, Ben, and everything fitted into place. I'm afraid it's time you took a trip in his car. I enjoyed our discussion. Goodbye."

Chapter 21

Gottingen, Germany
Friday, 12 February 1943 1415

Kessler sat up on the cell's bed demanding to see the commanding officer once more. The guards continued to ignore him with the occasional instruction to shut his mouth. They did nothing to hide their resentment for a man who had killed one of their comrades. Kessler's return shots had found their mark, he could hardly miss in such a confined area, and so another man was dead. Kessler felt no remorse, Muller had been shot in the back, and he would kill their whole squad if it would bring him back.

All his belongings and the decoded scientific papers had been taken, but he was still alive, and that was more than his own men would have allowed having lost someone in similar circumstances.

He pushed against a stone block, the granite was cold and unmoving, the wall thick enough to make an excellent air raid shelter. There was no escape here, and little comfort in knowing he was safe from the RAF if they strayed this way. There was nothing to do, and so he turned over and closed his eyes, accepting for now, he was in their hands.

The guardhouse was disturbed by footsteps and the metallic clang of barred iron doors. The guards stood to attention as Kessler raised his head to witness the arrival of an officer who shared his rank. The officer in command when Muller died.

"Major Kessler, my name is Sankt. I have some news for you."

"What is it?"

"You are charged by Admiral Donitz of endangering the security of the Reich, and I am to hold you here until arrangements can be made to return you to Lorient."

"I'm more interested in news of my adjutant, Captain Muller?"

"Your officer died shortly after reaching the hospital. I wish that could have been avoided-"

"You mean you wish your men hadn't overreacted and shot an officer in the back," Kessler replied coldly.

"I was about to say that your captain was not the only man to lose his life in the arrest. You could have surrendered, and in doing so would have saved two unnecessary deaths. My men were simply doing their duty. What did you expect when you chose to run? If there is any blame to be apportioned for this incident, it is with you. You bear responsibly for what has happened this day, Major Kessler."

Kessler turned his back on the military policeman, there was only one man he considered responsible for the death of his closest friend, that man was Admiral Donitz, and he would even that score, however long it took.

"How long have I been here?" Kessler asked.

"Three hours."

"And so you have known of my adjutant's death for hours? I should have been informed immediately. He was under my command," Kessler said slowly, controlling his anger.

"The boy you shot had just turned twenty-one, and he was under my command."

"He was old enough to carry a rifle, Major Kietel, and many younger men are sacrificed for our country every hour of every day. Muller was a decorated veteran and many years my friend. I will avenge him, you can be sure of that."

"I'd be careful with your threats, Kessler, as you seem to have run out of friends. No-one is banging on my door to have you released. On the contrary, the navy is particularly keen to put you on trial."

Kessler remained silent; he still had a mission to complete.

"I have to reach Berlin," Kessler said. "You have taken my papers. They are proof of the development of an advanced enemy weapon. You must have read them and seen the letter written this morning by Professor Lenz?"

"The papers are evidence of your illegal access of classified material, and they link you to the murder of a naval radio clerk. I have been warned about this story of yours and am assured you are very much mistaken."

"Then the admiral is a fool."

"You can tell him that at your court martial."

"You have no right to transfer me to Lorient. As an SS officer I am not subject to Wehrmacht or naval regulations, and if I am to be court-martialled it can only be before an SS court. I demand this matter is put before one."

"It is out of my hands, but I hope the admiral treats you with the same compassion you have shown for the young man you shot down today."

Before Kessler could reply, another solider entered and saluted his officer.

"Sir, a porter from the university has asked to see you. He has a message from a professor there."

Sankt glanced towards Kessler, "You would think given the importance of your new weapon, the professor might have come in person. I will see this porter and give him some advice for his professor on his choice of friends."

Kessler could only watch as the jail door slammed shut and he was left with the sullen guards once more.

Kessler paced around the small cell, shouting for someone to fetch him food and drink. The news of Muller's death weighed on his mind, he tried to put aside the guilt he couldn't help but feel. All he could do is make sure Karl's death was not in vain.

Orders to open up were barked from outside, the police major appeared in the door frame before being pushed into the room. The guards raised their rifles, but an elderly man calmly pointed a Luger at their major's head, and his eyes told them he would use it.

Kessler lent forward, his hands on the bars.

"That one has the keys," he said pointing to a sergeant.

"Open the cell door," the porter ordered. The man looked to his officer, who feeling the cold barrel of a Luger on his temple, gave a careful nod of his head.

Kessler ushered the soldiers into the cell removing their belt kits and weapons. The porter addressed the newly captive military policemen.

"I am sorry it has come to this, Professor Lenz does not know I am here, although it was his reaction on hearing of this man's arrest that convinced me to act. I earned an Iron Cross in the Great War and know good officers from bad. This is a good one. If I am wrong, I will accept my fate."

"You can count on that, grandfather," Major Sankt replied.

Kessler slammed the door shut and threw the keys onto a nearby table. He pointed at the major and waved him forward. Kessler leant forward forcing the man to come close.

"I must continue my mission, where are my papers?" Kessler demanded.

"They are in my office safe across the courtyard."

Kessler had carefully memorised the outside area on arrival. Sankt's office was close to a main gate guarded by two sentries, and the likelihood of more inside a large gatehouse. It would be necessary to take the major along to retrieve the documents.

"Major Kessler," the porter said. Kessler turned to him.

"I need those documents. We must take him to his office-"

"Sir, one moment..." The porter replied he drew closer and whispered, "The professor has sent copies. I have them here."

Kessler stood back, so the porter was acting on the instructions of the physics professor after all.

He turned back to the cells, "Major Sankt, do not try and follow me and do not take action against this man," Kessler said, "Do you understand?"

The major was unmoved and answered immediately.

"I will carry out my duties according to the law."

Kessler ignored the reply; Sankt would do his duty whatever that meant for the old man. He rattled the cell door to make sure it was locked and then left the room with the porter following behind.

The porter already had an escape plan. A small van was parked close by the entrance to the guardhouse and Kessler easily slipped into the back unseen. The porter was known to the sentries, he told Kessler they drank in the same bars and they had listened to his war stories many times, but more importantly they knew there were few men more devoted to the Nazi cause.

They were waved through, and Kessler was free once more, he forced himself to put his regrets over Muller aside, and focused on Berlin, he owed it to his comrade to deliver this weapon to the country they both loved.

Kessler ordered the porter to stop beside an army Kubelwagen parked up in an area surrounded by bars and restaurants.

"I can take you onto Berlin, sir," The porter said. "It is a four hour drive, but it would be a privilege-"

"No, my friend, they will be searching for this van soon enough," Kessler interrupted. "I want you to hide somewhere safe and send my thanks to your professor. This will be resolved within the next few days, and I will send men to protect you both. Is there somewhere I can contact you?"

"If you leave a message with the professor, it will reach me."

"Thank you, now go. If you are caught before I can report to SS Headquarters, they may decide to shoot you. I would simply be rearrested, but it is more dangerous for you."

The porter nodded, called out a salute, and continued on alone.

Kessler turned his attention to the Kubel, the door was unlocked, and he ducked under the canvas top. He found the light switch for the dashboard and placed his dagger into the ignition switch. The car's straightforward design meant the switch directly linked the battery and coil, a tap on the hilt and a strong turn broke the switch and the engine turned over and started first time. It was four hours to Berlin, nothing would stop him now.

Chapter 22

Charles Rae left the room without a second glance as Vadim pocketed Lily's phone, the smile gone.

Lily's eyes were glassy, her breathing fast. She was that girl in the ambulance again, hope fading as she realised they were about to die.

Ben had accepted the position. It was a simple fact, there was no point debating it, it was happening, and he had to find a way out. He focused on Vadim, and had to ask the question.

"Did you kill my brother?"

Vadim turned and spread out his hands, "Does it matter?"

It mattered to Ben, and he knew he was looking at Simon's killer. He let his head drop.

As Vadim issued orders to his men, Ben controlled an overwhelming sense of outrage - like Simon, and Munro they were to be sacrificed for some crazy belief about messages from the past. As Lily was pushed forward, she spun and launched herself at Vadim, kicking out at the Russian, who stepped away easily, and slapped her hard across the face. Ben flinched, but let it go, he wanted them to think he was broken, to drop their guard and give them a real chance of escape.

"I have to kill you and make it look like an accident," Vadim said to Lily. "Do something like that again and I forget my orders and death will not be easy."

He looked thoughtfully at Ben then licked his lips, nodding to Ben's guard, who held him tight.

"Do you know how the boss is to cover up the killing?"

Ben didn't respond.

"If your brother got out of hand, we place a hosepipe from the exhaust pipe to his car, a common enough suicide, his mind was unsettled."

"Fuck you!" Lily replied.

"You will be playing that part, both of you will die in his car, but only one will be suicide, you will have taken this girl with you," he said to Ben, "murdered her as you murdered your brother and the other scientist. The police will believe it, the boss will make sure."

"Get real, nobody will believe that," Lily shouted.

Ben watched as the man smiled, a smug grin, as though he was savouring what he was about to tell them.

"You know nothing about this man," he said nodding at Ben, "He fell out with his father and ran away to join the army. A father who died recently leaving everything to his older brother."

"So what?" Ben replied, "I never expected or wanted anything from him."

"How hard will it be to believe you resented, even hated your brother. You hardly see him, then shortly after your father's death, you turn up and bad things happen."

Lily looked at Ben, "No-one will believe this," she said.

"This man is perfect, a criminal history for assault, the father is dead, so he went after the brother he always hated."

"I'm only here because Simon contacted me, he wanted me to be here," Ben replied.

"You are here because the boss wanted you here. We investigated your brother and found you. Most victims are killed by someone they know, you have history, the police will be happy."

Ben didn't reply.

"You don't understand, you think you are here because the university called you, told you your brother was unwell? No-one from the university called anyone, the boss called you, you have come to help us -

and to die"

Vadim nodded, two men held Ben leading him out of the castle, through the gardens, and back to a trailer loaded with Simon's car. They knew their jobs well, there was no chance to escape, the men expertly held Ben, as Vadim covered them all with a compact Sig-Sauer pistol.

They placed him in the driver's seat beside Lily. A thick blanket was wrapped around his body as he was tied to the seat by worn leather straps.

"This will be over quickly." Vadim said, "New cars remove most of the poison. An old car is better. Thirty minutes will finish you, and I will be watching."

With that, he lent over, started the ignition then slammed the door shut.

Ben started to cough as the acrid smoke built up rapidly in the space around them while Lily fought desperately against her bonds.

"Can you move?" Ben spluttered.

She nodded, leaning forward, her hands and feet were bound with cable ties.

"The cigarette lighter, turn it on," Ben ordered.

Lily pushed the lighter into the dashboard.

"Wait until there's enough smoke to cover us, hold your breath as long as you can." Ben said.

"For what?"

"Untie my straps, do it slowly."

She undid the leather straps holding him to the seat and he pushed the blanket onto his knees.

"Use the lighter to burn the cable ties," he held out his hands.

Ben watched her pull out the cigarette lighter, she looked into his eyes.

"Do it," he said ready to pull his hands apart as hard as he could.

She held the red hot element against the cable tie, and he jerked away, trying not to scream as his skin burnt alongside the cord. The tang of burning plastic added to the noxious atmosphere, and Ben held his breath trying to stop the smoke's debilitating effects as Lily attacked the thick tie. Sweat poured down his face as he fought to stretch the weakened cable, just when he thought they would need the lighter again, the cable gave way. Ben took a gulp of air and choked as the fumes caught his throat.

His hands were already at his ankles, he jabbed the lighter back into its holder then held it against the tie, his legs were protected by his jeans and the bond burnt through immediately - his hands and feet were free.

The exhaust fumes were thick, and he opened the side window to clear the air, Ben caught movement from Vadim and his men who had been chatting over a cigarette. He slammed the car in gear, and it lurched back off the trailer's ramp. Shouting at Lily to open her window, he gunned the car forward knowing there was a single track leading down from the house. There would be no second chance to escape these men.

The fumes cleared as Lily coughed violently having torn the tape from her mouth. Ben fumbled with the switches trying to find the headlights - he heard her scream a warning, and felt the sudden change of surface beneath the tyres. He found the headlight switch in time to see they were heading for a large stone gatepost. Ben tugged the wheel hard, fighting to change the direction of the heavy old car. The tyres found grip avoiding a full frontal impact, but there was a horrendous jolt as they glanced off the gatepost, smashing the rear passenger door and wheel arch.

Ben righted the car then stamped on the throttle. The old Rover shot forward, responding to the steering. The only major problem was a broken headlight on the left side, but the car was running and taking them away from the castle. Ben checked the mirror and saw Vadim running back up to the house, and a gleaming Audi saloon. They had little time as they couldn't hope to out pace a modern, performance car.

Lily nursed a bump to the head caused by the gatepost impact while Ben had avoided injury by bracing against the steering wheel. With her hands and ankles still bound, Lily was forced to position herself as best she could, and Ben was glad the car only suffered that glancing blow as anything more substantial would have ended their escape before it began.

Ben pushed the car through the tight bends with tall, dense pine trees screening them from their pursuers on either side.

Ben shouted a warning to Lily before braking hard and reversing sharply onto a rough access road. The car landed in a shallow ditch as he killed the lights. There was just enough moonlight to make out the way ahead and Ben pulled Lily out of the car and carried her to the cover of trees beyond a low fence. They had just reached the treeline when a car roared past.

Ben ran back to the car and pulled out a shard of glass from the broken headlight to carefully free Lily's ties.

"What now?" Lily asked.

"Can you walk?" Ben asked in return.

"I think so."

"We need a phone - we need to contact the police."

"I know," she replied, "I can't believe we got away."

"We haven't yet, we couldn't have outrun them and our only chance was to get off the road, we have to move now."

"Where to?"

"Back to the castle. We've travelled less than a mile. When we were dragged out of the van I noticed the keys were left in the ignition, if we get back quickly, we have a real chance to escape."

"What about Rae?" Lily said. "Do you believe what he's saying?"

"We get out of here and let the authorities deal with him-"

"And the time loop?"

"Munro read the paper and wasn't convinced... I don't know."

"But Munro didn't know about the link to the Large Hadron Collider..."

"Yeah, and thanks to Rae, he never will. Now come on, we need to go."

Ben was already walking.

Lily nodded as Ben peered into the trees, they would provide excellent cover, but it would be slow going with Lily through tree roots in the darkness below the canopy. Ben was trained to fight in shadows, without Lily, he wouldn't have considered the risk he would have to take now.

"We'll have to use the road, we'll have to run?" Ben said.

They made for the road anxious to get moving as Vadim would surely turn back at any moment.

"Get off the road if you hear a car," Ben instructed.

There was little immediate cover at the road side, and they would be easily seen, but there was nothing to do but move.

Ben started to run, taking Lily's arm and pulling her along, as though she was a recruit struggling to keep up during a yomp in the marines. They both coughed, and Ben felt sick from the fumes, but he urged her on; unable to settle for a slower pace when every extra second on the road could cost them everything. A couple of minutes passed slowly as Ben waited for the sound of a car to signal their luck had run out. Eventually, the tree line gave way to the outline of a castle above beech hedging that lined the roadside border.

Should they go through the gates and up the driveway? Ben decided it was worth taking the time to approach the van from cover. He led Lily through an open doorway into the castle grounds, and they moved quietly along a wall, sheltering in its shadow.

As they approached the castle, the crumbling coat of arms was illuminated by an uplighter, and it provided a perfect reference point for the path that led to the old greenhouses where they'd been taken from the van.

Movement through the large windows, and voices from the castle made them wait before moving slowly through the garden to the greenhouses where the van came into view.

Ben signalled for Lily to stay put, took a gulp of air, and then moved silently towards it. He covered the short distance quickly and lay flat against the cold, white bodywork before edging to the driver door. That was when he heard footsteps on the gravel.

He kneeled and cocked his head until one eye could see the older of the men who brought them here coming his way. He was well-built, probably fast and powerful. Ben automatically went for the handgun he'd so often carried, strapped to his right thigh. He found his leg instead, and realised he'd never been unarmed this close to an enemy. He clenched and unclenched his fists, all the hours of self-defence training would be put to the test. He shaped his right hand to deliver a open palm strike. It was easy to damage the small bones of the hand throwing a punch. He remembered a black belt whose technique faltered in the heat of a real fight, not enough to lose, but enough to suffer broken metacarpals in his right hand.

The man approached, he was going for the cab, so Ben crouched and waited close to the driver door.

The guard stopped. Ben's heart started to race - had he made a noise, given himself away? Then he heard the flick of a lighter, as the man paused momentarily before smoke rose from a cigarette.

The man continued on, and as he turned to open the van door, Ben surged forward pivoting his body to slam his hand, and full bodyweight, into back of the head.

There was a reason most combat sports disallowed strikes to the rear of the skull. Spinal cord injuries could cause loss of co-ordination, temporary or permanent loss of sight, paralysis and even death. Ben didn't wait to find out if any of those symptoms applied, as he immediately transitioned to a choke, blocking blood flow to the brain, and held on long after his opponent's body had gone limp.

Using the van as cover, Ben pulled the body and hid it behind bushes for the gardeners to find. His arms felt weak and clumsy from holding the choke on tight, and he shook them out as he made his way back to the van.

There wasn't enough light to see if the key was in the ignition, so he tried the door. It opened with a noisy clunk, the cab light came on - the key was there - and he quickly slid in and flicked the light to off. There was a large paper label attached to the key, and he could just make out the registration number scrawled with a black permanent marker alongside the name of a hire company. He waved frantically for Lily to join him and winced at the noise as she crossed the gravel track.

"We're good to go," he whispered. "Let's get out of here."

Ben waited until Lily was safely in the passenger seat before trying the ignition. The diesel engine fired up immediately, and the fuel gauge climbed half-way, which was more than enough to cover a couple of hundred miles.

Lily was ashen-faced as Ben carefully selected reverse and gently fed in the clutch. He would move off as normally as possible as it might give them a few extra seconds before anyone realised something was wrong. Ben tried to control himself, he wanted to dump the clutch and stamp on the throttle to reach the open road before Vadim could return and block their only way out.

They reached the gateposts and gratefully looked into darkness on both sides. Checking the mirrors showed there was no activity from the castle, so Ben gunned the van to the right, the opposite direction from their initial escape, and then floored the accelerator.

Road signs indicated they were on an A-road twenty-five miles from the bridge at Ballachulish where they could join the main A82 that lead north to Fort William or south to Crianlarich through Glencoe.

Ben drove fast along the loch side road looking in the moonlight for the rudimentary box steel bridge that would put them within ten minutes of the Highland's main town.

"North or south?" Ben asked.

"North," Lily said. "I've got a friend in Fort William who can help us."
Ben followed the signpost.
"Fort William's fine, but we need to stop and make some calls," he said.
Lily nodded and he felt her looking at him.
"What?" he asked.
"You saved my life," she said quietly.
Ben took his eyes from the road for a moment, "We saved each other."

Chapter 23

The hire van passed under the steel bridge and looped back onto the A82. As they reached a roundabout, Ben looked down towards Glencoe. It might be safer to head South through the towering stone walls of the famous mountain pass, then further on, to be lost in one of the towns and cities of Scotland's central belt. But Fort William was only twelve miles away, and better still, they were only minutes from a hotel in the small town of Onich. Ben followed a familiar route over the bridge and skirting alongside a loch, before turning into the car park of a hotel that sat on the water's edge.

"I've stayed here before," he said, "there's a bar at the rear. We can use their phone."

"Do you think it's safe to stop?" she asked.

"If they'd taken the same road, they'd have caught us by now. They had to make a guess, and must have chosen south."

He opened his door to get out of the van, but Lily stayed where she was.

"Ben, when Simon said he was responsible for Ohrdruf, he must have meant the time loop. He wasn't losing his mind at all. He knew about the messages."

"Munro said he'd been acting weird," Ben replied, "you said that yourself."

"If he believed in the time loop, he would be working on the biggest discovery in physics for a generation," she replied. "That would explain so much..."

"It would, if he believed it," Ben replied stepping out, "but we don't know for sure."

"But you saw the messages in my office, and Rae-"

"We saw some files created today on a computer - do we really know where they came from?"

"But Rae said they got a response from the past, and we saw the messages ourselves," Lily insisted. "Simon must have believed it, and he was just too smart to be fooled by Rae or anyone else."

"He was ambitious, so maybe part of him wanted to believe. I'm totally out of my depth here, but the simple explanation is those messages have been around for sixty years. They were sent sixty years ago, by people sixty years ago, and because Charles Rae believes otherwise - people are dying today."

"You're going to call the police?"

"You don't want me to?"

"They're sending another message tomorrow," Lily replied. "We have to stop them."

"We'll tell the cops, it'll be their problem after that."

"Simon wanted his papers published, he didn't trust the police, and anyway, they won't believe any of this, not in time to stop that message."

"People are dead, we need a very good reason for not going to them right now," Ben replied.

"I believe we have to stop the message and make everything public, publicity is the way to be safe, and I don't trust a government that spies on its people. Every phone call made, every email sent. Do you think it's OK for them to do that?"

"I understand why they think it's OK."

Ben considered her for a moment, he focused on the mainly black and gray tattoo that wrapped her lower arm; it was striking, with hints of colour on small flowers. He'd never seen one like it before, probably done to her own design. The current tattoo craze had passed him by; it was an act of individual self-expression that seemingly every individual wanted to express. Every other guy in the marines had them and they were a part of life, like the banter and smell of body odour.

He'd never felt the need to get inked, and he'd never believed in conspiracy theories either. Politicians, and senior figures in the forces and police, rarely controlled events, they spent most of their time reacting to them. She wanted to believe the worst about a police state, but in reality, crooks and terrorists were the target, not pretty, middle-class academics, however many tattoos and pins adored their faces and bodies.

"I want the cops to know about Charles Rae, if anything happens to us, I want them to know where to look."

"I agree, as long as you take me to Fort William, I need to try and stop that message."

Ben nodded, and they made their way to the hotel. He tried the door, and they carried on through a narrow hall to the bar. They passed a handful of guests leaving the bar, and their glances made him realise they both looked pretty rough, and so he tidied himself as he walked. Lily stopped at a mirror, but seemed unconcerned by her appearance, and only spent a moment fixing her hair. It wasn't an issue anyway, the area was full of outdoor people, and the local hotels were accustomed to the sweat and dirt that came through their doors.

Ben tried to find the pay phone, it had been on the far wall, he turned to the bar, looking to see if it had been moved, but found the room had gone silent, and everyone looking at them.

Lily stepped forward and hesitantly asked, "We're looking for a phone; our car's broke down."

"Everyone has mobiles these days, not had a public phone in here for a long time," the barman answered.

"You got a phone we can use?" Ben asked.

"Yeah, sure, there's a phone in the office on the way out, but you'll have to wait until I close this place up, be ten minutes or so."

Ben nodded, "Anyone got a mobile we can borrow now?"

"Not much of a signal around here," a local said.

"OK, no problem," Ben said, "we'll wait."

He steered Lily over to sit on a fixed bench by the exit, and watched as the barman stepped out through a door behind the bar.

Ben pulled out a chair facing her,and sat on the edge.

"Ben, can I ask you something?"

He nodded, he'd been waiting for her to ask about Simon.

"Was it true? I mean, what Vadim said about your father..."

Her voice trailed off, he turned to her, and she looked away before reluctantly meeting his eyes.

He shrugged, "He lost his business, and started drinking. It came at the worst time, as I was about sixteen, and didn't exactly sympathise. He started slapping me around, and I never backed down, so one day I decided to get away, and left school to enlist in the Royal Marines. I think that really got to him, he'd always expected me to follow my genius brother to university, and I was leaving it all behind to run over hills with a gun. I never spoke to him again."

"Did Simon know?"

"Simon was nine years older than me and he'd just got his PhD. He stayed away because he knew things weren't right, probably didn't want to accept his dad was a scumbag, he died six months ago, and we'd barely been in contact since. The truth is, I hardly knew Simon, we weren't that interested in each other."

"You never talked at the funeral?"

"I never went to the funeral. It wasn't deliberate, I can be hard to contact, the best way is usually my mobile, but I don't always carry it. I missed a few calls from Simon, and that was that."

"Rae used Simon," she said lowering her head.

"Yeah, but he's not using me," Ben replied standing up, he caught her eye, "Something's wrong."

There were wires running up the wall next to a spirit rack with bottles and optics, but Ben was more interested in an old telephone junction box half-way up the wall. The oval box with single central screw joined a wire that disappeared through a hole in the door frame to the room behind the bar. Ben had noted there was another door into that room next to the toilets in the hall.

Ben called to one of the men, asking where the barman was, and waited for an answer he already knew. He motioned to Lily to stay, and made his way out to the hall.

The other door was slightly ajar, and Ben cocked his head to listen.

"Yeah, I'm sure it's her," the barman was saying into the receiver.

Ben pushed into the room, and the barman spun around. They looked at each other for a moment, there was a kitchen knife at the end of a worktop that ran the length of the wall. The barman dropped the phone, and went for it. Ben slapped his hand away, and forced him back against the wall, his right forearm over the man's windpipe as his left hand roughly held the wrist. Ben's weight pinned him against the wall, and he was ready to put the man down using knees to groin or stomach. The controlled aggression of the assault shocked the barman and he stopped struggling .

"Who were you calling?" Ben asked increasing the pressure on the throat.

"The police," the man gasped.

A man's voice called in from the bar, "Scott, you alright?"

"Why were you calling them, Scott?" Ben hissed.

"The girl, she's been on the TV. There was a murder in Edinburgh, the TV said she's a witness, they're looking for her, the tattoos and piercings, it's her?"

"OK, that's fine; we wanted to call the police, that's why we're here."

He released the pressure, "I'm going to let you go now, don't do anything stupid."

Ben pushed him back into the bar, following him in; the drinkers got off their stools and moved towards the door, towards Lily.

"Scott, has called the police," Ben said, "that's OK as we want to talk to them."

One of the men, a tall, heavy man with a florid complexion, moved closer as though he was going to pull Ben over the bar. Ben had no doubts he could do it, he looked like a manual worker, someone used to heavy lifting.

"We're going to wait on the police outside, none of you need to get involved."

The man kept getting closer, "We're already involved."

He threw a roundhouse punch at Ben's head. People tended to say their piece before attacking, and this guy was no different. Throwing a punch halfway through a sentence was always a surprise, but at the end of some announcement was when to expect it, and Ben was ready.

He blocked the punch, and used his other hand to deliver a palm strike hard to the face. The nose would be broken, and the pain enough to drop him to his knees.

"Lily, let's go," he shouted, "everybody else, stay where you are, the next guy gets more than a broken nose."

He stared them down for a moment, and when no-one moved he took Lily's hand, and led her out to the van.

"What now?" she asked.

"We can't stay here, even if you wanted to, that lot in there might grow some balls, especially when the big guy's back on his feet."

Ben opened the passenger door for her, and made his way around to the driver's side.

"Did you learn to fight like that in the army?"

"Let's just say my dad encouraged me to learn self-defence. You still want go to Fort William?"

"Yeah, let's go, I need to think."

He nodded, and they pulled onto the road heading north for the short drive to the tourist town just 12 miles away.

Chapter 24

Edinburgh, Scotland
Monday, 8 May 2017 00:16

Andrew Shaw had taken his leave from the police and booked into the Marriott hotel close to Edinburgh airport.

There was nothing more to do at the observatory or Professor Munro's home, and if DCI Whyte chose to keep him at a distance, he could rely on Special Branch to keep him informed on what was now, officially, a double murder investigation.

Shaw called room service, ordered a beer and sandwich then flicked the TV channel to Sky News. The Edinburgh murders were topping the bill with the Ohrdruf story falling down the order behind more tales of economic woe.

His phone beeped on a side table, the beep that came with the arrival of email. The phone screen wasn't great for reading anything more than the briefest of mails, so he opened his laptop, pressed his right thumb on the fingerprint reader, then provided two more passwords before he could access his secure email.

The background reports on Ben Millar and Lily Taylor were attached, it was quick work by London, but then Ohrdruf was a top priority even without the deaths of two British physicists.

DCI Whyte would no doubt have requested similar checks on his witnesses turned suspects, but MI6 had much better access and would have scanned records held by their employers, banks, telephone companies and Internet providers before the police had applied for the first warrant.

Shaw started to read the report when his phone rang for a voice call just as there was a knock at the door. He answered the call first and put it on hold while his room service delivery was placed on the main table inside the room door.

"Shaw," he said resuming the call as he removed the lid from the club sandwich.

"I've got something else for your report on the Edinburgh murders," a female voice stated.

Shaw recognised Sylvia's accent immediately, it was a product of private schools, wealthy parents and the stereotypically privileged background that had filled Whitehall posts for centuries. None of which mattered as he knew she was also one of the most capable analysts in the service.

"Shaw, can you hear me?"

"Sorry," Shaw managed, "you've caught me grabbing a bite to eat."

"OK, just listen," she replied. "You should have already been told this, but your Special Branch escort copied down the wrong number for your mobile, so he called us instead."

"I'm listening," Shaw replied.

"The suspects were just spotted at a hotel in a place called Onich-"

"And?" Shaw said putting down the sandwich.

"And it will take much longer to tell you if you insist on interrupting..."

"Sorry, please continue."

"It's near Fort William, up in the highlands. The police are there now, with many more on the way."

Shaw poured the bottled lager into its glass with his free hand.

"I only managed a quick look at your report. Ex-Royal Marine, rose to sergeant.. He's nothing like his brother then?"

"Quite. His military record is excellent, he only left because of an injury; he was rated first class."

"What happened to him?"

"Training exercise, broke both his legs and took months to recover. The doctor's seemed to have written him off, but he was kept on to see how things panned out. After another few months, he chose to quit. Judging by his current job, he must be fully fit again."

"Marines are tough bastards, definitely fully fit to be working as a diver. He was recently deported from Zambia?"

"He'd been working as a freelance diver on a gas platform off the coast of Mozambique. It seems he picked up some girl volunteering with the VSO and they travelled to Lusaka together."

"What went wrong?"

"The local police picked him up for loitering, which equates to being out after 11pm over there. He got in a fight with a white ex-pat over treatment of other arrestees. It seems some ex-pats were having a bit of fun riding with the police and deciding who to pick up. There was some rough stuff handed out to a few of the locals and Millar stepped in and punched the ringleader out. After a bit of a beating he was given the option of facing a trial or accepting a stiff fine and leaving the country that day. He wisely chose the latter course."

"Yeah, I wouldn't fancy a Zambian jail house," Shaw replied.

"As that's all we have, we're looking for any associations that might have led them to flee north, I'm keeping an open channel with the police, and I'll call you back when we have something."

Shaw replaced the phone, raised his glass and took a mouthful before pouring the rest down the sink of the en-suite bathroom. The beer tasted good, but he needed a clear head. Millar and the girl were running for a reason, and as events unfolded, the more Shaw began to wonder if Professor Millar's telephone confession really was the farce everyone had been so happy to believe.

Chapter 25

Kessler slowed as he approached a small farm. A troop of Hitler Youth saluted as his jeep passed. He returned the gesture and scanned their smiling faces. He wondered where his thirteen year-old son, Harald, was at this very moment? He was a beautiful boy, strong like his father, with his mother's looks and fair hair. Was he in a camp like this, up north near his home in Hamburg, or back from school and out with his friends causing trouble? The remains of a camp fire sent thin, grey smoke drifting upwards. It had dispersed by the time it reached the top of the trees.

Harald was too young for this war, and he would live in a better time when the madness finally ended. Germany had come too far in the last decade to be defeated by enemies to the east and west. Europe had been consumed by his country's blitzkrieg tactics, a new mechanised warfare that devastated enemy armies and delivered great victories wherever the hand of the Reich had fallen. That was two years ago, and the Red Army had regrouped after an initial rout that could have delivered Moscow and ended the war on the eastern front in one hammer blow. As it was, the Russian winter had come to save its miserable people, trapping German troops in mud and ice, where they froze and died against a determined foe that numbered men in the millions. Despite this setback, his people had achieved too much for it to end in defeat once more, they could not fail, the consequences for the civilian population would be truly dreadful.

Kessler shook his head to clear out those thoughts. German forces were the best in the world and would prevail against all enemies, but that applied to fighting armies of men. No nation, however strong, could stand against a super weapon with the power to level a city. It was his duty to continue the mission and ensure the importance of the Enigma message he carried was recognised.

The kilometres passed as he drove deeper into the heart of his country, the lights from a distant vehicle occasionally flashed in his rear mirror despite the blackout covers. Kessler pulled over and switched off his own lights. Was it possible he was being followed, and a road block waiting up ahead?

A heavily laden army truck soon approached, struggling to maintain its speed as the driver crashed through the gears to maintain momentum.

Kessler stood on the centre of the road waving a flashlight slowly across his chest. The brakes squealed as the truck was forced to a shuddering halt.

The driver lent out of his cab, Kessler's uniform was illuminated in the headlights.

"Can I help you, sir?"

"I need a ride."

The driver looked to the abandoned car.

"Do you want me to try and fix it, Major?"

Kessler didn't want to explain the broken ignition lock or anything else and made to climb aboard.

They joined a convoy of military trucks on the approach to the first city of the thousand-year Reich. It wasn't long before they were queued on the busy roads. In normal circumstances, Kessler would have made a fuss and ordered the driver to overtake regardless of the oncoming traffic. Today it was wiser to accept the delay and blend in as just another uniform among the many thousands stationed in and around Berlin.

He bade farewell to the driver close to Central Berlin, and made a call to his old friend and commanding officer, SS-Colonel Werner Armin, a man he could count on under any circumstances.

It was a cold evening as he made his way past the magnificent statue of Fredrick the Great and walked quickly towards the many bars and cafes on Unter den Linden.

Kessler enjoyed the warmth as he entered a small restaurant on the main government thoroughfare of Wilhelmstrasse. It had been years since he'd eaten here, and only the staff had changed. Kessler ordered the pork knuckle with sauerkraut, and his usual glass of red. The food was good but could hardly be enjoyed as he was anxious to meet the colonel.

Thirty minutes after his call, a staff car pulled up outside the cafe, Kessler recognised the only passenger, and wiping his mouth, walked out to welcome him.

The driver held open the rear door, and Kessler embraced his old commander who'd stepped out from the car.

"It's good to see you, it's been too long, far too long," the SS colonel said. "There is no time for friends anymore."

"Thank you for coming," Kessler replied.

"Kessler, I have followed your progress. Partisan activity has dramatically deceased in your sector, and I have let it be known that is no coincidence."

It was his peripheral vision that first alerted Kessler something was wrong, the speed and direction of the incoming cars. Kessler stared into the colonel's eyes, the man reacted and turned outwards - there was no betrayal, he was obviously surprised, and so Kessler pulled him close and placed his documents in the deep, inside pocket of the colonel's great coat.

Waffen-SS soldiers lined up on either side, their automatic weapons firmly held and trained on Kessler. The colonel shouted orders for the soldiers to stand down, standing between them and Kessler.

Kessler stood flat-footed, he would not run and risk bringing fire on the colonel, and anyway, he was with the SS in Berlin, and that was exactly where he wanted to be.

He raised his hands and waited as a young captain with a resolute expression approached. The man was readying himself to deal with the delicate task of arresting a senior officer.

"Major Kessler, you are wanted in connection with the murders of two German soldiers. You are to be taken before an SS court."

"Major Kessler has murdered no-one, and who authorised I was to be followed-" The colonel shouted at the captain who flinched but stood his ground.

"I will come with you, Captain," Kessler interrupted, "I can explain my actions."

The colonel lambasted the captain once more as Kessler was ushered into a waiting car.

"I am sorry, sir, but I have my orders," he said as they started to pull away from the kerb.

The colonel shouted at the leaving car, "You will be released within the hour-"

Kessler sat next to a captain who looked anywhere but at his captive, in contrast to the two soldiers he faced, who never took their eyes from him.

"Will you be good enough to tell me your orders, Captain?" Kessler asked.

The captain considered the request, taking a moment before answering.

"My orders are to detain you and take you before a judge. That is all."

"You know nothing of the charges?"

"Very little, it is not my concern. This is a routine matter, you understand?"

"A routine matter, sir," Kessler snapped. "I am still your superior officer and earned my rank, Captain."

"I apologise, sir... Please, no more questions we are approaching our destination."

The car turned sharply into a narrow gateway that opened up into a large courtyard.

Kessler was drawn to the tall, thin young officer in flowing robes climbing the wide stairs two or three at a time. The man was an official of the SS Legal division, the Hauptamt SS-Gericht. They had arrived at Berlin's SS court.

As the car drew up, Kessler took it on himself to open the door and step out first. He wasn't going to be naval lawyers called for an explanation. Kessler stopped beside them, "Tell the Admiral, I will be him soon enough."

y ignored him and continued to protest, the judge, leaving the chamber, waved them away.

ank you, you timed that well," Kessler said.

ou doubted me, Kessler?"

d be interested to know what changed the judge's mind quite so quickly."

nim held out the paper, "We have powerful friends."

essler read the contents and looked back to the colonel.

The Reichsfuhrer? You went to Himmler himself?" Kessler asked, they were talking about one of the e most powerful men in the country.

"Of course, and he wishes to see you this afternoon, so we had better find you a decent uniform."

ordered out like a criminal, and the arrest party followed hurriedly after him. The capta
he knew he was in control of the situation, and there was no need to overreact. Kessler
sentries were posted every twenty metres around the court, and both men knew there was
escape.

Kessler was led into the building through a grand hallway and past a huge, stairway und
ceiling. They entered an empty courtroom and Kessler was shown to a wooden bench as his
stepped back to stand at either side of the exit.

The captain sat a few rows behind as court staff filed in, followed by a female stenographe
up her position to the front. Two naval officers joined them and sat to Kessler's left.

The court was instructed to stand as the young legal official entered. It was the man Kessler
hurrying outside, and who was announced as an assistant judge. Kessler noted his rank, he was a
lieutenant, was this the most senior man in Berlin? He knew the SS legal department's headquarte
in Munich, but expected a few senior judges to be on hand to hear cases regarding the higher ranks
kind of judges who knew their job and would not be intimidated by admirals, however elevated.

The court sat around him, Kessler remained on his feet, What is going on here?" He asked interru
the shuffling of papers on the surrounding desks.

"You are charged with conduct unbecoming of an SS officer, Major," the judge said without looking
it was doubtful the man was twenty-five years old.

"I will defend myself against all charges, but it is customary to have the time to prepare a defence. So
ask again, what is going on here?"

One of the naval officers stood up, "If I may answer the Major, your honour?"

The judge nodded.

"Major Kessler has deluded himself into thinking he carries information vital to the war effort. The
information concerned is already known to the high command and has no value. It provides no excuse for
the killing of young German soldiers-"

"That is of no consequence here, I came to Berlin to make my report, and I will face any accusations
put before this court after preparing a defence."

The naval officer slammed his fist on the desk, "This man breached communications security vital to
the naval effort," he shouted. "His irresponsibility has led to the deaths of two men and an emergency
change to the naval Enigma ciphers. Admiral Donitz demands to know how security was breached, and
we will return Major Kessler to the SS court when we have that answer."

Kessler stood up to argue, but the judge cried out for silence and both sides sat down and waited for
the assistant judge to speak.

"Major, you are under the jurisdiction of this court, and there is a request before me to allow your
questioning on a naval security matter. You will be well-treated and returned here within ten days. I grant
the application, and on your return you will be given sufficient time to arrange legal representation. Do
you have anything to say?"

"This is highly irregular. I wish to appeal to a senior judge. You are out of your depth, Lieutenant."

The Assistant Judge dismissed the court, "He is yours, for now, Gentleman. I expect him back here in
ten days' time."

"Hold that order!" was shouted across the court. Kessler turned to see Colonel Arnim striding into the
chamber. He carried a single sheet of paper, which he placed in front of the judge. If the judge was put out
by this interruption he hid it well enough, lifting the paper which he quickly read. The colonel waited for
a response, his eyes fixed on the bench.

The judge stood and spoke, "Major Kessler is released to the custody of Colonel Arnim; he is free to
go."

The captain and his troop stepped back and saluted as the colonel and Kessler passed them by.

The naval lawyers called for an explanation. Kessler stopped beside them, "Tell the Admiral, I will be seeing him soon enough."

They ignored him and continued to protest, the judge, leaving the chamber, waved them away.

"Thank you, you timed that well," Kessler said.

"You doubted me, Kessler?"

"I'd be interested to know what changed the judge's mind quite so quickly."

Arnim held out the paper, "We have powerful friends."

Kessler read the contents and looked back to the colonel.

"The Reichsfuhrer? You went to Himmler himself?" Kessler asked, they were talking about one of the three most powerful men in the country.

"Of course, and he wishes to see you this afternoon, so we had better find you a decent uniform."

ordered out like a criminal, and the arrest party followed hurriedly after him. The captain let it happen as he knew he was in control of the situation, and there was no need to overreact. Kessler had already noted sentries were posted every twenty metres around the court, and both men knew there was no chance of escape.

Kessler was led into the building through a grand hallway and past a huge, stairway under a domed ceiling. They entered an empty courtroom and Kessler was shown to a wooden bench as his guards stepped back to stand at either side of the exit.

The captain sat a few rows behind as court staff filed in, followed by a female stenographer who took up her position to the front. Two naval officers joined them and sat to Kessler's left.

The court was instructed to stand as the young legal official entered. It was the man Kessler had seen hurrying outside, and who was announced as an assistant judge. Kessler noted his rank, he was a second-lieutenant, was this the most senior man in Berlin? He knew the SS legal department's headquarters were in Munich, but expected a few senior judges to be on hand to hear cases regarding the higher ranks - the kind of judges who knew their job and would not be intimidated by admirals, however elevated.

The court sat around him, Kessler remained on his feet, What is going on here?" He asked interrupting the shuffling of papers on the surrounding desks.

"You are charged with conduct unbecoming of an SS officer, Major," the judge said without looking up, it was doubtful the man was twenty-five years old.

"I will defend myself against all charges, but it is customary to have the time to prepare a defence. So I ask again, what is going on here?"

One of the naval officers stood up, "If I may answer the Major, your honour?"

The judge nodded.

"Major Kessler has deluded himself into thinking he carries information vital to the war effort. The information concerned is already known to the high command and has no value. It provides no excuse for the killing of young German soldiers-"

"That is of no consequence here, I came to Berlin to make my report, and I will face any accusations put before this court after preparing a defence."

The naval officer slammed his fist on the desk, "This man breached communications security vital to the naval effort," he shouted. "His irresponsibility has led to the deaths of two men and an emergency change to the naval Enigma ciphers. Admiral Donitz demands to know how security was breached, and we will return Major Kessler to the SS court when we have that answer."

Kessler stood up to argue, but the judge cried out for silence and both sides sat down and waited for the assistant judge to speak.

"Major, you are under the jurisdiction of this court, and there is a request before me to allow your questioning on a naval security matter. You will be well-treated and returned here within ten days. I grant the application, and on your return you will be given sufficient time to arrange legal representation. Do you have anything to say?"

"This is highly irregular. I wish to appeal to a senior judge. You are out of your depth, Lieutenant."

The Assistant Judge dismissed the court, "He is yours, for now, Gentleman. I expect him back here in ten days' time."

"Hold that order!" was shouted across the court. Kessler turned to see Colonel Arnim striding into the chamber. He carried a single sheet of paper, which he placed in front of the judge. If the judge was put out by this interruption he hid it well enough, lifting the paper which he quickly read. The colonel waited for a response, his eyes fixed on the bench.

The judge stood and spoke, "Major Kessler is released to the custody of Colonel Arnim; he is free to go."

The captain and his troop stepped back and saluted as the colonel and Kessler passed them by.

Chapter 26

Fort William, Scotland
Monday, 8 May 2017 00:25

Street lights reflected on the surface of Loch Linnhe as the Renault van left the cover of the trees and the road opened out towards Fort William.

Ben and Lily had sat in silence on the dark, windy road from Onich, but he felt her looking at him, guessing she was dealing with some internal debate.

"We have to stop that message," Lily said as they passed a seafood restaurant on the loch shore.

"I know, you've said," he replied. "Do I keep following this road?"

"I'll tell you when to turn off."

"You're sure it's that important, Simon thought the effect of any messages would already be part of our past?"

"But that relies on there being no free will," Lily said. "Think about it - if they are already part of our past, then Rae must survive to send those messages to complete the loop. He can't get terminal cancer, can't be run over by a car, he simply can't die before those messages are sent or that link is broken. It can't work like that. You heard Munro describe timelike curves where cause and effect breaks down, we have the contamination at Ohrdruf immediately after his first message, if the details of how to build the bomb are sent tomorrow, who's to say what could happen next?"

"What do you think could happen?"

"I don't know, but when the particle accelerator generates these mini-black holes, information gets dragged into them, and the closed time curve they follow sends that information to an earlier point in time. That information can be acted upon and create a reaction, an event, and there will be a resultant effect. My guess is feeding those messages into our past can change our present, and Ohrdruf's sudden radioactivity could be nothing compared with what's to come."

Ben concentrated on overtaking a slow moving car, and then glanced at Lily, "How do we stop the message."

"I've visited CERN, I know some of Simon's colleagues, and I know the guy that runs Simon's experiments. We have to find him as he'll be unknowingly sending Rae's messages."

"You got a name?"

"Clive Adams, Simon supervised his PhD, and he's worked with him ever since, he'll be cut up about Simon's death..."

"So he's unlikely to run an experiment any time soon."

Lily shook her head.

"The LHC cost somewhere between £3-4 billion, so if it's up and running, nothing is going to stop the work schedule, life goes on."

"So what do we do, just call up CERN and talk to this guy?"

"Yeah, we explain what has happened and stop any further messages being transmitted."

Ben slowed for a junction.

"That sounds like a plan."

Lily gave a few more directions, and they were soon approaching a large detached house slightly elevated from the others in a quiet cul-de-sac.

"I don't like this," Ben said pulling over, "involving someone else after what's happened to Munro."

"Neither do I, but what else can we do?"

Ben shrugged, "We haven't been followed. It's safe enough for now"

The house was a new build in a largely traditional style despite the majority of the stone work on the facing wall giving way to large glass panels. During the day the interior space would be flooded with light. At night, a dimly lit section of the open plan lower floor was visible from the road, and there was little sign of life.

They reversed out of the dead-end street and parked the van behind some similar vehicles outside a builder's yard. They walked the short distance back to the house, then followed recessed lights up the paved driveway, triggering a security light at the front door. Lily pressed the doorbell, they exchanged glances when the expected two-tone ring turned out to be a loud sample of music. Ben recognised it from the radio, it was current and by some boy band. More lights came on upstairs, followed by the sound of footsteps. The door opened, and a heavily-built man stood there groggy-eyed wrapped in flowery silk dressing gown.

"Lily, what are you doing here?" he said before pulling her close for a hug, "Come on in, good to see you."

They followed him into the open plan area, there was more glass to rear of the room and Ben guessed there would be good views towards Britain's highest mountain, Ben Nevis.

Lily introduced Rory Moffat to Ben, who half-smiled at the man's appearance, the red hair, broad shoulders and large frame looked comical draped in the slightly fussy and very feminine gown. Rory noted the look, "Hey, it was all I could find, I didn't want to risk you pressing the doorbell again."

"What's with that?" Lily asked.

"Present from one of Kath's relatives in the States, that's my wife," he explained to Ben. "You record your own message with music, sound, whatever. We have a rota, this week it's my daughter Amy's turn."

Ben looked sharply at Lily - she hadn't mentioned a family.

"Sorry to turn up like this, but we really need your help," Lily said.

"I can see that," Rory replied. "Frankly you look like shit, and I'm sorry Ben, but I guess you've looked better too."

"It's not been a good day..." Lily said.

Rory sat them in the living area for a moment as he used a switch to shut the curtains.

"OK, fire away, I've got plenty time to listen, Kath and the girls are away with her mum for a few days," he squinted at a large wall clock, "Looks like I've been in bed all of two hours. I thought you were the cops; some emergency at the hospital. I'm just off-shift, so they wouldn't have bothered me unless it was something really bad."

"Rory's a consultant at the local A&E department," Lily explained.

"OK, so what brings you here?" Rory asked.

"Something really bad has happened," Lily replied. "You remember Simon Millar, the physicist?"

Rory nodded, looking at Ben.

"He's Ben's brother and he's dead. James Munro is dead. The people who killed him just tried to do the same to us - we were lucky to escape."

Rory's large, cheerful face was suddenly serious.

"Dead, when?" Rory asked, "and I'm so sorry about Simon, Ben."

"A few hours ago. They were going to kill us and blame Ben for the murders," Lily replied.

"For once, I really don't know what to say," Rory said.

"I'm sorry we're here, I wouldn't have come if I'd known you had a family," Ben said. "They'll be trying to find us."

"What about the police, have you called them?" Rory asked.

"No," Lily replied, "we will, but not yet."

Rory nodded slowly, "I need a coffee, I'll make three, then you better tell me everything."

"Can you turn on the news," Ben asked.

Rory nodded, flicking a remote control at the large plasma screen on the wall.

Lily was about to speak, but Sky News was showing footage of a reporter standing in front of the royal observatory's west tower. Volume bars appeared on the screen as sound filled the room.

"...What actually happened here tonight at Edinburgh's Royal Observatory remains unclear, but at least one member of the academic staff is dead- presumed murdered, and sources tell us it was a prominent and well-liked scientist who worked here in the observatory. There are also reports of another attack only a few miles away and that is thought to involve another university employee from the same department. There are limited details at present, and police are unable to confirm a link to the scenes behind me, but they will be holding a press conference at 8AM. Police Scotland are still searching for a missing witness, seen driving away from the scene. Her name is Lily Taylor, she's a research assistant here at the University, and they are urging her to contact them, as there's some concern for her safety. we'll be back with live coverage on the breaking news for this tragic story..."

The image switched to the news reader in the studio, they stared as Lily's picture stared back at them from the screen.

"...Now for a roundup of our other top stories, German authorities are baffled by the nuclear contamination in the town of Ohrdruf, around 300 kilometres from Berlin, thought initially to be the after-effects of a suspected dirty bomb attack. A least five people have lost their lives..."

Rory hit the mute button and dropped the TV control on his knee.

"Jesus, what are you guys involved in?"

Lily looked to Ben then shrugged her shoulders, "We're involved in both of those stories."

Rory blinked looking from one the other as though waiting for someone to give up the joke.

"Simon thought he was responsible for the nuclear contamination in Ohrdruf because of a message transmitted during one of his experiments at CERN."

Ben rested his head back on the leather seat and let Lily talk while he took in the full height of the building, up past the mezzanine upper floor to the ceiling where it met the exposed, chrome chimney of the wood-burning stove. They listened as Lily explained.

Lily covered what had happened to them after leaving the observatory with the police close behind, then the meeting and subsequent murder of James Munro, and the escape from Rae's men. She talked for five minutes, stopping frequently to answer Rory's questions, and concluded by returning to Ohrdruf.

"As I said, there is a possibility the Large Hadron Collider has effectively ripped a hole in spacetime, allowing Rae to send messages back in time. He's attempting to get his hands on a hugely valuable treasure missing since the early 1940s."

Rory sat forward his head tilting towards Lily then Ben obviously trying to make sense of what he was hearing.

"No-one is sure about any of this," Lily continued, "but the CERN experiment produces black holes. Charles Rae found messages mentioning Simon's present day experiments in a wartime archive."

"What archive?" Rory asked as he got up and walked to the window to make an unnecessary adjustment to a closed curtain.

"A wartime archive - as in Second World War," Lily explained. "Simon can't have believed it, so he authorised another message as a test. Rae replaced a meaningless test message with one that offered to trade a valuable work of art for wartime nuclear technology. Ohrdruf was the centre of Nazi nuclear research in the late 30s and early 40s. You've just seen the news, it's become a nuclear hazard shortly after the message was sent. The particle accelerator has opened up a link to the past. That's the reason Simon claimed responsibility for the radiation at Ohrdruf. Our immediate problem is Charles Rae intends on sending another message tomorrow, and we need to stop him. The last message caused Ohrdruf, who knows what effect the next one will have."

Rory took a deep breath, "This can't be real?"

"The new LHC particle accelerator has the power to generate energy levels unseen since the beginning of the universe - the beginning of what we call time. Some people believed its operation could even destroy our planet, and tried to stop it in the courts. No-one knows what these black holes can do, no-one even knows if they are black holes, that's the point, no-one knows much about any of this... but we do know the messages exist," she said.

"And Rae doesn't believe they can change the present," Ben added, "My brother told him any past actions caused by the messages would already be part of our present."

"But we know from talking to James Munro that cause and effect can theoretically break down in what are called closed timelike curves," Lily explained, "where time loops back on itself. Simon discovered Rae had sent a message to the Nazis containing nuclear research, then almost immediately Ohrdruf becomes radioactive. The news agencies are reporting a terrorist attack, but why an attack there? There is nothing in Ohrdruf to attack. Simon must have suspected the message changed the research carried out there in 1943, and has left a radiation signature we can detect now. He must have realised he was wrong about our ability to affect the present."

Rory blinked repeatedly.

"You really believe this?" He asked Lily.

"Why not? Serious physicists talk openly of parallel universes, the so-called multiverse with its branes, and all kinds of exotic features such as the need for eleven dimensions to make sense of string theory. This could just as easily be accepted as the one of the many hundreds of extraordinary things we take for granted. Your computer has millions of transistors on a tiny chip, if you'd told the creators of the 'bombes' used to break Enigma during the war what was possible now, do you think they'd have believed you," Lily said.

"Are you convinced, Ben?" Rory asked.

"I don't share my brother's background," Ben replied, "But Charles Rae believes it, and that's why there's a body count."

"Rory, I wish there was another explanation, but Simon believed it at the end, so I must stop Rae from sending anything else," Lily said.

"Why not contact the police?" Rory asked.

"By the time they react the damage will be done."

Rory paced across the room, "What are you going to do?"

"Right now, we just need a phone and somewhere to think. You were the only person I knew within a hundred miles, but Ben's right, I shouldn't have brought us here. I'm just glad Kath and kids are away."

"It's not the best situation, but no-one followed us," Ben added.

"Forget it, you've had a bad enough night already," Rory replied, "I'm glad the family are away though. I treat the result of accidents and drunken attacks every week, but I rarely know the people involved. I'd met Simon a few times and that's enough to leave me feeling pretty edgy. God knows how you both must feel."

Rory left them disappearing up the stairs.

"I really shouldn't have brought us here," Lily whispered to Ben, "I can see that now, the kids could have been here..."

She stopped short as Rory skipped back down the stairs. He'd changed into jeans, a t-shirt, and was carrying a pile of clothes.

"Ben, Some of that stuff should fit you. They're a bit tight on me. If you guys need a shower, there's a bathroom at the top of the stairs, make yourself at home."

Lily sat forward straightening out her hair, "Thanks."

"Feel free to use the phone or computer, it's hidden behind a partition over there."

A white Apple iMac sat on top of a transparent glass desk with a comfortable office chair to the front and a thin built-in book case on the wall to one side.

Lily sat at the computer and started it up.

"We shouldn't use the phone," Ben said. "I don't want anyone to be able to trace us here. It could put you in a bad position with the cops."

"Lily's an old friend – you've both been abducted and nearly killed - why would I stop you using the phone?"

Lily walked through, "I've got a few numbers I could try."

Ben handed her the cordless phone.

"Rory's taking this pretty well," he whispered.

"Yeah, he's fine, but if he wasn't who could blame him."

Lily keyed the first number. There was a slight pause as the networks made the connection.

"CERN laboratory, can I help you?"

"Hello, I'm trying to contact Dr Clive Adams. I've managed to mislay his number. I was hoping you could connect me?" Lily said in a very professional voice.

"Hold, please," came the reply, followed by, "There's no reply at his extension."

"Could you give me his mobile number?" Lily asked.

"I'm sorry, I can't give out that information."

"I've visited him at CERN, I should be on record. My name is Lily Taylor, and I really need to speak to Clive urgently about an experiment he'll be running tomorrow. It really is most important."

"Hold, please."

They could hear the sound of someone speed-typing in the background before the phone cut to background music. Ben had heard all visitors to CERN were security checked in advance.

"Ms Taylor, I can see you've visited us a number of times. Clive Adams is not expected back until Tuesday afternoon. I cannot give you his number, but I can leave a message for him if you wish?"

"If you just tell him I called and need to talk to him urgently. I'll try again later, thank you."

Lily ended the call, "He wasn't there, they work all kinds of hours, so there was always a chance, but he won't be back at work until tomorrow afternoon. I can't even leave a number for him without my phone. We need to contact him before then."

"What about email?" Ben asked.

"I don't have it, I could call back and ask for it, but I doubt they'd give his personal one out," she replied.

Rory looked from one to the other, a smile spreading on his face.

"What?" Lily asked.

"I'll take you," Rory said stepping forward. It was Ben and Lily's turn to stare.

"Lily, you remember my old VW camper van?"

"Yeah," She replied.

Did something pass between them? Ben pretended not to notice, but got the feeling Rory was helping more than an old friend.

"Well, I just had it refurbished, and it looks brand new. It's easily big enough to hide two people, and from what you've told me, we need to stop any more messages and get this under control."

"We're a thousand miles from Switzerland," Ben said.

"Eurotunnel," Rory replied. "We just need to get to Folkestone, and I reckon that's a ten-hour drive. I can book the ticket online, and we can be in France in less than twelve hours, that still gives enough time to drive to the Swiss border by tomorrow afternoon."

"But the van," Lily asked. "What if it's checked?"

"I've never been searched on the way out, maybe once or twice on the way back, but never, ever on leaving the UK."

"It won't go well for any of us if you are this time," Ben said.

"It'll be fine," Rory said. "I'll stick my skis on top of the van. I'm a hospital consultant; customs have no interest in people like me, they never do. I go climbing and skiing in the Alps every year, a trip like this is totally normal for me."

"You're sure you want to do this?" Ben asked.

"Of course I'm sure," Rory replied, "Lily's explained how important this is. One of you will have to drive on the way down as I need some sleep, but it'll work fine."

"If you want that shower, Lily, you better go now, we leave for Switzerland," Rory said looking like an excited schoolboy.

"What do you think, Ben?" Lily asked.

There was silence for a moment.

"The way I see it, you don't trust the authorities to do the right thing about the time loop, and we have no evidence to back up anything so far. The cops and press won't believe a word we say, so if this gives us a chance to stop the message, and get evidence to back our story, then we go."

Chapter 27

Berlin, Germany
Friday, 12 February 1943 20:10

Colonel Arnim's car drew up outside the old Prinz Albrecht Hotel. Kessler knew it well, having stayed there as a guest, and then visited as an officer when it became SS headquarters in 1933.

The colonel led the way into the large, vaulted reception hall, and a brief telephone call had them waved through security.

They were ushered to the elevator, the guard inside was told to take them to the old penthouse apartment that was now the office of the head of the SS, Reichsfuhrer Hienrich Himmler.

Kessler had met the Reichsfuhrer a few times before, the last was in Berlin after his field promotion to major and the Iron Cross, first class, that went with it. He was about to confront someone with immense power, a man who reported directly to the Fuhrer, someone who could restart the nuclear programme immediately. The guards snapped to attention as the elevator doors opened. Kessler noticed something about them, in a wartime army where full colonels could still be in their twenties, these men were all much older than the average. They were a modern day praetorian guard, they would be the men who purged the SA in the night of the long knives, men like himself who'd received their SS dagger before 1933.

"Gentleman, this way." Said an adjutant rising from his desk to usher them in.

They entered a well-appointed room whose facing wall was adorned with a large oil painting depicting an armoured knight on a white horse with his lance raised in victory. Himmler was known to appreciate this type of imagery, and the gallantry of past times had become the inspiration for the virtues of loyalty and strength that founded their brotherhood.

The opposing wall had a single SS crest above a large oak writing desk. The Reichsführer rose with a smile on his thin lips and indicated for them to sit in the chairs laid out across from his own.

"Major Kessler, you have had an interesting day, please sit, can I offer you something to drink, some coffee, perhaps?"

"Thank you, sir, and my thanks for your intervention today."

Himmler nodded to a steward who poured a cup for each of the men.

"I'm not unknown to intervene if I believe one of my men has been treated harshly, but it usually occurs after a sentence is passed. Colonel Arnim insisted on putting your case before me. He was told to wait until after the court's decision, but he made such a fuss about the papers you carry. You have a friend in Arnim, Major Kessler."

Kessler nodded to the colonel, "Yes, sir."

"You told the court you wished to make a report, please do so," Himmler ordered as he sat.

"You have inspected the papers I was carrying, sir?"

"Yes, but I want you to explain the killings that have Admiral Donitz so hot in pursuit."

Kessler took a sip from his cup and cleared his throat.

"Sir, yesterday morning I was informed that a signal bearing my name had been sent using the naval Enigma. Admiral Donitz was livid his system had been used without permission and held me responsible. I knew no more than the admiral, and in my role as head of security, I naturally offered to investigate the matter."

"From his order to have you arrested I can see some disagreement followed."

"The admiral would not allow access to the full text of the message, and accused my men of having breached operational security in using naval Enigma codes. That was, of course, absurd."

"So you arrested one of the admiral's radiomen, extracted the full message, and then had him killed to cover it up?"

The colour had drained from Colonel Arnim's face, the Reichsfuhrer showed no emotion, and Kessler wondered just how dangerous a situation he was in. His only regret was Muller's loss, and total honesty was the only approach.

"I asked my men to get the Enigma code as being the intended recipient gave me that right. The admiral would not listen to reason, and so I acted. I am responsible for what followed. The radio operator was officially murdered by his lover, a local man, who I subsequently hanged in the town square. My men questioned the operator about his sexual activities, and he gave up the code, he was a weak man, a homosexual and so already vulnerable to blackmail. In such a sensitive position, he is no loss."

Himmler considered the explanation for a moment, "It seems there is no case to answer here. A delinquent is dead and his murderer dealt with," he said, "and so you finally read the message?"

"Yes sir, it was a proposal to trade advanced weapons technology for the Russian Amber Room. I felt the only possible action was to have the documents inspected."

"And the Admiral disagreed?"

"I assumed that was his position, and so decided to take matters into my own hands."

"Yes, and the result is the killing of more men. I am also the chief of police, Kessler, and I cannot be seen to allow my men to be gunned down when performing their duties, it won't do."

"Shot in self-defence, sir," Kessler said calmly, "the police overreacted and shot my adjutant in the back. I returned fire and held them off before negotiating a surrender to allow my comrade to receive medical care. It was too late for him, but I do not regret my actions, I had to bring the documents to Berlin."

"Is there anything else I should know, any more unfortunate acts of self-defence?"

"I escaped from the police and made my way here. I was helped by a university porter, a Great War veteran. I hope he will not suffer for assisting me."

"Let us finish your report first," Himmler replied, "and so we come to the message."

"Yes sir, the sender wants to exchange the Amber Room for a dossier on a super weapon, an atomic bomb powerful enough to win the war."

Himmler stopped him, "I finally understand why the admiral would have no interest here. Our scientists led the field up until war broke out, and they concluded it was not possible to create a weapon within ten years. You look to have made a wasted journey, Major."

"Sir, the source sent technical documents to prove the value of the material, I have just arrived from Gottingen, they have been verified by an expert, Professor Lenz. The professor has assured me the documents are genuine and that the Americans could have the weapon within months. He gave me a letter to present his findings, the original message and documents are also here," Kessler said handing over the papers Colonel Arnim had held for him.

The Reichsfuhrer got up from his seat, picked up the documents, opened the letter and wandered towards the balcony doors.

"The professor said months?" He asked. "You are sure of that?"

"Yes sir, he says what has been provided in that message is enough to restart our own programme, and with access to all the papers promised, it is possible we could eclipse their efforts."

Himmler leafed through the pages.

"We could build a weapon quickly?"

"That is what he says."

"The Amber Room is quite a request. A room panelled in amber and precious stones from the Winter Palace in St Petersburg, it was removed by our troops during the advance to the east. Did you know it was a gift from Frederick Wilhelm I of Prussia to Peter the Great? It is of German origin, not that it matters, but it is an item of significant value and beauty."

Himmler walked behind his desk and picked up the telephone to call the outer office, "I need information on the Amber Room. It was located in St Petersburg before being seized for the Reich, find out where it is now."

He replaced the receiver, "What do we know about this source?"

"Very little, sir. We have someone with high-level access to a key enemy weapon system and to our top secret naval Enigma codes. I cannot understand how this can be.

This person wants something they would be unable to sell openly, so either intends to keep it or sell to a private buyer. I have no idea what motivates the offer of information or why the message was addressed to me personally. All I can say is that the information looks to be genuine and could be of tremendous value."

"I agree, the identity or motivations are not immediately relevant, but we must acquire the dossier. The message mentions the terms of exchange, what do we know of these lawyers?"

"Nothing as yet, I sent men to investigate, I haven't had an opportunity to make contact since-"

There was a short tap on the panelled door, Himmler's staff officer entered, "Sir, I have issued orders to find the Amber Room. We will receive a report this evening."

"Thank you Ernst, please stay. Major, I have a mission for you."

"Sir." Kessler snapped to attention.

"I have read your file. Your record is exemplary, and the colonel here could not be more confident of your abilities. I want you to go to Switzerland. You will have control over the Amber Room and my authority to exchange it for the information. Is that clear?"

"Yes sir, however, it is possible Admiral Donitz will order my arrest again."

"You are reassigned to the SS-Heinrich Himmler, Major. As members of the SS we are already outside military and civilian law, I will give you papers that make you answerable to me alone, any actions taken on this mission will be considered legitimate if they are being carried out in the furtherance of my orders, and you have my orders to do whatever is necessary to secure the dossier.

Ernst, issue the Major with the documentation he needs and make his status known to all police units, you have my full support, I want that dossier."

"I will get it, Reichsfuhrer," Kessler replied.

"As for the admiral, I will let him know of your new circumstances."

"He has been negligent with this message," Kessler could not help adding.

"Understand the position, Major. He has good political connections, and the Fuhrer favours him, so it will do him no lasting harm. Now, you have your orders," Himmler said, "and I have my next appointment, good day."

Chapter 28

Fort William, Scotland
Monday, 8 May 2017 01:20

Ben followed the red camper van down towards the town centre. Two police patrols had passed them in the five minutes it had taken to reach the central railway station. The patrol cars were travelling slowly, but ignored the white van, Ben guessed they were looking for a classic Rover. Moving the van was a risk, but the alternative of leaving it close to Rory's home was unacceptable.

As arranged, Rory took the first exit at a roundabout on Fort William's south side and parked up to wait for Ben who continued to take the second exit down towards a loch side car park. Ben slammed the van door shut, and turned towards Rory and Lily on the opposite side of the dual carriageway about 100 metres away.

He didn't look back, glad to leave the link to Rae behind. He was about to vault a barrier and run between the traffic, when another police car cruised past, he gave an apologetic wave and staggered slightly as though drunk. Ben walked on slowly ignoring the hard stares from the cops. The borrowed baseball cap and upturned collar on his rugby shirt hid much of his face, and whatever description the police had for him didn't match his new look as they continued on without stopping.

He waited until they were out of view, before quickly crossing to the camper van.

"That was close," Lily said, "let's get going before they come back."

Ben volunteered to drive first as he wasn't ready to sleep. They were underway, passing Rory's hospital within minutes, although the doctor wouldn't have known as he was already snoring softly.

"He worked hundred-hour weeks as a junior doctor, he can fall asleep in a heartbeat," Lily said.

"You look tired yourself, try and get some rest. This'll be a long drive," Ben replied.

She nodded, but he could see sleep wouldn't come easy for her.

Ben concentrated on twisty roads lit up by the camper van's headlights. Rory said the electrics had been upgraded alongside the suspension and brakes. If so, then the original light must have been awful as he struggled to match the speed limit with their limited range. The van had none of the aids that gave modern cars their effortless speed and handling. Fifty miles per hour felt plenty fast as he headed north, away from their destination, and over to the east of the country for the trip down the A9 which the satellite navigation decided was a longer distance, but a faster route. That suited everyone as it meant avoiding Onich where the locals would be outnumbered by police.

A couple of hours later Lily finally let sleep take her as they approached Glasgow. Ben usually chose the A1 for trips down south, but decided to switch back west again to join the M74, totally avoiding the old jurisdiction of the Lothian and Borders Police, which had joined with all the other Scottish forces, to become a single, unified force in Police Scotland.

The double murder of Edinburgh scientists would be on the front pages of every newspaper later that morning, and he wondered if Rae's planned frame up could ever have succeeded in branding him a killer. His friends would have fiercely defended his innocence, but with the right forensics and no obvious alternative, was it possible Rae could generate enough doubt for the story to be accepted? That plan would have tidied things up nicely for Rae, but he must be worried they'd told others what had happened by now, and so who knew what his next move would be?

They would have to call the police and put their case as soon as the message was stopped, whatever the initial reaction, they would be believed eventually.

He glanced back to the Rory who'd left money on top of the dashboard for fuel. Lily had good friends, and this one was sleeping close to her, Ben wondered if they had once been lovers? It would explain why Rory dropped everything to help her, but that didn't always follow, he'd never remained friends with any of his ex-girlfriends. Ben focused on driving, and kept the company of the heavy goods vehicles that increasingly outnumbered the cars as the night wore on.

They headed down past the Lake District and followed the M6 to Manchester and Liverpool. Five hours had passed and Ben was feeling the weight of the night's events, he knew he could tough it out and go on for hours without rest, but his eyes ached, and his mind was beginning to drift. The speed had crept up to the van's maximum of 80 mph, and all he could see through the windscreen was identical sections of tarmac repeated over and over again. The effect was becoming hypnotic, and it would be best to pull over soon. Rory stirred in the rear, sitting up on the wooden floor, he checked his watch, "Are you the only driver so far?"

"Yeah," Ben replied.

"That's a good effort, I'll take over for the rest of the trip. Get your head down, and that's doctor's orders."

Ben pulled over onto the hard shoulder of the motorway, he didn't want to stop somewhere so conspicuous, but Rory insisted as it was still seventeen miles to the next services. They swapped over, and Ben settled down on the floor still warm from Rory's body and close to Lily. The movement of the van had his eyes closing the moment his head hit the ground.

Ben woke with a start, Rory pulled his hand away quickly "Whoa, it's me," Rory said. "Jesus, you're jumpy."

Ben came to his senses, the memories hit hard as he realised where he was and why.

"Are we at the tunnel yet?" He asked quietly.

"Well, we're in Folkestone," Rory replied. "The Eurotunnel entrance is a couple of miles away, and the train leaves in forty minutes, so we're right on schedule."

Ben's right hand was numb from lying cramped on the makeshift bed. He shook it out as Rory offered him a cereal bar.

"Is it time for us to disappear yet?" Lily asked. She looked tired, but stronger than yesterday.

"You ready for this?" Ben asked.

"Yeah, as Rory has been repeatedly telling me for the last half hour, we'll only be stopped to check the ticket, I don't know if he's just trying to convince himself."

"Not at all," Rory boomed. "I've smuggled the occasional bottle of malt, this might be a bit of a step up, but we'll manage. Now does anyone need the loo before we start?"

Ben and Lily lay side-by-side on the van's floor, Rory started to load his suitcase and camping gear above them, leaving a small gap to the front of their faces. They would have to remain this way for at least an hour without much light. Ben's hand touched Lily's by mistake, he made to pull away, but she held on. He squeezed back - he felt at hoome in the dark, but maybe she needed the support.

There was a thud as the van's door slid shut, and the suspension compressed under Rory's weight. He told them to stay quiet and motionless as they moved off towards the first hurdle of the new day.

Rory gave a commentary as they approached the ticket booth, he sounded relaxed and jovial as he chatted with the female officer at the gate - letting her in on the few glorious days skiing he was going to enjoy. Within a minute, the van pulled away and then slowed on the approach to the enclosed carriage that would transport them under the English Channel.

The camper van moved slowly before coming to a stop. The driver door banged shut as Rory locked up and left them. Echoing voices gradually faded leaving only muffled sounds from the outside world. They lay next to each other fearful of making any sound until, a short time later, the carriage shunted forward before moving smoothly as the engine took the strain. He whispered to Lily to make sure she was coping then settled in for the short crossing in a sealed carriage up to twenty-four miles below the sea.

Chapter 29

Meyrin, South-East France
Monday, 8 May 2017 21:15

The entry into France had been as smooth as Rory predicted. They'd driven straight out of the Eurotunnel carriage, and were waved past passport control by officials who gave the van nothing more than a cursory glance.

The rest of the day was spent driving on and on, enduring a monotonous journey through the hedgerows and tree-lined roads that framed vast areas of flat agricultural land. The scenery barely changed, occasionally broken up by small, but similar towns.

Satellite navigation indicated forty miles to their destination across the Swiss border to the CERN campus at Meyrin. The Volkswagen had covered over 470 miles from Calais, following the E17 through Reims, and on to their current position. The soaring alpine mountains lay ahead, but they did nothing to lift Ben's spirits, with almost a full day on the road and snatched sleep, it was just like being back in the forces. Lily just sat back staring outside, her hands constantly touching her hair or face.

As they reached the border, they found an abandoned checkpoint, its guards long gone as only random customs checks were carried out since Switzerland joined the Schengen zone with other signatories inside and outside the European Union. They passed onto Swiss soil having covered hundreds of miles with a final marathon driving shift put in by Rory who talked and smiled continually.

"Has anyone thought about how we're going to find this guy?" Ben asked.

"He lives close to the CERN campus," Lily replied quickly. "We'll find him."

"You know the address?" Ben asked.

"He should be in the telephone directory either the paper version or online. Rory, can you stop somewhere so we can check."

"And if he's not in there?"

"We drive to CERN and find him there," Lily replied.

"If it comes to it, I'll go into CERN and ask to see him," Rory chipped in.

"I thought you were going skiing?" Ben replied.

"No point in bringing you all the way here to leave you at a dead end, and anyway I'm as involved as anyone now, the police will have to find out about me, that was obvious from the start."

Rory pulled over into a service station. There was a small cafe close by and they parked up after paying for fuel. The cafe was busy enough with groups of travellers and the occasional lone businessman, all of whom were filling up on coffee, sandwiches and pastries. Rory ordered coffee and food for three in passable French, while Ben and Lily poured over the telephone directory they'd picked up next to a public phone.

Lily flicked the pages and scanned the entries looking for Adams under Geneva.

She sat up, "Look he's here." Her finger was over the number they needed. "I thought he would be - he's lived in Switzerland for years now."

"OK, call him," Ben replied standing up and squeezing through the gap behind her chair towards the toilets. "I'll be back in a minute."

The toilet was bright and clean, the lighting and fixtures all looked brand new, maybe fixed up for the winter season. Ben washed his hands and checked his appearance in the mirror. He looked tired but acceptable, the swelling on his jaw hardly noticeable. Another customer in outdoor clothing entered the toilet jolting him back to the present as he self-consciously stepped away from the mirror and used the hand dryer. When he got back to the table, Lily was talking into Rory's mobile.

Rory watched her expectantly; his head cocked to one side trying to catch the conversation.

Lily noticed Ben, and gave him the thumbs down. He sat next to her as she listened on the phone.

"This is the fourth try," she said, redialling the phone.

"Come on, what's going on?" Rory shouted.

"Nothing, there's no answer, but we've got his address," Lily said as she put the phone down.

"With two physicists dead, maybe he's in hiding," Ben muttered quietly.

Rory left some euros on the table as they drained their cups, before making their way to the van.

Inside the cafe, a man in his late twenties thumbed the telephone directory. He was dressed in typical outdoor clothing, and none of the customers had paid him much attention, certainly none of the targets who were just leaving the service area. He switched on his phone and typed a message on the touch screen and clicked 'send'. The secure mail program sent the short email back to London. A silver Mercedes M-class with French plates pulled out slowly behind the camper van. It blended into the background as although the Swiss legislated to protect the environment, the environmental zeal didn't quite extend to going without the largest of luxury vehicles.

The driver, an attractive woman in her forties nodded to him as she switched to become the lead surveillance vehicle. The man finished his coffee and hoped things had gone to plan. The van would be wired, and listening devices fitted to expose what the hell these people thought they were doing. The van's old locks took seconds to open, easily allowing the small, magnetic microphone to be placed behind the cabinet that stored the gas cooker.

He paid his bill admiring the cashier who was far too pretty to stay working in this kind of place for long, and looked forward to catching up to a safe distance in the powerful BMW M3 saloon that was his for the duration of the mission.

Rory followed the sat nav through a pretty suburban area with a mixture of traditional wooden houses and modern apartment buildings. The device announced they'd reached their destination, and Rory slowly followed the street numbers before parking across from Clive Adams' apartment.

"Well, this is it," Rory said stretching out his arms.

Ben and Lily walked over to the apartment block and tried the intercom. After a few tries, there was still no reply. They guessed which flat corresponded with the button they were pressing, and finding no lights on, tried some of Clive Adams' neighbours. Lily was told Adams had left on Friday evening with luggage. Lily thanked their anonymous informer, and they walked back to Rory's van.

"We'll just have to wait for him," Lily said.

Ben tapped her shoulder, and pointed to Rory, he was fast asleep, slumped over the steering wheel.

"We might as well wait here," Ben said, happy with the observation point.

"It's quiet enough," Lily agreed, and went around shutting the van's curtains. She woke Rory and moved the semi-conscious doctor into a more comfortable position.

"You weren't joking about him being able to fall asleep," Ben said.

"He's sure to need it," Lily replied, "Let's keep the lights off and try and get some ourselves, we don't want to draw any unwanted attention."

They both settled down, but Ben watched the apartment out of his window, he'd given himself 'stag' duty, and would stay awake until the early hours just in case Clive Adams arrived during the night.

Chapter 30

Ben woke to find Lily shaking him, "What time is it," he asked.

"Seven thirty, what time did you get to sleep?"

"Rory took over at 0500," Ben replied rubbing the back of his head.

"Clive arrived a few minutes ago, he's up in his flat right now."

Ben sat up to find Rory beaming back at him, "I'll leave you guys here, I'm off to find some breakfast, and I need to phone Kath. I sent her a brief text last night, but she needs to know what's happening."

"We'll call you from Clive's when we're ready to leave," Lily said as Ben slid the side door open and they left Rory to explain himself to his wife.

Rory waved as he pulled away, Clive Adam's apartment faced them across the road as they waited for a metallic grey BMW to pass before stepping out onto the road.

Lily tried the intercom, they heard a man's voice in reply.

"Clive, it's Lily Taylor from Edinburgh, can I come in?"

There was a long pause before Adams replied, "Lily, is t-that really you? The police are looking for you, hold on."

The lock clicked, and the entry door opened a fraction, pushed inward by the wind. Ben opened it fully to find Dr Clive Adams waiting for them at the doorway of his ground floor flat.

"Lily, what on earth are you doing here, and who's this?" Adams said nodding at Ben.

"This is Simon's brother, Ben. Can we come in?"

Adams gestured for them to enter and Ben followed Lily through a short hallway passing doors on either side, leading to a large room currently stacked full of numbered boxes.

"Moving out?" Lily asked.

"Yeah, I've got a new place, a chalet up the mountains."

"Sounds good?" Lily replied.

"It's just a house move, seems important until something like this happens."

He turned to Ben, "Simon was a friend, I'm s-so sorry he's gone."

"Thanks, and I'm sorry to ask, but we'll need your help," Ben replied wondering if the slight stutter was normal for the man.

"I'll do what I can," Adams replied.

Despite the two sets of skis and a snowboard piled next to the boxes, Adams didn't look as though he spent much time outdoors, he was a tall man with pale skin, and his long, thin legs didn't suggest regular exercise.

The open plan room was partitioned into a kitchen area and a comfortable lounge by a breakfast bar where they were invited to sit. Ben let Lily repeat their story, she covered the ground quickly, and Adams was given a full account. Unlike Rory, Adams listened intently and didn't interrupt.

"Why come here and take the risks you have?" Adams asked. "The police will be trying to find you."

"It's about the experiments you ran for Simon."

He looked puzzled, "What ones?"

"The ones that sometimes produce Centauro effects - you're running one today," Lily replied.

"Well, t-they can all do that, but the only experiment scheduled for today has already taken place, the data is being downloaded now."

Lily and Ben exchanged glances, "Clive, are you aware of Simon changing some sort of error message?" Ben asked.

"He had an idea to add some identification markers, he kept the details to himself, but they weren't important, just some meta data, an addition to the real results."

"Could we get a copy of them?" Lily asked.

"I suppose so," Adams replied, "but why would you want them?"

"It's hugely important we get them," Lily said. "We should be able to read them."

"But only if we can access the decryption engine on Edinburgh University's physics grid," Ben added.

"There's a program on one of the servers called the decryption engine," Adams said. "It's owned by Simon."

"It's probably just a copy of the programs," Lily said.

"I don't think so," Adams replied. "It's stored in the c-cloud, so is a shared resource."

"What? Does that mean anyone could access it?" Ben asked.

"No it's a private system."

"Can we login remotely?" Ben asked.

"Where can we get access?" Lily added.

"Through there," Adams replied pointing back to the hall where they had entered. "I have a home office and full access to the CERN network."

"Is it connected?" Ben asked pointing to the crates.

"My computers will be the last thing I pack. Follow me."

They made their way to the spare room converted into an office. Two widescreen monitors sat side-by-side displaying a UNIX login screen with the CERN logo. Adams entered a few user names and passwords until he got far enough in for Lily to take over. Lily slid into his seat and started to move expertly through the system.

"I'll be back shortly," Adams said. "I'm supposed to join a conference call, um, but I'll make an excuse to get out early."

Ben held his breath, if they could log into the network they would see exactly the same data they had accessed from Lily's office the previous day. He watched as Lily navigated through familiar screens, everything looked identical so far, but the crucial part was the data. Lily pointed to the screen and slowly turned to him.

"This is it, audit records generated by us last night - this is the same database," she said, "and there are four new messages, the last will be what was sent today."

Ben stared at the screen, "Can you access them?"

"I'll try," she replied, clicking to reveal a menu on the first message. Lily chose the 'decrypt' option, and lines of text appeared one by one. The full message text was there to see. Ben crouched next to Lily as they read the document. Like the others it was intended for a Major Kessler.

THE AMBER ROOM IS TO BE WELL PACKED AND UNLABELLED, INSTRUCTIONS WILL BE GIVEN ON DELIVERY, THE TRANSFER MUST BE COMPLETED WITHIN 30 DAYS, THE PACKAGES WILL BE INSPECTED, ANY DISCREPANCIES AND THE DOSSIER WILL BE DESTROYED. ANY DELAY WILL RESULT IN A SIMILAR PENALTY.

Ben re-read the message.

"Rae must know the British could read Enigma," he said. "They would surely take action to stop this?"

"But maybe not at that time, this is what the Bletchley code-breakers called SHARK - the German U-boat code. They were locked out of that for long periods during the war - my bet is that this message was sent to arrive during one of those periods. It must be why Rae chose SHARK as it was the hardest code for the allies to break."

"But surely they would break it sometime later?" Ben asked.

"Not necessarily, messages sent a week, a month ago just weren't worth the effort. It was where the U-boats were today that mattered," Lily said, "Let's check the next message."

Lily selected the second message repeating the commands to display the text in English.

"It's using Abwehr settings, look, the decryption engine categorises the encryption type if it recognises the key from other messages."

"The Abwehr, that was Nazi intelligence, wasn't it?" Ben asked.

"Yeah, that's right."

"What's Rae doing sending a message to them?"

"We'll soon see."

Lily scrolled the screen down to view the message.

ATTN: CAPTAIN BRANDT

YOU ARE TO OPEN NUMBERED ACCOUNT WITH ONE HUNDRED YEAR LEASE ON A LARGE DEPOSIT VAULT. THE ACCOUNT NUMBER IS TOP SECRET. USE YOUR CODENAME AS THE PASSWORD ON THE ACCOUNT. INSTRUCT LAWYERS TO EXPECT DELIVERY OF ITEM FROM SS-MAJOR PETER KESSLER.

DEPOSIT FUNDS IN ACCOUNT TO COVER ANY CONTINGENCY, RETAIN 2.5% FOR EXPENSES. YOUR DISCRETION IN THIS MATTER IS REQUIRED.

Ben finished scanning it first. Rae was sending a message to an Abwehr agent in wartime Germany.

"Rae's trying to co-ordinate the delivery through two different Nazi agencies and an intermediary," Ben said.

"This message looks like an order coming from one of Brandt's superiors over a normal channel, he'd do it without hesitation."

Lily switched back to the browser and typed the name of the law firm into the search engine. She followed the first link to the lawyer's website. A basic page loaded - there was a company crest and links to view the site in multiple languages. The site held minimal information and was tastefully styled - the image and reserve expected from such an organisation extended to the web. Although there were offices in every Swiss canton, the main office was in the financial capital, Zurich.

"Established in 1901, it says they're one of the oldest firms in the country," Ben read aloud. "If the account exists and we can find the number and code name, we'll be able to access it. If we can get to the vault first and find the Amber Room, it'd be headline news all over the world. Rae would have nowhere to hide."

"Hold on, let's read the last message," Lily said.

COMMERCIAL BANK OF SWITZERLAND: 5427585281.

Ben stopped - the only movement was the screen cursor that blinked in the decryption engine's search box.

Lily slumped in the chair, "Ben-".

"It's a reply," he said leaning forward resting both hands on the table.

Lily stared at him, "Ben, this is a reply... from 1943."

Chapter 31

Geneva, Switzerland
Tuesday, 8 May 2017 07:37

Andrew Shaw was first through passport control and emerged onto the main airport concourse to find Alexandra Parsons among a line of drivers waiting to pick up the Monday morning business travellers from Charles De Gaulle. Alex looked typically stunning in a smart trouser suit, and Shaw noted the envious glances from a couple of fellow passengers who were being led away by a nicotine-stained, overweight and very male taxi driver.

She called out to him.

"Good of you to pick me up," Shaw offered.

"Not at all, glad of the excitement."

Shaw wondered just how quiet things were here. Alex had lived in this area since finishing an expensive education high up in the Alps at Rougemont, a school whose alumni included the late Diana, Princess of Wales. Shaw smiled at his memory for trivial information, he didn't know Alex well, but like her school's most famous former pupil, she made more of an impression than most.

"As for excitement, that's the last thing I want. I want a short, straightforward surveillance to explain what's going on, followed by a quiet arrest," Shaw said.

She rolled her eyes then flicked her long dark fringe away from her face. "I'll bet you do. You're not exactly playing it safe. I was talking to Sylvia, and she's a bit concerned about all the potential 'excitement' if this mission goes wrong. I hope you know what you're doing?"

Shaw smiled, "So do I."

They walked quickly to the short stay car park next to the terminal building. Alex held up a key, and the deadlocks on a black Range Rover Sport shot back with a solid clunk. Shaw placed his overnight bag on the back seat and buckled up.

"Have you any idea what the targets are doing?" Alex asked as she started the engine.

"In a word, no...," Shaw replied.

"No wonder Sylvia's worried, where do you want to go?"

"To wherever that red Volkswagen van is."

The car pulled away smoothly, it was comfortable, but Shaw had spent far too much of the last day transported around in soft leather seats.

"What have I missed?" He asked.

"We knew from the bug in their car that they were going to a CERN physicist's home. We had plenty time to get the place covered," Alex said. "While the targets waited overnight for the physicist, Clive Adams, to return, we found an empty apartment across the road, and Adams just got back as I arrived to pick you up," she looked at her watch. "That wasn't much more than ten minutes ago..."

"What do we know about, Adams?" Shaw asked as they pulled up behind traffic at the car park's exit barriers.

"Very little, there's no criminal record, we've no file on him."

"How long will it take to get to the house?" Shaw asked, hoping the scientist lived close to the CERN complex, which was only a few miles away.

"Twenty minutes," Alex replied. "Andrew, is there a link between the Ohrdruf confession and the Edinburgh murders?"

"That's what we're here to find out."

She shot him a look.

"I'd tell you if I knew more."

"Is the brother involved in the killings?"

"The police seem to think he's involved."

"And you?"

"No, something else is going on here."

"I hope you're right," Alex said.

"How come?"

"If not, we might just have another dead British physicist on our hands, and there's a bit of a run on them right now."

"True enough, but what better way to destroy my career than facilitating a high-profile killing abroad?"

"Well, you must have been pretty sure to let them run?"

Shaw thought for a second, "Nothing adds up. The police were ready to sling our targets in jail, but we'll let them lead us to whatever they've got themselves into."

Alex shrugged as she accelerated hard towards the motorway.

Chapter 32

Geneva, Switzerland
Tuesday, 9 May 2017 08:01

Ben re-read the message over and over again. Could it really have come from 1943? Did the account number represent a vault containing a missing treasure? His eyes scanned a web article on the LHC, it was something out of science fiction. The particle collisions occurred under extreme conditions, they were trapped in a super fluid environment colder than deep space, but producing temperatures 100,000 times greater than the heart of the sun. The LHC was built to find the Higgs boson - the God particle – named after the Edinburgh university physicist, someone who had worked with his brother and James Munro, the man who first proposed its possible existence. The evidence pointed to it already having achieved that goal, so why shouldn't the existence of a time loop be an unexpected triumph?

"The timestamp on the reply is identical to the one on Rae's original message," Lily said.

"You think this is real?" Ben asked.

"James Munro stated an event could happen in the same instant as the cause, or an event could even cause itself," she replied. "Rae's message created the reply."

Ben walked over to the window.

"The real proof of whether this comes from wartime Europe will be if the Amber Room is in a vault corresponding to that account number. Now that would be something..."

"It would be more than something," Lily replied.

Ben rubbed his face and winced, the dull pain a reminder of Vadim and the fact they were lucky to be alive. He looked out the window and back to Lily.

"Whatever the effect of this message, at least the streets aren't lined with Swastikas, but we have to stop any more messages, you were right - we don't know what damage they would do."

Lily nodded and returned to the screen.

"What are you doing now?" He asked.

"I'm searching for the name, Brandt, in the decryption engine archive, and there are twelve matching messages."

Ben watched as Lily loaded the first on screen and they scanned the contents. It was orders for Captain Brandt to report on the movements of a suspected British agent. Lily skipped to the next. This was more promising – Brandt's message to a high-ranking Luftwaffe officer. A consignment had been deposited in Commercial Bank of Switzerland to a supplied account. As they read through the remaining messages, three related to Brandt arranging banking services for senior German officers.

"Rae found his bag-man," Ben said. "This was late '43 - before D-Day - but some Nazis must have been nervous enough to begin stashing whatever they could in the world's most accommodating banks."

"Brandt was setting this sort of thing up for others, and Rae decided to become a client," Lily said. "They were all high-ranking officers, so Brandt wouldn't refuse them."

"He probably shared their views, and he was profiting, I think we know enough," Ben said, "but what now?"

"There are three messages left, and we need his codename, if Rae has it, it must be in one of them."

They scanned the next two messages; they were situation reports on Geneva operations containing nothing of interest.

The final message was dated, 9 Sept 1943.

Gerhard Brandt (Asche) killed as the result of enemy action in central Geneva.

"Asche - that's his codename! We have the password for the vault!" Lily said excitedly.

"Rae didn't count on anyone else reading these messages," Ben replied.

"Brandt was perfect - Rae also knew he would be dead within the year and so couldn't get any ideas about the vault after the war," Lily said, "you have to hand it to him, it tied things up nicely..."

"And he didn't have to do the killing directly for a change," Ben added.

Ben's attention was drawn to the screen as an instant messaging application popped up a window on-screen. The sender was identified as Kevin. Ben scanned the text.

> Clive, Got your mail, rescheduled your experiment to run @ 0800 as requested, heard about Simon Millar, terrible news. The experiment failed, and an error occurred almost immediately?

The application sat with the mouse cursor blinking, waiting for a reply.

"Lily, check Clive's sent emails," Ben said.

"But it's his personal-"

"Do it, He never told us the experiment failed, and I want to know why he rescheduled it."

Lily opened the email application, and they read the most recent mails and found one addressed to Kevin Porter. It had been sent the previous night.

Kevin,
As discussed in our call, could you get in early and run the experiment at 0800, you can find the files in the usual directory.
Many thanks
Clive

Clive Adams
Project Leader
LHC CERN

"Why would he change the schedule?" Ben asked.

"Could be anything, but it looks bad if he sees us reading his mail-"

"Hold on, I've got an idea," Ben said angling the keyboard towards him, and typing a reply to the instant message.

> Thanks for doing that. I couldn't believe when I heard about Simon. As there was a problem this morning, can we run it again? It was Simon's work, and in the circumstances I want to do it properly. If I upload a new file how quickly can you re-run?

Ben clicked to send. Lily looked at him, "Why do you want him to run it again?"

"You said the decryption engine has a store of Enigma keys, correct?"

"Yes?"

"I want to send a new message to Brandt, then resend Rae's messages with a different Enigma setting?"

They were interrupted by an immediate reply.

> OK, I can do it now, just send me the file, or I can do it tomorrow morning if it can wait?

Ben typed a reply

> File will be there in a minute, I'd like to do it now.

There was a brief pause before they received the reply.

> OK, just mail me the file, and I'll set it up. If it fails again, we'll know soon enough.

"What's the plan?" Lily asked.

"We need to send Brandt a later message, tell him to send a new account number as the security of the old message is compromised. Then we resend Rae's messages using an Enigma code we know the Allies had broken. It will let them take action on any emerging Nazi nuclear work initiated as a result of the messages, it's the best way to balance any impact the messages could have on our timeline."

Lily started typing.

She looked up. "It's done, the file's gone, and when he runs the experiment it will send Rae's message again, but this time the allies will be able to decode it."

The instant messaging program displayed a new entry.

> File received, started experiment. If you need anything else, I'll be around until at least 4pm.

"That was amazing," Lily exclaimed.

"What?" Ben asked.

"Your idea, to send new messages. We'll refresh the data, and if it's worked then Brandt will have replied before his death. We will have a reply to your message - I won't need to see the contents of any vault to know the time loop is real after that."

Ben held his breath, there was no point trying to understand the physics, instead all he imagined was a simple boomerang, where messages were thrown back in time and returned with the possibly of taking off your head.

Lily refreshed the decryption engine, moments later the screen updated.

There was a new message.

The message was highlighted in bold text just the way an email program would display unread mail.

Lily raised her hand to her mouth: she was trembling. "Even after the last message... I didn't dare hope there would be anything there. It's wonderful."

"Wonderful?" Ben asked.

"Yes, wonderful. What it means for science, a real breakthrough, who would have believed it?" She started to laugh.

"Believed what?" He asked.

"That we split time to stop the Nazis splitting the atom."

Ben forced a smile.

"The only good thing is there's only one LHC, and it's surely impossible to build another like it," he replied. "Even at that, if it's possible to change the past, then our future has no meaning. Do you think our governments will be able to resist this? We'll pick up the papers tomorrow and find Saddam Hussein still in power in Iraq, and a close ally in the war of terror, that's what this could mean, Lily, it could change everything..."

"I know, but let's enjoy the moment, however briefly; it's like landing on the moon, Simon and Rae might have been Armstrong and Aldrin having got there first, but while Simon feared the effect existed, and Rae hoped it did, we know for sure."

Lily opened the message and viewed another ten digit account number, Ben noted it down.

"Can you delete it, make it unrecoverable?" He asked.

"Yeah, you sure you've copied it down correctly?"

He nodded repeating the digits out loud to check.

"OK, I've deleted the message and its system signature, it's gone for good." She said.

"If that's true, then Rae has done all this for nothing," Ben said. "He'll have no access to the vault, so will have to come looking for us."

"There's one more of Rae's messages to read," she said as she loaded it.

"What have we got?"

"He's sent a nuclear dossier, and it looks like the real thing. Why would he do that? That dossier arriving in Nazi hands in 1943 could have helped them build a bomb."

"Because he believes it makes no difference to the present," Ben replied. "We can thank Simon for that - he only understood the stakes after Ohrdruf. But why send the dossier and Amber Room delivery instructions together? Surely he'd wait until he had some confirmation on the Amber Room?"

"It's decrypted using a different Enigma key. I'll check it," Lily said as she quickly typed the commands and waited for the result.

"It's encrypted with a later key, that key wasn't used until a few days after Rae's deadline in 1943. He sent the dossier at the same time as the demand, but no-one would try a future Enigma key to decrypt a current message. So the message wouldn't make sense until after the date it came into use... it's quite clever really."

Ben moved to the Window, "Lily, I think we should leave."

"What's wrong?"

"A BMW passed us as we crossed the road... It's parked on the corner."

"They seem to be the national car here, are you sure - they all look alike?"

"It's the same one, an M3, and I'm just wondering if it's the same one at that cafe we stopped at too."

"Who do you think it is?"

"I don't want to find out. We'll have to go, let's see if there's a way out through the back and meet Rory away from here. We've put Clive in danger."

Ben walked towards the door as Lily left the computer and peered down on the street below.

"You're sure?"

Ben joined her looking out, "Yeah 100%, let's go."

Chapter 33

Geneva, Switzerland
Tuesday, 9 May 2017 08:02

The Range Rover's satellite navigation led them around the airport's perimeter and the road towards CERN. They passed by a variety of small bungalows and flat-roofed industrial units in quiet streets below the white-peaked mountains to the north.

Shaw had little time for the scenery or the crisp, tidy suburbs surrounding Geneva, his thoughts were on the apartment and what the two targets could want with the scientist. He might have joked with Alex about another murder, but if he was wrong about Millar his career was over, the police would crucify him if they ever discovered he'd allowed murder suspects to leave the country.

Alex's phone started to ring; she held it in the palm of her hand as she answered on speaker.

"Alex, Reid here, you alone?"

Shaw recognised the voice.

"No, she's not, what's happening?"

Martin Reid was all of 5' 7" and weighed 140lb. He didn't look ex-army, let alone ex-SAS, he simply didn't attract attention, a skill that had saved his life on numerous tours of Northern Ireland. Shaw was glad he was on the case.

"That you, Shaw?"

"It is," Alex replied for him.

"OK, we have another team on the ground here, are you aware of any other interest in the targets?"

Shaw took the phone from Alex.

"Negative, Martin, I don't know of any other interest."

"Two men just got out of a blue Audi, which then moved off and took up position at the end of the street. These guys look like pros - specialist police, military or something worse..."

Shaw lent over Alex and checked the sat nav.

"We are 3 km from your position, where should we come in from?"

"Loop around, don't come directly into the street, there's a real chance of compromise here, I've got our people to fall back for now," Reid replied, "Alex knows where we are."

"OK, we'll be with you shortly. I'll make a call and see what I can find out about the new arrivals." Shaw added before nodding for Alex to hang up.

He checked his watch, he'd just have time to make that call before they got to Reid, they needed to find out who else was involved and call up whatever backup was available in Geneva tonight.

"We'll be with the surveillance team in a few minutes," Alex said.

"Good, I don't like this, who else knows our targets are here?" Shaw asked.

"What do you want to do?" Alex asked.

"If this gets out of shape, the only thing we can do is snatch anyone we find in that apartment, we can't let anyone walk away."

Chapter 34

Geneva, Switzerland
Tuesday, 9 May 2017 08:04

Ben moved quickly back to the lounge, pausing a moment for Lily to catch up. Adams sat forward on one of the two leather sofas that faced each other in the centre of the room.

"We may have been followed," Lily told him. "We need to get out of here right now. Is there a way out the back?"

Adams visibly paled.

"Clive, I'm so sorry," Lily said. "It isn't safe here, you need to come with us. You should stay with friends for a couple of nights..."

Adams didn't seem to be able to comprehend what was being said to him, after a few seconds silence he mumbled, "Through there... the back door."

He pointed to a door by the kitchen, his eyes bulged, and hands were held behind his back as though he didn't know what to do with them.

He gestured for them to keep moving, Lily was already on her way, but as Ben followed he sensed something was wrong. He glanced to his side and saw a blur of movement. He shouted a warning to Lily as he threw himself back towards Adams. The blow struck his right shoulder, just missing the collarbone, Adams held a claw hammer in his right hand. In moving backwards, Ben had taken a lesser impact from the handle rather than the head. He whipped around, following his left elbow as it struck Adams' jaw, the hammer fell as the physicist was sent crashing into boxes full of kitchen utensils which scattered around him.

He heard Lily gasp as he held Adams down and punched him hard in the face. The pitifully one-sided fight was over in a few seconds and Ben stood over a beaten man.

Ben pulled Adams violently up to a sitting position.

"WHY!" Ben screamed in Adams' face. Ben was fully in control of his emotions, but Adams didn't know that and recoiled in fear. There wasn't much more than a whimper in reply. Ben grabbed the front of his shirt.

"Are you working for Rae?" Ben shouted. "Tell me right now, are you working for Rae?"

Adams looked stricken, and shot a look towards the front door.

"Who's coming here!" Ben demanded, picking up the hammer and holding above Adams' head. "Tell me, or so help me God!"

Any resolve Adams had to hold out deserted him.

"Rae's men, they're coming for you. I had no choice, I had to keep you here until they arrived, I didn't know about the killings until it was too late, I wanted to get out, but he won't let me."

"They're coming here now?" Ben asked carefully.

He glanced at Lily who stared back at him. Adams was nodding vigorously.

"Lily, open the back door," Ben ordered.

"If you had nothing to do with Simon and James, what have you to do with?" Ben asked.

"They gave me money, lots of it, to change some pretty unimportant diagnostics," Adams sobbed. "No-one cared about them."

Lily had opened the door into the garden. Ben threw the hammer down and made his way towards her.

He turned back to Adams, "They cared enough to kill two people, and I wouldn't trust your new friends, you know too much."

Lily put her hand on Ben's arm, "Let's get out of here." She said it quietly without looking at him.

"I wasn't going to hit him with the hammer," he said in a whisper sensing her shock at the violence.

That wasn't quite true, he hadn't hit him as there was no need, but it would have been no trouble as he felt nothing for a man complicit in his brother's murder, a man who tried to stall them knowing full well they would have been taken and killed.

Ben took one look back at Adams before stepping out into the garden. There was no time to think, they had to move as they were finished if caught here.

Ben and Lily crossed to an alley that ran behind the apartment building. As they turned to the left, Lily stopped dead. She touched Ben's arm, but he had already seen the movement as someone had stepped off the path. Without a word, he guided Lily in the opposite direction. They had covered thirty metres and almost reached the end of the alley when a gate was noisily kicked open behind them.

Lily looked back. Ben grabbed her arm and urged her on. There was sudden crack and Ben's right arm lifted as he was spun around.

Lily steadied him, and he was able to stay on his feet. Ben could feel the blood spreading out onto his shirt, he looked behind to see two men, one had pushed the other's gun down, and now both men were running towards them. He felt Lily pulling him away and they lurched onto the main street and out of their attackers' line of sight.

There were more gunshots, he heard shouts of 'Police', and screaming all around them. Pedestrians were backing off from them to find cover in the shops and doorways. Drivers stuck in traffic abandoned their cars while those further back leant on their horns unaware of the danger ahead.

"We have to get across the road quickly," Ben said to Lily.

"Last thing I want to do is stay around here," she shouted pulling him.

"Look!" Lily shouted.

Ben could see that the traffic hold up was caused by a double-parked VW camper van barely twenty metres away. Rory was frantically waving at them, and Lily urged Ben on before pushing him into the already open sliding door. Ben fell in head first and twisted trying to avoid landing on his arm, the effort failed to shield him from a fierce pain that left him lying in a sweat trying not to move. The VW pulled away, amid shouts and screams, a line of its bright red paint marking a white van as Rory pushed his way out into the traffic.

It was at that moment Ben realised Lily wasn't there.

He scrambled forward and lent out of the open door to see her bundled into a powerful Audi estate that had reversed along the pavement until blocked by the wall of traffic. He could hear himself shouting over and over again. Rory looked back and realised what had happened and spun the wheel while Ben shaped his body trying to protect his arm once more.

Rory turned towards the abduction point, revving the engine hard, going up and down the gears, trying to find a way through the traffic to Lily. They lost the Audi almost immediately as there was no way through cars abandoned across the street and pavements. Ben watched helplessly as it disappeared around a far corner, he looked to Rory - Lily was gone.

Chapter 35

Central London
Saturday, 13 February 1943 1056

It was a rare occurrence for Colonel Edward Timmons to report to the prime minister directly, but this was the second such summons in as many days.

His car passed through checkpoints that became more frequent the closer he drew to the heart of a government that still commanded an Empire.

The prime minister wasn't as well protected as he should have been, but the man wouldn't listen to reason and insisted on running the war from the capital - 'Why should Londoners stay if I leave?' - was the usual argument, ignoring the fact that he'd become a symbol of the struggle against the Nazi regime, his life as vital to his country as that of the King's.

The sentries checked the car carefully, and Timmons noted there was no joking or exchange of smiles, he was glad to see these young soldiers knew the importance of the man in their charge.

The car turned into Downing Street, pulling up well before the famous black door of Number 10. Timmons preferred to use one of the many anonymous entrances, and waited for the driver to open his door.

Timmons was met by one of General Brooke's staff officers, Captain John Ames. The general had recently been promoted to Chief of the Imperial General Staff (CIGS), the new head of British army and an architect of the allied war. Ames was an affable man who had an easy way with people, and it appeared the loss of his left leg below the knee during the flight from Dunkirk had done little to change his temperament.

He followed Ames along a corridor and into a drawing room where four men were seated at a conference table including the CIGS himself. Timmons knew the others well enough, they were all at the top of their professions, each one a knight of the realm: Sir Richard Dees, a permanent secretary attached to the war cabinet, Sir Stewart Menzies, head of MI6 and Sir David Petrie, head of MI5.

"Has the PM arrived?" Timmons asked.

"No, change of plan, he's still at Chequers," Ames replied, "He returned from Tripoli midweek, and has come down with something, we've to continue in his absence."

Petrie shifted in his seat, "As my diary is rather full, can I ask what's so important to call us together this morning?"

Timmons sat in the chair that Ames had offered and started to undo the straps of the worn, brown leather briefcase he'd carried for more than twenty years. The others waited as he pulled out numbered copies of the ULTRA decrypt responsible for his early start that day. Timmons passed the papers around the table.

"Gentlemen, we are all busy men, but I was telephoned this morning from Bletchley Park about a message one of my officers felt required immediate attention. I informed General Brooke, and that's why we are here now."

"Who else knows of this message?" Petrie asked as he started to read.

"It will be included in the daily ULTRA messages you all receive," Timmons replied.

"Who exactly is your man in Bletchley Park?" Petrie asked, "It's my responsibility for keeping the lid on tight there."

"It's all above board. My man's working there on secondment, he's a naval officer-" Timmons replied.

"That may be, but we can't have loose cannons somewhere like Bletchley. You should know that,

Colonel," Petrie insisted.

Timmons knew MI5 wouldn't like his contacts on their turf as each intelligence agency jealously guarded their own little fiefdoms, and his Special Operations Executive was considered an upstart and potentially damaging newcomer by many of the others.

"The officer concerned knows my position and that he can talk to me freely," Timmons replied patiently. "Now, let's consider the matter in hand."

Petrie was about to retort when General Brooke cut in.

"Colonel, please continue..."

Petrie looked sour but gave way and started to scan the document once more as Timmons cleared his throat.

"Gentleman, we have a serious situation. The enemy has been offered a trade. They are to exchange a treasured work of art for some of our most valuable, top secret plans. I have codenamed the sender of this message, VIPER, and he has already passed classified information in the form of the message before you now. That information alone is of significant value to our enemies. If the Germans agree to his terms, and I'm sure they will, then VIPER has promised to send the full blueprints of the atomic bomb currently being constructed in the United States."

The concern caused by the weapon's mention in a German signal was obvious around the table. If the Nazis could obtain this type of weapon with the tide of the war finally turning against them, they would use it against London.

"Do we know anything about this VIPER?" Dees asked. "Bad enough as this is, if he's British and these are American secrets, well, I don't have to explain the damage this will cause."

"We have no idea of his nationality," Timmons replied.

Do we even know if these plans are the real thing?" The civil servant continued, "It could easily be some kind of confidence trick."

"All I can tell you is that he'll hang if he's one of ours," Petrie added.

"Yes, Sir Richard, they're real," Timmons replied. "One of our top scientists working on the atomic program codenamed, MANHATTAN PROJECT, has verified the documents, he is unaware of the context under which he examined them, but he was suspicious and he's been told not to mention them on his return to the States."

"Can we trust him to keep it quiet?" Petrie asked.

"I'd imagine you have a file on him at MI5, I'd suggest you check it, but he's back in England to bury his youngest son who lost his life in a Hurricane over Kent. He seems a good sort."

"If he's due to return soon, might be worth delaying him, at least until we know what we're up against, and what we're going to do about it," General Brooke suggested.

"The atomic plans or the American reaction are not my immediate concern," Timmons said. "It's unlikely they could make use of the information in time to make a difference. The issue now is ULTRA. I don't need to tell you of its continued importance to our operations, we have let men go to their deaths to protect it."

General Brooke lent forward.

"Yes, we all know the importance of ULTRA, but how is it affected?"

Timmons thought the general looked more than tired. The man carried a heavy weight, but then again he'd probably looked better himself.

"The message was sent over DOLPHIN, and the code-breakers were able to decode it. Naval encryption keys changed shortly after the VIPER message was intercepted. I fear there is a direct link and the Germans are wondering how someone with top-level allied secrets could possibly know the settings to send a message. We were already out of the U-boat cipher, SHARK, and as a result of the code rotation we are now locked out of all naval signals. That may be the case for a significant period of time."

There was a stunned silence as members of the meeting digested what the loss of their prized signals intelligence meant. Eventually, Richard Dees spoke up, "When did you find out the keys had changed?"

"Bletchley realised there was a problem yesterday when all naval traffic failed to decrypt," Timmons replied, "The German navy take Enigma security extremely seriously, more seriously than the other services who all consider it unbreakable. A message sent to SS Major Kessler will be seen as highly irregular and may well have triggered the key change. We just have to hope there's no loss of faith in the Enigma system as a result."

Petrie stood up pushing back his chair, "Any interruption to ULTRA will cost us men and equipment, the losses in the Atlantic may well rise to levels last seen in 1941, but bad as that is, we have someone with inside information on projects that have the absolutely highest level of security. We are looking at someone with a top security clearance. VIPER is the right word, we have a traitor very close to home."

"I don't think we need panic unduly," Dees said, "One thing I do remember from the atomic briefings is that we are many months from a weapon, that's if it's possible to produce one at all. Even if the Germans obtain these blueprints, well, it's not a simple process, and any threat would be too far in the future to affect the conduct of the war. So whatever we do, we cannot risk anything that would raise further questions over ULTRA."

"I take Sir Richard's point, but if there is the slightest chance the enemy could use this technology to further their weapons programmes, then we would be forced to take action regardless of the consequences, and even at the risk of losing ULTRA completely," General Brooke said.

"You mean fail to cover our tracks? Let the Germans know we're reading their signals?" Petrie exclaimed. "I cannot see the PM countenancing that."

"I'll call the PM and find out," Brooke replied. "If you could all stay until after I've spoken to him, the final decision must come from him, but I tell you now - he will not allow atomic progress by the Nazis - whatever the cost."

Timmons couldn't believe what he was hearing.

"But we can't risk ULTRA," Timmons said. "Our scientists have stated that it will be at least a year before they're ready to test a weapon, and the Germans must be many months, if not years behind our efforts. ULTRA is winning the war for us now, and I urge whatever steps we take are mindful of that fact."

"I'm afraid, Colonel Timmons, that's not quite correct." Menzies had spoken for the first time, "If I may, General?"

Brooke nodded to Menzies who, unlike Petrie, looked quite calm. Timmons put that down to his diplomatic experience before he became a spymaster.

"Since 1941, we have been working alongside our American friends on the construction of a weapon so powerful, it has the potential to change warfare as we know it. The Germans have also been working on a weapons programme. We have interviewed many of the scientists who fled from Germany on Hitler's rise to power. We know they have made progress, but the question is: how far have they got? What we do know is they have test laboratories and facilities for atomic research. The MANHATTAN PROJECT data could be all they need to move their work on quickly. We simply have no idea how far they are behind us."

"Are you saying they could develop a weapon before us?" Timmons asked.

"No, I'm saying we do not know their capabilities, but we cannot underestimate them, their industrial resources are formidable," Menzies replied.

General Brookes held up the message, "I visited the Amber Room before the Bolsheviks took power, it was quite extraordinary. Do we know its current location?"

"All we know is that the Nazis had it removed from the Winter Place in St Petersburg," Timmons replied. "Its current whereabouts are unknown. Requesting it as payment for the documents makes very little sense, it's bulky, obvious - why not ask for enough gold to buy a few Amber Rooms or something easier to move such as diamonds?"

"Good God! This VIPER could sink us," Petrie exclaimed. "He could sink us, and for what, a pretty museum piece?"

"Whoever VIPER is, he must be on the inside. It would be wise to keep any investigations as quiet as possible, we don't want to tip him off we're onto this," Menzies said.

"Where would you suggest we start?" General Brooke replied.

"We can start by compiling a list of anyone with access to atomic weapons research, and cross reference it with those who have knowledge of ULTRA. We fully investigate any matches," Menzies suggested.

"I'd like MI5 and MI6 to work closely together on this one-" Petrie said before being interrupted by a knock at the door. Ames answered and walked back to the table to pass General Brooke a note. The general read the message in the way a card player examines his hand, leaving the page face down as he looked back around the table.

"This is a message from the PM, we are to stop the proposed trade whatever the cost and by all means available. Colonel Timmons you are directly responsible for ensuring this SS Major does not deposit the Amber Room with any Swiss lawyer or bank."

Timmons took a moment to light a cigarette, "If that's the position, let's see what we have on Kessler."

Chapter 36

The Range Rover screeched to a halt in the underground car park. Shaw was out of the car, and moving quickly towards the surveillance team's borrowed apartment.

The last few minutes had been a nightmare; the distant sirens screamed that out. His better judgement told him they should be out of the area immediately, but he needed to know what the hell had gone wrong and now. Events were never fully under control on any operation, but he was in the middle of a full-on disaster, and far worse, a very public disaster on foreign soil.

Alex moved to the front leading Shaw down a spotlessly clean hallway with thick carpets, and heavy panelled doors.

She knocked on the second door and entered a large, square hall with Shaw close behind. They walked through the third of four doors into a drawing room with views over the street towards the target address. Agents were straightening out the room, their gear packed in black rucksacks and stacked by the door. Radio chatter filled the background, the voices calm, the exchanges were short and professional, there was no hint the op had just crashed around them.

Shaw's phone began to buzz, just as ex-soldier and lead watcher, Martin Reid stepped into the room. Shaw's phone stopped.

"I was calling you," Reid said pocketing his own mobile.

"What's happened?" Shaw asked.

"We need to get out of here. The area will be crawling with cops in three to five minutes."

Two other officers, seemingly happy with the look of the rooms and apartment, shouldered the rucksacks and started to make for the exit, Reid was last out as the party of five walked back down towards their cars.

"This is where we are," Reid explained as they headed down the stairwell. "Two men turned up at the apartment. We've sent images to Vauxhall Cross for facial recognition, but right now we don't have positive ids."

"Go on..." Shaw said.

"Our targets split up, the doctor dropped the others out front, before heading off in the camper van. I had to let him go as we only have enough people to watch one group. Approximately twenty minutes after they entered the apartment, the men turned up and entered the property. Our targets must have realised something was wrong as they left the building from the rear. We had the whole building covered, but they pinged our man on the way out and changed direction to walk away from him. The new arrivals appeared from the apartment both carrying shorts. There was a contact with our targets."

"Any casualties?" Shaw asked.

"None of our men were injured, but Millar took a round in the arm and is walking wounded. The female was snatched by the men before they made off."

"Snatched, how?" Alex asked.

"Our agent fired two rounds in the air and shouted 'Police'. He was trying to give the targets time to escape. The men returned fire before going after the targets. We slowed them down, but the girl slipped as she went for the van, and they were able to grab her."

"And Millar?" Shaw asked.

"Millar got to the camper van, and in the melee that followed, we couldn't tail either vehicle and maintain cover. We had to let them go, the only positives are we have a tracker in the van, and we lifted the apartment owner, Clive Adams."

"Is he in one piece?" Shaw asked glancing over at Alex who was listening intently.

"We checked the apartment after the men fled, he's taken a beating, but it's nothing serious. He's on his way to a safe house now."

"Good," Shaw replied, "is it close by?"

"There's a house on the lake, Alex knows it."

He looked to Alex who nodded.

"OK, I need to see him, has he said anything yet?"

"No idea, this is all recent history."

"OK, at least we can still track Millar," Shaw said.

"If he stays with the van, the device is standard issue with GPS and audio capture."

"That's something," Shaw mouthed as he climbed back into the Range Rover, watching as Reid jumped into a larger Land Rover Discovery. As they exited up a ramp and onto the street, a TV news van with an array of satellite and communication equipment sped past. The operational objective had crossed from simple surveillance to full-scale damage limitation. If any hint of their involvement emerged it would result in a serious diplomatic incident, and one Shaw couldn't explain away. The priority now was to protect the reputational risk to his agency, his country and himself, and that meant the capture of everyone involved or ensuring their silence.

Chapter 37

Harry James pushed his food around his plate. The canteen food was nourishing, but he doubted it would match the tables of the many nearby London clubs, such as Brooks, Whites and the Carlton. According to the pilot who flew him out of Dublin, despite rationing, their members still enjoyed the most extravagant dishes.

James would try and verify those claims as soon as possible, maybe Colonel Timmons would take him to lunch and explain exactly what was so important to remove him from his posting in the Irish Republic with immediate effect.

After draining his teacup, he lit up a cigarette and pulled out papers from his briefcase, he stifled a cough as he lay out his report on the table. Last night's hastily arranged flight had left him restless and unable to sleep, so he'd spent the early hours writing up some notes on his contacts in the Irish Intelligence services, which he'd drop off before leaving the building. The dining room was becoming busier and tables around him were dotted with occupants, James kept an eye out for a familiar face, but hadn't recognised anyone as yet. It was still early and maybe he'd have time to catch up with old friends after he found out what the fuss was about.

As he read over the last file, there was just under an hour before the appointment with Timmons at the War Office. He'd heard SOE had been running things out of Baker Street, but maybe Timmons wanted to stay closer to the powers-at-be.

A slow walk around St James Park, down the bomb-damaged Mall, and back by Birdcage Walk ensured a timely arrival. A good walk was preferable to some smoke-filled waiting room that would just drag out a morning he'd expected to spend quietly in his Dublin office.

On arriving at the War Office on Horse Guards Avenue, he was directed up the staircase to the second floor where a clerk would show him where to go.

He made his way up and offered his papers to a young civil servant who sat behind a battered desk. The phone was picked up, and James announced.

"Please follow me, Captain James. The Colonel is waiting for you."

The War Office apparently contained over one thousand rooms, it was an impressive building by any standard, but Whitehall was surrounded by so many impressive buildings where so much of the nation's and the world's history had been made. How many of them would be left standing at the end of the latest chapter being written by the Luftwaffe?

They turned into a spur off the main corridor before his escort stopped and rapped on a door. There was a shout to enter and James was left with sound of leather padding on stone as the clerk returned to his station.

James cleared his throat before opening the door and walking into the centre of the room. There was an older man on the opposite side of a large writing desk.

"Captain James, good of you to come."

James studied the Colonel - he was tall, lean and looked bloody awful with dark eyes and a yellow tinge to the skin. His tweed jacket was an old friend, worn leather patches at the elbows and a small repair to a rip above a side pocket. The scarring on the neck was severe and typical of wounds hastily stitched in the field by surgeons stretched to the limit by the butchery of the Great War. The scars placed the man instantly.

"Dockyard politics," James replied.

"Pardon me?"

"I attended a lecture you gave on dockyard politics in Glasgow," James explained.

"Ah, yes, good men our Bolshevik friends on the Clyde, they'll have lined up to fight the fascists, and good luck to them."

The colonel indicated for James to take a seat, "Would you like some refreshments, tea perhaps?"

"No thanks, sir, I'd like to know what's important enough to put me on a plane from Dublin to London with a few hours' notice."

James instantly regretted his tone, in truth, he'd wanted out of Eire for months, but would have liked the time for some simple farewells.

"You're here under my orders," Timmons replied. "You have applied to join the Royal Marine Commandos, is that correct?"

"I've been trying for nearly a year, sir."

"Why so keen to leave MI5?"

"I was a soldier first, sir, and there's plenty soldiering to do right now."

"You've been refused because of your work in Ireland, what were you doing there?"

James looked impassively at Timmons.

"Sir, who do you work for now if you don't mind me asking?"

"I run missions overseas; I was head of Section D at MI6 until that became part of the Special Operations Executive. I know the kind of work you've done - Donal Keogh, was your first job."

James considered the last remark, that episode had been hushed up, relations between the British and Irish governments were already bad enough, and it was unthinkable that James' involvement in those killings should ever become known outside the service, if Timmons knew about that, he would know everything.

"Britain was always going to keep a close eye in its own backyard," James explained. "The threat of invasion with the Irish Republic as a possible bridgehead was enough reason for someone like me to be on operation there. We had to ensure Irish neutrality did not include turning a blind eye to refuelling of aircraft or U-boats within their territory."

"And the dead men-"

"Not an innocent among them. All Provisional IRA - all caught in contact with Nazi agents. My orders were to discourage any co-operation..."

"Very effectively it seems."

"Sir, why am I here?"

Timmons opened a dog-eared folder and flipped over a photograph of a German officer.

"Mean anything to you?"

James slid the photo closer; a fit-looking German officer was caught glancing towards the camera as he waited by a car on a busy street.

"Should it?" James replied shaking his head slowly at the washed out image, "I can't make much of it, I'm afraid."

"It's the only recent one we have of him. It was taken last year, the name's Kessler, does that help?"

James could feel the old man watching him closely as he picked up the photograph again.

"I see it now, that's Kessler," James replied, "he's still thin as a razor."

"He's come to our attention and is currently stationed in France. He's been utterly ruthless in dealing with the French resistance, and you've faced him before?"

"He was ruthless in the ring. I fought him in Berlin in the 1936 Olympics where he went on to take the silver. So Kessler's the reason I'm here?"

"He's involved in something big, and your name came up when we cross-referenced him across departments. You've shown that you can fight a dirty war and that's what's required for Kessler. All you need to know is that this show could cost us the war, and you might just be the man I order to kill him?"

James made eye contact and nodded, he could follow orders - he had always done that.

"One more thing, James, unless you took the gold, I take it Kessler beat you in Berlin?"

"A lucky left hook, Colonel, and I always wanted a rematch."

Chapter 38

Geneva, Switzerland
Tuesday, 9 May 2017 08:14

The VW van stopped short of the corner they'd last seen Lily, cars were blocking the way and the Audi was long gone.

"We've lost them," Ben said.

"I know," Rory replied quietly as he reversed into a turn before heading away.

Ben doubted Rae's men had been aware of their efforts to give chase, they would be more concerned avoiding the local police than worrying about any threat they could pose.

"What happened?" Rory asked.

"Rae's men turned up. Adams was working for them," Ben started to explain.

Rory looked back again, "You're hurt."

"It's my arm, I've been shot."

"Christ! Put pressure on the wound, you have to control the bleeding, and raise your arm if you can." Rory ordered as he accelerated hard taking a turn towards the city centre.

"I already am," Ben replied.

They made rapid progress through the increasing heavy traffic until Rory followed a sign for parking close to the city's main railway station.

"Hold on, Ben," Rory shouted back.

He edged into a multi-storey car park and took his ticket at the barrier before driving upwards to the deserted top level. Jumping out of the van, he pulled the sliding door open, sat across from Ben, then shut the curtains and opened his medical bag. Ben sat forward and winced at the pain. Rory pushed him back into the bench seat, "Sit still, we need to fix you up."

Rory expertly slipped on surgical gloves and started to examine the blood-stained arm. Surgical wipes removed the blood to reveal a small gash just below the deltoid muscle.

"It looks like a nick, but it's difficult to tell as there could be a wound cavity, how's it feel to move it?"

"I'll cope," Ben replied as he glanced down, blood seeped from the wound as he tensed his arm.

"It looks worse than it is," Rory said slowing rotating the wrist and forearm while checking Ben's reaction to the movement.

"I'm just angry I lost Lily," Ben said.

"I'll patch you up. There's going to be some swelling, but I'd say you've been lucky."

"Too right," Ben agreed as Rory filled a syringe.

Ben gritted his teeth as a needle plunged into his shoulder then relaxed as the burning sensation in his arm started to fade and Rory went to work. It was over in a few minutes, the arm was stitched, dressed and set close to his body in a sling.

"Thanks..." Ben said.

"You'll be OK, are you allergic to anything?

"No.

He pressed two packs of tablets into Ben's hand, "These are painkillers, take one every four hours; these are antibiotics, three a day before food."

Rory peeled off his gloves and added them to a waste bag, then tore open an antiseptic wipe and methodically cleaned his hands.

"We need to get moving," Ben said.

What about your other shoulder?" Rory asked. "That's a bad bruise."

"A blow from a hammer," Ben replied. "I was lucky with that one, I backed into it, and only got caught with the shaft."

"What the hell happened back there?"

"Adams is on Rae's payroll, he'd set up any message Rae wanted for the LHC, and he was stalling us until Rae's men got to the apartment," Ben replied. "When we tried to leave he came at me with a hammer, and I had to take him out. We started to run, and this happened."

"Was Lily hurt?"

"She pulled me away from them - she had to be OK."

"What about Adams?"

"I left him on his back, he knew the men he called would have killed us too."

Ben sat up and started to move his arms in small circular motions, his shoulder was numb, but he could use the arm.

"There's something else," Ben said.

Rory sat forward.

"We logged into the decryption engine. We saw Rae's messages and replies - real replies from 1943."

Rory shook his head, "Lily's what's important here, and nothing else matters until she's safe."

"Everything else is the reason we're here."

"We must focus on getting Lily back first," Rory replied steadily.

"I know," Ben replied, "but you have to listen to this: Rae asked for a numbered account to be set up. A number was in the reply we saw from 1943, but that message suddenly appeared, it hadn't existed until Rae's message had been sent, but exists now and has, in effect, since 1943."

Rory leaned away and started to pack his medical kit away.

"Ben, even if I accept this is all possible, that doesn't help get Lily back."

"No, that's not true as it gives us exactly that."

"I don't see how?"

"We impersonated Adams and managed to get the experiment repeated. We sent a new message back in time ordering a new account number. As soon as it was sent, a new reply immediately appeared in the decryption engine... it was as Munro had explained, cause and effect acting as one."

Rory lifted his head, "What was in the message?"

"I told you... the new account number, and Lily deleted all trace of that message from the system. Rae will know another message had been received, but he won't be able to read it. He will want that account number, and we can trade it for Lily."

"There's a problem with that," Rory replied.

"What?"

"He won't want any witnesses left when he finally gets it."

"I know, and if I'm dead he can try and pin all the murders on me, but that's just another reason for him to accept a trade."

"No-one's going to believe any of this, Ben."

"Not any time soon," Ben replied.

"So we need to contact, Rae?"

"He runs a company, and so we find a number and get a message to him. We have to do it before anything happens to Lily."

"And you think he'll meet us and release her just like that?"

Ben slowly pulled out a folded sheet of A4 paper.

"If the Amber Room could be found who knows what it could be worth. If Rae's believes it's waiting for him in a Zurich vault," Ben said holding out the sheet, "he can't collect without this account number so he'll deal with us to get it."

"If that's true, what now?" Rory asked.

"We get out of Geneva," Ben replied. "We've already stayed too long."

Chapter 39

Lake Geneva, Switzerland
Tuesday, 9 May 2017 08:25

Shaw unclipped his seatbelt as they pulled up at the entrance to a large lakeside house. Solid, wooden security gates closed smoothly behind them, a metallic clang disturbing the burble from a centrepiece fountain as they hit their stops.

A number of cars were parked outside a stable block bordered by gardens that led down to the lake with a boathouse on the water's edge. MI6 had chosen a beautifully calm and confident part of Switzerland to hide away.

There are safe houses, and there are safe houses, Shaw thought as a Dauphin AS365 N1 helicopter came in to land at a helipad marked out close to an outdoor tennis court.

"Not bad," Shaw said, "how long have we been using this place?"

"A few years," Alex replied. "The owner's a retired barrister who spends half the year in the Caribbean. He worked for the service once upon a time and lets us use this place - I don't know the full details."

Shaw followed her through the hall to a large half-panelled room that enjoyed views across Lake Geneva through leaded windows. Clive Adams PhD was seated at a dining table. His manner was reminiscent of a sulking child, and one used to getting its own way. Adams glanced between Shaw and the agent who stood over him.

"Dr Adams, I've got some questions for you," Shaw said as he pulled out a chair opposite the scientist.

Shaw searched through the contents of his pockets without a glance at Adams. He checked his phone before setting the volume to mute.

"I demand to see a solicitor, you've no right to keep me here," Adams blurted out.

Shaw looked directly at Adams for the first time.

"There's no need to be unduly alarmed," Shaw said looking the man over, "but I'm afraid I need some answers."

"Not without my lawyer," Adams repeated, "You have no right to keep me here."

"One question would be - did you know two of your colleagues were murdered in Edinburgh last night?"

"Of course I did, I worked with Simon daily, and I knew James quite well," Adams replied immediately.

"That wasn't too difficult, but this one might pose more of a problem. Did you know you were sheltering the murder suspects of those same colleagues?"

"Of course not, that's outrageous! Lily and I were friends of Simon Millar. How could I possibly suspect she was involved in those deaths? Who are you people anyway?"

"I have two murders in Edinburgh, you are found with the suspects in your home, and we pick you up in the middle of a major firearms incident. I work for the British government, and I expect your full cooperation. You can forget about your rights as you're here until I get the answers I need," Shaw said making a show of looking to the guard.

He waited as Adams digested his position.

"I'll answer what I can, but what will happen to me?" Adams replied.

"It depends what you tell me, but I'm not here to arrest anyone, I need to know what happened, and if you help me, I may be able to help you."

Adams slowly nodded his head, "OK, ask away."

"Why did they visit you?" Shaw asked.

"They wanted access to a computer. I know Lily, so why would I refuse."

"They travelled all the way from Edinburgh to use your computer?"

"I had no idea where they came from, or their motive. If you're correct and they were involved in my friend's murder then they no doubt had their reasons, but they didn't share them with me."

"Ben Millar is your friend's brother."

"Well, I'd never heard of him, so I wouldn't know."

Alex walked back into the room; she tapped his shoulder and bent down to whisper in his ear.

"Excuse me," Shaw said as he stood and followed the female agent out of the room.

They walked up a wide stairway to the upper floor and into a sitting room where a table was laid out with numerous laptop computers, electronic devices and a web of cables and power supplies.

"The mike in the doctor's van picked up a conversation you need to hear," Alex said, nodding to one of three technicians.

An audio feed started to play, and Shaw stared at the small portable speakers as he strained to listen to the poor sound quality.

As the recording finished, the room fell silent with all eyes on Shaw. He thought for a moment, if any part of what he'd just heard had the remotest chance of being true, he'd have to act and quickly.

"No-one else hears that tape," he said, "and Alex, where's the surveillance team?"

"I'll get them for you," she replied speed-dialling a number, and spoke briefly before passing to Shaw.

"It's Martin Reid..." She said as he took the phone.

"Where are the targets now?" Shaw asked.

"The tracking device led us to a city car park - they were still with the van," Reid replied.

"Can you take them in now?"

"There's a risk we'd be pinged by locals, this place is pretty busy. I'd rather wait until we can take them cleanly?"

"OK, follow until you are happy to snatch them. I need to talk to London. Just make sure we don't lose them."

Chapter 40

Scottish Highlands
Friday, 19 February 1943 2307

Harry James settled in to an empty cabin on the sleeper train from Inverness to London King's Cross. It was five days since he'd left Ireland, but every hour had been put to good use by the Royal Marine Commandos instructed to give him a thorough weapons and fitness refresher on a short schedule.

The hard physical exercise had quietened his mind to the danger he'd face on operation in occupied Europe. While he'd hoped to serve in a standard unit, wearing a uniform and joining the hundreds of thousands that were gathering in the south for the inevitable push back into mainland Europe; his was a spy's war, and this was an important job, everything about Timmons' manner conveyed a sense that Kessler must be stopped whatever the cost.

He lay back in his bunk, and listened as the rain lashed the carriage. He let the tiredness wash over him, the waiting was over, tomorrow would bring the assignment that would finally put his stamp on this war.

The train drew into King's Cross a few minutes late. James had risen early and spent the remainder of the journey reading one of yesterday's newspapers. Sleep had come easily, a combination of recovery from the marines and a comfortable sleeping compartment.

As he stepped out onto the platform, he spotted Timmons immediately. The thin figure, smoking a pipe, was drowned in a raincoat too broad for his shoulders.

Timmons raised his hand in a single wave and walked away leaving James to follow on. A female driver sat behind the wheel of a Humber staff car, Timmons sat in the rear leaving an open door. James pushed his single case into the car first then sat by Timmons slamming the door behind him.

The car sped off and James felt himself peering at the driver, he'd rarely been driven by a woman, and this female was barely that, just out of her teens and a real beauty if a touch severe.

"Pleasant trip?" Timmons asked.

"Yes, train travel agrees with me," James replied.

The driver opened her window, Timmons' pipe fumes seeming to favour her for some reason, it was strong tobacco doing battle with her equally strong scent and prevailing.

Timmons made an apology and tapped the pipe outside the car letting tobacco and ash fall to the road.

"There's been a development with your old opponent," he said stowing the pipe in its leather pouch.

"I'd guessed as much, sir. I've been expecting your call at any time."

"Let's take a walk, we can cut across St James's Park and get some air," Timmons said, before smiling at his driver who sharply turned into Horse Guards Road to comply with what must have been a change of plan.

They were dropped on The Mall, and James was glad to stretch his legs after the long journey. He considered the damage a small number of German paratroopers could do here. The targets were irresistible: senior officers from all services, politicians, self-important civil servants and all of them walking around the park largely unprotected. Timmons seemed unaware of the danger, but these were the very people who ran the war for Britain's survival, and they were sitting ducks.

James walked side-by-side with the special operations man. Timmons moved quickly to business.

"We've had some information that relates to Kessler, and need to move quickly. I wanted to let you know what you're getting into."

James nodded as he lit a cigarette.

"This stays between us."

"I understand, sir. How reliable is the intelligence?"

"The source is impeccable. You're aware of ULTRA?"

"It's the product of our code-breaking efforts, I've no idea of the details, but I was involved in vetting Bletchley staff before my posting to Ireland."

"ULTRA has become quite a success, and we have become rather protective of it. Petrie considers it unwise to send you overseas as the little you know about it is enough to change enemy signal procedures overnight. That's if you were captured and made to talk, and of course, you carry other secrets..."

"Did you bring me here to drop me from the mission, sir?" James asked.

"No, I brought you here because I want to send you into Switzerland - Zurich to be precise. I want you to get there before Kessler, but you have to understand if this mission is to be sanctioned, then you can't allow yourself to be captured."

James took a long drag on his cigarette, and they walked in silence before he answered.

"You have something?"

"Potassium cyanide, it comes in a glass vial," Timmons replied without hesitation. "It's quite safe until you bite down."

"That's agreed then," James said.

Timmons smiled, seemingly satisfied with their understanding. James smiled back at the cold bastard, a man who'd let a slip of a girl determine when he could enjoy a pipe, thought nothing about extracting the word of a man to take his own life.

"You can only be there to identify Kessler, MI6 agents are already on the ground, and you'll work with them as a spotter."

Timmons stopped and turned to him.

"I know you wanted a more direct role, but we need you to do this."

"I understand," James replied trying to hide his disappointment of another posting to a neutral state, "now what about Kessler?"

"Major Kessler has been approached to exchange a Russian treasure called the Amber Room for a dossier of top-level allied research."

"Who's supplying the dossier?" James replied.

"That's the question we're working day and night to answer. His codename is VIPER and is most likely to be one of our own people. The information offered is so highly classified it can only mean a top-level penetration by someone like a senior scientist or intelligence officer. The message was sent to Kessler using the German Enigma system, and that opens up even more questions. How the traitor managed to do that is still unexplained, but there may have been some earlier contact and the means of communication arranged in advance."

"I thought we had the Nazi spy rings here under control?" James asked.

"So I'm told, but our traitor may know that too and avoid compromised channels."

"Do I need to know what the dossier contains?"

"Part of it was sent as proof in Kessler's message, it's contains top secret atomic weapons research. These weapons have the power to end the war and their possession is considered decisive by both sides. That should explain the importance of this mission."

Timmons paused as a couple on horseback trotted past.

"We know the Germans have carried out parallel research, but we have no idea how advanced their efforts are. This dossier may be all they need to make the breakthrough. They can hit London at will with their rockets. They would only need to do so once with an atomic warhead. Those are the stakes we're playing for."

"So I identify Kessler and let MI6 deal with him?" James asked.

Timmons nodded, "Kessler is to deliver the dismantled Amber Room to a law firm in Zurich. Our traitor has instructed the firm to act as intermediaries, and they will coordinate the exchange. I want you to go to Zurich and watch the lawyer's office for any sign of Kessler. We have men there right now, and you will join them."

"I understand, sir."

"Good," Timmons replied looking at his watch and picking up the pace, "I'll drop you off at a safe house, any other questions?"

"Why the Amber Room, I know it's supposed to be a wonder of the world, but it's a strange request-"

"You're not the first to ask that question," Timmons interrupted, "that's just another question on the list."

They crossed the road out of the park and Timmons stopped to buy a newspaper.

"I intend on getting you into Zurich as soon as possible, I had intended on flying you in via Lisbon, but it would take too long and there's a possibility you'd be recognised as one of us on arrival. Don't worry we'll think of something."

Chapter 41

Geneva, Switzerland
Tuesday, 9 May 2017 08:29

Rory slowly slid the van's door shut and locked up. He sighed as he traced his fingers along the scratches and dents that marred the panels.

"Rory, you have a family, you should cut out here," Ben said.

"I'm part of this until we get Lily back, and anyway, you're hardly fighting fit."

Ben tested the range of motion in his shoulder and arm; the pills were easing the pain, it was something he could deal with. His thoughts returned to Lily as he looked through a thick steel mesh down to the streets below. Was she close by, held in one of the buildings, or passing by in the back of a truck? She'd have to deal with the fear they'd shared together such a short time ago, but it would be worse this time. She was facing it alone.

Rory indicated he was ready.

"Can I carry something?" Ben said.

"Let's give you some time to heal," Rory replied walking off with a heavy rucksack.

Ben followed, and was glad they were finally putting distance between themselves and the van. It stood out among the sleek lines of modern vehicles, and the Swiss police had to be looking for it by now.

Ben's arm cost them time, but at least it was properly patched up, and he hadn't been forced to fix it himself.

They dropped down two flights of stairs and out onto a busy street signposted Rue de Alpes. Shoppers and tourists walked by, but no-one gave them a second look. They joined the crowd moving towards the main railway station. It was a scene of utter normality, and despite having no idea what troubles lay behind the impassive faces of the passersby, Ben almost envied these people and their everyday problems and lives. His legs felt weak, but he pushed through it to match Rory's pace.

They entered the railway station and made for a cafe with Internet access. It was time to start tracing Rae, and they sat either side of the closest available computer.

Rory had just fetched coffee and sandwiches, when his phone started to ring.

Ben continued to search the web as Rory took the call, but he knew something was wrong the moment he heard Rory's voice, and he turned to see the obvious shock on the doctor's face. Rory held out the phone.

"Ben Millar, just the man I was looking for."

It was Charles Rae.

"You've found me," Ben replied angling the phone for Rory to hear.

"I hope I haven't upset, Dr Moffat. I was just congratulating him on his daughters, such beautiful girls, he must be so proud."

Rory shook his head as though unable to accept what he was hearing.

"Let's talk about Lily," Ben replied coldly.

"She's being most helpful, and was good enough to provide the good doctor's name and details."

"I want to speak to her," Ben said.

"She's safe for now, although one of my men has taken a fancy to her, he'll be sure to look after her provided you don't do anything stupid, like contact the police."

Ben's mouth tightened, and he let himself breathe before continuing.

"I have nothing more to say to you until I know Lily is OK."

There was a brief pause on the other end of the phone, Ben listened intently then he heard a voice.

"Ben, I'm well-" It was Lily.

Rory heard her voice, and called her name, leading to raised heads from the screens around them, but the reply came from Rae, "She doing fine, now your request has been satisfied - let's move on."

"Just make sure nothing happens to her," Ben said through gritted teeth.

"Let's not be unpleasant," Rae replied.

"Yeah, people die when you get like that."

"Let's concentrate on the task at hand. Now, the decryption engine reports a message was received from my man, Brandt, in 1943, and Lily has told me it contains a new account number. I want that number."

"When Lily is released unharmed, you'll get it."

"We'll have to meet and arrange a trade."

"What's on your mind?"

"I'll send men to pick you up."

"You'll have to do better than that," Ben replied without humour.

"That was a bit obvious," Rae conceded. "We must meet in Zurich."

"Go on," Ben said.

"It's not exactly safe for you to travel. Are you happy to risk Lily on your ability to get to Zurich unmolested?"

"I'll get there," Ben replied, "but only if I agree to your plan."

"You want Lily, and I want the account number. I have to verify the number is correct and so we have no option but to meet in Zurich. We will enter the bank together, and when I have access to the vault, Lily will be freed."

"I'll have my own conditions, but when can this happen?"

"This very day of course," Rae replied.

"It will take at least three hours to get to Zurich. I can't get there until sometime after seven."

"The bank closes at five for normal customers, but vaults can be accessed up until ten. We can access it today if we have a claim of ownership accepted before nine, so I will meet you there at eight-thirty - this is not a day to be late."

"Call back on this number at eight," Ben replied.

"And if you're picked up by the police?"

"Then you'll have to rearrange your calendar as the exchange will be delayed. But I want Lily freed as soon as possible, so we'll try for tonight," Ben said, "and Rae, if Lily is harmed in any way I guarantee you will never get the number."

"And if you fail to provide it, then Lily will suffer, and that will be just the start of your troubles and those of your friend, the doctor. But you've done surprisingly well so far, let's hope your luck holds for a few hours more," Rae said before ending the call.

"Giving up my name," Rory said, "what was she thinking?"

Ben handed him the phone.

"She had no choice," Ben explained.

"Things are different now - he knows about my wife and kids."

There was nothing Ben could say, it was less than a day since they'd met, and he knew Rory wasn't easily scared, but a threat against his family was something else, and it had shaken him.

Ben clenched his fists, he felt responsible for losing Lily, he should have held onto her, he'd lost focus and lost Lily - he couldn't drop his guard again.

Rory spent the next few minutes trying to reach his wife - leaving multiple messages for urgent return call. Ben waited until he finally stopped dialling numbers.

"Rory, this is what I was worried about. I want you to go home."

"I can't" Rory replied.

"I'll get her back," Ben said.

Rory took a moment.

"My family are with friends, they'll be safe enough for now. You need help, there's no way I can walk away from this."

Ben could see Rory's mind was made up.

"We have to get to Zurich," Ben said.

"There's a train leaving in ten minutes," Rory replied pointing to the station's departure board.

Ben sat on his own while Rory bought their tickets, the station was busy enough for them to blend in with other passengers moving between platforms.

They boarded the 15:55 TGV to Zurich with a few minutes to spare and were relieved when the train glided out of Geneva exactly on time. Swiss trains, unlike their UK counterparts, kept to their timetables, and that meant they would arrive in Zurich at 19:03.

As the TGV gained speed, Ben pushed back into the modern, comfortable seat. He laid his head against the window and on any other day, would have easily slept as the vibration massaged his forehead, but rest didn't come easy, as he knew what he had to do, and he only had three hours to come up with a plan to do it.

Chapter 42

Andrew Shaw stood back as his colleagues worked around him. The operations room was quietly efficient. Everyone concentrated on their part in what had become a major incident, and if the recording from the doctor's van was to be believed, then they had stumbled upon the most astounding scientific discovery in living memory.

Dr Adams bounced about unhappily on his seat. It was unlikely he'd noticed the camera which relayed images of his every move. Shaw studied the face and wondered how deeply Adams was involved. If he had knowledge of the time travel messages then he was doing a decent job denying it, but there had been no pressure yet. The man's life was being painstakingly dissected, and the results collated on the screens around him. Adams would soon find the online world left a digital trail, and unless he had taken great care, there was little he could hide.

Shaw called over to one of the agents responsible for monitoring the surveillance.

"What's the latest on the targets?"

"They boarded a train for Zurich. We have eyes on them, sir."

Shaw heard his name and looked up to see a hand in the air belonging to a young, immaculately dressed Asian man sitting behind a laptop. Shaw recognised him, he'd worked undercover for long periods and was in this team as a bit of a break.

"Sir, We have an Echelon intercept from Dr Moffat's mobile, he's been contacted by Charles Rae, I've got the transcript here."

The Echelon system captured a range of electronic signals, such as mobile phone conversations and email messages, flagging those of interest based on key words and phrases. Shaw took the papers and scanned them quickly.

"My man, Brandt, in 1943..." Shaw read out, "Well, we have a confession, it would never stand up in court, but at least we know for sure."

He paced up and down as he read the rest of the document.

"Rae has been ruthless so far, we need to find the doctor's wife and kids and bring them into protective custody. The husband will be joining them shortly."

Shaw placed the papers back on the desk, "Is there anything else?"

"Yes, it's about Dr Adams. We ran his phone records - he made a call when the targets were in his apartment. The number dialled was to the same unregistered mobile that called the doctor's phone. It looks like Adams called Charles Rae and directed the gunmen to his apartment."

Shaw nodded and walked to a window, he took in the lake while he considered the information. Rae talked about sending messages to 1943 as if he'd done something as simple as sending an email to a friend. Rae's indifference to his actions was simply astounding as he must have known there was some risk in what he was attempting. Despite those risks, he chose to continue in the hope of making a profit. Even without the murders, his actions were dangerous and unforgivable.

It was clear Millar and his friends were caught up in the whole situation. Rae was responsible for the Edinburgh killings and now held Lily Taylor to ransom for an account number she and Millar had effectively requested almost seventy years earlier.

He ignored the absurdity of that thought and considered his next move. Everyone involved would be in Zurich later that day, and it was Shaw's job to ensure the situation was neutralised before the day's end.

Chapter 43

Red light illuminated the faces of the pilots, and if they were concerned about the operation it didn't show. The aircrew of the Halifax bomber were used to the risks they faced on raids into Germany, and Harry James supposed a delivery job over a neutral country might be seen as a good day out, even with the constant danger of enemy fighters en route. He expected a sense of tension, but the men around him seemed relaxed and simply concentrated on their dials.

Sitting in dark shadows intensified the incessant drone of the engines, which hummed and vibrated through the airframe with monotonous regularity.

The short journey from No.10 to St James's was enough time for Timmons to plan Harry's entry into Switzerland: 'You've parachuted before? Five years ago? Well, that's good enough. We'll see what can be done about some practice jumps.'

Timmons arranged the jumps, one before dark and another just after. The latter had just about broken James's leg as he braced and braced for a landing that he knew must come, but still arrived unexpectedly. On tonight's jump he hoped to fall onto snow which would reflect light and offer a softer landing, he hoped for snow, grassland - anything other than solid rock.

The aircrew sergeant leant over and shouted, "Ten minutes, repeat, ten minutes to target."

James raised his thumb in acknowledgment as the sergeant started to check his rigging. He just had to survive the jump, or more precisely - the landing. There was a small risk of trouble on the ground, but nothing to what he could have faced in occupied France. How many others had taken a similar journey to that country knowing their capture would mean torture and death?

Where did Timmons find his volunteers? They were mostly civilians with no military background - amateurs who faced the Nazis with a few weeks of basic training, a fluent second language and a cyanide pill. It took sheer guts or total madness.

James felt almost guilty his mission took him to another neutral country. There would be no searchlights and no German patrols waiting to deliver him to the Gestapo. All he should expect was a MI6 man to take him onto Zurich, or in the worse case, detention by the local militia.

The sergeant shouted out for five minutes to the drop zone, so James checked his weapons were secure. A silenced Sten machine gun and an Argentinian Ballester-Molina pistol - standard SOE kit. One final check came with the three vials of cyanide that sat in a small, padded box cradled in his outstretched hand, he wanted to throw them away as soon as possible, as if he had to die, it would be under enemy fire - he would not allow himself to be taken alive.

The plane shuddered as it banked into a turn, as she levelled out the sergeant beckoned for him to stand. James took a deep breath and shuffled over to the man.

"Right, know what you're doing then, chum?"

"Yes."

"Is that right, well I heard you've only done this a couple of times before," he said with a broad grin. "Listen, when you feel a tap on your shoulder, remember to push yourself away from the door as hard as you can, you'll clear the aircraft that way and the parachute will take care of the rest."

James nodded, the sergeant continued, "Must be important if they're sending untrained men to make this kind of jump."

"It would be better to forget this," James replied, a little more sharply than intended, but that was the nerves. Not that it mattered as the sergeant wasn't offended, he muttered something about loose lips and patted James enthusiastically on the back, before pulling the door open.

James grimaced and stepped into the door frame, He looked out into the darkness, the roar of the wind and engines were almost overpowering. He blanked his mind and waited for the count: Three-two-one and he was in the air, the sergeant shouted something after him, but it was lost in the wall of sound, he couldn't be sure, but it sounded like good luck.

Chapter 44

As Andrew Shaw walked back into the large drawing room of the splendid lakeside house, Dr Clive Adams' eyes followed his every move as the MI6 agent returned to stand before him.

"When will I be released?" The physicist demanded.

Shaw smiled.

"Fifteen years, give or take a few..."

"What the hell do you mean by that?" Adams replied suddenly on his feet. The guard took a step forward, but Shaw signalled for him to stand down.

"We know about the call from your apartment to Charles Rae," Shaw let that statement linger before continuing. "It's quite obvious you're involved in multiple murders, the question is - how deeply?"

Adams looked blank; Shaw could see his mind racing to calculate his position, whatever he knew, Shaw wanted it fast.

Shaw slapped his hand down hard on the table. The impact shattered the silence and Adams jumped back, before finding his chair and holding on to steady himself. The colour had drained from his face, exaggerating the dark swelling around his mouth.

"You're an accomplice to murder," Shaw shouted. "You called in the men who shot Ben Millar, and kidnapped Lily Taylor; two people who went to you for help... two people who trusted you."

"But-"

"Shut up," Shaw said. "When I ask you to talk, you'd better tell me everything. Lily Taylor's life may depend on it."

Shaw walked back and lent back against the marble fireplace, he waited until Adams' panic was barely concealed, his hands visibly shaking, his world turning on its head.

"Now, talk. Tell me everything..."

Shaw looked out as the helicopter skirted Lake Geneva passing close to Lausanne. It was the first time he'd raised his head during the flight, the high mountains were visible to the south. The snow-topped Mont Blanc Massif rose up from behind a colossal wall of stone, then fell to a tree line leading all the way down to the lake. There was no better way to see this country, but Rae's dossier had Shaw's full attention, and the luxury of the ride and the spectacle of the surroundings were wasted on him today.

On what he'd read so far, Shaw was glad he'd arranged protection for Rory Moffat's family. What had started as a routine precaution was now looking essential. There was ample evidence that Rae's activities in the antiquities business were suspect to say the least, and this had coincided with the recruitment of former Russian soldiers, most of whom had served in the Vmypel unit, an outfit Shaw remembered from his days on the Russian desk.

They were a special forces unit specialising in deep penetration and covert action. Its men generally spoke multiple languages, and like the SAS, they would fight behind enemy lines in wartime. After the disintegration of the Soviet Bloc, Vmypel was attached to the Militsiya, who despite the name were not a branch of the military, but part of the civilian police. Many of its officers left in protest, although some including Rae's man, Vadim Tarasov, stayed on according to the document's sources.

His phone vibrated on the empty seat next to him.

"Shaw," he answered.

"Andrew, its David Sykes, what have you uncovered?"

Shaw cleared his throat.

"What have you heard so far, sir?" Shaw replied to the head of his section.

"I've read the Millar/Rae transcripts, I know all about the time loop messages, what I need to know is what we're doing about it?"

"We have one suspect in custody and Millar is under surveillance right now. Millar is travelling to a meet with the man behind all this, Charles Rae, and when that happens, I intend on arresting everyone present and transporting them to UK territory quietly, and without delay."

"Get them into custody ASAP. Do we know where Charles Rae is?"

"No, but the transcripts tell us he's heading for Zurich to trade the girl for the account number in Millar's possession."

"Rae is known to us, he has provided useful information in the past," Sykes added.

"I'm reading his file now."

"We might be able to deal with someone like Rae. Once he knows we're involved, he'll know to follow whatever line we give him."

"He is responsible for two actual and a few attempted murders," Shaw replied, "he'll know he has to answer for that."

"This situation is unique, and it can never go before a court. If there is any truth to this new technology then it must remain top secret, and that is your overriding priority."

"Yes sir."

"This whole thing is so hard to believe, what'd you make of it?"

"I don't know what to make of it."

"Nor me, we're dragging the experts in now, but we have to treat this seriously until we're told otherwise, and more importantly, we have to keep a lid on it."

"I understand. What does that mean for Millar, Rae, and any others?" Shaw asked.

"I'm sending a RWW detachment to Zurich. They are to be used if there is any risk of this going public. There are no limits on keeping this quiet."

Sykes rang off, and Shaw knew exactly what had just been authorised. The watcher, Reid was ex-RWW, the Revolutionary Warfare Wing was better known inside MI6 as 'The Increment', a team made up of veteran SAS and SBS soldiers on loan from the UK's elite special forces. They were the military wing of MI6 and few intelligence officers had anything like their weapons or combat skills. When government ministers claimed MI6 had never carried out targeted assassinations, either past or present, they were factually correct – it was the increment's job to kill in defence of the realm. Shaw had his orders: no publicity and no holds barred to keep it that way. He knew his conscience could accommodate giving the command to wipe out Charles Rae and his men, but the others were caught up unwittingly, and he didn't yet have Sykes' detachment that allowed him to accept collateral damage quite so easily.

Shaw's eyes fell back to the dossier. The intelligence on Vadim surmised the reason he transferred to the police was simply to share in the money being made from the crime networks that filled the void in the chaos of the post-communist state.

Vadim was 23 years old when either through carelessness or betrayal he ended up in a Moscow prison for two years on corruption charges. The prison was massively overcrowded and brutal in the extreme. Vadim rebelled against it, and ended up serving three of his first six months in solitary confinement. The expectation was, as ex-police, he would be targeted by other inmates, but by the time of his release he bore the military epaulet prison tattoos on his left shoulder which marked him as a gang leader. All of his present associates, also working for Rae, were known to him from his time in the Vmypel or other ex-military men he met in prison.

Rae was linked to three deaths and the possible involvement in three more. In all cases, the victims had been involved in the antiquities trade. There was no direct evidence of Rae dealing on the periphery of the law, but then there was little to go on as his buyers were thought to be as private and secretive as their supplier.

All the victims had been severely beaten or tortured before death including a gallery owner in his fifties who was left nailed to the floor of his premises to be found by his aides and a young wife the following morning.

Ben Millar and his colleagues were in a dangerous situation, and when Adams started to talk, one statement had stayed with Shaw. According to Adams, Ben Millar and Lily Taylor escaped from an attempt to frame Millar in a fake murder-suicide. Adams used this as his excuse to explain the fear that led him to follow Rae's orders without question.

If this was a simple police matter, the evidence against Rae was beyond doubt and orders for his arrest would have been flashed across Europe, but this was nothing like a simple matter, and the world had become more complicated, the kind of complication that comes with weapons of mass destruction.

Shaw threw the report onto the opposite seat, it had made uneasy reading, he was about to have some of the world's best soldiers at his disposal, but they were dealing with tough, experienced and ruthless mercenaries - arresting those kind of men without incident would require as much luck as careful planning. Shaw was anxious to get to Zurich, anxious to take control of the operation. He would easily arrive before Millar and Moffat, and knew the whole situation along with his own future, would rest on the decisions he would make. It wouldn't be long now, Berne was to their left, and there were more mountains ahead. Shaw took a moment to savour the view, before returning to make plans.

Chapter 45

The parachute's circular dome deployed, abruptly slowing the rate of descent, Harry James's relief at the sound of canvas ruffling above him gave way to the need to pull hard against the risers and steer towards the flaming beacon far below. His vision began to adjust to the cold, pale moonlight and locked onto the vivid colour of a target, so conspicuous in the spectrum of grey that surrounded it.

His attempts to steer were clumsy but adequate, the terrain was farmland, mostly flat with a sparse covering of trees. There was none of the expected snow to cushion the landing, so he focused on a featureless spot and braced as the ground seemed to accelerate towards him. He landed well short of the beacon, but more importantly, he did so without injury.

The parachute whipped up around him as he scrambled to find some cover with his Sten gun at the ready. It was a couple of minutes before he was satisfied it was safe to gather the mountain of silk and drag it towards a stream in the dead ground between small rolling hills. The field shovel made easy work of the soft, rich soil, and he quickly buried the parachute and covered his tracks.

The next priority was to find his contact. The procedure was simple enough - they had thirty minutes to meet before both parties would break off - for James that would mean finding his own way to Zurich.

During the descent, he'd kept his eyes on the beacon until the last moment and marked its direction as lying north of a large solitary tree. He shouldered his rucksack and took a bearing before moving off. He stopped every few paces to listen out for the man he was to meet.

As he crossed a rough track, he spotted torchlight and slowly moved to cover. The light continued to bob up and down with the motion of a holder who was walking on without a care. James covered the distance between them, staying low and expecting to find a local stirred up by the beacon which still glowed on the horizon. As the outline of a man approached, James heard some muttering - spoken in English.

James stepped out, his machine gun on the target, and his torch aimed directly on the face. The man was dressed for the city, wearing a heavy overcoat over a dark suit. James barked at him in German to stand still.

The man raised his hands and spoke out, "Schlange, Schlange!"

James recognised the codeword, it translated to snake or viper, and let the torchlight fall, before stopping on a pistol in the man's hand."

"James?" He was asked.

"Put the gun on the ground," James said.

The man went down on one knee slowly, and carefully dropped the pistol as ordered.

"It's bad enough having to drive out here without getting a gun stuck in my face."

James peered into the moonlit terrain, after he was satisfied they were alone, he lowered his weapon.

"Your name?" James asked.

"Clarke, Donald Clarke. I'm attached to the consulate."

An armchair spy, Shaw thought.

"Pick up the gun, tell me why that beacon is still blazing, and then why you're staggering about with a torch like you've just returned from the village pub?"

"Sorry, but this is a bit of a rush job, best get going and try not to press our luck as the local police might just decide to turn out."

"What's the plan now?" James asked.

"We get back to my car, and I'll drive you to Zurich." Adams replied plainly.

"Lead the way," James said, "and turn off the torch - there's enough light if you let your eyes adjust."

"Don't mean to complain, but it would have been easier all-round to have put you on a plane."

"And that would have alerted every intelligence officer watching Zurich airport that a new man had arrived."

They climbed to the ridge of a hill where Clarke pointed to a car sitting on a narrow, single track.

It was a short walk, and they quickly reached the car.

"How long before we clear this road?" James asked.

"There's one way out, and it's about two miles, but we can't carry any speed, so it'll take ten minutes."

"This is a dead-end road?"

"Yes, but a very quiet one, especially in the middle of the night."

"What if the beacon attracts company?" James asked.

"Well, I have diplomatic immunity."

"When did you know you were picking me up?"

"That would have been yesterday afternoon."

"Well, that being the case, you might have lain off the whiskey I can smell on your breath," James snapped, "the beacon should have been extinguished as soon as you heard the aircraft overhead. Your torch will be visible for miles, and you now tell me there is only one way out. If we're stopped I'll shoot you myself - you're not immune from a bullet."

Clarke looked over, "If we're stopped I'll do the talking. We took the wrong turn and got lost in the dark, I'll think of something, don't worry, old boy."

"Are you fit to drive?"

"I only had a couple before I left, I'm fine."

What time will we get to Zurich?"

"Around midnight."

Clarke had been able to walk in a straight line, so hopefully he'd drive in one too - James decided to follow the man's plan for now.

"OK, let's go - you drive while I get some rest."

"As you wish," Adams replied with a patronising smile.

After leaving the minor road, James relaxed the grip on his Sten. He patted his pocket; he was still carrying the vials of poison, and knew he couldn't throw them away. There was the promise to Timmons over the secrets he could be forced to reveal. He'd treat this as enemy territory, take extreme care unlike his chauffeur, and with luck he'd hand them back to Timmons before the week's end.

Chapter 46

The twin engines of the Dauphin roared as the pilot flared the rotors slowing the helicopter to a hover. It drifted slightly before touching down on the centre of the helipad, fifteen metres from the black saloon car that sat waiting on the perimeter.

Andrew Shaw waited for the pilot to give the all clear before walking directly to the car, a privilege that came with the €6000 per hour a helicopter like this cost to hire.

The driver passed a message from Martin Reid giving the number of a room in the Hotel Schweizerhof overlooking Bahnhofplatz and the main exit from the central railway station. The team of watchers were in place.

They sped out of Zurich airport past the terminal building and on their way to the city's other key transport hub and the shortly arriving Ben Millar.

Shaw's phoned buzzed, it was Sykes' secretary, and he waited a moment to be put through to his boss.

"Andrew, we have some new developments."

"I'm listening, sir."

"The technical people have decided there is every possibility this is for real..."

"Really," Shaw replied, "they actually believe this?"

"That's their judgement, we also have strong corroborating evidence from our own archives supporting the time loop hypothesis," Sykes replied. "Our files show that there was mole hunt in 1943 for a suspected traitor with high-level access. The traitor was codenamed VIPER. An operation was ran to stop the trade in Zurich, and ordered by Churchill himself, no less."

"Do we know what the operation concerned?"

"High-level secrets were offered in return for a Russian national treasure. We've found a number of documents and are looking for more. Not all of the files are transferred to computer, so we'll have to go back to the indexes, and that'll take time, but this is top priority and the foreign secretary is calling for updates."

"Are you briefing him?"

"Oh no, come on, Shaw. I'm much too lowly for that."

Sykes had reached as high as he'd ever go in the service, but he'd never miss the opportunity to impress a senior politician given the chance.

Shaw settled back in his seat.

"The details of the mole hunt were only known to a handful of men at the time," Sykes continued. "Those involved such as the chief of staff, General Brooke, were determined to keep any security breach under wraps as they were concerned about the effect it could have had on intelligence sharing with the Americans, and just as important, whether it would cast German suspicions over the Enigma cipher machine. The only people who could have any hope of sending an Enigma message, outside the German military, would be based at Bletchley Park, and that is where the hunt started. It was considered a remote possibility that the traitor was a member of the one of the security agencies as people from that group would have had access to all the material. A decision was made to recall a MI5 agent stationed in the Irish Republic, as while he had some knowledge of Bletchley Park, he knew nothing of the work at Los Alamos. The man was particularly suitable as he could also identify German operatives involved in the trade. This agent would report directly to the joint intelligence committee headed by the prime minister or

General Brooke; no-one else was notified of the existence of VIPER, or of any arrangements to act against him. The net would be cast to cover the scientific community, in addition to intelligence staff.

VIPER's other possible profile was of an academic with access to Enigma through Bletchley, and who would have friends or acquaintances at Los Alamos. It was thought unlikely individuals would have worked on both projects, but it was investigated and found there were certainly friendships across these teams as almost all of the participants were trained at the relatively small number of elite universities in Europe and the US. It was normal for the top men to take positions in these institutions as part of their normal career progression, making new contacts on the way.

The man who fell under most suspicion was the Cambridge mathematician, Prof. John Hare, there was no real evidence, but the man lost his job and was made an outcast. He committed suicide in 1945. The hunt ended as that was seen as an admission of guilt.

It only leaves me to tell you that the operation to stop the trade was aborted. An MI5 agent failed to intercept Major Kessler in Zurich and no-one knows what became of the Amber Room," Sykes paused to take a breath, "Have you got all that, Andrew?"

"Yes, just about, sir," Shaw replied, he was reeling from the thought that Rae, Millar etc. could have sent Enigma signals that Churchill himself would have shuffled through with what could only have been rising alarm, "This possibility raises so many new questions..."

"Which won't be answered by people like us," Sykes replied. "Now, make sure you're careful with this, it looks like our last crack at this ended in failure in 1943. I do not want history repeating itself, is that clear?"

"Yes, sir," Shaw replied ending the call as his car crossed a bridge over the Limatt towards the old town.

He stowed the phone in his pocket, the call had been over a secure line and the little computer that was his mobile phone, effortlessly handled encryption light years beyond anything the warehouse-size computers of Bletchley Park, the Bombes, could have ever hoped to break.

The transcripts from the VW van disclosed Ben Millar had re-sent Rae's messages on an Enigma setting known to have been broken by the code-breakers in wartime Bletchley Park. Could the resending of Rae's messages that very day, have allowed the allies to decode them and ultimately forced Churchill to act?

If so, Millar and Taylor had put those messages in Churchill's hand, and time no longer flowed inextricably forward, it had been shattered by man's never-ending curiosity in the shape of the Large Hadron Collider.

Chapter 47

Approaching Zurich, Switzerland
Tuesday, 9 May 2017 11:50

Ben had been a tourist the last time he'd travelled on the Golden Pass line from Lausanne to Zurich. The beauty of the scenery was undiminished, but his feelings about the journey couldn't have been more different. Travelling gave you time to think, and he was thinking about a coming confrontation that was firmly stacked against them. He'd seen action many times in Iraq and Afghanistan, but this was different, he wasn't part of a small, heavily-armed patrol who watched each other's backs. He was wounded, and sitting next to a civilian who was becoming more and more withdrawn.

As the train slowed on the approach to the Zurich station, passengers gathered their belongings, and prepared to disembark. Ben glanced at Rory, who looked tense and pale.

"You OK?" Ben asked.

Rory nodded in reply.

"You sure?"

Rory looked around checking there was no-one close by.

"Where do you want me to start?"

"This is a tough situation," Ben replied.

"You can say that again. We have science altering history, murder, and the threat of more death to come. As you say, things are tough." Rory turned away to face the platform that was drawing up outside.

"We've been trapped with our thoughts for the past three hours. I know how you feel," Ben replied. "I'm trying to keep my focus on getting Lily out, that's all we can do right now."

Rory nodded dejectedly and reached up to grab his rucksack from the luggage rack. The train pulled up, and they joined the queue of passengers waiting for the doors to open. As Ben glanced out to the platform - his heart jumped - the fleeting eye contact, a meaningless exchange between passing strangers. Ben stared out impassively, pretty sure he'd given nothing away, but he had seen that face before.

Someone was waiting for them.

He followed Rory along the aisle towards the exit. Ben couldn't trust Rory's reaction so would tell him when they were out of the sight of prying eyes. Rae knew they were coming here, they'd had few options to travel here in time for the meeting, and he should have expected the main transport links to be covered.

As they stepped onto the platform, they made their way up an escalator to the station's main hall. It was a vast area, the walls topped by huge semi-circular windows looking out on the evening sky.

The station was busy, only an hour or so after the evening peak at the end of the business day. Ben directed Rory to a station cafe where travellers were expected to pay high prices for average food and the convenience of being close to their departure point.

Ben led the way and squeezed into a table with only two of its normal complement of four chairs remaining, the others having been crowded around an adjacent table by a large group of bleary-eyed backpackers.

"Nice spot," Rory observed his voice almost drowned out by the noise of the coffee machine as it steamed and gurgled its way through the endless production of caffeinated drinks.

"Don't react," Ben said as he stood and called over to the barista to add two more to the queue.

"We're being followed."

"Are you sure?" Rory replied casually stifling a yawn and looking around them.

"He's over there looking at a timetable. I've seen him before..."

Rory glanced across, "OK, I haven't, there's no possibility you're mistaken I suppose?"

"I'm sure."

"I hope I didn't sound dismissive, but I don't like the news."

"That makes two of us," Ben replied.

"It has to be Rae," Rory said.

"He's the only one who knows we're coming here," Ben agreed.

The coffees were brought to their table and Rory took a quick sip before picking up the menu.

"What do we do now?" he asked.

"I think we should move quickly," Ben replied. "Rae only has so many men, and they must be spread thin."

"Go on," Rory said.

"Put your bag in left luggage then try and slip away, I'll meet you in Hotel St Gotthard, it's on Bahnhofstrasse and is only a couple of minutes away. I've stayed there before. We can meet in the lobby bar."

"What about you?"

"If he stays where he is, I'll give you a few minutes, then go to the toilet and see if I can find a way out the back."

"If he comes after me?"

"I'll follow on, and we can both deal with him."

"Why don't we just get a taxi, and then jump on a tram, you know, shake someone off like the movies?"

"There's no time, we've got to act now," Ben replied before gulping a couple of painkillers down with a mouthful of coffee.

Rory put the menu back on the table, "I suppose we can forget about the food then?"

"Are you really hungry?"

"No, being shit-scared suppresses the appetite. I've only been really scared a few times in my life, and this is becoming one of them. Coincidently one of the last times also involved Lily."

"What happened?"

"Nothing sinister, we were several thousand feet up on a climb. I'll always remember her happily hammering in the pitons; that has to be ten years ago as I haven't used them for an age. Anyway, she overbalanced and fell fifteen feet slamming into the rock below an overhang, it took ten minutes to reach her, and even with a helmet she was out cold."

"You'll climb with her again," Ben said.

"I hope so."

Ben had no intention of making that rendezvous in the St Gotthard, he'd get a message to the hotel when he could, but it was Ben who had the account number and there was no need to risk them both. Rory's taxi and tram idea was a good one, but Ben had already decided they should separate.

"See you in the bar," Rory said as he stood and drained his cup.

"Look after yourself," Ben replied hoping that there was a single man, and when they split, he would target him.

"Can I have your phone," Ben asked.

Rory pushed half of his wad of notes across the table and then the phone.

"Just in case," Rory said.

"Thanks, and I'm sorry we've met under these circumstances," Ben said slipping the cash into his trouser pocket.

"Yeah, me too, I'll deposit the bag then find that hotel bar."

"It's to the right as you leave the station... on the main street. You can't miss it."

"See you soon," Rory said as he turned to walk away.

Ben's eyes followed him as he asked a railway worker for directions. The man glanced over at Rory but kept his position exactly as Ben hoped. Ben sipped the last of his coffee, his peripheral vision trying to catch anything out of place. There was nothing to see, but more men would be on their way.

After Rory had time to get clear, Ben left twenty francs on the order slip, got up and walked slowly to the rear of the cafe looking a bit too obviously for a toilet. The toilets were separated from the main eating area by an outer door and a corridor with facing entrances to the male and female restrooms. Ben poked his head into the gents, then the ladies, both were empty but windowless, he walked fast towards the only other door marked 'Staff Only', and through into the kitchen. It was an L-shaped space, with a long serving counter to the front. He looked around the corner and could see a chef busy reading orders that were hung up in a row towards the front of the cafe.

The back door had been left open, no doubt to provide some respite from the kitchen heat. Ben smiled, it was all too easy to slip away. He passed through the back doorway into a small yard stacked with empty boxes and crates.

He kept on moving until he was out of the cafe premises and standing in a service lane. He casually looked both ways, and could see busy streets on either end of the alley that ran under a wide railway bridge. He walked towards the station's main entrance with its fountain and tram stops at the head of the affluent Bahnhofstrasse.

As he started to move, a can rolled over the road behind him, Ben took a slow look over his shoulder to find an empty street. He was only twenty metres from the corner to the main station plaza, in moments he would merge with crowds stepping off the escalators that led to the station's underground platforms.

On reaching the corner, he took a step out of the alley, then stopped and stepped back in. His eyes widened as a bulky figure with a shaved head filled the alley only ten metres away. The man pulled up in surprise. They faced each other for a split second before Ben turned to run.

He jumped out in the path of an oncoming car causing it to swerve violently. The screech of tyres came a moment before the heavy crunch of an impact behind him.

It was another few steps before he risked a glance over his shoulder and found no-one in pursuit. A large BMW motorcycle was laid out on the road, the front of the bike was badly damaged as though it had been picked up by some giant hand and smashed down hard on its front end. The rider was on his feet, hopping back and forth in pain, he was injured, but it didn't look serious. There was a Saab saloon, its body unmarked, but it had stopped at an angle to the pavement, black tyre marks showed it had skidded to a stop under heavy braking. People stood around, looking down to the ground in front of the car, the driver was pointing at Ben speaking Swiss-German at breakneck speed.

Ben jogged back to the accident scene to check on his pursuer. As he closed he scanned around him - it wasn't the man on the platform.

"Is he OK?" He asked bending down to get a better look. No-one answered and Ben removed the injured man's iPod earphones. This was too much for the elderly Saab driver who grabbed at his shoulder babbling for him to come away. Ben pulled forward roughly and felt for a pulse on the wrist.

He couldn't find one, so grabbed the neck, hoping for a sign of life, he repositioned two fingers repeatedly, until he found an output. He slapped the man's face hard, and waited as the eyes opened slowly, coming to a focus on Ben.

"Who are you?" he asked.

There was no reply, as the man closed his eyes in obvious pain.

Ben was aware of the motorcyclist above him, "An ambulance is coming," he said.

He needed to know who this man was so checked the jacket pockets, there was a heated stream of dialogue from the Saab driver again who looked outraged as Ben plunged his hands deep in the pockets hoping for something that would identify him. The injured man pulled at Ben, who responded by moving his knee to control the arm. The driver was shouting at Ben, who couldn't understand a word, apart from

General Brooke; no-one else was notified of the existence of VIPER, or of any arrangements to act against him. The net would be cast to cover the scientific community, in addition to intelligence staff.

VIPER's other possible profile was of an academic with access to Enigma through Bletchley, and who would have friends or acquaintances at Los Alamos. It was thought unlikely individuals would have worked on both projects, but it was investigated and found there were certainly friendships across these teams as almost all of the participants were trained at the relatively small number of elite universities in Europe and the US. It was normal for the top men to take positions in these institutions as part of their normal career progression, making new contacts on the way.

The man who fell under most suspicion was the Cambridge mathematician, Prof. John Hare, there was no real evidence, but the man lost his job and was made an outcast. He committed suicide in 1945. The hunt ended as that was seen as an admission of guilt.

It only leaves me to tell you that the operation to stop the trade was aborted. An MI5 agent failed to intercept Major Kessler in Zurich and no-one knows what became of the Amber Room," Sykes paused to take a breath, "Have you got all that, Andrew?"

"Yes, just about, sir," Shaw replied, he was reeling from the thought that Rae, Millar etc. could have sent Enigma signals that Churchill himself would have shuffled through with what could only have been rising alarm, "This possibility raises so many new questions..."

"Which won't be answered by people like us," Sykes replied. "Now, make sure you're careful with this, it looks like our last crack at this ended in failure in 1943. I do not want history repeating itself, is that clear?"

"Yes, sir," Shaw replied ending the call as his car crossed a bridge over the Limatt towards the old town.

He stowed the phone in his pocket, the call had been over a secure line and the little computer that was his mobile phone, effortlessly handled encryption light years beyond anything the warehouse-size computers of Bletchley Park, the Bombes, could have ever hoped to break.

The transcripts from the VW van disclosed Ben Millar had re-sent Rae's messages on an Enigma setting known to have been broken by the code-breakers in wartime Bletchley Park. Could the resending of Rae's messages that very day, have allowed the allies to decode them and ultimately forced Churchill to act?

If so, Millar and Taylor had put those messages in Churchill's hand, and time no longer flowed inextricably forward, it had been shattered by man's never-ending curiosity in the shape of the Large Hadron Collider.

Chapter 47

Approaching Zurich, Switzerland
Tuesday, 9 May 2017 11:50

Ben had been a tourist the last time he'd travelled on the Golden Pass line from Lausanne to Zurich. The beauty of the scenery was undiminished, but his feelings about the journey couldn't have been more different. Travelling gave you time to think, and he was thinking about a coming confrontation that was firmly stacked against them. He'd seen action many times in Iraq and Afghanistan, but this was different, he wasn't part of a small, heavily-armed patrol who watched each other's backs. He was wounded, and sitting next to a civilian who was becoming more and more withdrawn.

As the train slowed on the approach to the Zurich station, passengers gathered their belongings, and prepared to disembark. Ben glanced at Rory, who looked tense and pale.

"You OK?" Ben asked.

Rory nodded in reply.

"You sure?"

Rory looked around checking there was no-one close by.

"Where do you want me to start?"

"This is a tough situation," Ben replied.

"You can say that again. We have science altering history, murder, and the threat of more death to come. As you say, things are tough." Rory turned away to face the platform that was drawing up outside.

"We've been trapped with our thoughts for the past three hours. I know how you feel," Ben replied. "I'm trying to keep my focus on getting Lily out, that's all we can do right now."

Rory nodded dejectedly and reached up to grab his rucksack from the luggage rack. The train pulled up, and they joined the queue of passengers waiting for the doors to open. As Ben glanced out to the platform - his heart jumped - the fleeting eye contact, a meaningless exchange between passing strangers. Ben stared out impassively, pretty sure he'd given nothing away, but he had seen that face before.

Someone was waiting for them.

He followed Rory along the aisle towards the exit. Ben couldn't trust Rory's reaction so would tell him when they were out of the sight of prying eyes. Rae knew they were coming here, they'd had few options to travel here in time for the meeting, and he should have expected the main transport links to be covered.

As they stepped onto the platform, they made their way up an escalator to the station's main hall. It was a vast area, the walls topped by huge semi-circular windows looking out on the evening sky.

The station was busy, only an hour or so after the evening peak at the end of the business day. Ben directed Rory to a station cafe where travellers were expected to pay high prices for average food and the convenience of being close to their departure point.

Ben led the way and squeezed into a table with only two of its normal complement of four chairs remaining, the others having been crowded around an adjacent table by a large group of bleary-eyed backpackers.

"Nice spot," Rory observed his voice almost drowned out by the noise of the coffee machine as it steamed and gurgled its way through the endless production of caffeinated drinks.

"Don't react," Ben said as he stood and called over to the barista to add two more to the queue.

"We're being followed."

"Are you sure?" Rory replied casually stifling a yawn and looking around them.

"He's over there looking at a timetable. I've seen him before..."

the occasional 'Police'. People were looking out for the cops, it was a busy area, and they would be close. There was nothing in the pockets, no papers of any kind, Ben felt inside the jacket and momentarily froze - he slowly pulled a pistol from an under-arm holster.

There was a gasp as someone saw the gun which Ben quickly stuffed into his jacket pocket. He became aware of the silence as people stepped away from him, he knelt and picked up the earpiece, and following the wire, removed what looked like a small radio, it was time to go.

An ambulance approached, lights flashing, he turned to sprint away. People shouted after him, but no-one followed. The police would soon have his description and he had to get out of the area fast. As he rounded the next corner he slowed to a walk, and breathed deeply to repay the oxygen debt. It was time to find somewhere to hide up and contact Rory, if he wasn't already taken.

He flagged a taxi and asked to be taken to Zurichhorn - the popular park on the east bank of the lake. Once they were moving he put on the earphones and fumbled with the radio's switches to hear nothing but a static hiss.

The taxi pulled in on Bellvuestrasse, next to a car park, which was busy with walkers and joggers. Ben handed over another twenty francs before walking along a wide path that led down towards the casino. Ben looked for some cover in the park's trees and bushes to make a call to the St Gotthard hotel. The radio and headphones were dropped into a litter bin, and he was quickly out of sight of the road.

Chapter 48

Zurich, Switzerland
Tuesday, 23 February 1943 0850

The legal offices of Weider and Unster were situated near the Bourse on Bleicherweg. Donald Clarke had taken a suite in a first-rate hotel situated directly opposite the practice across a wide, triangular plaza.

Harry James followed Clarke through the hotel lobby which opened out impressively on either side of a smooth revolving door. On the left was the reception desk of panelled wood and attentive staff.

Cigarette smoke filtered out from a lounge filled with sumptuous armchairs, ornate wall panels, and attendants ready to jump at the wave of a hand. The clientele sheltered from the global conflict in luxury and James' appearance was of another rich man making his way, and his money, in a neutral state surrounded by the madness of war.

Clarke collected the keys to the suite, before hurrying James upstairs to be introduced to the other members of the team. James shook each hand in turn, trying to remember the names, but knowing they would stick soon enough over their days together waiting to intercept the Amber Room. James pulled a heavy curtain aside and looked out of bay windows across the plaza. If there was any glamour in intelligence work, it wasn't to be found here, but the room was very comfortable and that was something, it certainly beat lying in a mud-filled Irish bog.

It had just turned 0900, and the room was thick with cigarette smoke as the men took it in turns to watch the newly opened offices. James settled down in a comfortable leather chair and found a copy of John Buchan's The Thirty-Nine Steps; a book that had regained popularity after Robert Donat's film of the same name was released shortly before the war.

The MI6 men would call him forward to check each new arrival, and while the agents would come and go after short shifts - Harry would be there all day, every day, as the only man who could positively identify Peter Kessler.

James felt the thickness of the book, he would have to ration it, a half-hour a day of the small, dense print should see it last a week. He joined the others at the window and scanned the passing faces intently. He didn't have the war he wanted, but he had his duty, and there'd be many an infantry soldier happy to trade their place in the coming battles for an office hour's vigil in a luxury hotel. James put his disappointment to one side, frontline combat was only one facet of war, and for the moment finding Kessler was as important as the taking of any beach or bridgehead when the push back into Europe finally came.

Two days passed without incident. They had settled into a routine and found the law office accommodated around ten appointments each day. Visitors were photographed and reports compiled. James carefully inspected each man through binoculars, but the latest ULTRA intelligence reported the Amber Room was still in Germany, and so Kessler wasn't expected quite yet. James felt confident they'd be ready when Kessler showed himself, having had four days to practice the routine and get to know the ground.

James glanced across at Donald Clarke who spent his breaks trying to relieve the others of spare change on an improvised card table. He also took a drink around lunch and towards the end of the afternoon. James had already spoken to him about that. The whiskey bottle was no longer in the centre of the table, but a sour smell clung to Clarke, as it did to the dedicated alcoholic.

James played a hand or two which allowed him to keep an eye on Clarke and pass a bit of time. It had just struck one o'clock when Clarke donned his hat and raincoat; the lawyer's office closed for an hour from one, but the partners invariably had lunch with favoured clients in one of a number of restaurants close by.

James, chaperoned by Clarke, would follow on and get a look at anyone they met. He was glad of the daily walk as his ULTRA knowledge confined him to the hotel, and if he had to go out, he would always do so armed with an escort.

Clarke was waiting in the lobby, and they walked out onto the Bleicherweg which was reminiscent of Mayfair's affluent terraced streets and town houses. The contrast between London and neutral cities such as Zurich and Dublin was the apparent normality of everyday life - at night lights shone brightly from windows while the blitz had left London in darkness with the smart houses of the rich boarded up and vacant while the poor had little choice but to take their chances among what little they owned. All of Europe lived under the shadow of war, but here, at least on the surface, people went about their lives without a sense of constant concern for themselves or their loved ones.

If Germany obtained the atomic bomb, and used it to win the war, it would simply be a matter of time until the neutral countries were forced to bow, no city in the world would escape Nazi domination.

Clarke had received the location of the lawyer's lunch engagement on the lobby phone before indicating it was time to leave. James turned onto the main boulevard, the rain had eased, so he walked casually, glancing into the lawyer's offices as he passed. The firm's name was displayed on a small plaque that could be easily missed; a simple brass plate with both partner's names and a year indicating the firm was approaching its fortieth year.

The lower window panes were opaque,and sat in well-cared for frames adorned with highly polished brass fittings. James was tall enough to see over into the interior of a large room with a young, homely secretary shuffling through boxes of papers. There were papers everywhere. Most were arranged neatly on a large oak table, each one tied with a coloured ribbon. Others were piled high in bookcases that circled the room. The decor was dull, expensively dull. There was no pretence here, high-class lawyers providing professional services at a price. James wondered if VIPER had been one of their lunch guests in the recent past. It would have been a mistake if he had left any knowledge of his identity as the time would come when one side or the other would press the partners hard to name their client.

As the fifth day came to a close, with nothing to show but a procession of elderly Zurichers attending to their legal matters, James had resigned himself to another night with the BBC World service when he was called to the window once more. A car pulled up outside the target building, and two men stepped out. The smaller and stockier of the two lent forward to say something to the driver who then drove off. A tall, thin man in his thirties causally glanced up and down the street before striding into the office.

"It's Kessler," James said immediately. "He's here."

Chapter 49

Zurich, Switzerland
Tuesday, 9 May 2017 12:01

Andrew Shaw looked out in disbelief from the first floor window down onto the mass of people crowding Bahnhofstrasse. One group of tourists were asking a passerby to take photos with a SLR camera. Shaw turned to Martin Reid then shook his head before speaking, "Run that past me again..."

Reid repeated the explanation, Shaw knew he wouldn't make excuses, but this was bad.

"We were covering all exits from the station. The targets separated and Millar tried to slip out on the west side, one of our men was in place and picked him up."

"I thought we had our best men on this?"

"We have..."

"Then how were they spotted?"

"Millar is an ex-bootneck, he must have seen something, and ordered them to spilt. No idea how he ended up face-to-face with our man."

Shaw glanced outside to watch the tourists gawping in the glow of expensive shop windows as the last of the evening's commuters hurried past.

"And then our man gave chase and got run over... Why didn't he just break off?"

"He had to make a split-second decision, and he made the right one. I told him not to lose Millar, your orders were to arrest them..."

"Have you heard anything from the hospital, do I know this guy?"

"I don't think so, but he's a good man. A motorbike fractured his left arm, but the real problem was he suffered a heart attack. Doctors are saying it's likely to have been caused by the impact to his chest when the bike hit him – they think he may have an undetected heart defect, but he's an ex-para - so that sounds unlikely to me, but you never know."

"Millar took the gun?" Shaw asked.

"Yes, and the comms kit. He left the holster, but our people got there in time to cut it off it before he was loaded onto the ambulance."

"So our man is clean?"

"Witnesses saw the gun, but he'll deny all knowledge."

"If there's no direct proof then it doesn't matter what the Swiss suspect. That's the only good thing about this. What was he carrying?"

"A Glock 23, untraceable."

"What's happening with him now, does he need anything?"

"The doctors want to observe him for a day or so, and he'll be transferred to a private hospital after that. He's able to talk, but he'll stick to his cover. The consulate is sending someone over, there's no rush because as far as UK government's concerned he's just a management consultant who's had a bit of a bash."

"Where's Dr Moffat?"

"Sitting in a hotel bar, he made his way there after a bit of a detour, I assume he's waiting for Millar."

Shaw stood and fetched his jacket.

"This has gone far enough, I'll bring him in - we need to find Millar now."

"You might want to talk to Sykes about that - he's been in touch."

Shaw stopped and faced Reid.

"What do I need to know?"

"He asked to be informed directly of any events regarding Millar as you'd be out of the loop while travelling."

"Go on..." Shaw said.

"I reported when Millar skipped. Sykes considers Millar and his friends to be a problem."

"Does he have a solution?"

"The increment team are to dispose of them."

Shaw knew this would be a considered response, but he'd expected it to be targeted at Rae. Reid wasn't fazed by the order; after all, he'd been one of the 'state assassins' the IRA learnt to fear in the 1980s. Shaw found his phone and looked up Sykes' number.

"That's the same plan as the man who started all this, only this time with even less chance of success. When will the increment take action?"

"As soon as Millar meets with the doctor and the girl. Once they're together, Millar is to be framed for their murders."

Shaw held the ex-soldier's eye.

"This is a mistake and I'm going to stop it. Will you let me know of any other developments?"

"You've been involved in the distasteful stuff before..."

"This is unnecessary, and it's crazy to do this here. Making Rae disappear is fine, he has enemies, and it won't be a massive shock to anyone that matters, and he's got it coming, but to dispose of these people, and then try to frame one of them just won't work."

"Keep your phone on," Reid said as he got up and walked to the door.

Shaw took the mobile from his pocket and clicked the dial button.

"Andrew," Sykes answered, "any news?"

"I just got here. I know how the targets are to be dealt with. Can we talk about it?"

"There's nothing to say," Sykes replied. "Charles Rae came up with the plan and tried to execute it in Scotland. It would have been better if he'd succeeded."

"And where does that leave Rae?"

"We'll have to bring him in. He's the driving force behind all of this, and frankly we need what's in his head."

"And his men?"

"Them too."

"What about Millar and friends, surely we could make them see things our way?"

"They simply can't be trusted. I know this is difficult, but Rae's people know what happens in the big, bad world, and people like that can be relied on. They know the consequences. The others will talk to the media the first chance they get, and we can't allow it. Millar carries the can and that ties things off nicely."

Shaw took a deep breath, "Sir, this is too risky. If it ever got out that we took out a doctor, an ex-serviceman and a female academic, we'd be finished."

"Are you losing you nerve, Shaw? The real risk is the world finding out about the time loop. We have to accept this sort of thing when the secrets we're protecting are this important. Now can I count on you to do your job?"

"Yes sir," Shaw replied trying to keep any reluctance from his voice.

Chapter 50

Ben sat on a secluded bench close to the water's edge. The light was fading and the few people still left in the park stuck to the lighted pathways. He turned Rory's phone on and checked the battery. It was a quarter full - more than enough for the calls he needed to make.

As the phone made a connection to the roaming network, he pressed it to his ear and watched as a large sailing boat slowly glided past on the shimmering waters of Lake Zurich, its hull reflecting the city lights in the darkness. He looked up the number of the Hotel St Gotthard using the web browser on Rory's smartphone and dialled the number.

"Hello, can you put me through to the lobby bar? I want to speak to a Dr Rory Moffat."

"One moment, sir," a receptionist replied.

Ben massaged his injured shoulder, checking to see where he most felt pain.

A male voice came on the line, "Sir, I have Dr Moffat here, I will transfer you now."

Ben was barely able to say thanks before he heard Rory's voice.

"Ben?"

"You OK?" Ben asked.

"Yes, where are you?"

"It doesn't matter, now listen - we were being followed - I got away from my tail, but there's a good chance they'll have someone on you."

"I haven't seen anyone."

"You're not meant to. I literally ran into the guy, and he wasn't the one I recognised in the station. I want you to leave the country and go to your family. Call a cab to the airport now, and watch your back all the way."

"What about Lily?"

"I've got a plan to get her out. I'll get her to contact you as soon as she can."

"Ben, get serious, I know you're an ex-soldier, but what plans can you possibly have to deal with these people? You need help."

"Rory, I've got this covered. Whatever happens, you'll be able to tell the police everything. Just do as I say, I've got to go."

Ben hung up, he just hoped Rory made it back to the UK without incident.

Ben scrolled down to the last incoming call belonging to Rae. He would have to make contact at some point, but that bastard could wait, and he'd already know Ben was in town. He switched the phone off and turned his attention to his jacket pocket. A quick look both ways confirmed he was well-hidden. He pulled the gun out and laid it on his lap, the black surface shone where it picked up light. There was a faint smell of oil, and the gun was clean and dry. Ben angled it to see 23 stamped on the casing along with the country of manufacture: Austria, a Glock 23, whoever the previous owner had been, his gun wasn't far from home. The British Army were using the highly rated Glocks to replace the Browning pistols he was accustomed to. He hit the release, and freed the oversized 15 round magazine. He turned the gun so the grip was facing up, and pulled the slide back to let the chambered round fall into his palm. He released the slide catch, and aimed the weapon out across the lake. His shoulder ached, but he was satisfied the gun was in good order, and he could use it. He reloaded, chambered a round, and stuffed the Glock in his jacket, then started walking through the trees towards the city centre. He had over an hour before his meeting with Rae at eight-thirty. That was all the time he had left to stack the odds in his favour, and patting the arm that had taken the bullet for luck, he thought he might just have the plan to do so.

Chapter 51

Zurich, Switzerland
Thursday, 25 February 1943 12:58

Donald Clarke and Harry James watched from the hotel room as the MI6 men moved into position to tail Kessler.

Clarke turned to James, "Bloody typical. You can spend weeks in some flea-ridden shit house waiting for something to happen, as soon as it's a five-star hotel, the bastard turns up earlier than expected."

James smiled, Clarke really did look injured at having his comfortable suite taken from him so soon. Clarke dropped his hat on the floor, and needed a couple of steps to steady himself as he scooped it up with both hands.

"Another heavy night?" James asked.

"All in the line of duty. I was keeping an eye on the opposition at the casino, looking for new faces, your man Kessler wasn't one of them though."

James flirted with the idea of joining the chase, but he was fully conscious of the orders to avoid anything that risked his capture.

"You better get going then," James said as Clarke prepared to leave him in his gilded cage. The MI6 man needed no extra prompting and left to join the others.

James looked down on Clarke's car sitting outside the hotel, exhaust fumes billowing, ready to follow Peter Kessler. James waited for one last glimpse of Kessler before writing up his report and waiting for the order to return home. Maybe with this job behind him, he'd get his wish to serve in a uniform once more.

Kessler appeared twenty-five minutes after he had entered No.23 Bleicherweg. He paused briefly to pull up his collar against the rain, and waited for his larger colleague to join him. They walked off at a pace looking around at every car as through trying to spot a taxi. Holding the cigarette in the corner of his mouth, James struck a match as his countrymen started to move. Kessler was at the centre of a box, with men to his front and rear, and he would find it difficult to 'break out' and lose his watchers.

James decided to allow himself a walk to Lake Zurich and gaze out upon the clear water and the surrounding mountains before he returned to a bomb-scarred London. As he opened the window to let the room breathe, he found three empty whiskey bottles behind the curtain. James shouldn't have been surprised in a service that was full of drunks. The cigarette dropped from his mouth as he glanced back out of the window. Kessler was walking past the hotel heading in the opposite direction. Where were the MI6 agents? Was Kessler alone?

The staircase flashed by as he pounded recklessly down the steps, taking three or four at a time. James could feel the weight of the pistol in his suit jacket as he narrowly avoided tripping over the raincoat in his hands.

He slowed, panting for air, entering the lobby and walking quickly towards an exit and the street outside. How on earth could Clarke let this happen? A sideways glance stopped him dead. Kessler was being directed to a telephone booth on the other side of the room. James turned back to the stairs, hoping he hadn't been seen.

He took the time to put his raincoat on before heading across the hotel lobby, then outside to look for a cab. He was taking a risk as Kessler could duck out through the rear of the building, but it was riskier trying to follow him closely as he had already shown he could evade a team of men and would surely pick up a single man - especially one he'd faced across the ring, even if it was in the distant past.

There were a number of taxis parked up close to the hotel, James only spoke a few words of German, so tried French as he needed someone to understand his instructions fully. The second driver he spoke to nodded vigorously, and James slid into the cab.

James was gambling everything that Kessler was calling for a car to pick him up, so he had his driver reverse back from the hotel ready to follow when it hopefully arrived. He passed the driver a wad of francs which was easily two day's pay and promised the same again when he was dropped off. They waited for Kessler to appear, or for any sign of the British agents. James could only wonder how he'd lost them.

A long, black Mercedes glided to a halt and was met by the concierge who held the rear door open for the oncoming Kessler. He tipped the man and the car pulled away.

The cab was already moving, following on a few cars behind. James was impressed with his driver, the man drove carefully, keeping the Mercedes in sight. Only once did he ask him to pull back fearful of Kessler's counter-surveillance skills. They followed the Mercedes onto Seestrasse heading south-east out of the city on the lakeside road. They were forced to fall back as the traffic thinned, and they passed affluent residential villas which faced the lake across the wide boulevard.

They had barely covered five miles before the Mercedes turned into a private drive and James urged the driver to go straight on and to drop him around the next bend. Kessler's destination was a large mansion set far back on the right, away from the water's edge.

James could see movement from the tall upper windows, and a sentry patrolling the courtyard as the Mercedes parked up beside two large trucks before the driveway passed out of view.

He instructed the cabbie to continue on and stop at the entrance to a lakeside park and marina. The driver was paid in full with a bonus to deliver a note to the Grand Hotel for Clarke.

The park was busy with families strolling through the grounds, and the occasional cyclist touring the lake. James tracked back along the boulevard to the top of the private drive to see the mansion more clearly through the hedging and shrubbery of its grounds.

He continued past the gothic stone gateposts and found there was no way to approach the house from the roadside unseen. As he reached the boundary with the next property, James looked both ways then pulled himself up and over the six foot wall into a thin strip of woodland that screened the house from its neighbours. He crawled into the middle of large rhododendron bush, the sound of breaking branches loud in his ears as waited for a signal he'd been heard or seen.

He let a full minute pass before inching forward, becoming acutely aware of the information he could be forced to reveal. He checked for the cyanide vials and felt the weight of the gun in his hand. Should he remain in this fairly safe position until the cavalry arrived? Donald Clarke would move quickly when he received the note, but Kessler could move at any time and being followed earlier may have spooked him. He might have viewed it as business-as-usual in a neutral city where spies kept a close eye on the other side, but it would have reminded Kessler he faced hostile forces here, and it would be wise to conclude his business as soon as possible.

The gardens provided cover right down to the rear of the mansion, and so James felt confident enough to make his way carefully down to an old stable block built along the rear boundary wall. The car was parked to his left alongside two large unmarked military-style trucks. A moment passed before the sentry drifted into view, he wasn't patrolling anywhere other than the area around the vehicles, and that could only mean they contained something worth guarding - was the Amber Room 25 yards away?

James had his chance for real action. If he could destroy the Amber Room, any deal with VIPER would be off - possibly for good. James could succeed by destroying the trucks and their contents, but he would need to be sure the Amber Room was present, and that put the sentry in his way.

He'd left the gun's silencer behind, and without a commando knife, he'd have to improvise. Loosening his belt, he looped the thin strap around each hand until he had a tight grip on the ends. James muttered a short prayer and then moved forward keeping the sentry out of sight behind the trucks.

His footsteps crunched softly on gravel, echoing in his ears, as he slowly approached the closest truck. There was a door from the house to the stables facing him, and so he circled around to the offside for cover. He pulled the belt tighter, the sentry was still 20 paces away - if he was detected more than a split-second before his belt crushed the man's windpipe, he'd be gunned down. He willed the sentry to come closer, but couldn't delay for long as every second risked the arrival of the man's comrades. The stone-chipped driveway shimmered in the sunlight, the rain having washed off the dust, there could be no silent approach and James fought against the urge to rush the man. Suddenly he froze at the sound of voices, the sharp bark of a German officer had the sentry running, and it was to open the doors of the truck. James fell to the ground and rolled underneath a heavy axle as men climbed into the cabs of both vehicles. He waited until the feet disappeared and everyone had climbed on board before emerging at the rear and climbing over the tailgate as powerful diesel engines burst into life. James just had time to steady himself before the truck started to reverse down to the road. He gripped the strapping that held a number of wooden crates steady in the load bay. The crates came in different sizes, but the volume was mostly made up by the width and height as none had a depth of more than a foot. They were perfect for carrying panels. James found a toolbox tied down by leather straps and fumbled inside until he found a large screwdriver. He inspected the crates more carefully, each one had a number and a ticket stapled to its side. James could make little of the ticket, other than this one was section four of a total of 18. A quick count revealed the need for two trucks as there were only eight large pieces here. James found a crate that was damaged at a corner and carefully levered it open. Removing a handful of tightly packed straw revealed some sacking and yet more packing material. The screwdriver ripped through to the cargo which sparkled yellow/orange when exposed to light. He ran his hand over the surface, the rich colour gave it warmth, but it was cold and smooth as marble. Intricate patterns were inlaid in the amber, adding to the decoration, and James felt for the rough edges of precious stones, but could find none within reach.

Would it be enough to destroy the cargo of this truck? Surely one half of the Amber Room was worthless to VIPER? His eyes fell on metal ammunition boxes strapped to the floor. He opened the clasp to find it full of 9mm shells. A smaller case was marked with an army stamp, he opened it, revealing German Model 24 stick grenades. The detonators would be packed separately as they required inserting prior to use. He searched the boxes and found the fuses in sacking close by. The grenades had a fragmentation sleeve designed to send deadly shards of shrapnel over a wide area. They would need to be removed as while they were devastating to any soft tissue in range of the blast, there was no guarantee they would do any damage to the contents of well-packed wooden crates. James would have to consider how best to use them and fast as they were slowing for the heavier traffic - they were heading back into Zurich, and he guessed they would only move the Amber Room for one reason – they were making a delivery.

Chapter 52

Andrew Shaw walked briskly past the stone lions and under the assorted national flags that decorated the entrance to the Hotel St Gotthard. He quickly followed the red carpet up the handful of stairs into the main lobby.

The lobby bar was to his right, and he ignored the MI6 agent who was comfortably seated in a soft chair, quietly reading a German print newspaper. Dr Rory Moffat was seated at the bar, and he glanced blankly at Shaw before returning to his coffee cup.

Millar had used the doctor's mobile to call the hotel, but he hadn't said anything to narrow down his location, and he'd immediately turned the phone off on ending the call. The man would make a decent spook.

Shaw took the stool next to the doctor who drained his cup, and shuffled in his seat.

"Can I offer you another, Dr Moffat?" Shaw asked.

The barman, having overheard, approached to take the order.

"Nothing for me..." Rory replied. "I'm sorry, but I can't seem to place you?"

Shaw ordered a diet coke and asked the barman to serve them at a side table.

"Please join me, it's much more comfortable over there, and we have a mutual friend in Ben Millar."

Shaw watched Rory closely as he followed him over to the table indicated.

"I need your help," Shaw said sitting down.

"And you are?" Rory asked.

"I work for the British government."

"Police?"

"I work for the security services, my name is Andrew Shaw," he said holding out his hand, which Rory shook cautiously. Shaw noted the man's strength, and decided he could be a handful if he knew how to use it.

"I would like to find the last person to shake your hand about 200 metres from here, less than fifteen minutes ago."

"Who are you talking about?"

"Our friend, Ben Millar - the man you have smuggled past border controls in three countries. The man who absconded from a murder scene in Edinburgh last night and the man who has left a trail of dead bodies in his-"

"Ben's no murderer, any fool would see that," Rory snapped.

"I'm here to help, Doctor. I wish to find Ben and take you both into protective custody. The same protection currently enjoyed by your wife and children in London."

"My wife and kids are in Reading..."

"I had them transferred to London. All precautions are being taken for their safety."

Shaw could see the anguish on the doctor's face.

"Why should I believe you?" Rory asked.

"I can let you call your wife. She's being watched over by the police at a safe house... try not to look so worried, your wife and children are as safe as the Royal family."

"I need to see them."

"That will happen, but I need your help with Ben Millar now."

"I've no idea where he is," Rory replied sitting back as the barman delivered Shaw's drink.

"He advised you to go home."

"If you have us bugged then you'll know just as much as I do," Rory replied.

"Are you are aware of the magnitude of what you're involved in?"

"Are you? How much do you know?"

"We know about the time loop, we recorded some of the conversations in your van."

"When?"

"We've trailed you all over Europe. Once we realised Millar and Taylor had been in the Western Highlands, and her local doctor friend had suddenly decided to drive off to the continent on a ticket bought the same night. It was a reasonable guess they were with you."

"How long have you followed us?"

"From The moment you entered France."

"You saw the shooting... the kidnap, and you did nothing?"

"My men fired shots to give Millar and Taylor time to get away."

"Not quite enough time."

"Those agents may have saved their lives, but we have to find Millar as Charles Rae will surely kill them when he gets what he wants."

"Ben knows that, he just wants Lily, he's smart enough to figure something out," Rory said.

"Millar's military training might help, but however smart he is, it won't be enough. Are you sure all he wants is the girl?"

"He's managed to give your men the slip, so I wouldn't underestimate him."

"Did you know he has a gun?"

Rory faltered, "No."

"He took it off one of my men, what's to stop him going after Rae - his brother was murdered, an attempt was made on his own life and Lily's too, how do you know he won't want to take revenge? Do you really know him at all?"

"He just wants an end to all this, and to have Lily safe."

"Whatever his motives, Rae is surrounded by mercenaries. They are all experienced soldiers, and much of that experience is outside the Geneva Convention. However good he was, and his record says he was good, he's injured, outnumbered, and they will take his gun and kill them both. We must get to him first. Will you help me find him?"

"I understand what you're saying. If I tell you what I know, what happens next?"

"You will be taken back to your family in the UK, be debriefed, and we will arrest Charles Rae. You don't have a choice. Ben Millar will not survive a meeting with Rae, and the girl is only alive as bait. Rae is not aware of our involvement and is trying to tie up loose ends. For him to stay in the clear, he can't let any of you survive. "

"Ben has something they need-"

"Then they will torture it out of him, or make him watch as they torture Lily. However strong you think he is, they will break him."

Shaw waited for a reply, the doctor was thinking hard, the tension written on his face. However tough the medic's day job was, he wasn't prepared for anything like this.

"We're running out of time, Doctor, where can I find Millar?"

"He's to phone Rae later," Rory said quickly, "he's to meet him at the Commercial Bank on Bahnhofstrasse. Ben has an account number for a vault there."

"To claim the missing Amber Room," Shaw said, "and to solve a seventy-year old mystery..."

"What mystery?"

"The identity of a traitor," Shaw replied.

Shaw waited as the doctor spun his wedding ring around his finger.

"Are you feeling OK?"

Rory nodded, "I can't believe any of this, but if the Amber Room is in that vault-"

"Then the world will have changed forever," Shaw said quietly, "but before we concern ourselves with that, let's worry about Ben and Lily."

"Go on?"

"I want you to go and tell him that I know he's not responsible for any of the killings or events of the past 24 hours. My goal is to arrest Rae and return him to the UK."

"What can I do?"

"As Millar has a gun, and I don't want anyone else harmed, I want you to go and tell him that as soon as Lily arrives with Rae, my men will move in, and he is not to react to them."

"I really don't have any choice, do I?"

"Not if you want him to live, but if you do this, he'll know he's not alone. If he pulls that gun on Rae's men or my team, he's a dead man..."

Rory let his hands fall to his sides.

"I hope you know what you're doing," he replied.

"Charles Rae won't see us coming, we'll get you all out of there."

"When do I start?"

"When we locate Millar, I'll ask you to take a walk down Bahnhofstrasse. You'll contact him and wait for Lily Taylor to appear. After that, get your head down and leave the rest to some of the finest soldiers in the world."

Chapter 53

Zurich, Switzerland
Tuesday, 9 May 2017 12:29

Ben checked his watch for the tenth time in as many minutes. He'd stood at the tram stop for quarter of an hour, waiting as locals jostled to board the trams and no-one seemed to notice as he held back watching the entrance to the bank. With just over an hour to go before his meeting with Rae, he was on his own - all he had was a plan that gave Lily and him a chance to walk away with their lives.

A trip to the shops with Rory's money had left him looking presentable, the bruises and stubble marginally offset by the clean white shirt, the dark blue travel suit, and new shoes.

The waiting had left him feeling cold, his hands were trembling, and he rocked back and forward to generate some heat.

The time had come, if there were lookouts outside the bank, he'd failed to spot them. His decision was made and tightly gripping the pistol in his jacket pocket, he made directly for the entrance, not sure whether the spasmodic shakes he was trying to control were nerves or his plummeting core temperature.

The usual mixture of locals and tourists stood between him and his destination. Customers were drifting in and out of the famous street's fashionable restaurants and beer halls, and no-one paid any attention as he walked through the crowd.

Ben put one foot in front of the other, and kept his thoughts on Lily who had no-one else coming for her. The bank's neighbour was a fabulous jewellery store where his annual salary could easily be spent on a single, small purchase. He window shopped for a moment, as he took in the bank's cameras and security guards. Would he be searched on entry? Would they need an overt search to know he was carrying a gun? The security systems had to be state of the art, and while the Glock felt good, pressed tight against his lower back, he stopped momentarily, forcing himself to place the gun in a litter bin, pushing it all the way to the bottom of the refuse.

Automatic doors slid silently open as he climbed the three steps to the bank entrance. Two security men in dark suits, much more expensive than his own, looked on impassively as he crossed to a modern reception desk, a glass island, in the large empty hall. The atmosphere was sterile, intimidating and designed to let you know whether you belonged.

One of the two bank clerks, or huissiers, looked up from the desk. Like the guards he was immaculately dressed, and looked slightly concerned, wondering if someone who looked to have been in a fistfight, could be a client of his bank.

Ben smiled, however good so many of the clients would look on the outside,and however many expensive suits and watches they wore, a good number would be criminals of the worst kind.

"Can I help you, sir?" The man said first in German then repeated quickly in English when there was no immediate reply.

"I wish to claim an account here?" Ben stated.

"You have an appointment, sir?"

"I'm afraid not, this matter has come about unexpectedly."

"If the account holder has passed away and you are a beneficiary, you will require the appropriate documentation-"

"I'm told the account has its own instructions in these circumstances. Unfortunately, I can only spend a short time in Zurich and need this matter resolved this evening," Ben said. "Is that possible?"

The man gave a tight lipped smile, "If you could give me the account number I will make an enquiry."

Ben slowly repeated the number and watched it noted down.

"There is a waiting room, just over there," the huissier said pointing over Ben's left shoulder. "Please make yourself comfortable, Mr...?"

"Millar, my name's Ben Millar."

One of the security men opened a door for him, and Ben entered a darkened room which gradually lit up as his presence activated wall lights and a large candelabra at the centre of an elaborate baroque ceiling.

The first thing Ben noticed was the smell of leather from the numerous chairs and sofas. A highly polished side table was set out with bottles of water, fruit, and magazines from around the world. Ben fumbled in his pockets for Rae's contact number, whatever happened with the account it would be needed for what followed. He poured a glass of water and drained it, then took a single bite out of an apple, before tossing the remainder into a bin.

Five minutes passed, the large wall clock announcing each second with a movement easily heard above the ambient noise. Ben waited, controlling his breathing, it was another fourteen minutes before the door opened and he was called.

"Herr Millar, one of our partners will see you in his office, please follow me," the huissier said.

Ben followed him along a brightly lit corridor lined with paintings and other pieces of what he assumed to be original art. Given the quality of the furniture and finish, it seemed unlikely they would skimp on the trimmings.

They approached an elevator, and his escort inserted a key which activated a button below to call the car.

They glided upwards, stopping at the third floor, and continued on to a large arched door with the bank crest carved into thick, dark wood.

A single knock announced their arrival as the door was held open for Ben to enter. The room had a definite period feel, and one could imagine it had changed little while serving generations of wealthy clients. The only outward concession to modernity came with technology - a complex, multi-function telephone sat next to a LCD computer monitor and keyboard. They were strangely as at home in this setting as they would be in an Apple store.

Two men stepped forward to greet Ben, the huissier introduced the partner, Alain Wegel. He was a distinguished looking man, Ben guessed he'd be in his fifties; his hair was greying but collar length and well cut. Although a few stones overweight, his modern suit was tailored to hide the excess. Ben had expected someone less stylish, a drab accountant, but the other man fulfilled that stereotype. He was thin with a pinched face, and barely smiled as Ben shook his hand.

"Ah, Mr Millar, please come in... sit down, sit down," Wegel said.

"It's very good of you to see me at such short notice," Ben replied sinking into yet more expensive leather.

"We are at your service. Now, how can I help you?"

"The account number I gave at reception?"

"Of course, and you wish to make a claim?" Wegel replied.

"Yes," Ben said, he couldn't help wondering if Major Kessler had sat in this very room sixty years ago carrying out his orders to arrange the deposit of the Amber Room, orders given by a man as yet unborn, and who was due here with Lily as his captive within the hour.

"Very well, what credentials do you offer in support of your claim?" Wegel asked.

"I believe there are instructions on the account that specify a password. When the correct password is given along with the account number, they are to be considered proof of ownership."

Wegel read a paper on his desk and slowly nodded.

"You are correct, this account is slightly unusual and the instructions pre-date our current procedures, so we require an independent witness to verify your password. Herr Gisler is a notary from a local solicitor's office. He was here on other business, but has kindly agreed to act in this matter. The terms of the account allow us to deduct any administrative charges, and that clause will cover his professional services. I can of course arrange for another witness if you would prefer?"

"I'm happy with Herr Gisler and thank him for his time."

The notary gave a curt nod.

"Very well, I would ask you to write down your password clearly in capital letters - please space them out. I will open the envelope which contains our copy. We then cover our password to compare with yours. We will do this letter-by-letter until the full word or phrase is in view. If there is a deviation, the correct password is resealed as only one attempt can be permitted, and the account can never be claimed in your name again. Do you understand?"

"Perfectly," Ben replied.

Ben wrote out the password on the thick sheet of headed paper. Herr Gisler took out the bank's copy and carefully placed a thick sheet of paper on top so no-one could read the content. He placed the sheets flat on the desk. Ben passed over his version, face up in plain view.

"Please begin when you are ready," Wegel instructed.

Ben clearly enunciated the letters of Brandt's codename as the lawyer then revealed the matched character, and nodded for Ben to continue. After shuffling the papers momentarily, Gisler looked up, "The passwords match, Herr Millar's credentials are in order."

Ben smiled, quite unable to believe the comparison was successful as Wegel held out his hand.

"Congratulations, I am very happy to welcome you to our bank."

Ben took his hand and thanked the lawyer who gave another small bow.

"Would you like some refreshment, Mr Millar, coffee perhaps?" Wegel asked while scribbling his signature on some papers and passing them to the lawyer to be countersigned.

"No thanks, but is there somewhere I could make a private phone call?"

"We have rooms on the ground floor. They are fully equipped with telephones, computers, and faxes - every communication device you could need. I will have you escorted to one directly, but first, would you like to know the state of your account?"

"Very much," Ben replied.

"At the latest exchange rate in British pounds sterling, the balance is £1,836,738 on deposit and the contents of vault number sixty-seven."

"Are the contents catalogued?" Ben asked, surprised at the cash balance.

Wegel moved back to his desk and rifled through a few papers, "The contents consist of eighteen numbered crates, and that is the extent of the information we hold."

Ben held his breath for a moment, eighteen unmarked crates, any one of which proved the existence of one of the most extraordinary scientific discoveries ever made.

"But surely someone must know," Ben asked. "The vault must have been accessed over the years?"

"The vault is opened periodically to check it is in order." His eyes strayed back to his papers, "The items have been disturbed on less than ten occasions."

"Is that all - in over seventy years?" Ben asked.

"Yes, the first time was when the building was rewired, the others all occurred in similar circumstances, such as changes to the security or safety systems."

"Has anyone else has tried to claim the account?"

"There have been no attempts until this very day."

"The vault's contents have never been disturbed in all that time?"

"Of course, the account had the funds to meet any expenses, so there would be no change in status.

Shaw stepped out of the hotel onto Bahnhofstrasse. The doctor had agreed to help, knowing
ation gave Millar his best chance of surviving his next encounter with Charles Rae.
y main street provided plenty of cover for the watchers to blend in with tourists and shoppers
wed in and out of the charming side streets.
icked up the doctor's position and held the distance at twenty metres. He was ahead to the right
track in the wide semi-pedestrianised zone where the only significant visual obstructions
equent trams.
fat knew Millar was to meet Charles Rae at the Commercial Bank, but not the time, as a phone
be made to arrange the last minute details. Shaw's team were in place, including the increment
yone was ready for the most dangerous part of the operation to begin.
ntinued to move south towards the bank until its main public entrance was visible from the
Paradeplatz, close to the headquarters of the larger global banks such as UBS and Credit Suisse.
sed the tramlines and moved slowly down the wide thoroughfare lined with more of the classy
international brands that made Bahnhofstrasse famous around the world.
h probability of compromise made Shaw edgy and he continually scanned the area looking for
heard Rory Moffat's codename on the radio.
C is drawing attention from police. A patrol just had a good look at him. He's really wound up,
pinning like a top - he's staring at every face that passes him, over..."
ng we can do but watch and wait, over and out," Shaw replied.
had every right to feel tense, to be honest he was doing well, it wasn't exactly his line, and he
Rae's men would place no value on his life. Shaw closed to within ten metres, there were too
ole here, the radio crackled again.
olice are coming back, and this time they're making for MEDIC, five metres behind you at four
hey are going for MEDIC."
laced himself in the path of the cops. There was no question of allowing an arrest, so Shaw
ards the hapless doctor, greeting him loudly in English.
sorry I'm so late. You'll have been thinking I wasn't coming," Shaw said for all to hear, then
tly, "You've drawn the attention of the police, keep facing me and we'll walk away from them."
ook Moffat's arm, and they casually drifted away from the cops about the same instant a young,
rist stopped the policemen to ask directions in the same Home Counties accent he'd last heard
final radio check. Shaw kept the doctor moving until they were clear.
s," Rory said, "but I'd have thought of something."
ok totally stressed out, just try and relax," Shaw urged. "We've got everything covered."
fine..." Rory replied his voice trailing off, Shaw switched on - there was something in the
sion, fear? Chatter filled Shaw's earphone, and as he looked behind he found they were
d by three men, the one with shoulder-length hair he knew was Vadim Tarasov.
started to break away, "Well, thanks for the directions, nice to meet up with a fellow Brit," he
g his best to play the innocent trying to escape the trouble of which he had so suddenly become

here you are, my friend," Vadim snapped. "This man has an appointment, and you will come

Some vaults and deposit boxes have been passed down through families for centu[r] this account is not unusual."

"I have one more question, how easy would it be to transfer the account to some

"There is a standard procedure to follow, but it can be completed within an hou transfer papers have your signature, it would take immediate effect. Do you plan to

"Yes, please have the papers prepared?"

"This evening?" Wegel asked.

"Is that possible?" Ben replied.

Wegel gave a sigh, "But of course, can I help with anything else?"

"Yes, I want to see the vault, and I'll be inviting some guests."

Andre[w]
his coope[

The bu
as they fl[

Shaw [
and easy [
were the

Dr Mo
call woul[
unit. Ever

They c
corner of
Shaw cro
shops and

The hi
Millar. H
"MED[
his head [

"Nothi
MEDI
knew the
many pec

"The [
o'clock. [

Shaw
strode to[

"Hell[
more qui[

Shaw
female tc
during th[

"Than
"You
"I'll b
voice: te
surround

Shaw
said, doi
aware.

"Stay

Chapter 54

Zurich, Switzerland
Tuesday, 9 May 2017 12:34

Andrew Shaw stepped out of the hotel onto Bahnhofstrasse. The doctor had agreed to help, knowing his cooperation gave Millar his best chance of surviving his next encounter with Charles Rae.

The busy main street provided plenty of cover for the watchers to blend in with tourists and shoppers as they flowed in and out of the charming side streets.

Shaw picked up the doctor's position and held the distance at twenty metres. He was ahead to the right and easy to track in the wide semi-pedestrianised zone where the only significant visual obstructions were the frequent trams.

Dr Moffat knew Millar was to meet Charles Rae at the Commercial Bank, but not the time, as a phone call would be made to arrange the last minute details. Shaw's team were in place, including the increment unit. Everyone was ready for the most dangerous part of the operation to begin.

They continued to move south towards the bank until its main public entrance was visible from the corner of Paradeplatz, close to the headquarters of the larger global banks such as UBS and Credit Suisse. Shaw crossed the tramlines and moved slowly down the wide thoroughfare lined with more of the classy shops and international brands that made Bahnhofstrasse famous around the world.

The high probability of compromise made Shaw edgy and he continually scanned the area looking for Millar. He heard Rory Moffat's codename on the radio.

"MEDIC is drawing attention from police. A patrol just had a good look at him. He's really wound up, his head spinning like a top - he's staring at every face that passes him, over..."

"Nothing we can do but watch and wait, over and out," Shaw replied.

MEDIC had every right to feel tense, to be honest he was doing well, it wasn't exactly his line, and he knew the Rae's men would place no value on his life. Shaw closed to within ten metres, there were too many people here, the radio crackled again.

"The police are coming back, and this time they're making for MEDIC, five metres behind you at four o'clock. They are going for MEDIC."

Shaw placed himself in the path of the cops. There was no question of allowing an arrest, so Shaw strode towards the hapless doctor, greeting him loudly in English.

"Hello, sorry I'm so late. You'll have been thinking I wasn't coming," Shaw said for all to hear, then more quietly, "You've drawn the attention of the police, keep facing me and we'll walk away from them."

Shaw took Moffat's arm, and they casually drifted away from the cops about the same instant a young, female tourist stopped the policemen to ask directions in the same Home Counties accent he'd last heard during the final radio check. Shaw kept the doctor moving until they were clear.

"Thanks," Rory said, "but I'd have thought of something."

"You look totally stressed out, just try and relax," Shaw urged. "We've got everything covered."

"I'll be fine..." Rory replied his voice trailing off, Shaw switched on - there was something in the voice: tension, fear? Chatter filled Shaw's earphone, and as he looked behind he found they were surrounded by three men, the one with shoulder-length hair he knew was Vadim Tarasov.

Shaw started to break away, "Well, thanks for the directions, nice to meet up with a fellow Brit," he said, doing his best to play the innocent trying to escape the trouble of which he had so suddenly become aware.

"Stay where you are, my friend," Vadim snapped. "This man has an appointment, and you will come

Some vaults and deposit boxes have been passed down through families for centuries, so the period of this account is not unusual."

"I have one more question, how easy would it be to transfer the account to someone else?"

"There is a standard procedure to follow, but it can be completed within an hour if necessary. Once the transfer papers have your signature, it would take immediate effect. Do you plan to do so?"

"Yes, please have the papers prepared?"

"This evening?" Wegel asked.

"Is that possible?" Ben replied.

Wegel gave a sigh, "But of course, can I help with anything else?"

"Yes, I want to see the vault, and I'll be inviting some guests."

too."

Shaw waved him away, "Now listen, I just heard him speaking English and stopped to ask my way. I don't have time for this."

The smile flattened, and a nod of the head preceded the expertly applied elbow lock that sent a sharp pain the length of Shaw's arm.

"Go easy," he said coughing and trying to catch a breath. Vadim nodded, and the pressure eased, "You need to come with us."

Shaw nodded, he could hear Martin Reid's voice in his ear standing down his colleagues, the increment soldiers were moving in, but this was a covert mission and a fire fight in central Zurich was out of the question.

"Look, I don't know what this guy has done to you, but it's nothing to do with me," he tried to explain. "I just want to go..."

Vadim shook his head, and they were ushered down a side street. Shaw was frisked at the door of a Mercedes limousine and could only watch as the doctor was pushed into another car and driven off.

Vadim Tarasov opened the Mercedes' door.

"Look, you're making a mistake," Shaw said once more.

His arms were held to the front of his body, and a thick cable tie applied to his wrists. His guard tested the bond was tight, before pushing him into the car.

Vadim sat up front and looked back at him.

"I have an excellent memory, but then, it is only yesterday I saw your face at an observatory in Edinburgh."

Chapter 55

Paradeplatz, Zurich, Switzerland
Tuesday, 9 May 2017 13:10

Ben took another drink of water before composing himself for the call to Charles Rae. He laid his hands on the heavy triple-glazed window frames. There was a catch at shoulder height, he turned it and the window opened slightly before stopping against a latch. The low, air-conditioned hum was replaced by loud street noise as the room was exposed to the outside world.

Ben was ready to make the call and dialled the number. It was answered on the first ring as he looked out at the square below.

"Ben Millar."

"I've picked up a couple of your friends, but still no sign of you?" Charles Rae replied.

Ben sat back on the window sill, they'd got Rory, he bit his lip, it was too much to expect for both of them to have gotten away.

"I hope you're treating them well?"

"Oh yes, but we have more important matters to discuss."

"We have an exchange to negotiate," Ben replied.

"Let's stop the pretence. If you want to see your friends again, you will follow my instructions precisely."

"Things have changed," Ben said.

"Don't try and play me."

"I have claimed the account," Ben paused to let that sink in. "There are eighteen unmarked packages in a vault over which I have full control. You should remember that I wasn't particularly close to my brother, and I've known the others for less than twenty-four hours. Luckily for you, I value their safety above the contents of this vault, but not above my own life, so do we negotiate, or do I take my chances with the police?"

"Where are you?"

"I'm calling from a private room inside the bank."

"You really are a surprise package. What exactly do you want?"

"I want to speak to Lily and Rory first."

"Very well," Rae replied, "one moment..."

Ben listened intently straining to hear their voices, "Ben?" she said, "Ben, are you alright?"

"I'm fine, have you been harmed?"

"No, I'm with Rory, we're both fine..." she said.

"I'm going to get you out of there."

"You've heard her," Rae cut in. "Now, what have you got planned?"

Ben took a moment, he'd heard her voice, and she sounded OK for now.

"I want you - in person - to bring Rory and Lily into the bank, and ask to meet me here. This place is full of people and cameras, and even you won't do anything stupid with so many witnesses around. There's a drive-in garage at the rear of the building, I'll expect you as soon as possible."

"Anything else?" Rae asked.

"The account has £1.8 million pounds in cash, plus the contents of the vault. I will keep the cash, and I want a small percentage of the vault's value to be split between Lily, Rory and myself, say a maximum payment of five million pounds between us."

"Keep going..." Rae replied slowly.

"I want the three of us to be able to move forward in life without looking over our shoulders. We will be compensated for your actions and you'll get our silence in return. Taking the money will make us accomplices, and that should give you some comfort in the deal."

"What about the police looking for you in the UK?"

"They won't be able to convict me of Simon's death or any other, and of course, I'll be able to afford the best lawyers."

"This is quite unexpected... and dare I say it, welcome..."

"I want you to bring Lily and Rory here. They will leave first, when I know they are safe, I will transfer the vault contents to you, then it's my turn to leave, and we have no further contact until you pay the five million back into the account here after you have sold the Amber Room."

"Your friends know nothing of this idea. What makes you think they'll agree to go along?"

"What's the alternative? There is nothing to be gained by opposing you. You'd have us killed without a thought. I'll convince the others we have no choice, and they'll have to agree. I can disappear to a comfortable life and forget all about you."

"And if I refuse?"

"Why would you? It puts you in the clear. Our only alternative is to let the world know about the time loop, and your crimes. We all come out with something this way."

"But only if you keep your side of the bargain."

"We don't need each other as enemies. We both profit from this and I don't need to see you brought to justice - it won't bring Simon or James Munro back - the money will be enough."

"OK, we'll talk more face-to-face," Rae said ending the call.

Ben had bought some time; Rae would be suspicious, but he believed in the power of money and would assume everyone had a price. Even if he believed Ben's story, he would want to keep the money and ensure their silence, as anything else was a risk. Ben put a pair of scissors that were lying on the table into his pocket, he wished he had the Glock, but the scissors would do for now. Unless Rae was a total madman there could be no killing here - the thought gave him little comfort.

The phone on the table started to ring. Ben crossed the room and answered, one of the huissiers at the front desk told him Rae was due to arrive in the underground garage. Ben asked for vault transfer papers to be drawn up and for a meeting with Wegel in the coming hour. Ben shivered and pulled himself together; they would be as safe under the bank's high-tech security blanket as anywhere else. As he ended the call there was a sharp knock on the door, it was all happening so quickly, it was already time to go.

Chapter 56

Zurich, Switzerland
Thursday, 25 February 1943 13:48

The military trucks, with their precious cargo, turned off the main road into Zurich towards the Bourse and the bank's depository. By Kessler's reckoning, he should be on a flight back to Berlin by late afternoon. If all went to plan, he would report a successful mission to the Reichsfuhrer that evening.

His strategy of a small five-man team had worked perfectly so far, each man hand-picked from his command in France, good men like his fallen comrade, Karl Muller.

Once the will of the Reichsfuhrer was decided, control over the Amber Room had been secured with minimal fuss, and the wretched thing would soon be in a Swiss vault and no longer his concern.

Despite warnings about the cat and mouse games played with enemy agents in Zurich, he couldn't quite shake off the feeling that the attempt to follow him was more than chance, but it was only natural to be cautious on such an important mission.

Suddenly Kessler had to brace against his door, the truck had skidded in a turn, the road gleaming with spilt fuel.

The driver needed no rebuke; the tight bends were difficult even when the surface was good. He was more concerned about the heavy clunk from the cargo bay.

Harry James stared at the tools strewn across the steel floor. He'd left the toolbox unsecured, and the noisy crash had almost stopped his heart.

He quickly finished off re-sealing the partially opened crate as he needed to get away and summon support.

The truck shuddered on for a moment, but the driver started down-shifting, causing it to slow to a crawl. James had to get out and find cover. If they'd arrived at the final destination he would call for help, if not, he would try and re-board to avoid losing the Amber Room.

With the truck still moving, he straddled the tailgate before climbing down and finding a foothold. The truck steered off the road and he braced against heavy braking before pushing away and landing heavily on a gravel track. His left ankle twisted and collapsed under his weight. Ignoring the pain, he focused on trying to reach a shallow ditch only a handful of yards away. Just as he was about to drop out of sight, he doubled over from a hefty kick that caught his hip. He curled up to protect himself from further blows, but hands pulled at him until he was thrown on his back. The hard faces of soldiers in civilian clothing looked down on him. Kessler stood to one side and watched as the others covered him with drawn pistols.

"I know you," Kessler lent closer, "but where do I know you from?"

"Quarter finals, 1936," James gasped.

"I remember, a strong left jab, but I was the better boxer. Your name is Harry... Harry James?"

James nodded as he was pulled to his feet.

"There wasn't much in it - you were saved by the bell in the second round."

"I don't share that recollection," Kessler laughed, "but we find ourselves as opponents once more. Why are you here?"

"I'm based here. I recognised you in town, and arranged to have you followed. You were an SS officer in 1936, and I wondered what exactly you were doing in Zurich?"

Kessler considered him for a moment, scanning James's face for the lie, James held his gaze, it was a good story – he almost believed it himself.

"You are a British spy," Kessler mused, "I seem to bring bad luck for you. This will certainly be our last contest."

"Can I have a cigarette?" James asked pointing to his inside jacket pocket.

Kessler nodded as James pulled out the grenade hidden in the folds of the jacket, he wrapped the pull cord around his index finger ready to activate the five-second fuse. Every gun was pointed at his head.

"If you fire, you will all die with me," James shouted.

"What do you expect to achieve?" Kessler asked calmly.

James didn't know how to answer that question, he desperately wanted to live, but he couldn't be captured.

"Drop the grenade, and we will have our final bout," Kessler said stripping off his jacket and throwing it to one of his men.

"I'm afraid I can't do that," James replied.

"You know what, it's no longer important why you are here," Kessler said lunging for the grenade.

His men gripped James' arms, but he still managed to separate the cord from grenade's body as Kessler pulled it from his hands.

"Five seconds can be an eternity," Kessler said, before tossing it into a ditch where it detonated harmlessly.

"Search him," Kessler ordered.

His men pawed at James' pockets pulling out his revolver and the cyanide vials.

"Interesting," Kessler remarked, "these are usually given to the poor souls that drop from the skies into my sector in France. They carry them for a reason, and that reason is to keep their secrets. What secrets do you keep, Harry James?"

Kessler stretched out his arms and threw a few punches in the air.

"Let him go, let's see how he fights now."

The soldiers pushed James towards Kessler, who missed with an uppercut as they came together.

James threw a feint, unable to move quickly on the injured ankle, and tried to finish the taller man quickly with an over the top right hand.

Kessler circled away, then immediately moved back in with a series of vicious blows to the body and head. He caught James with a left hook that dropped him to his knees.

"I am still the better boxer."

He motioned to one of his men, "Phone the house and have him taken there, we will see what he knows when I return."

Blood trickled from James mouth as he was pulled upright. He watched as drops fell on the dust and gravel, soon to be washed away by the rain.

Chapter 57

Zurich, Switzerland
Tuesday, 9 May 2017 13:12

The rear of the Mercedes limousine had room to transport six in comfort. Shaw sat alongside Vadim who carefully watched his every move. Charles Rae faced him, busy with the imminent arrangements to exchange people for a vault containing a treasure lost to history.

Rae finished his phone call and gave orders for the driver to take them back towards Bahnhofstrasse. He finally turned to Shaw, who returned his gaze impassively; there was little point in continuing the deceit of the hapless tourist. They knew he was more than that.

"Your name is Shaw," Rae stated.

Shaw flinched slightly, the last thing he'd expected to hear was his name. He forced himself to relax, and didn't respond. His mind running over the possibilities and realised David Sykes must have made contact with Rae - it was the only way he could know about him.

"I don't care if your real name is Shaw or not, that name will do for now," Rae continued.

Rae watched Shaw closely as he waited for a reply.

"David Sykes has been in touch, you'll find we're on the same side now."

"That means we can lose the cable ties," Shaw replied holding up his wrists.

"Vadim, cut our friend loose," Rae ordered.

The driver slowed as they approached a junction, Vadim leant forward holding out a doubled-edged dagger, he pushed Shaw back into the leather seat and quickly cut the cable that held his wrists.

"Vadim is as precise as any surgeon. Just don't give him cause to cut anywhere else," Rae warned.

Shaw rubbed his wrists.

"Don't look so concerned, you're a British agent... if you were anything else you would be in serious trouble," Rae said. "You have nothing to say? No questions to ask?"

"You seem to have everything covered," Shaw replied.

"You were at Clive Adams's apartment near CERN and prevented my men intercepting Millar."

"Was I?" Shaw replied.

"You're free to call Sykes... he will explain the situation. Our partnership is best for all."

"What exactly have you been told?" Shaw asked.

"In exchange for the Amber Room, I will ensure there is no publicity around the CERN discovery and no-one else talks."

"You will eliminate the others?"

"I simply want to make a huge amount of money from the Amber Room, a little recognition for finding it would also be quite fitting, but most of all I want peace of mind, and if that means the others must die - then they must die."

"You really think you'll find the Amber Room?" Shaw replied.

"If you can believe the events at Ohrdruf occurred as a side effect of my message, why not believe it has put those adorned panels safely in a vault."

"And your peace of mind?"

"I have worked with intelligence services many times. You do what's necessary. Millar and my captives have simply got too close to the flame and will get burnt. I intend on remaining fireproof."

"What now?" Shaw asked.

"You can do what you want after I have the Amber Room, but for now I think it would be a good idea to keep you close... it will discourage the possibility of... friendly fire."

Shaw studied Rae; he knew the type of man he was dealing with, unrelenting and ruthless. He was reminded of Sykes.

"So you know who I am," Shaw said, "but I know what you've done. You've unleashed an unbelievable phenomenon that poses so many new questions about our world, but you use it to satisfy greed, you use it to contact the Nazis... I think you can forget about the Nobel Prize, Mr Rae."

Rae sat back and laughed, Vadim flashed his golden smile.

"We share the same goal, no publicity around this phenomenon: agreed?" Rae asked.

"It would be better out of the headlines," Shaw replied.

"I did what was necessary, Shaw. Simon Millar thought of the fame the discovery would bring, but he was afraid to believe what he could see with his own eyes. He was so afraid to be made a laughing stock. He was someone who would keep my discovery a secret, someone whose vanity drove him to be the first to explain the impossible."

"If he was so worried about his reputation, why send a message about the Amber Room?" Shaw replied. "That's not likely to commend him."

"He never sent that message," Rae said laughing once more. "After a few days of gentle pressure, he agreed to repeat the experiment that brought us together in the first place. However he would only agree to send a basic message that contained a cryptographic signature. Even if someone could decode that message it had no meaning other than as a unique marker that Simon would take as proof. However he asked me to encode it using Enigma so we could search the archives and see if it really was possible to send messages through time. I encoded a message, one with more interesting text, and that has brought us together now."

"Let me guess, he found out and was going public?" Shaw asked.

"We used his university's computer system because of its computational power, but I funded and controlled the decoding software. Every access was logged, and I knew immediately when he'd found evidence of the real message. It was always a risk he would, but it was a risk worth taking to speed up the process. Something made him go snooping and that was his undoing."

"To get to the point," Shaw said, "he threatened to expose you, and so you killed him?"

"Of course... and for the same reason it will end the lives of three others shortly," Rae said. "This is a big game, which I'm happy to turn over to you and your people as I'll have taken what I want from it."

Shaw chewed his lip - it was inconceivable this man would be allowed to walk away from the murders in Edinburgh and the death and chaos of Ohrdruf.

"You've implicated yourself in the murder of prominent British scientists and attempted murders of others. But worse, your action is suspected to have caused the radiation leak at Ohrdruf, people have died there, have you considered that?" Shaw replied.

"I listened to the great Professor Simon Millar. He was convinced that even if we could send messages back in time, any reactions were already woven into the past... that our actions were already a part of history. According to Simon, we had already affected the present."

"His work was never peer-reviewed, I have a feeling that despite whatever else he may have said, on that point, he was totally fucking wrong, and had realised it when he phoned the police to take responsibility for Ohrdruf."

"Without my intervention we would never know about the loop's effect as no government would have ever sanctioned those tests. I have given you a window to the past, and now I have an agreement for full legal immunity and guarantees of no future action against me or my men. By the end of this day, I will have met all my obligations, in other words – we have a deal."

"I don't think it will be quite that simple," Shaw replied.

"Don't talk down to me, Shaw. We can be trusted to remain silent. We will keep our side of a bargain.

The only problem is Millar and his friends, but then we have Her Majesty's Government's blessing for how to deal with them... You don't look too happy, Shaw?"

"I'd prefer another way."

"Millar is asking me to buy him off, to offer compensation for his troubles so far."

"And...?"

"He's not serious, and then there's the girl and his doctor friend, too many people know about this. My plan is simple - anyone who discovered the time loop, and especially my involvement - cannot be given the opportunity to talk."

"I'd need to talk to my people, I want no killing here." Shaw said.

Rae's eyes narrowed.

"That decision has already been made by your superior," Rae replied, "and I'll have to mention to Sykes that you seem a little out of your depth. Millar is the obvious candidate to take the fall for the murders, there's no 'Plan B'."

Shaw could see why this quick fix solution was attractive to Sykes, he'd seen informers and agents cut loose in circumstances that would lead to certain death. It was something that happened and bad luck on those who outlived their usefulness, but he didn't have to like it.

"Shaw, one more thing, I have documents that fully catalogue the current situation. It includes audio recordings of Sykes accepting the proposal to eliminate Millar and the others. If anything should happen, the evidence will be sent to specific journalists who are no friends of the security services."

"I understand," Shaw replied accepting this further restriction on his ability to act.

The driver opened the partition that separated him from the main body of the car, "Sir, the police are stopping cars up ahead. Will I re-route to avoid them?" the man asked.

"Drive," Rae said, "the Swiss don't keep rich men from their money."

Chapter 58

Zurich, Switzerland
Tuesday, 9 May 2017 13:20

The elevator announced to all in the car they had reached the basement, and the doors opened to a floor split in two sections; the majority for car parking, and a loading bay large enough to take three or four delivery trucks. On the far wall, a heavy, steel roller door was firmly closed, its polished surface reflecting the bright fluorescent lights onto clean, whitewashed walls. As Ben walked forward, a glance behind showed a security station sealed behind thick glass. There was a bank of monitors in front of two security guards and cameras that covered every angle. A black limo suddenly filled the largest screen. Ben felt a knot in his stomach as an electric motor whined into life. The door juddered and began to rise.

Ben took a deep breath, every sense was razor sharp - he was ready.

Two cars slowly made their way into the car park. The leading Mercedes had darkened rear windows, it came to a stop, and Charles Rae, Vadim, and another man got out and walked towards him. The second car, a black Mercedes 4x4 M-Class with similar darkened windows stopped behind the limo, its occupants staying where they were for now. The roller door slowly descended until it came to rest with a dull clang, shutting them all inside.

Rae looked at ease, he gestured to Ben as though they were old acquaintances. Ben felt the hard steel of the scissors in his hand.

"What a day this is," Rae exclaimed, "it's so exciting, wouldn't you agree, Ben?"

Ben looked to the cars, "Where's Lily and Rory?"

"If you'd be good enough to wait for us over there, we have some business to discuss," Rae said to Ben's escort.

"There is a private room you could use, sir," the man offered.

"No, wait by the elevator, we'll join you shortly."

Ben opened his hands offering no objection. The bank employee nodded and said he would wait on their call.

Rae moved closer to Ben to ensure they wouldn't be overheard.

"Although we have an agreement, I feel it's necessary to remind you of your position," Rae hissed.

Vadim smiled, and led them to the M-Class. Ben glanced over his shoulder - they were shielded from the bank security cameras by the cars. He tensed himself, ready to fight if he was to be dragged into one of them. Rae gestured for him to look into the big Mercedes and Ben watched as the rear window lowered smoothly. The dark glass fell away to reveal Lily, her hair pushed onto her face by the hand firmly holding her neck. The sight of her filled Ben with relief and then anger, she stared into his eyes, all he could focus on was the knife held closely to her throat. Ben moved towards her, but Vadim stopped him, "Easy now, or your girlfriend's pretty white dress will stain red. Do not move - I will search you."

Ben froze, he couldn't take his eyes off Lily, any other time she would have made the dress look wonderful, for now, it was a hateful way to display Rae's control. Vadim quickly removed the scissors and showed them to Rae who shrugged, "Best return them - how else do you expect people to remove the coupons from their bearer bonds?"

Charles Rae started to walk away, Vadim indicated Ben should follow, but Ben continued to stare into the car, Lily had been pulled back and Rory was now visible, sitting in a third row of seats, another knife close to his waist.

Ben stood out from between the cars and shouted at Rae's back, "We're going nowhere without them."

"You're in no position to make demands," Rae replied keeping his voice low.

"If you want that fucking vault, get them out of the car right now, it's your choice," Ben shouted.

"Quieten down?" Rae replied, looking to Vadim.

"You need me to sign over that vault to you and no matter what happens I won't do that until they're safe."

"Do I have to make you?" Vadim asked.

"That would cause a whole lot of trouble," Ben replied.

"Gentleman, there is really no need for unpleasantness. I have a solution," Rae said smoothly, "I will release your friends to the custody of my companion here," Rae said pointing to the unknown man.

"Why would I agree to an insane idea like that?" Ben said.

"There is reason enough," Rae replied, not quite hiding his annoyance, "This man is a member of the British security services. He's tracked you since you entered France. Your friends will leave with him, they can do so now."

Ben looked the man up and down dismissively, "He's just another hired thug - you can do better than that."

Rae laughed, "Just another thug, maybe, but a government thug. Ask your medic friend, surely you'll believe him?"

Ben stooped down to the car, "Rory, what's going on?"

"Ben, you were right about being followed. He's MI5 or MI6 or something..., his name's Shaw."

"Is this true?" Ben asked Shaw.

"Yes, we watched as you visited CERN, you lost us when Ms Taylor was taken by our host, but we latched onto you again at Geneva station. I do work for the British Government."

"You know about the time loop, why we're here?"

"Yes, we know pretty much everything."

"Rory, are you sure?" Ben asked again bending to the window. Rory nodded.

"Why is Rae going to let you walk out of here just like that?" Ben asked.

Rae answered first, "Because, I don't need sovereign states as enemies. They know all about it, and so the game is up, but I get the Amber Room and immunity for my silence. In return no-one knows about the link to the past."

Ben looked away from them, not trusting himself to speak clearly through the anger he felt at Rae's causal confidence and, worse, his country's apparent complicity in murder.

"Is that how things are?" Ben eventually asked Shaw.

"I was brought in to investigate the radiation contamination in Ohrdruf. I was in Edinburgh when you absconded. It is likely the Enigma messages sent from CERN have changed our present and caused that incident. This is a unique situation and we need time to deal with it - the potential consequences are unknown."

"So what? You cut a deal with killers and look to exploit it yourself?" Ben said.

"The stakes are above any individual; we have to make the best of a bad situation," Shaw replied.

"What happens to us?" Ben asked.

"Look, you all need debriefed before you decide on your actions, I want you to hear the case for secrecy-" Shaw said.

"Take Lily and Rory away from here, I've got a vault to sign over," Ben interrupted.

"No!" came a shout from the car, it was Lily, "Ben, we can't leave you..."

There was a short scuffle. Ben looked into the car to see Rory held down. Rae stepped over and barked at his men. Ben could see the bank security men looking uneasy behind the glass.

"Lily, I need you and Rory to go, you've been through enough... don't worry about me, I can work something out with them."

"Work what out?"

"Something that keeps us alive - Shaw is right – we can't just blurt this out to the world, we need to listen first."

"Do you really believe our government, any government, can be trusted with this?" Lily replied quietly.

"What choice do we have?" Ben asked. "Rory, tell her there's no need for all of us to remain here."

Shaw moved over to the M-class.

"I'll take them," Shaw said to Rae, "and the car."

"Whatever gets this done," Rae replied gesturing to his men to get out of the vehicle.

"Let the bank staff know I'm coming back in, I'll hand these people over and be right back," Shaw said sliding into the driver seat.

"You'll have to catch up, I've waited long enough, and we're going to the vault right now," Rae replied.

Lily shouted out, "Be careful."

Shaw quickly reversed flashing his lights for security to raise the door. He nodded to Rae then gunned the car forward up the exit ramp. Ben felt hugely relieved to see them go, but it was mixed with anger over the immunity deal. Simon's and James Munro's memories demanded justice, and the knife held at Lily's throat just increased his determination they would get it. He'd find a way to make Rae pay, but right now, he had to focus on living to see another day.

Vadim walked beside him as they caught up with Rae who stood with the huissier by the elevator. Rae ordered his other men to wait for them in the basement while they got an elevator to the first floor. The huissier walked a discreet distance ahead. Ben shot a glance at Vadim then turned to Rae, "I'm surprised your thugs can carry guns in here."

"I'm sure there's much that would surprise you. Switzerland is closer to the States than it is to Europe on gun control. My bodyguards have carrying permits for their weapons. Swiss citizens serving in the militia are able to keep their assault rifles at home, and it would be considered rude to search clients," Rae replied.

"I suppose we must all mind our manners."

"So you gained control of the account, very clever," Rae said.

"Remember our deal and you'll have it soon enough."

"You are proving to be a resourceful man."

"Why this bank?" Ben asked. "You're known here?"

"You should be reassured as I'm hardly likely to try anything untoward here. Don't take the attempts on your life personally, they fitted an earlier plan that you've forced to evolve. I chose this bank as I'm good customer here... having a three zero account helps..."

"Which means what?" Ben asked.

"It means I have a large amount of cash on deposit. The number of leading zeroes on an account signifies the value of a particular account and customer - it helps the staff sort the wheat from the chaff."

Ben was taking the events of the last forty-eight hours very personally. It was hard enough to be so close to these men and not try to take them out. Images rushed into his head, flashbacks about Simon, all the good memories. He stared at Rae - he would kill him if he got the chance. The justice he wanted could not come yet, so he bit his tongue, and tried to keep his temper while he waited for a chance to escape. Vadim was close behind and watching him. It seemed the mercenary sensed something of his mood.

They walked on in silence, Ben knew they were close to Wegel's office and this charade would soon be over. The sound of their footsteps on the marble floor was broken by the buzz of a phone. Their escort answered his mobile and spoke quietly in German. The man stopped and turned to face them.

"Herr Wegel has informed me there will be a slight delay in drawing up the transfer papers, he asks me to assure you that it is nothing serious, but we must first review all the paperwork before transferring the vault and contents. The arrangements are taking slightly longer than he hoped, and so he wonders if you would like to inspect the vault while you wait? We will let you know when transfer documents are ready."

Ben's face betrayed nothing, but he thanked Wegel for whatever procedure had slowed things down. It was more time for Lily and Rory to increase their distance from Rae, and more immediately, whatever they had in mind would have to wait until the vault was signed over.

Rae agreed with the idea enthusiastically, "Yes, let's go now, I've been looking forward to this for over seventy years," he said with a wink at Ben.

They were led down a flight of stairs, the new floor had a security checkpoint and their escort had to swipe his identity card and enter a number for access. He confirmed the vault number with the security staff, and waited briefly for two keys to be passed over.

"This is your key, Mr Millar, I had it retrieved from a deposit box once your claim was accepted, you can retain it or leave it here, whatever is most convenient," he explained.

Ben could feel Rae's eyes on the key as it was passed to him. He pocketed it; Rae would have to wait to take possession a little longer.

With the keys in hand and the first security procedure cleared, their escort placed his thumb on a reader outside two heavy metal doors, he stood back as there was a sharp click, and the doors opened smoothly to reveal a brightly lit, windowless corridor. It was almost as though they had entered another building. Like the basement, this area was more industrial with polished steel and painted concrete, rather than the smart minimalism of the reception area, and both were a world away from the careful charm and stylish decor of Wegel's office.

"This way, Gentlemen," the huissier said, "we are entering the most secure area of the bank. It houses the majority of our safety deposit boxes and vaults. Our depositors can rest assured that we have the most advanced security and safety systems in place. Your items are safe from theft, fire and flood while they are in our care-"

"Yes, I've heard that speech before, and I wouldn't be a client if it was any other way," Rae replied brusquely.

He then added smiling at Ben, "This bank, unlike many others, has been very stable from as far back as the 1940s. It protected its pre-war clients from the Nazis, who passed a law condemning German citizens to death for possessing foreign currency in a Swiss bank account, and then its post-war Nazi clients when the American authorities tried to track down what they had hid away over the mountain passes."

"One more thing, sir," their escort replied. "I would like to apologise for the bright lighting and bland surroundings, it is a security measure - there is nowhere for intruders to hide."

Chapter 59

Andrew Shaw gunned the Mercedes into the hotel car park, screeching to a halt beside Martin Reid and two increment soldiers who were waiting at a rear entrance. He led Lily Taylor and the doctor up a staircase and into the hotel suite overlooking Bahnhofstrasse. The soldiers took up position on either side of the door and carefully watched the new arrivals.

"Who are they?" Lily asked.

"MI6," Rory replied, "and they know everything."

"The messages, the time loop... everything?" Lily asked looking at Shaw.

Shaw nodded.

"And the murders? you know, Charles Rae is responsible?"

"Yes, all of it," Shaw replied.

"What about, Ben?"

"I'm going back to the bank now," Shaw replied, he turned to Reid, "Look after these guys, make sure nothing happens to them... I'll be back as soon as I can."

Reid nodded to the bedroom, "You've got a visitor."

David Sykes stepped into the doorway, "Come in here, I need a word."

Shaw walked into the room with Sykes closing the door behind him.

"I'm taking over, Shaw, and I've left Reid in charge here. I see you've picked up two of the three strays – at least something has gone as it should have."

"Ben Millar claimed an account, and they're accessing a vault. I need to go back."

"I know - Charles Rae has been in touch, I'll meet him as you have another job to do." He motioned through the door to Lily and Rory.

"You still want them taken out?"

"Nothing else for it, this story cannot come out."

"I don't know what the plan is, but nothing can happen here," Shaw said.

Sykes took his overcoat from the back of a chair.

"Things haven't gone well, and you'll be lucky to keep your job. But you know the plan right now, just make them disappear, and I'll try to forget some of the many errors you've made in the last few hours."

They entered the main suite, and Shaw could see Lily and Rory lying on the floor, a soldier standing over each one, both hooded and tied at both wrist and ankle.

"This isn't necessary," Shaw called after Sykes.

"Just get on with the job, and have it done by the time I return."

The door slammed shut, Shaw shook his head and looked to Martin Reid who stared back impassively.

"OK, get the hoods off them."

The increment men looked to each other and Reid but didn't move.

Shaw kicked a chair towards them.

"Get them off now," Shaw shouted, "and put them on the chairs."

Reid nodded. The civilians were lifted to sit up, and their hoods removed.

He expected tears or curses, but was met with a quiet sadness - disbelief that they were anything but safe.

"You two, wait outside," Shaw ordered.

Again the men looked to Reid.

"Guard the door, and don't be too obvious."

The men followed the order, and Shaw turned to Lily and Rory.

"What's going to happen to us?" Lily asked.

The knee-length, off the shoulder white dress was too short for a bride, but it would be perfect for a sacrifice.

Shaw sighed, "You're seen as a risk, you know about the messages – you sent one. No-one is ready for what you know to be made public, and one solution is for you, Rory and Ben to disappear."

Rory sat forward, "Why don't you say killed because that's what you mean? How could I have trusted you?"

"What kind of people are you?" Lily said, "You're as bad as criminals like Charles Rae – no, actually you're worse because, like so many others during the time those messages were received, you're just carrying out orders."

Shaw walked over to Reid, "I'm not following that order."

"You got a better plan," Reid asked.

"There's no certainty to any of this, what if they find an empty vault and all this is bullshit? These people don't have to die, do they look like a threat to anyone? If they didn't know before, they know now what will happen if they talk."

"Sykes told me to expect this, he told me to slot you too."

Slotting the SAS term for killing a man, Reid was a couple of weight classes below him, but Shaw knew he was deadly with or without a weapon.

Shaw took a step towards him, and found the barrel of a 9mm Browning high power pistol pointed at his head.

"It's like that?"

"Have you got a plan?"

"I want to talk to these two, and see if I can find a good reason to call off Sykes' order."

Reid looked to the others, his aim never leaving Shaw, "You've got five minutes."

Shaw pulled up a chair next to Lily and Rory.

"We're all in danger, so listen carefully - is there anything you know that could point to this whole thing being a hoax?"

Lily shook her head, "No, I think the messages are real, surely you know that yourself?"

"How, I don't know what's in that vault."

"The British agent mentioned by Kessler in one of the messages, Harry James, surely he must have filled reports?"

"Who's Harry James?"

"He was sent after Major Kessler in 1943."

Shaw pulled out his phone.

He dialled Sylvia's number at Vauxhall Cross.

"I can't believe what you've found," the MI6 analyst answered on hearing his voice.

"Sylvia, I need your help – can you look up a wartime agent, name of Harry James. He may be the guy sent to try and stop the transfer."

"I've already identified him, and I'm trying to find out what his involvement actually was. Some of the reports from that time were copied to microfiche, but the registry are looking through the index for any of his original reports from that period."

"Found anything so far?"

"No, I'd be sure to call you if I had."

"That's important, can you repeat that to Martin Reid?"

"What..."

Shaw held the phone out for Reid who had already lowered the gun, as he passed the phone, Shaw grabbed the gun, and twisted it down, breaking Reid's grip and simultaneously kicking him hard between the legs - just the way his instructors had taught him to disarm an opponent. Only Reid had blocked the kick by twisting his hips, and had made no sound.

Reid was still on his feet, with Shaw holding the gun over him. He picked up the phone, Sylvia was still there.

"Sylvia, things have gone wrong here. Sykes wants to leave a trail of bodies, possibly including mine. I'm going to try and resolve this, and stop the killing. If you can find anything that helps, will you call me?"

There was a moment's silence.

"Of course I will, now try and be careful, Andrew."

Shaw pocketed the phone.

"I'm getting too old for this," Reid said.

"You let me take the gun," Shaw replied.

"I don't know what you're talking about."

Shaw smiled.

"You weren't falling for the phone call?"

"I still don't know what you're talking about, but as you have my gun, I assume you have some idea of what to do next?"

"Call the two outside in here, once you're all tied up, I'll be taking these two back to the bank, an ex-marine called Ben Millar needs some help."

Chapter 60

As they were led past barred rooms with rows of shiny deposit boxes, Ben wondered if they contained anything as potentially sensational as the vault that drew closer with every step.

Despite everything, Ben realised he wanted to see what was in there just as much as Rae. They were looking for physical proof that a message sent to the past had taken the Amber Room out of the flow of time and kept it safe for the present. They were witnesses to the unravelling of time itself.

They approached yet another gate, only those with private vaults could pass this point. The barred pens of the shared vaults were replaced by solid steel walls. Their escort explained that the contents of these vaults were registered under a single account, and only the account holder and their guests could gain access. The escort slowed, "Number sixty-seven - Mr Millar, can you insert your key in the right-hand lock."

They were faced with a large double door of polished steel with keyholes on either side. Ben's key made a solid click when inserted into the lock. The escort inserted his copy on the other side.

"Please turn the key to your right."

Ben held his breath as the dual keys engaged and turned smoothly together. The silence was broken by the metallic clang of multiple bolts springing back into the door.

"After you, sir," the escort said while effortlessly pulling one of the heavy doors towards them.

Rae stepped forward, "If you don't mind, I've waited a long time for this..."

Ben indicated for him to go first, not that it mattered as Rae was already entering the vault.

Motion sensors activated the lighting and an audible hum became noticeable from the air conditioning that kept the room at a constant temperature and humidity. Ben could feel the dry cool air from the vault on his face and hands.

They all stared at the outlines of the packing crates. Each covered in canvas sheeting, they were all rectangular with a shallow depth consistent with holding paintings or panels. The crates came in various sizes, some quite small, others over two by three metres in size, and at the limit of what the doorway could physically accommodate.

Rae pulled back a sheet from the nearest crate disturbing a fine layer of dust that floated in the still air. The wood was pale and dry, with a few marks and indentations over its surface. At any other time, it would have thrilled Ben to think what discovery lay here, but his eyes were on Vadim. Like the others, he was transfixed by the contents of the vault. Ben had calculated his best chance to make a move would come with the opening of that first crate.

There were no visible cameras inside the vault and no means of opening the crates either, Rae was running his hands over the next one, examining it closely, totally unaware of others around him. Ben's chance would come soon.

Another buzz from the phone echoed up to the high ceiling and the huissier answered his phone once more, the sound broke the vault's spell, and Vadim stared Ben down, he was back on guard, at least until the first box was opened.

The huissier put his phone away and turn to Rae, "Your guest has arrived, Mr Rae. Would you like him to join us?"

"Yes, show him in," Rae replied.

Ben almost smiled – Andrew Shaw was returning and that meant Lily and Rory were safe in British hands.

The huissier continued, "The papers have been drawn up and are ready for signing, would you like to proceed to Herr Wegel's office to complete the transfer?"

"No, have them brought down, we can do it here," Rae ordered.

"Very good sir, I'll inform Herr Wegel and bring your guest right down."

"And send something to open these crates," Rae called after him.

Rae tested the strength of one of the wooden straps that spanned the length of the crate, it was nailed down fast, and there was little movement.

"This has to be the Amber Room," Rae said. "What else could it be?"

"Whatever's in there isn't worth the lives of the men you've murdered," Ben replied, "and I don't want to be around you any longer than I have to, I'll sign the vault over, and then I walk out of here..."

"We're witnessing history - we've made history, all of us together, and I want you to see what we've done, so you must wait a little longer."

Ben fell silent as steps once again approached the vault.

"Your guest is here," the huissier had returned, but he hadn't brought Shaw. "I'm afraid, Mr Millar, will have to go to Herr Wegel's office to complete the papers, it is our procedure."

"It seems Mr Millar will have to leave us," Rae said nodding to Vadim, "My aide will accompany him. Now where are the tools to open these?" Rae asked pointing to the crates.

"I have arranged for two of our staff to help with the unpacking of your items-"

"No, just bring the tools, we can unpack them ourselves, and bring them quickly, I've asked for them three times now," Rae snapped.

Ben walked out the vault followed by Vadim and the huissier who hurried along. Ben had expected to see Shaw, but found a man who returned his glance with cold, intelligent eyes. He didn't strike Ben as another of Rae's mercenaries. The man was older, slightly overweight and had a look of authority about him, he was someone used to getting his way. Whoever he was, Ben had a feeling he was bad news and that his time was running out, he had to find a way out and fast.

Chapter 61

Zurich, Switzerland
Thursday, 25 February 1943 14:04

A black Mercedes-Benz 170 pulled up behind the truck containing the Amber Room. Harry James' hands were placed before him and securely bound before two men dragged him forward until his head was jammed against a rear white-wall tyre.

A kick, that was more of a push, turned him over to face Kessler who was watching as James was squeezed into the car's cramped rear seat. The Mercedes started up but could hardly be heard above the rattle of the trucks' engines. James turned to sit upright and squinted at Kessler through his swollen right eye. The SS-major was scowling at his watch; Harry smiled, at the very least, he had disturbed their delivery schedule.

As they pulled away, and Kessler climbed aboard a truck, James realised his only hope was the taxi driver getting the details of the house to Clarke, who after losing Kessler, would surely be desperate to find his fellow agent.

It couldn't have taken more than ten minutes until they made the turn into the driveway and came to a stop in the old stable yard.

His captors dragged him down steps into a cold, damp cellar where his feet were untied, and he was thrown against a wall.

One of the men flicked a light switch, and James was immediately drawn to a hook in the centre of the high ceiling; it was not an original feature. A mound of plaster lay below it, trodden into the worn flagstones. He thought he could hear movement in the floor above. Was this the Swiss headquarters of the Gestapo or SS in Zurich? Whatever happened to him, at least sending the address meant that Clarke would know where to look when his own men disappeared.

The two guards checked the room, and seemingly satisfied, left him to the sound of heavy, steel bolts slamming home from outside.

James tried not to think, he had accepted he would die, and cursed himself for not swallowing Timmons' death pills when he'd had the chance. Whatever he told them, he could not mention ULTRA, he would stick to his story of spotting and following Kessler, but as a new arrival in Zurich they could hardly be expected to believe him, and they would make him talk.

He knew his duty, and started to look around. Was there anything here he could use to take his life? The hard fact was he couldn't rely on Clarke coming in time, the man was a drunk, and even if he got the taxi driver's message, could he plan an effective rescue? James should have reported him when he had the chance – this wasn't a game, amateurs like Clarke led to incompetence and death.

He thought of Buchan's Thirty-nine Steps, Richard Hannay escaped from a cellar with the help of some handy explosives. In this cellar a loop of wire was all that could be found, the cord was thin – it would be perfect. He blanked his mind to the horror of what he was about to attempt. If he could attach the wire to the hook, then what he carried inside his head would never pass his lips.

It took only three attempts to loop the wire onto the hook. James laughed out loud, it had to be a butcher's hook, he could hardly miss – it might have been nice to try and fail, but his time had run out - there were no excuses left.

He took the other end of the cord and wrapped it around his neck, he would dive forward, the wire was thin, and his weight would be enough for it to crush his windpipe, and with God's mercy, give him a quick death.

Harry James shut his eyes, said a prayer, and got ready to make good his promise to an old man in an ill-fitting raincoat.

He stepped onto a chair. He would treat this like a parachute jump: follow a countdown and clear his mind before stepping out.

James' countdown had ended, as he was about to jump he heard the bolts on the door pulled across, he let himself fall, and almost passed out immediately from the pain as the wire bit into his flesh. The door burst open, and he quickly felt hands pulling him up, and coughed hard as the wire was removed and thrown to the floor.

"Christ, you're a lucky man Harry, if you'd taken the cyanide there'd be no coming back."

James' focus cleared to find Donald Clarke smiling down on him. He grunted his thanks, unable to speak clearly as the wire had ripped at his throat. There were two of the others standing over them, Sten guns at the ready.

"Can you walk, Harry?"

James tried to get up, he felt weak but was on his feet.

"Right, let's get out of here," Clarke ordered.

Clarke went ahead with the two men supporting James under each arm. They turned down towards the road, passing the door, where the trucks had been parked.

They were twenty yards from the open road, when fire came from the main house. They started to run, the MI6 agents pulling James on until they were only moments away from the cover of the house's outer wall.

Clarke was shouting for them to run, and James pushed forward, when his right leg gave way, he didn't understand what had happened, his legs wouldn't respond, and he fell flat on his face. He felt his thigh, covering his hands in blood. He lay on his back, and tilted his head towards the bark of a German officer to see at least five men with machine guns firing on their position. Clarke and his men were pinned behind the wall, and he could hear shouts for him to crawl.

James realised this was the end, he'd been a soldier most of his life, and this was a soldier's death under enemy fire, the only problem was the Germans were not targeting him - they were trying to keep him alive.

A sustained bout of fire from the road covered Clarke who dived close to James.

"Harry, just a few feet, for goodness sake man, try!"

James met Clarke's eyes, "Kill me, I can't be left to talk," he rasped.

"No, I can't do it."

"Come closer," James said his strength failing.

Clarke leaned over him and heard Harry's final words. Tears ran down his cheeks as he levelled the revolver at James' head.

"I'm sorry," he whispered.

James smiled; this was a soldier's death.

He never felt the bullet that took his life, or saw that Donald Clarke and his men retreated without further loss.

Chapter 62

Zurich, Switzerland
Tuesday, 9 May 2017 13:43

Charles Rae cocked his head out of the vault and waited until Millar was through the final security gate and out of sight. When he was sure he couldn't be overheard he turned to his guest, "Why are you here?"

The man waited until they had stepped into the vault before answering, "What we have agreed carries a risk, and I want to make sure nothing goes wrong."

"You know my men are reliable, Sykes."

"There have been too many mistakes and Millar must disappear the moment he leaves this building. He shouldn't have gotten this far, and his face will be on camera, so I have to ensure no tapes from this location are handed to the police."

"We didn't allow Millar into this bank. He was already here. We would have dealt with him in Geneva, but your men helped him escape. What can you do about the cameras?"

Sykes gave a small laugh, "I will talk to Herr Wegel, once he finds Millar is a suspected killer - he will hand over the tapes."

"We have a small problem with Millar," Rae said.

"And what is that?"

"He only intends on transferring the vault to me, there's money too."

"How much?"

"£1.8 million."

"That would make a nice down payment to add to my cut of the Amber Room."

"You'll get your share," Rae replied, "I was surprised when you asked for it."

Sykes lent forward and frisked Rae, who pulled back saying, "I'm not wired."

"This will top up my pension fund rather nicely, and for doing what I'd do in any case. You can view it as an insurance policy on my future actions where you're concerned."

"And I'm sure it will be money well spent, but we've all underestimated Millar. What about the others?"

"My man has them. He'll follow orders, and as long as Millar can be blamed for the killings... then there will be no questions from anyone that matters."

"What about the rest of our plan?"

Sykes tapped his fingers on the largest crate.

"As discussed, you get the glory of recovering the Amber Room, I get a substantial cut, and the UK government gets to worry in secret about what dangers the world faces from the ability to send messages to the past. This plan gives us all exactly what we want."

Chapter 63

Ben scratched his signature with a beautifully balanced Montblanc fountain pen then let it drop on the table. Wegel and the huissier added their signatures in turn.

"That concludes the transfer of the vault and contents," Wegel said. "You have transferred the vault to Charles Rae, retaining control over the account's funds as specified. What now, Gentlemen?"

"My business is finished," Ben said. "I'm leaving."

"Very good, thank-" Wegel started to reply, but was interrupted by Vadim, "We need to go back to the vault."

It was not a request and the threat was obvious. Wegel rather uncomfortably called for the huissier to escort them out. Ben wondered if Wegel would intervene, to say that of course he could leave if he wished, but the man looked away. In that instant, Ben realised no help would come from within the bank, and he was on his own. Vadim thanked Wegel for making the arrangements then added, "We have a van coming to remove some of Mr Rae's possessions. Please make your security aware."

"Of course," Wegel replied, ignoring the incident of a few moments ago. "If you can give my assistant the vehicle details, and when we can expect it to arrive, access will be arranged."

"They are on their way now, and we will be transferring the contents this evening," Vadim replied.

The huissier reappeared, and Vadim leant close to Ben and whispered, "You go nowhere without permission... understand?"

Ben looked him straight in the eye and nodded, with the vault signed over, his only protection was the money in the account as he knew they would want such a substantial sum too. There was a possibility Shaw and MI6 would stop any further killing. They knew what Rae had done, but they had made one deal to accommodate murder, any more killings would just be bargained off against the greater good of keeping the time loop secret. Charles Rae looked too relaxed, too confident of his position. They were in as much danger from the British Government as they were from Rae. Simon had been right to want to publish everything, it was the only way to protect anyone with knowledge of his work. They were part of the biggest story on the planet, a story that people like Shaw were determined would never be told.

Chapter 64

The huissier led Ben, closely followed by Vadim, back to the vault corridor. They passed a couple of late clients being shown to their valuables, before reaching the vault door where the huissier nodded politely and withdrew once more. Ben entered first then fell to his knees as Vadim punched him in the kidneys. Rae looked up, "Leave him, he can wait, I'm about to open a crate, we're unpacking history."

Vadim lifted Ben to his feet then pushed him to the far corner where he tripped and just avoided striking his head as he landed among the crates.

"Our business is not finished," Vadim said turning away.

Ben decided to test their arrangement with Shaw, "You can't really expect Shaw to let you walk away?"

Vadim stopped mid-stride, "And how is that, Millar?"

"Rory and Lily will make sure the police know who to look for, you'll be hunted for the rest of your life."

"Your friends will already be dead." Vadim said slowly waiting for Ben's reaction.

Sykes shot an irritated look at the Russian.

"What does it matter if he knows?" Vadim said shrugging his shoulders, "Shaw works for Sykes here... who is being paid twice to do what his country requires."

Ben stared at Sykes waiting for him to contradict the man.

"Shaw works for you?"

Sykes' lip curled at the question.

"Mr Sykes has done what is right for all concerned," Vadim continued, "well, maybe not all."

"You mean Sykes is a murderer, who takes bribes from scum like you," Ben said.

"You were in the wrong place at the wrong time, that's all there is to say." Sykes stated coldly.

"I always knew spooks were incompetent, your useless intelligence nearly got me killed a couple of times," Ben replied, "but you're a mercenary too, the worse kind who'll kill innocents for money."

"I protect the status quo, the individual doesn't figure, especially ones who would tell every tin-pot dictator they could influence the past. Can you imagine the sudden interest in high-energy physics around the world? Your friends intended to publicise classified information, and that's put you where you are now."

"The new accelerator at CERN cost billions, and took decades to build, it can't proliferate," Ben shouted. "That's your excuse for killing a doctor and academic who've hurt no-one?"

"Countries have billions, they have good minds. Who says they need another CERN? Who knows what technology is required to repeat this effect if it becomes the primary goal?" Sykes asked.

Ben shook his head, "One more question, what cut are you taking from the Amber Room-"

Ben didn't get to finish as Sykes moved quickly and kicked him hard in the stomach, the blow left him lying out on the crates. Rae shouted about being careful not to damage the contents as Ben raised his head to find Vadim smirking down on him. The mercenary drew his gun, levelled it at Ben's chest, and mimicked a shot, his hand rising with the mock recoil as he blew away imaginary smoke. It was intended to let Ben know - that when the time came - it would be Vadim who ended his life.

"Enough!" Rae shouted, "Not here, and anyway we need him alive to recover the money."

Rae turned and faced one of the smaller crates, "Leave him, and help me open this."

Vadim moved forward to help, but Sykes barked an order, "I'll do it, you watch him." He said pointing to Ben who was still in the centre of a heap of toppled boxes.

Ben wanted Vadim to think he was beaten, to drop his guard, so he laid there, head down, gathering himself to make an attack, to try something, as there was nothing to lose... if he was going to die, this was as good a place as any.

Chapter 65

Zurich, Switzerland
Tuesday, 9 May 2017 14:07

Andrew Shaw led Lily and Rory into the front entrance of the Commercial Bank of Switzerland on Bahnhofstrasse. He explained he'd arranged to meet an account holder, and a call to basement security confirmed they were members of the party viewing vault sixty-seven.

As they waited to be led down to the vault, Lily pulled Shaw's borrowed raincoat tight.

"You actually have a plan?"

Shaw raised his head slowly, "It could do with a bit of detail, but it's been a long day."

"I suppose we should thank you."

"I've had to do things I'm not proud of. That isn't required here, and once you're all in custody, you'll be safe enough. As for the plan, that's simple – it's to get you both, and Ben Millar, out of here. We can worry about what follows after that."

"Why should we trust you now?" Rory asked.

"You don't have any choice," Shaw replied as his mobile started to ring, it was Sylvia's number. He drifted away from the others to answer the call.

"Andrew, where are you?"

"I'm waiting in reception at the Commercial Bank's head office on Bahnhofstrasse."

"Thank God, I'm not too late I may have found something."

"Go on..."

"Harry James died in 1943 under enemy fire. An MI6 agent named Donald Clarke found James was being held in a villa on the eastern side of Lake Zurich. James was killed when they tried to get him out, and Clarke filed a report about the death. He's noted James tried to tell him something about a booby trap as he lay dying, but he'd injured his throat, and Clarke couldn't make it out."

"What does that tell us?"

"What if James booby trapped the Amber Room?"

"Sykes is with the others opening what they think is the Amber Room right now."

"Well, you might want to warn them, and Andrew..."

"Yes."

"I was talking to Martin Reid. If the people you're risking everything to protect managed to send the message to 1943, then that message sent Harry James to Switzerland, and led to his death. They might have done what they thought was best, but there's a direct consequence here, and no-one will argue with Sykes if they don't make it back – just thought you should know."

"Thanks, can you do me one more favour? Call Alex and send her to pick up the two I have with me at the bank's reception – tell her to take them somewhere unofficial and safe."

Shaw ended the call, and walked back to the others, he stopped by Rory, "I can understand why you're not feeling like trusting anyone right now, but I need you to stay here as I need to get Ben out. There's someone coming for you, her name's Alex, and she'll look after you until I can make contact again."

"What's to stop us walking out of here, and going straight to the police or the press?" Rory asked.

"I won't stop you, but this is a dangerous situation. I was just told Lily and Ben's message changed the past - it led to a wartime MI5 agent being reassigned and ultimately killed as a direct result of that message. He may also have booby-trapped the Amber Room before he died. I have to go and warn the people in that vault."

"OK, let's go then," Lily said as she called over to one of the huissiers. As the man made to escort them to the vault, Shaw blocked Lily's way, "You're not coming with me."

"We don't have time to argue - you're not leaving us here."

"Oh, Lily," Rory exclaimed.

"No, I want to go, and right now. We need to warn, Ben."

Lily walked away from them without looking back. Their escort started to lead the way, and if he was concerned by the conduct of vault sixty-seven's latest visitors it barely showed.

The sound of footsteps behind Lily echoed in the large, empty hall.

"I haven't got time for this," Shaw said taking Lily's arm.

She pulled away, "Rory can stay and wait for this Alex person if you want, but I'm going to make sure you really are here to protect Ben."

"If I didn't want that then you'd be dead by now. How can I get Millar out when I've got to watch over you too?"

Rory touched Lily's shoulder, "He has a point, Lil."

She spun away, "You were just asking how we could trust him."

Shaw let out a sigh, "Rory wait here for Alex; tell her we'll meet at the corner of Tiefenhofe. Lily let's go - you're going to follow me anyway, and we can't wait any longer."

Chapter 66

Ben Millar rolled onto his side, Sykes' kick had winded him, but he wasn't badly hurt. Vadim motioned for him to stay on the floor, and Ben could hear Charles Rae calling to Vadim from behind the stack of crates. Vadim stepped back to glance at Rae while keeping an eye on Ben.

Rae's voice boomed out, "Look, we actually have it... we are witnessing the first glimpse of the Amber Room in nearly seventy years-"

An explosion roared in the confined space of the vault.

Ben cradled his ears, he closed his eyes tight, trying to deal with the intense pain from the blast's pressure wave. For the first few seconds, he looked out on the darkened room, unable to comprehend what had happened, but he became aware of the flames and thickening smoke, and staggered to his feet moving towards the bright lighting that still functioned in the main corridor.

Other than his head and ears, he felt no obvious pain, the main sensation was an overpowering smell, a mixture of an acrid, chemical stench, and strong perfumed incense that burned the back of his throat. Ben held his breath and made it to the vault door, alarms sounded all around, but they were muffled and seemed far away as though he was hearing them in a dream. It took no more than a ten seconds after the detonation for the fire systems to activate. Gas pumped into the vault suppressing the fire, followed by a deep vibration as an extraction system cranked up to expel the smoke. Ben stood with his back against a wall looking in on the vault. Lying behind the crates had saved him from the direct force of the explosion. There was movement inside as the smoke cleared, Ben crouched to get a better view, he looked into a face streaked with blood, the glint from the gold in clenched teeth meant there was no mistake - Vadim was still alive.

Ben staggered back into the vault and straddled Vadim's body, the Russian twisted, but his right side was trapped under a large crate. Ben pinned his left arm, pawing for his shoulder holster. Ben pulled out the pistol and stood back up, slowly moving back, with the gun aimed at Vadim's head.

Vadim turned to face Ben, the smile was still there - he was almost daring Ben to pull the trigger.

"Two men in Edinburgh are dead because of you, and... Lily and Rory," Ben shouted hardly able to hear his own voice.

"What do you want? I should say sorry?" Vadim spat.

Ben made out the words and wanted to blast that smug smile from his lips.

"You deserve to die," Ben said his finger on the trigger.

"Then do it, fuck you, Millar, go on... do it!"

Ben steadied his aim, he had never killed a defenceless man, and there'd be no mercy if their positions were reversed. He tightened his grip as he became aware of movement in the corridor outside.

He spun around to find the MI6 agent, Shaw in the doorway. He levelled the gun once more, this man had lied to, then killed Lily and Rory. His betrayal was a worse act than anything Vadim and Rae had carried out, they were simply criminals, but this man was supposed to protect the very people he'd calmly taken to be slaughtered. Ben raised the pistol, Shaw was also a defenceless man, but one he was certainly able to kill. As he adjusted his aim, Shaw was talking words he couldn't hear, he started to squeeze the trigger, then saw Shaw wasn't alone, he recognised the white dress. The gun fell as Lily ran towards him throwing her arms around him.

Chapter 67

Shaw called for Ben and Lily to move, pulling them out into the corridor. Bank security guards were running towards them shouting orders. Ben couldn't make out what was being said as nothing registered above the painfully repetitive screech of the alarm system. He stuffed the gun in his pocket as a guard came towards him, he spoke, but Ben pointed to his ears and the man stepped back. Ben touched the ear and dropped his hand to see it glistening with blood.

"Need to get out," Ben said, the guard nodded and motioned for Lily and Ben to follow another man out through the security checkpoint into the loading bay. The steel roller door was open, a small crowd gathering outside attracted by the noise of the alarms, and joined by a number of uniformed police. Lily led Ben to sit on some steps, he wanted to fade into the background, but as the only person who looked to have suffered injury, all attention was on him.

Another guard said a few words to Lily before pointing to Ben, he was telling her to wait where they were. Ben had made out a few words, but stared back at him blankly showing no sign of comprehension, they needed to move and soon, they needed to be gone before Shaw or anyone else appeared.

A few passersby lined the street and the bank's security men formed up to control access to the building in what must have been a planned emergency drill.

"Lily, time to go," Ben said.

"Shh, not so loud, can you hear me?"

"Yeah, just about, that OK?" He replied lowering his voice as best he could.

Lily nodded.

"We have to get away from here. Simon was right: we have to go to the press, we can't trust anyone."

He stood and took her hand, leading her past guards more preoccupied with keeping people out rather than in. An ambulance turned into the lane that ran behind the bank, and that gave perfect cover to join a small group who were drifting off towards the front of the building, and Paradeplatz, where a fire engine's siren howled to announce its arrival. Ben checked behind them, convinced he'd find Vadim's trademark smile, but they were alone, and in the noise and confusion, they became part of the crowd. He crouched down at a car's side mirror, and wiped away the worse of the blood and dirt that smeared his face and ears with his jacket sleeve. Lily helped, before nodding her approval.

Ben started to move, "Look for a taxi," he said scanning the area. It was just then he was aware of someone coming towards them from the left, and so he took the first turn, pulling Lily down a quiet one-way street. The road branched no more than thirty metres away, and as he reached the corner, his hand went to Vadim's gun, and he turned to face whoever was behind them.

Somehow he'd expected Vadim but found the man from the vault, Sykes, standing there. Ben started to back away and Sykes, wrapped in a three-quarter length raincoat, followed awkwardly with an obvious limp.

Ben looked around - there was no point in running, they'd walked into a dead-end. Ben's trigger finger rested on the guard, and the gun was pointed at Sykes' chest through his jacket in the gangster style of countless movies. Sykes stopped, and seemed to be considering the situation, as though trying to read Ben. If he thought Ben would falter after failing to pull the trigger on Vadim, he'd be very wrong, Ben had been ready to kill Shaw, and now he thought of it - where was the other agent?

"What'd you want?" Ben asked.

Chapter 67

Shaw called for Ben and Lily to move, pulling them out into the corridor. Bank security guards were running towards them shouting orders. Ben couldn't make out what was being said as nothing registered above the painfully repetitive screech of the alarm system. He stuffed the gun in his pocket as a guard came towards him, he spoke, but Ben pointed to his ears and the man stepped back. Ben touched the ear and dropped his hand to see it glistening with blood.

"Need to get out," Ben said, the guard nodded and motioned for Lily and Ben to follow another man out through the security checkpoint into the loading bay. The steel roller door was open, a small crowd gathering outside attracted by the noise of the alarms, and joined by a number of uniformed police. Lily led Ben to sit on some steps, he wanted to fade into the background, but as the only person who looked to have suffered injury, all attention was on him.

Another guard said a few words to Lily before pointing to Ben, he was telling her to wait where they were. Ben had made out a few words, but stared back at him blankly showing no sign of comprehension, they needed to move and soon, they needed to be gone before Shaw or anyone else appeared.

A few passersby lined the street and the bank's security men formed up to control access to the building in what must have been a planned emergency drill.

"Lily, time to go," Ben said.

"Shh, not so loud, can you hear me?"

"Yeah, just about, that OK?" He replied lowering his voice as best he could.

Lily nodded.

"We have to get away from here. Simon was right: we have to go to the press, we can't trust anyone."

He stood and took her hand, leading her past guards more preoccupied with keeping people out rather than in. An ambulance turned into the lane that ran behind the bank, and that gave perfect cover to join a small group who were drifting off towards the front of the building, and Paradeplatz, where a fire engine's siren howled to announce its arrival. Ben checked behind them, convinced he'd find Vadim's trademark smile, but they were alone, and in the noise and confusion, they became part of the crowd. He crouched down at a car's side mirror, and wiped away the worse of the blood and dirt that smeared his face and ears with his jacket sleeve. Lily helped, before nodding her approval.

Ben started to move, "Look for a taxi," he said scanning the area. It was just then he was aware of someone coming towards them from the left, and so he took the first turn, pulling Lily down a quiet one-way street. The road branched no more than thirty metres away, and as he reached the corner, his hand went to Vadim's gun, and he turned to face whoever was behind them.

Somehow he'd expected Vadim but found the man from the vault, Sykes, standing there. Ben started to back away and Sykes, wrapped in a three-quarter length raincoat, followed awkwardly with an obvious limp.

Ben looked around - there was no point in running, they'd walked into a dead-end. Ben's trigger finger rested on the guard, and the gun was pointed at Sykes' chest through his jacket in the gangster style of countless movies. Sykes stopped, and seemed to be considering the situation, as though trying to read Ben. If he thought Ben would falter after failing to pull the trigger on Vadim, he'd be very wrong, Ben had been ready to kill Shaw, and now he thought of it - where was the other agent?

"What'd you want?" Ben asked.

"I need you both to listen to me. Things aren't as they seem," Sykes replied. "Everything I said earlier was for Rae's benefit. I've been working undercover, infiltrating his group for some time."

Ben's hearing was returning, and he wanted to believe him, wanted to think this man and his country hadn't really sentenced them to death.

"Don't listen to him, Ben," Lily said pulling his arm, "he ordered us killed."

"Don't be hysterical, you were tied and bound as we do with all captives until we're one hundred percent sure about them. It's standard procedure."

"It's OK," Ben whispered to Lily, she moved closer, and gave him a reluctant smile.

"Well, you were pretty convincing earlier, but less so now," Ben replied to Sykes. "What happened in there?"

"A German stick grenade dropped out when Rae removed some of the packaging, I recognised it immediately, and jumped away, but he moved towards it. I'm glad he did as his body took the blast and saved my life."

"What about Vadim?"

"Dead – we're the only survivors, it wasn't a powerful explosion, but a detonation in such a small space was enough to finish the others."

"Unfortunate," Ben said watching Sykes carefully.

Lily stepped forward and asked, "Where's Shaw?"

"Looking for you, he helped me out of there, then he went one way, I went the other. He told me you came to warn us about a possible booby trap." He looked at Ben, "If Lily hasn't already told you: records were found from a mission to stop delivery of the Amber Room in 1943. It failed, and the agent was killed in action. Booby-trapping the crates may well have been his final act."

"Go on," Ben said showing no signs of relaxing his aim.

"The authorities in 1943 thought they had a traitor on their hands, someone with access to both nuclear secrets, and knowledge of the Enigma code breakers. It had to be someone very senior, and this traitor wanted the Amber Room in return for selling out the allies. He was codenamed VIPER, but you already know that."

"Tell me anyway," Ben said.

"When you sent that second message with Enigma settings known to the allies, you caused a sensation in 1943. Churchill himself ordered the transfer of the Amber Room to be stopped at all costs. The whole thing shook trust at all levels in government, military, and civil service. Your message was the direct cause of a MI5 agent working in Ireland to be sent into action to stop the transfer. We thought his mission failed, but he left a traitor's payment for VIPER. A payment that VIPER collected in vault sixty-seven this day, as we now know the man who supplied those documents to the Nazis was Charles Rae."

Ben smiled, if the grenade that killed Rae was there because of the message they had sent from Geneva yesterday then Simon had his justice.

"What happens now?" Ben asked. "What happens to Lily, Rory and me?"

"We get back to the UK," Sykes replied "You'll get medical attention and return to your lives after being debriefed."

"Just like that?"

"Of course, you'll be expected to keep quiet, and will be subject to the official secrets act, as are all UK citizens whether they have signed it or not. You'll see the need for secrecy, but even if you didn't, who'd believe what you've got to say anyway?"

Sykes manner was assured, and looked at Ben's jacket to see if he was still covered by the gun. He was.

"Did you kill, Vadim?" Ben asked.

Sykes paused for an instant, and Ben detected the ruthlessness behind this warm, new facade.

"You saw him... alive?"

"All I want is an answer for now," Ben replied.

"Vadim and Rae had to be... eliminated. We couldn't allow the Amber Room to appear suddenly on the black market, it would raise too many questions. They would never have accepted that. There was no choice in their case."

"Meaning there's a choice in ours?"

"Yes, I've no doubt you'll come to appreciate the situation and do what's best for your country, now please point that gun somewhere else before we have an accident, we're safe here for now, but the Swiss authorities are all around us."

"Maybe we'd be better off with them," Ben followed Sykes' as he moved sideways clearly frustrated the gun was tracking him.

"Keep still," Ben said as he brought the Glock from under his coat.

As Ben finished speaking he realised something was wrong, Sykes had turned him ever so slightly for a reason. He wanted to look around but daren't take his eyes off Sykes as it could be a feint. Was it something MI6 taught their officers, to unnerve and possibly unarm opponents? Ben found the answer a split-second later, his forearm was forced down as his wrist was twisted using the gun as a lever to break the finger left in the trigger guard. He automatically head butted his attacker as Sykes lunged at Lily, punching her with all his weight as she fell to the ground. Sykes's hands were on his throat and his head was forced back to look into the eyes of someone he'd liked better dead.

Chapter 68

Zurich, Switzerland
Tuesday, 9 May 2017 14:17

Ben's face was in the gutter, Sykes and Vadim held him down, and he'd been a fool for failing to put a bullet in their heads.

Vadim pulled Ben up by the hair, his hands smothering Ben's mouth and face. Ben tried to bite him and received a hard strike to his injured arm that made him gasp in pain. Lily's eye's opened, as she and Ben were pulled behind a row of parked cars, hidden from the road – literally a dead end.

Vadim tied Ben's arms then walked away, quickening his pace. Moments later an Audi A6 pulled up beside them, and Vadim got out tossing the keys to Sykes.

"Put him in the boot," Sykes ordered.

"That space is taken," Vadim said as he roughly gagged Ben and tightened the cable ties on his wrists, "but we can make room for one more."

Ben was dragged to the rear of the car, and Sykes opened the trunk. Lifeless eyes stared back at them, the man must have been in his sixties, he'd been well-dressed and affluent - the distinguished face was grey and hollow - devoid of life. The position of the head on the shoulders could only mean the neck was broken, there was a sharp smell of urine, and Ben was fighting the horror of being forced to lie beside the body to wait for his own death.

"Who is he?" Lily gasped, blood seeping from a cut above her left eyebrow.

"I wanted his car, he is just a man in the wrong place, at the wrong time," Vadim replied with a grin, "Do not worry, you will travel with us up front."

Vadim roughly pushed Ben to the lip of the trunk. Ben let himself fall to the ground landing heavily unable to break the fall, screaming into the gag as Vadim stamped on him.

Vadim pulled him up, Ben was on his knees, he had to try something - they were dead if forced into the car. He lent forward on the balls of his feet, and when Vadim was above him, he sprung up with all his strength, leading with his good shoulder trying to topple the mercenary.

Vadim sidestepped the attempt, and tripped Ben sending him sprawling into the car. Ben's face landed on the dead man's chest, and he reared up trying to escape being trapped with the corpse.

Ben spun around kicking out and connecting with Vadim's ribs. The Russian swore then pointed Ben's Glock at Lily's head.

"Get in or she dies," he spat.

Ben stared at Lily and stopped struggling. Just as the trunk door was about to shut, Vadim and Sykes spun away from the car allowing Ben to jam his heel in the sill. He recognised the voice, and kicked out against the lid for it to open fully.

It was Shaw calling to Sykes, and Ben fixed on the dagger hidden against Vadim's wrist.

"What happened?" Shaw asked.

"I wondered when you were going to turn up," Sykes said.

"I'm here now."

"Millar had minor injuries after the explosion, he was first to recover, and he killed Rae, who was stunned but alive. He damn near killed the two of us. We should have dealt with him earlier."

"We're really going through with your plan?" Shaw asked.

"Rae was our agent, he's fed us intelligence for years, I've handled him in the past, and everything he's done has been with my consent. Millar killed him, but we can continue to work with his men."

"If you've known about this from the start, why didn't you tell me?"

"You've been in the business long enough to know better than that - things aren't always as they seem - you didn't know Rae was an agent because you didn't need to know. The man had contacts everywhere, and when he let me in on this, I didn't believe it, so I sent you in. Rae brought those Enigma messages to me, and I asked him to investigate. Rae and his men are working for us, the others have to be silenced," Sykes said motioning to Ben and Lily.

Ben strained against the gag. Was Shaw going to let this happen? His eyes met Shaw's who asked Sykes, "You're just going to kill them?"

"They need to disappear for the sake of national security," Sykes said sharply as though unhappy to have to explain himself again.

"Just like that?" Shaw asked.

"Of course, I'd have thought you of all people would want this all hushed up. Your actions, if reported, could be extremely embarrassing. I mean: you allowed wanted fugitives to leave the UK failing to disclose their location to the police, you were involved in a gun battle in Geneva, you disobeyed my orders regarding the girl and doctor, and finally you let yourself get captured outside this bank. This operation has been a farce, and that's why I've been forced to take control. But if we do things my way, there is a chance we can all come out of this with a bit of credit, and we'll have ensured a major scientific discovery remains as it should - top secret. Now, if you don't have the stomach to finish the job, we will handle it," Sykes said pointing to Vadim as he turned away.

"You're not in control, this operation is spinning out of control and I will not accept any more killings," Shaw said.

Sykes dismissed Shaw with a wave of the hand, "Put it in your report. We have to move, in case you hadn't noticed, we're not on home ground."

Shaw didn't flinch, "Fine, but I'm coming with you, and no action is to be taken against anyone until we are back in the UK."

Sykes took a moment then nodded, and told him to get in the car, but Ben noticed the signal to Vadim. Sykes had his back to Shaw, and there was no way Shaw could have seen it, it was a quick look, nothing more, but Vadim's knuckles whitened as he tightened his grip on the handle of the dagger.

Ben threw his head from side-to-side to warn Shaw as Vadim lunged forward, the dagger sliced through the air in a vicious arc towards Shaw's neck.

Shaw was ready, he shifted his weight, slipping the blade as it passed close by, then stepped forward into Vadim, smashing his elbow into the man's jaw. Blood splattered from the blow, and it was then Ben saw the pistol in Shaw's hand, he punched it into Vadim's face, and cocked the gun inches above the motionless mercenary's face. Shaw's eyes lingered on the car when he saw the crumpled body under Ben, and then he turned - too late - to find Sykes' gun levelled at his own head.

Lily kicked out and caught Sykes full on the hip, there was a silenced gunshot and Shaw fell back clutching his shoulder, she had done enough to spoil the aim, but Shaw's gun laid an arm's length from his body, and he was at Sykes' mercy. The agent kept the gun on Shaw, but turned to face Lily and Ben.

"This is going to work out," Sykes said as he kicked Shaw's gun away. "A double tap from an ex-marine, just the kill shot expected from someone like you."

"No-one will believe any of this," Ben said.

"You'd be surprised what people will believe," Sykes replied. "After, Shaw, we have some business to attend to, we'll work out how to transfer that £1.8 million, and don't worry, by the time I've finished with you, you'll beg me to take it."

Sykes turned back and sneered at Shaw, "Always second best, this operation will send me to the very top of the service. If you'd carried out my orders none of this would be necessary... Goodbye, Andrew."

Ben sat motionless as Sykes raised his gun once more, that was the last move the spy made. His head whipped back, and he was thrown against the car, he was dead before his body hit the ground.

The killing had happened so fast Ben could only blink as two figures approached holding out long, silenced pistols.

Ben pushed his legs out of the car then twisted to sit up on the edge of the trunk. Once upright he moved slowly, aware any sudden movement could bring fire his way, but he needed to get away from the soft flesh of the old man's ruined corpse. As he leant forward, he found Sykes at his feet. Ben steadied himself against the Audi, the face was unrecognisable, a large entry wound where there should have been an eye.

The solider moved forward quickly, and a nod from Shaw had him fire two shots into Vadim's head. Ben gave a wide smile for the first time in two days.

Lily lay on the ground sobbing as Shaw tried to comfort her. Ben was pulled forward then pushed aside as Sykes and Vadim's bodies were thrown into the boot space with their earlier victim. One of the men took Ben's arm and firmly put him in one of the rear seats. Shaw sat next to Ben. Within a minute of the shooting, the car slowly moved off into the night.

Once they were under way Shaw turned on a light. He pulled his shirt off his shoulder, he was wearing a bullet proof vest, if the bullet struck one inch to the right it would have hit flesh. He massaged his chest, "That was close," he said to Ben. "You look like you need some attention yourself."

"Where's Rory?" Ben asked.

"Safe."

Ben gave a hollow laugh, "But for how long? Sykes told me - we're all to be killed..."

"I've never subscribed to that plan," Shaw replied finally.

"But you considered it?"

"I'm not asking for your trust, Millar, but you and your friends are safe, you have my word on that."

"You'll let us walk away knowing what we know...?"

"Rory has kids and a career, he'll welcome his life back, that's all he wants now - his normal life. Both Lily and you will surely feel the same? You've lost family and friends, and nothing you do will bring them back. One day people will know what was discovered here - but not now."

"What about the police?"

"They'll be handled. If you open your mouths, you'll be discredited, and I can't guarantee you won't have an accident somewhere down the line. It's up to you what life you choose, but you'd be advised to work with us."

"Yeah, you made that point with Vadim back there. What about the time loop, what will happen?"

"I've no idea, but my guess is it will never be opened again, we would never know the true consequences until it was too late. Mankind has found yet another way to destroy itself, this time by sending radio messages to our grandfathers, it's astonishing and equally terrifying, but unlike the atomic bomb, no-one knows about it and we intend on keeping it that way."

"What made you suspect your boss."

"After the increment men were so easily sidestepped outside the bank, I knew Rae was being fed information. Ever since we saved your life in Geneva they'd been a step ahead. That all coincided with Sykes insisting on shadowing the case. I suspected him, but couldn't be sure, not until a few minutes ago."

"And the grenade in the bank, did our message cause that?"

"Must have been more than a grenade to do that, but a brave man died seventy years ago to stop a traitor selling allied secrets, he must have left his own message for VIPER, and it took seventy years to deliver it. I think we can close that case off now. We'll get you medical attention, there's an emergency doctor from Fort William who could be persuaded to do something for you."

Chapter 69

Zurich, Switzerland
Friday 12 May 2017 09:54

Three days had passed since the explosion in vault sixty-seven. The bank released a brief statement about a small, electrical fire in their Zurich headquarters, which was brought under control before emergency services entered the building. They went on to say no client suffered any loss during the incident, which was technically true if you only counted the living.

The Swiss media showed little interest in a story that did nothing more than prove some very expensive fire systems worked as expected. The shooting in Geneva reached the national news, but had been reported as a suspected falling out among foreign criminal gangs and quickly moved down the news order that day.

Ben Millar picked up the antibiotics he'd been prescribed, and thanked the nurse who escorted him to the end of the small ward, handing him over to a security guard, who politely asked Ben to follow him.

They walked through a corridor of matt black acoustical panels designed to retain heat, and more importantly sound. Light strips along the tops and bottom reminded Ben of something from the set of a science fiction movie, as did the toughened glass security doors that silently opened when his companion enter a pin number.

They turned the last corner, and Ben could see Lily Taylor sitting back, reading a book. She was in a large comfortable room with views down over a river, with a busy motorway in the far distance. The guard opened the door, and Lily looked up and smiled as the door slid shut behind him.

She was on her feet, "Ben, have they discharged you?"

He nodded, "Yeah, they're happy enough to let me go - from the hospital wing anyway."

"Have a seat," she offered, I've stayed in worst hotels."

Ben sat beside her, he had to admit, he'd also stayed in worst places, they'd been treated well so far, and Lily had been allowed to visit him for an hour a day before the nurses shooed her away.

"Any word on Rory," Ben asked.

"Only what Shaw told us when we got here, Rory's staying with his wife and children, but we'll be able to see him soon."

Ben knew every word they uttered would be recorded, but at least they were alive.

The door opened behind them. Andrew Shaw walked into the room helping himself to some toast left on a plate.

"Thought I'd drop in and see how the patient was doing," he said, "The doctor's aren't that interested in you, only surface wounds apparently. I suppose when the docs were getting years of surgical experience on six-month tours of Afghanistan, your injuries are a bit basic."

Ben stood up, "So, what happens now?"

"I told you before, I convince you to keep our newest scientific discovery secret, and the world goes on in blissful ignorance."

Ben looked to Lily.

"We agree," she said, "there's no need to threaten or detain us, we both understand."

"I'm glad to hear it, Dr Moffat has also seen the light."

"We have some questions though," Ben said.

"I'll answer them if I can."

"What about the police, am I still a suspect?"

Shaw poured a coffee, "That's all straightened out. Charles Rae is taking the blame for the two Edinburgh murders. The evidence is compelling, I helped design it, and the inquest will deliver the verdict we require."

"You're happy to let us go?" Ben asked.

"Pretty much, I will have to get your assurances on a few things, but you should be good to go in a couple of days, have you any idea what you'll do now?"

Lily took Ben's hand, "We're thinking about a holiday," she said.

Shaw raised an eyebrow, "Well, you both deserve it, and Ben I've had the deportation notice removed from your file, but I'd avoid Zambia for a while yet."

"What about Major Kessler, did you ever find out what happened to him?" Ben asked.

"Rae must have liked the look of him from signals in the archives, and he had a particular attribute Rae admired."

"And what was that?" Ben asked.

"He was hanged by partisans as he tried to flee occupied France after D-Day, so he wasn't going to be around to get any post-war ideas on Rae's vault."

Shaw got up to leave, "Good luck to the both of you, I'm sure I'll see you around."

He left without waiting for a reply.

Lily turned to Ben, "I wanted to thank you."

Ben took a seat beside her, "Finding me a cigarette would be thanks enough."

"Maybe you should give them up," she replied.

"Thank me for what?"

"You risked your life for me."

Ben thought for a moment, "Anyone would have done it."

Lily looked away, "Oh, I see."

Ben turned her back to him, "No you don't. It was the right thing to do, but there was something there, I didn't want you to get hurt-"

She put her fingers on his lips, "Want to take me for a beer when we get out of here?"

Ben smiled and looked down on the river, "I was thinking more of a holiday."

"Where'd you want to go?" she asked.

"Anywhere but Switzerland," Ben replied, "How about the Caribbean, I've never been there."

"I think that might be out of my price range." Lily replied.

Ben leaned close and Lily burst into laughter before hugging him tight.

Andrew Shaw put down the headphones.

"Did you hear that?" Sylvia asked.

"Did you get it on tape?" Shaw replied.

"Of course," she replied frowning.

"Well, I think they're entitled to a decent break after all this."

"Are you serious?"

"Why not, I'll catch up with Millar when he gets back, and he can transfer the money from that account to the crown. I might even offer him a job, but in the meantime, it won't hurt for them to make a dent in that balance first."

Sylvia shook her head, "And if anyone finds out?"

"Well, as the new section chief, it would come to me first, and that reminds me, with my pay rise I can afford one of those posh restaurants of yours, so ring one up and grab your coat, as a mighty fine lunch is on me."

Thanks for reading, I hope you enjoyed the book, and please leave a review if you can.

This edition is UK English.

I'd love to hear any comments you have and I can be contacted at thedecryptionengine@outlook.com

Phil Marks Oct 2016

Printed in Great Britain
by Amazon